THE LIGHT INFANTRY BALL

THE LIGHT INFANTRY BALL

HAMILTON BASSO

Novels

THE LIGHT INFANTRY BALL
THE VIEW FROM POMPEY'S HEAD
THE GREENROOM
SUN IN CAPRICORN
WINE OF THE COUNTRY
DAYS BEFORE LENT
COURTHOUSE SQUARE
CINNAMON SEED

Biography

BEAUREGARD

Biographical Essays and Social History

MAINSTREAM

Hamilton Basso

THE LIGHT INFANTRY BALL

1959 Doubleday & Company, Inc.

Garden City, New York

PART ONE

CHAPTER ONE

Urgent though his business was, a matter so pressing that it had demanded his rising before dawn and facing the day without so much as a cup of coffee, John Bottomley paused in the downstairs hall of his father's house to glance at the front page of the Pompey's Head *Morning News*. He always read the *News* first thing in the morning whenever he came in from the country to Pompey's Head, and when he saw the newspaper lying folded on a table that stood against the wall, he reached out for it almost automatically. He halfway checked his hand, telling himself he had best be getting along and that the others must not be kept waiting, and then, since by now he really wanted to see what was in the paper and since his haste in getting dressed had given him a few moments to spare, he picked up the *News* and brought it closer to the lamp that stood on the table with its wick turned low, casting shadows along the hall.

The *News* was delivered during the early morning hours, and John imagined that one of the servants who lived in the quarters must have brought it in—Celia's boy Rumford most probably, it being Rumford's responsibility during the winter months to lay the fires in the downstairs hearths and heat up the kitchen stove. A faint smell of woodsmoke drifting from the rear of the house gave sign that the boy was already about his chores. There was no sign of his presence, however, and the house was without a sound. Should Rumford be living up to his reputation he would most likely be snatching a few more winks in the kitchen, where the banked ashes in the iron range would have kept the room warm and cozy overnight, and at that early hour of morning the rest of the household lay deep in sleep. A catbird called from somewhere just beyond the front porch, and first one rooster and then another cut loose from the neighborhood of the barns, and the lamp cast just enough light for John Bottomley to read by.

The most conspicuous item on the front page of the *News* was an account of the Light Infantry Ball. Flanked on one side by a number of those commercial particulars that were of such interest to the business community (eight thousand bales of cotton traded in Liverpool and sixteen thousand in New Orleans; rice firm; corn dull; pork, bacon, turpentine, and rosin generally quiet in all areas), it was bordered on the other by a special dispatch from Washington, reprinted from the New York *Herald*. John noted the date of the dispatch, January 16, which meant it had been filed three days before, and read it through. "The administration adheres to its position in regard to the forts in Charleston Harbor and emphatically refuses to surrender Fort Sumter. The instructions to the commander of the fort were completed today. The exact nature of these instructions is not known, but enough is known to state positively that the fort will be defended in every emergency. Opinion here is that the ultimate decision must await the inauguration of the President-elect. It is not apprehended that any attack will be made on Fort Sumter at present."

John Bottomley chewed at his lower lip and thought, "I wish I could be sure there will be no attack. What those people up there don't realize is how far this thing has gone. They should realize it, but they don't," and not wanting to think about it any longer, wishing it were not there to be everlastingly thought about, almost to the exclusion of everything else, he turned his attention to the account of the Light Infantry Ball. It began by noting that the ball had taken place in the ballroom of Caledonia Hall, that three hundred guests were present, that the grand march had been led by ex-Governor and Mrs. Corwin Bottomley, that Mrs. Bottomley wore a rose silk gown in the latest Paris style, and that ex-Governor Bottomley, in his capacity of grand marshal, carried the silver cane presented to the Light Infantry by General Lafayette in 1825 when he visited Pompey's Head and spoke at the unveiling of the statue of General Robert Carvell in Montague Square.

John Bottomley did not like the editor of the *News*—George Upton Pierce Monckton, his name was, a splendid edifice that had tumbled down into Gup Monckton because of the way his initials fell—and on this January morning in 1861 John had reason to have hard feelings against the whole Monckton tribe. But it was not Gup Monckton of whom he was thinking. It was Gup's older brother Ules. Speak the name of Monckton in Pompey's Head, and it was Ules who first came to mind. It was he who owned the *News*. Gup was the shadow he cast. John Bottomley was constrained to admit, however, that the shadow knew his trade. The best news is local news. The subscribers to Monckton's newspaper would find the Light Infantry Ball considerably more entertaining than the administration's refusal to surrender the forts in Charleston Harbor, and certainly the ball was closer to home. Take himself, for instance—ex-Governor and Mrs. Corwin Bottomley were his parents. They lay asleep in their separate bedrooms, recovering from the festivities of the night just past. A few minutes before, when he had tiptoed down the stairs, John could hear his father snoring and his mother talking in her sleep—for an instant he had frozen where he stood, afraid he had roused his mother and that she had misread his footsteps, she being high-strung and nervous and full of fears, especially now that her younger son Cameron had so strangely disappeared.

John knew that his mother had not wanted to go to the ball. She had been forced to attend by her husband. He said it was her duty, by which he meant his own desire: the word "duty," with Corwin Bottomley, had a way of becoming synonymous with his own desire. The scene in the library was still fresh in John's mind. His father's dark, heavy face was flushed with exasperation, and there was a hoarse tone to his voice. He said, addressing his wife, "I must remind you, madam, that you are expected to lead the grand march. It is your duty, as well as your privilege. Shall we hide ourselves like a pair of runaway niggers just because a weak and trifling boy has absented himself from home?" John watched his mother try to speak, the effort resulting in only a few broken sounds, and then saw her give way to the hysteria that always lay so close to the surface—her face disintegrated and she broke into tears. John heard his father give a loud, impatient snort. There was a streak of Indian blood in all the Bottomleys, and in Corwin Bottomley perhaps a streak of Indian cruelty. Hard as John had tried to disavow the idea, he had been compelled to realize it was true. Corwin said coldly, again speaking to his wife, "Very well, then, stay home if you like. Just recollect that you will be here all alone," and John watched his mother's eyes grow wide and still with fear. She was terrified of being left alone in the house at night.

"Father," John said. "Wait."

Corwin shot him a black, censorious look. "You will oblige me by minding your manners," he said, and turned again to his wife. "And you, Virginia, you will please to stop this nonsense and get dressed for the ball. I must also ask you to compose yourself. Do you wish to appear in public looking as though you had been whipped?" and John thought that that was the way his mother did look, whipped, and there was nothing he could do. She was beyond his reach or any man's. All her life she must have been held in the grip of fear, seeing its shadow in the most innocent shape, and now she had Cameron's disappearance to bear as well. John knew that Cameron was her favorite, dearer to her than either him or his sister Missy, the youngest of her children, and Cameron's mysterious vanishing must have been the last straw. But the curious thing was that, once she reached the ball, his mother appeared to have forgotten Cameron entirely. Either that or she wanted to face down deliberately the rush of gossip that had followed in the wake of Cameron's disappearance (and this on the very evening when his engagement to Kitty Williams was to be announced), holding her love and her colors high.

The whole complicated nature of the trouble in which he found himself closed in on John Bottomley all at once. He had a sense of separation from the more fortunate run of men, seeing himself as from a distance, and for an instant everything was slightly unreal. He caught a glimpse of himself in the mirror on the wall—a slender man of moderate height with dark hair and gray eyes who looked older than his thirty years—and there was a certain unreality about that too. But most unreal of all was the obligation that lay immediately ahead of him. He had read enough in the *News* to know that the account of the Light Infantry Ball was admirably complete—the Light Infantry toast being proposed by Mr. Anthony Blackford; the first glass of Light Infantry punch being poured by Miss Cordelia Lake; the names of the eighteen young ladies whose year it was to be presented to society and the names of their escorts; the music provided by Major Wolfgang Weber and the Old Pompey Band—and yet the most startling event of the evening had been omitted. Nowhere was it mentioned that during one of the intermissions he and Ules Monckton had had words, that words had passed into insults, and that Ules Monckton had called him out to a duel. That was the reason for this early rising. He and Ules Monckton were going to fight a duel. It was absurd, it was unreal, and it was true. He could not believe that Ules Monckton would try to kill him—it was something his reason refused to credit—but since his reason could not be imagined to be identical with that of Ules Monckton, this could be his last morning on earth.

John replaced the *News* on the table, folding it with extra care so that his father would not know it had been touched (he could save somebody that tirade, at least), and left the house. He crossed the front porch, walked down the steps, and made his way to the stables. He kept close to the house, not wanting to be seen. His parents did not know about the duel. The morning was crisp and chill, and he could tell that it was to be one of those warm, golden January days that he sometimes used to dream about when he was going to school up North at the College of New Jersey in Princeton. It seemed a long time ago—school and the North and the College of New Jersey in Princeton—and for a moment, once again taken by a sense of unreality, he had a fleeting glimpse of all those twists and turnings that had led him to this present pass in time. Only a glimpse, however. Things came too much in a rush for him to sort out the details, and his mind was too full of his brother Cameron, Ules Monckton, Lydia Stanhope, and the Light Infantry Ball.

ii

The Light Infantry Ball was the high-water mark of the social season in Pompey's Head. Given annually on the night of January 18, it celebrated the anniversary of the Battle of Little Pigeon Marsh, one of the decisive encounters of the American Revolution and the occasion on which the Pompey's Head Light Infantry, a local militia regiment, went into action for the first time.

Pompey's Head was never without a considerable amount of social activity, even during the long hot summer, but from New Year's Eve to the night of the Light Infantry Ball there was some kind of dance or party almost every evening. The few old-fashioned planter families who still lived all year round on their country properties moved into Pompey's Head, staying with friends or relatives, and there was always a host of aunts, uncles, cousins, and other visitors from the whole length and breadth of the low country. It was commonly agreed that there were only two occasions when everybody who was anybody could be found under the same roof: the Light Infantry Ball in Pompey's Head and the St. Cecilia's in Charleston.

No one could remember a more crowded season. In addition to the numerous private entertainments, the newly formed Palmetto Rifles were having a theatrical, the older Indigo Guards had sent out cards for a masquerade (this after a parade of secession torches), the annual race meeting of the Jockey Club at the Six Oaks Course was going to run ten instead of the usual six days, and the Royal Italian Opera Troupe, with Mlle. Adelaide Cortesi, Prima Donna, and Signor Muscani, Tenor, was appearing at the Marlborough Theatre. Old Mrs. Percy Wyeth Blackford II, whose memories went back forever and who as a little girl had presented a bouquet of red roses to General Robert Carvell after the Battle of Little Pigeon Marsh, said that even the season of 1825, when General Lafayette led the grand march, could not compare with this. "But we didn't pleasure ourselves so much in those days," Mrs. Blackford added, speaking like the ninety-one-year-old Revolutionary relic she was. "I didn't own a ball gown until I was seventeen." It was noted, however, that Mrs. Blackford went about as much as anyone, getting names mixed up and confusing mothers with daughters and sometimes the daughters with their grandmothers, and it was common knowledge that she did not read her mail until she had first looked through all the invitations.

Among the invitations that especially pleased Mrs. Blackford, as it did everyone fortunate enough to be on the same list, was a card from Mr. and Mrs. Montague Williams for a supper and musicale. The date was Tuesday, January 15, three days before the Light Infantry Ball, and it was an open secret that at some time during the evening the engagement of Kitty Williams to Cameron Bottomley would be announced. In point of interest, since the Williamses and Bottomleys were among the wealthiest and most prominent families of the low country, the Williamses' party promised to overshadow even the Light Infantry Ball.

Crossing the stretch of open ground that lay between the gardens and the stables, John Bottomley could distinctly recall when his invitation to the Williamses' party had arrived. His memory focused upon the incident, not only because the arrival of the invitation could be regarded as the first of the series of nearer events that led to his quarrel with Ules Monckton at the Light Infantry Ball, but because it was on that same day that he saw his brother for the last time. That in itself was troubling enough, but what made it worse for John was that it was he who had provided Cameron with the money that had apparently made it possible for him to carry out the scheme that even then he must have had in mind. In the useless wisdom of hindsight, John told himself he should have known his brother was in more than an ordinary amount of trouble, that some kind of climax had been reached, and that instead of losing patience with him, in the belief that he had got himself into another scrape, he should have been astute enough to realize that Cameron was in the last extremity of despair.

On the day the Williamses' invitation arrived, John had been up since early morning, supervising some ditching that had to be done in his fields. He could call them his fields because they were a gift from his father. It never occurred to Corwin Bottomley that either of his sons would desire to be anything but a rice planter—in Corwin's view it would have been something akin to a resignation from the Family Royal—and so, upon John's graduation from college in 1851, when he was twenty, Corwin put him to work, under the eye of an experienced overseer named Wilson, on one of the oldest and most valuable of all the family properties.

During his years in New Jersey, John had developed two sets of ambitions. First he wanted to be an author like Mr. William Makepeace Thackeray and Captain Thomas Mayne Reid, his two favorite writers among those living, and then, without the idea of being an author ever completely losing its appeal, he wanted to be an architect. Three months before his graduation he wrote to his father asking permission to continue his studies abroad—more than anything, fired by some engravings he had come across, he wanted to see the ruins of ancient Greece and Rome. But there was more than the appeal of antiquity involved. A most elegant young lady from Philadelphia, Miss Clarissa Drew, had recently indicated that she was disinclined to accept his hand in marriage.

Corwin Bottomley replied by the next post. John took the letter to his room to read. There had been a big fall of snow the night before, the heaviest of the winter, and all day long it had been cold and gloomy and gray. John poked up the small coal fire that burned in his room, warmed his hands, and opened his father's letter. He saw that it was much longer than usual, running to five or six pages.

Feb. 5, 1851

My Dear Son:

We are moving into our new home today and I have just set down a moment to acknowledge your letter. No gentleman should regard his education as complete without some knowledge of "the lands beyond the sea," and I agree with our English Cousins about the salutary effects of the "Grand Tour." As you know, your dear Mother and I were in London & Paris in the winter and spring of 1840–1841, and

16

I often remember those distant scenes, especially the procession when we saw the young Queen, and so you can see that I understand your desire to "go thou and do likewise."

But at the present time it is out of the question. I have not begrudged a penny spent on your education, regarding it as my Duty to see that you were prepared for the position that you will someday be called upon to assume in our County & State, and it is not the dollars involved that cause me to deny my approval to your scheme. You are needed here at home. As you know, I am removing your Mother from our old family seat at Rosebank Plantation because of her ill health, caused the doctors say by the miasmas that are supposed to rise from the tidal swamps around Rosebank, though I myself have never been troubled by them and have often wondered if the doctors, including our old friend Dr. Carpenter, who brought you into the world, know what they opinionate so freely. Like the character in Shakespeare, I think that there may be more than they know of in their "philosophy."

John could hear his father speaking. He could see his fleshy frame and heavy features, and he remembered his habit of hunching his head forward when he spoke, fixing his listener with his small black eyes. John swallowed his disappointment, braced himself inwardly, and turned to the next sheet of his father's letter.

You must realize that this new house I have caused to be built in Old Pompey has subjected me to considerable expense. Were it not for your Mother's health, cojoined with the fact that when I am inaugurated Governor a few weeks hence I will have to do a great deal of entertaining in the way of receiving distinguished visitors, fellow statesmen, etc., I would have "thought twice" before spending upward of $50,000 for a new home.

Incidentally, I have decided to call our new residence Indigo. I was influenced in this regard by its standing on part of the hundred acres where your great-grandfather on my mother's side grew the first crop of indigo in this part of the state. You will be interested to know that I have sold one-third of the property (33⅓ acres) to Mr. Robert

Blackford, who is desirous of erecting a town residence to move into from his country place Mulberry during the winter season. Mr. Robert Stanhope is negotiating for a like parcel of 33⅓ acres. Mr. Peter Pettibone approached me in regard to the piece of land I am selling to Mr. Stanhope, but when I mentioned my price it scared him off as I knew it would. I must say that it does not displease me not to have the Pettibones as neighbors. Peter Pettibone hangs onto every penny like a leech and the Pettibones have never been of the front rank.

To return to yourself, I will now explain what I mean by saying that you are needed here at home. I am not as young as I used to be, though at the age of 60 I am still in my prime and except for a bad attack of colic this winter have never enjoyed better health, and the time has come for you to assume your share of responsibility. When I become Governor I will not have time to supervise all the details of managing our various properties, as has been the case heretofore, and I am looking to you to start "taking hold of the reins." When I was your age I was well impressed with the seriousness of life, and spent many a day under the hot August sun with chain and compass, marking banks, ditches, and canals, and otherwise running out the land.

John stopped reading long enough to poke up the fire again. Weather like this could finish a man. Never had he been more damnably cold. He would not mind having a taste of that hot August sun his father never missed an opportunity to mention.

It should not surprise you that I have given much thought to your future. It is my plan, when you return home, to settle you at Deerskin Plantation. The place wants looking after, and I am dissatisfied with the way it is being run. The overseer I have there, a man named McGaha, who used to work for Mr. Horace Prescot on one of the Prescot plantations near Port Royal, has been a great disappointment to me. Among other deficiencies, he drinks. I intend to discharge him and put Wilson in his place.

On Deerskin, which has a dwelling-place in good repair—I spent $500 on it only last year—you will learn the business of being a rice planter under Wilson. Though only a sand-hill white, Wilson has al-

ways been the best of my overseers, and it will profit you to be under his instruction. It is my settled opinion that every son, when possible, should go out and attend an experienced overseer to learn the secrets of success in that employment than which there is none more lucrative or profitable.

When I have satisfied myself that you have learned all that Wilson can teach you, it is my intention to put you in complete possession of Deerskin with no payment or obligation on your part except that you have remitted to me, through our factors Thrall & Lockhart, ⅓ of your annual income after expenses, with the stated agreement on my part to renounce this ⅓ amount upon the birth of your first male heir.

As you are aware, Deerskin is the source of all our family fortunes, being part of the dowry received by your great-great-great-grandfather Christian, one of the original colonists with Sir Samuel Alwyn in the Swan, upon his marriage to your noble Indian ancestress, Princess Mary, the daughter of Chief Tupichichi, who as you know once held the whole of the low country under his rule. It has always been my wish to have you follow in the footsteps of your ancestors as a rice planter and I hold it to be no less than your Duty. In this I expect you to agree. I have always tried to be kind and generous to my children, and all that I have ever asked in return is Honesty, Truth, and a cheerful willingness to comply with my wishes, which I have never formed without having the benefit of my children in mind.

John felt no inclination to read further. He wanted to be an architect or an author, and he was going to be a rice planter. He wished he had courage enough to tell his father that his life was his own, that he preferred not to have it so completely arranged, and that he was not one of his father's bondsmen. But even in the midst of wishing, he knew he was whistling at the moon. Nor did it help matters to say there were times when his father reminded him of Critias of Athens, Dionysius of Syracuse, and all those other tyrants of the ancient world. His years at college in the North had given him a slightly different way of looking at things. He was able to see they were all like Critias of Athens and Dionysius of Syracuse, those powerful planters who ruled the South. Their wills had never been crossed and on their separate monarchies their slightest wish was law.

In my proposal to put you in possession of Deerskin, I am not playing favorites. I expect to make a similar arrangement in favor of your brother Cameron. It is my intention, when he comes of age and also learns the employment of planter, to settle him on Cornwall, which as you remember adjoins Deerskin, and was the first land acquired by your great-great-great-grandfather Christian after he made his first turnout of rice. I get no pleasure in saying that Cameron continues to disappoint me. He does poorly in his studies, especially spelling and sums, and shows no sign of growing into Manhood even though he is now in his 12th year. Your Mother continues to indulge him to a degree that I fear will prove detrimental to his future benefit.

In planning for you and your brother, I have not neglected to provide for your infant sister Margaret. Upon her marriage she will be endowed with Persimmon Wood, which I purchased five years ago from Mr. Endymion Waites for $33,000 and which has already increased 25% in value by virtue of my having had the Left Branch channel dredged so that the Persimmon fields now get the full benefit of the pitch of tide. I read a paper about my Persimmon improvements to the Agricultural Society last Thursday evening and was greatly complimented by all the gentlemen present. The weather has been uncommonly warm, cloudy, and damp. We will scarcely have good weather for killing hogs till about the change of the moon, i.e., about next Monday. Old Pompey has been fortunate in having a little fair organized by the Agricultural Society. The exhibition was held in the old Mechanics Hall & on the grounds thereof. The show of machinery was pretty good, and there was a great variety of poultry from the little booted bantam up to the "Moley" and "Shanghai" giants. Some countryman brought in a "hairless horse" which he showed in a tent for 25¢ admission. It was a good sized well formed horse without a particle of hair on him except the beard.

John always liked hearing the local news and gossip and hoped that the rest of his father's letter would be taken up with it. But instead:

I of course had no way of knowing, until your Mother invited me into her confidence, that you have been unfortunate in a tender passion. I assure you that it is no more than once befell your father, among a host of other honest men, and I am confident that in times to come, when you look back upon it, you will come to the conclusion, even as did I, that Providence knows what is for our good, better than we do, despite our habit—natural, I suppose—of thinking to the contrary. Dwell on this reflection and be content to bide your time. Now that you are to lead the life of a Planter, it would be well to contemplate that no one of the Ladies (however accomplished, beautiful, and delightful) whom you are likely to meet in the North, especially the towns and cities, will ever be satisfied and happy in it. The old saw is "land should marry land," i.e., your neighbor's daughter, but except for Miss Elizabeth Paxton, who seems to be the only one among our neighbors' daughters who has been brought up with due regard to habits & education, we have no neighbors' daughters whom I would be pleased to see you wed. When you return I will arrange to have your Mother get up a party, and invite Miss Elizabeth, and we will see if your opinion of her happens to coincide with mine.

Your Mother has just sent word by old Jenny that my presence is required elsewhere. As you can imagine, the place is in an Uproar. Be diligent in your studies, especially Natural History & Botany. It is these that you will find most useful later on.

> *Sincerely your father,*
> *C. Bottomley*

John did not even think to argue. He returned to Pompey's Head, went to work under Wilson, avoided any entanglement with Miss Elizabeth Paxton, and ten years later, in January 1861, a bachelor of thirty, was owner and master of Deerskin. He lived alone in the small frame dwelling that stood on the property, looked after his crops, hunted and fished in season, took a toddy before three o'clock dinner and a double toddy at night, remitted his father one third his annual income, and often felt shut off from every drift and current of the world. He worked long, read much, and spoke little. Those who had known him before he went to live at Deerskin often commented on how much he had changed. It was surprising to have him turn into a recluse. There were those who held his Indian blood responsible, since the smallest touch of Indian blood was known sometimes to cause a man to do strange things, and there were others, much more numerous, who said it was because of his having been sent up North to get an education—truth was, to come right out with it, going up North had done things to John Bottomley, and not good things, either. It was no secret that he and his father had quarreled about secession, that he had expressed his doubts about the South's being able to emerge victorious in a sectional war, and that if Corwin Bottomley had not sensibly kept title to his people at Deerskin, John would have set them free.

So perhaps it really wasn't so strange that he had buried himself on Deerskin. It was a shame, though—before this trouble came up, John Bottomley was a pleasant, friendly, sociable man. People still liked him, despite what was being said, but it was plain that something had gone wrong somewhere. It might be that Indian blood of his, as some folks believed, but it would seem much more likely that it was because of his having gone up North to school. One thing, sir, I'll tell you: I'm damned if I'd send any son of mine up North to school.

iii

John Bottomley's withdrawal from society was so gradual that he was hardly aware of it. When eventually he realized the direction his life had taken, there was little he could do to alter its course. Nor did he want to. To move in society requires considerable effort, even on the part of the most adroit, and John had reached the point where the expense of energy seemed too disproportionate to what he received in return. It was easier to live in the country. At that remove it was not required that he suppress his thoughts, or half speak his mind, or avoid discussion, or run the risk, amid a round of calls and parties, of being thrown with Lydia Chadwick—Lydia Stanhope, rather, as he must now remember to call her.

But to balance these advantages there were disadvantages. The four hundred and ninety acres that comprised Deerskin Plantation lay thirty miles south and west of Pompey's Head. Bordered on the north by a small tidal stream called Little River, one of the tributaries of the Cassava, the property was enclosed on the south by a stretch of boggy lowland, inhabited only by frogs, mosquitoes, and waterfowl, that was known as Little Pigeon Marsh. To get from Deerskin to Pompey's Head involved a hard day's ride, in the course of which it was necessary to ford two salt creeks and then take a ferry across Little River at a hamlet called Bugtown, or else a more pleasurable, six-hour passage aboard a small packet, the *Serena Moore*, which made a twice-a-week round trip from Pompey's Head to the various plantation landings on Little River.

Six of these landings, the ones first met by the *Serena Moore* as she left the Cassava on her outward voyage and began the ascent of Little River, were attached to the properties of Corwin Bottomley. Including Deerskin, the Bottomley plantations spread across four thousand acres. Corwin's rice fields ran along the banks of Little River for three miles.

It was impressive and it was lonely. At Deerskin, John Bottomley had no near neighbors. Those closest were his brother Cameron, who was supposed to be learning the profession of rice planter at Cornwall, a plantation smaller than Deerskin and adjoining it on the west, and the various members of the Blackford family at Mulberry, five miles to the south. The Blackfords, however, were seldom in residence at Mulberry. They preferred to live most of the year in the new home Mr. Robert Blackford had had built in Pompey's Head. Cameron was also nearly always in town. He had shown so little inclination to be a planter that Corwin Bottomley had come to the end of his patience and was arranging to have him enter the firm of Thrall & Lockhart, the family factors. Corwin regarded the business of factoring as only a step away from trade, and it was difficult for him to adjust to the idea of any Bottomley's being even remotely associated with trade, but it was his hope that steady employment, coupled with Cameron's forthcoming marriage to Katherine Williams, would cause his younger son to settle down.

With Cameron and the Blackfords gone from the neighborhood, and Corwin's other properties being run by overseers, John Bottomley was required to live more and more alone. Weeks passed without his seeing anyone but Wilson, who still remained with him as overseer, and the plantation slaves. There were times at Deerskin when John felt he must be one of the most solitary men in the world, and the day on which he last saw his brother Cameron was one of those times.

If Cameron had had troubles, so had he. To say that, however, was no excuse for having failed to understand that his brother needed more than he had been willing to offer. The sequence of failure was too clear in his mind. When Cameron arrived he was sitting on his front porch. He had looked through the mail that had come up that morning on the *Serena Moore*—a letter from Thrall & Lockhart acknowledging his last shipment of rice, a notice that the Light Infantry was going to hold an election of officers two days after the ball, and an invitation from the Williamses to a supper and musicale—and had opened a small parcel that contained several copies of the *News*. He was still trembling inwardly because of what had just happened in the little plantation hospital called the sick-house. He had already had two drinks and had poured himself a third. He was trying to get enough control of himself to see what was in the *News*.

CHAPTER TWO

There was not much in the *News* to cheer a man. Gup Monckton
was at it again. He had clamored for secession, and secession he got,
and obviously secession wasn't enough. Now he wanted the forts in
Charleston Harbor. He also wanted the lesser forts, Signal and Lookout, that stood sixteen miles south of Pompey's Head, guarding the
mouth of the Cassava River. What Gup Monckton wanted, in plainest
terms, was civil war.

> No longer hoping for concessions, let us be ready to take the
> field. Our undecided sister states will never join us until we have
> indicated our power to free ourselves—until we have proven that
> the foreign garrisons who hold Forts Sumter, Lookout, and Sig-
> nal cannot close the portals of our commerce. The fate of the
> Southern Confederacy hangs by the ensign halliards of these
> fortifications. Let us seize the moment while the moment is ours
> to seize. The people will obey the call to war, and take the forts.

John helped himself to another swallow of whisky. He thought,
"And Gup's right, too. They will take the forts. The whole thing is
likely to blow at any moment," and let the newspaper fall to his lap.
From his place on the porch he could see the shadows on the lawn,
the stretch of rice fields beyond the lawn, and then the waters of Little
River. It was just after the noon hour, and the sunlight was without a
sound. The day being Saturday, and the last of the seed rice having
been threshed that morning, John had given his people the afternoon
off. And it was that, as he was eventually able to see, that had first
caused the day to go wrong.

Wilson, his overseer, had opposed the partial holiday. Though this was the slack time of year, with harvest over and the first spring sowing not until April, there was considerable work to be done—ditches and drains cleaned, sluice gates repaired, dikes mended, fields plowed, and the higher ground made ready for the annual planting of sweet potatoes, corn, oats, peas, and sugar cane.

But more than the press of work had entered into Wilson's calculations. When John announced his intention of giving the hands a few hours off, Wilson, speaking with the nasal twang he had brought from the upcountry and never lost, said, "It ain't for me to say, sir, but I wouldn't do it. You leave um idle and they'll be thinking up some mischief for sure. I've lived with um longer'n you have, sir, twenty-eight years come the first of next September, and effen I've learned one thing it's that you can't trust um. Not ever. Not man, woman, or child. I'll tell you this, sir—you leave um idle, and they get a chance to put their black kinky heads together, and first thing you know they'll be getting out of hand. And now with all these Yankee spies around, aiming to stir up trouble——"

"What spies?" John broke in, unable to restrain a burst of impatience. "Who has seen them? What trouble have they caused? Aren't things bad enough without our going out of the way?"

Wilson's face went set and suspicious. He looked at John for an instant longer than he would have ordinarily, and a kind of film dropped across his eyes. He was a small man, thin and wiry and burned by the sun. His coarse stubble of beard was shot with gray, and one of his front teeth was missing. He had been so long at Deerskin that he resented being crossed or corrected in any way. But, more than that, he did not like the way Deerskin was being run. He had not liked it almost from the day John arrived to take charge. He had objected to John's doing away with the stocks that used to stand at the far end of the quarters, and had then twisted it around as a personal affront when John laid down the rule that none of the people was ever to be whipped—as Wilson saw it, the implication was that he was one of those overseers who enjoyed using the leather. And he wasn't. No man could say the contrary, by God! Sometimes it had to be done, or else they would think it was them who was master, not you, but he didn't no more enjoy it than he would enjoy laying into some stubborn bullheaded mule.

John knew that Wilson had no savage leanings. Seen in the light of his occupation, he might even be called a humane man. John also knew Wilson's loyalty to Deerskin, his shrewdness in all things pertaining to planting, and his ability to get from the land the last possible bushel of rice—without Wilson it was foolish to imagine that he would have been able to keep Deerskin going. But that first rift had never been healed. Within a week of John's arrival Wilson decided the son was not the man his father was—too soft, too lax, too indecisive—and subsequent events merely convinced him that his first judgment was correct. There was never any open conflict—Wilson obeyed orders and did his work—but John knew that were it not for Wilson's devotion to Corwin Bottomley, along with the twelve-hundred-dollar annual wage he now received—considerably more than he could have earned elsewhere—he would have left him years ago.

John did not blame Wilson and bore him no grudge. It was not hard to understand why he had come to think of him as soft, lax, and indecisive, and in Wilson's background there was no Miss Clarissa Drew of Philadelphia and no Professor Adam Sedgewick of the College of New Jersey in Princeton. Wilson could not hear Miss Clarissa saying, "I disagree that there are kind masters, Mr. Bottomley. Merely to possess another human being is cruel," and neither had Wilson been present when Professor Sedgewick, in a final interview, had said, "Mr. Bottomley, let me speak plainly. Slave owning corrupts a man. It has to. The sooner your section gets rid of the institution—if it ever intends to—the sooner you will all be able to save your souls."

John looked at his overseer, taking in the rawhide boots and dark clothes and loose string tie that had become established as the official uniform of his trade, and found it curious, not for the first time, that after ten years of close association he and Wilson should still be almost strangers to each other. On the human plane they had never met. He said, "About those spies. There is always the possibility there may be Northern agents down here, but I doubt it. The people up

North don't need spies to tell them what's going on. They have only to read our newspapers. And what makes you believe that our people are likely to cause trouble? They've never seemed quieter."

"That's just it," Wilson replied. "It's the quietness I don't like. It ain't natural. It ain't to be trusted. Not with how that whole gang of Mr. Clay Vincent's took off to the swamps. Not with the way Mr. George Mayhew had four runaways all in one week. You leave um idle, sir, and they ain't no telling what'll happen. I wouldn't do it, sir."

John felt a kind of hopelessness. Half of what Wilson was saying was true—one of Clay Vincent's gangs had hidden out in the swamps and four of the Mayhew Negroes were missing—but what about the other half? Could the Deerskin people be trusted or couldn't they? He thought they could, and Wilson thought otherwise, and Wilson's belief that this was no time to trust any Negro, or, worse, to be indulgent, would be backed by practically every man in the low country. John had the sense of being driven into a corner. He was being asked to distrust the people on Deerskin because distrust had come to be regarded as one of the essentials of patriotism: because not to distrust them might now be interpreted as a sign of disloyalty to the South. He lost his patience all at once.

"What would you have me do, Mr. Wilson?" he asked. "Lock them up at night and fasten them each with a ball and chain? If that's your wish, I'm afraid I can't oblige."

An almost imperceptible rearrangement of the little muscles around Wilson's eyes made John realize that this time he had gone too far. He could tell what Wilson was thinking merely by the way he stood there, and what he was thinking was that this son of Corwin Bottomley was a fool. There was not a planter for miles around who was not taking extra precautions. Guards were being posted, doors and windows made doubly secure, and guns and ammunition kept close at hand. Everybody knew that what the North wanted was a slave insurrection. Northern spies were everywhere, even if this fool wouldn't believe it, and any night now the work of destruction might begin. But here at Deerskin, because of how soft and slack the place was run, nothing had been done. Nothing *would* be done. It was like he was being asked to let himself get murdered in his sleep. It was too jugging goddamn much, by God!

And John understood that it was too much. For years the fear of a slave rebellion had run like a fever through the South. Most of the time it burned feebly, almost unnoticed, a latent infection that men had learned to live with, but now in these past few months, because of secession and the increasing threat of war, it was raging more dangerously than ever before. John knew the fever well. His mother had always been ill with it—dangerously ill; brought to the edge of a cruel, wild terror that ripped the dark with nightmare screams—and if Wilson had come to be fearful of being murdered in his sleep, John could appreciate that too.

But what could he do? For ten years he had lived at Deerskin, and for ten years he had tried to deny what Miss Clarissa Drew and Professor Adam Sedgewick had both so intransigently affirmed—that in mere possession there is cruelty, and that no man who lived by slavery could ever hope to gain his soul. To satisfy Wilson—to distrust the people at Deerskin simply on demand; to lock them up when curfew came; to mount guard; to return to the whip—what would it mean except that Miss Clarissa and Professor Sedgewick had been proved right? If he was asking too much of Wilson, Wilson was asking too much of him.

He looked again at his overseer, thinking that the man's true center of vision lurked somewhere behind his blank impassive stare, and though on the surface nothing would seem to have happened—two men having a discussion, with their horses standing untethered nearby; the distant sound of an ax spacing itself in the flat bright light of noon; enough of a breeze to ripple the waters of Little River—it was clear that he and Wilson had come to a final parting of the ways. Wilson would remain at Deerskin, bound by habit and his affection for Corwin Bottomley and his twelve hundred dollars a year, but whatever still remained of Wilson's regard for him—not much, to be sure—had in the last few minutes been forfeited entirely.

John could not blame Wilson and neither could he blame himself. They were both casualties of the time. Knowing that the rift was now too great for words to make any difference, he said, "The afternoon off still stands, Mr. Wilson. Call in the gangs and get the women in from the cane field. And why don't you take the afternoon off too? You haven't been away from the place since weeks before Christmas."

Wilson's expression did not change. He was able to indicate, however, merely by a slight shift of position, that he understood their relationship had been placed on a new footing, and that, in addition, it was all right with him. Wilson said, "Thank you, sir. I been meaning to ask could I ride over to Bugtown anyhow. My brother-in-law that keeps the store there, the one's that's married to my sister Jane, he ain't been doing so good, and I been wanting to ride over and make um a visit. You sure it won't be no bother, sir?"

"Of course not, Mr. Wilson. There's nothing that needs especially to be done, is there?"

Wilson thought a moment. "No sir, not that I can think of. Not if you want um to have the afternoon off, that is. I ain't been to the sick-house yet, figuring that maybe you would want to do that yourself, and there's that loose rod we ought to look at on the threshing machine, but other than that, and maybe that cow with the lump-jaw——"

And maybe a hundred other things, John thought. The work on a plantation was never caught up with. He said, "We've done everything we can for that cow. And looking at that loose rod isn't going to help any. What we need is a new one. I was hoping it would come up on the *Serena* this morning, but it didn't. How many hands reported sick today?"

"Just one, sir, Cornelius J. It looks like the fever again. That makes three of um down in the past four days. Old Nellie, she's complaining of them same old pains, but she wouldn't go to the sick-house, and that girl of Rosella's, the one that they call Glory, she fell and hurt her arm. If you want me to wait——"

"Thank you, Mr. Wilson. I'll be able to manage."

Wilson hesitated briefly. "All right, sir. I reckon I'll be getting along then. I won't be long over to Bugtown. I'll be back by curfew. I'll be here to ring the bell."

"Don't hurry, Mr. Wilson. Have a good ride."

Wilson turned away abruptly, holding himself stiff and straight, like a man with a grudge who does not want it to spill, and once again John could tell what Wilson was thinking: that he had done everything in his power, that he had warned against giving them a chance to make trouble, and that he was now washing his hands of the whole thing. He strode off in a way that gave John the impression he was leaving Deerskin forever, and when he mounted his horse and reined it into motion without once looking back, John was sorry to see him go.

CHAPTER THREE

Watching Wilson ride off, John could not mourn the loss of a friend. Things would never again be the same at Deerskin, however, and never had he felt so alone. He walked to his horse, swung himself into the saddle, and looked for a time across the land. The long reaches of solitude seemed to have taken on a new dimension, and there was a larger immensity of silence and sky. And it must have been that, John often thought later—the feeling of aloneness; the sense of separation —that was responsible for what happened when he visited the sick-house. It must have been because he had been alone too long.

Tending the sick was woman's work. It was looked after on most plantations by the mistress or older daughters of the house. John never entered the sick-house, a small frame structure at one end of the slave quarters that had been fitted out as a hospital, without being conscious that here again he was being set off from the rest of his kind.

What was needed at Deerskin was a woman. John Bottomley's name rarely came up without the lack being mentioned, and one of the favorite topics of conversation in Pompey's Head, especially at meetings of the Wednesday Afternoon Ladies Society, was why hadn't he ever married. It was understood that he had been disappointed by a girl in Philadelphia, some Yankee bluestocking, but that was years and years ago, when he was going to school up North, and it wasn't as if he hadn't been offered a lot of opportunities to forget. Elizabeth Paxton would have him in a minute, and Isabella Vincent still opened those big black eyes of hers as wide as she could every time he came in sight, and there was that cousin of Kitty Williams from Savannah, Archer DeVere, who practically caused a scandal the way she danced with him at the last Light Infantry Ball. There must be somebody in whom he was interested. It couldn't be much of a life for him, buried out there at Deerskin all alone.

Because of his sister Missy, who was now eighteen, John was kept fully apprised of the gossip of Pompey's Head. The only thing that pleased him was that Lydia Stanhope's name was never linked with his. Nothing was ever your own business in Pompey's Head, least of all anything that even remotely resembled a romantic involvement, but apparently he had gone through that episode without its having caused any talk.

He had been wise to mask his feelings. He owed a debt to Miss Clarissa Drew. He could now think of Miss Clarissa without pain, even with affection, remembering her kindliness to the young Southern stranger who carried a letter of introduction from a distant Drew kinsman in Pompey's Head, but four years ago, when he fell in love with Lydia Stanhope, the memory of Miss Clarissa's refusal of him had barely healed over. He was not ever going to let himself be hurt in that particular way again.

No one, consequently, ever knew: no one but Lydia. For a few months, moreover, she had given him reason to hope. And then, to the speechless astonishment of all Pompey's Head (a speechlessness soon remedied), she married Senator Robert Stanhope, who had once represented the state in Washington, and with so little distinction that he was not returned. A widower with a young unmarried daughter (two others were safely wed), Senator Stanhope was old enough to be Lydia's father. His unmarried daughter Arabella was but nine years younger than she.

There are different ways of being hurt, and John had come to believe that this was the worst way of all—Lydia was married to Senator Stanhope and he was still in love with her. He did not think she knew. He had been careful not to let anyone divine his feelings. Unable fully to trust himself in Lydia's company, he did what he could to avoid her. The safest place was Deerskin.

34

John did not want to be in love with Lydia Stanhope. Much as he disliked to agree with the gossip of Pompey's Head, it must be true what they said—she had married the Senator for his fortune. And yet he was as much in love with her as ever. He would dream of her in the night, and wake from his dream, and stare into the darkness, wanting her in a way that brought his fist to his mouth. Nor did it help to tell himself this was madness. He no longer wished to contend with it. He would have said he had only his madness to live by. And so time after time he called her name—Lydia, Lydia, Lydia— and the sound was the source and echo of all his loneliness, its darkness and its heart. To speak her name was a way of reaching out to her, of giving some partial shape and definition to the vision of beauty that lay deep within him, beyond the grasp or containment of words, and as he rode down the river road toward the slave quarters he reached out to her again—reached out, seized on nothing, and heard the sound of the vision collapse upon the silence and the sky. He put his horse into a gallop and did not rein up until he reached the slave quarters. His horse was sweating a little, and so was he.

ii

The sound of his horse announced his coming, and when he reached the quarters, slowing down to a walk, a number of Negro children tumbled out of the cabins to watch him ride by. They waved to him and he waved back, and then, as if touched off by his appearance, the children began running and shouting all over the compound, scattering chickens and dust and dogs. A small, bent woman came to the door of one of the cabins, the crook of her back showing higher than her wrinkled, ancient face—Aunt Mim, her name was, a former field hand no longer able to do any work and just living out her days. She called out something in a high, unintelligible cackle, directing her voice toward a small boy who was scampering close to the horse's heels, grinning as he ran. John raised his hand to her, and then to an old man who sat huddled beneath a torn felt hat in the front door of a cabin nearby, sunning himself, and the old man, who used to be the plantation carpenter and still helped around the place in various small ways, rose stiffly, took off his hat, bowed, and kept his head uncovered until John had ridden past.

The cabins stood in a single line, twelve in all, housing thirty-nine people. Built of wood and with sharply angled roofs, each had a wooden slide or grating to admit light and air. John had rarely seen any of these used as they were intended. Even during the hottest weather they were nearly always shut. Nor was this because the Negroes were afraid of fresh air, as some people said. That was part of their fear, since they believed the fever was borne on the wind, but their real dread, their terror, was of duppies or ghosts. These evil spirits were everywhere. They killed hogs, destroyed chickens, sickened the cattle, curdled milk, and caused babies to be stillborn. They could not get into a sealed house, however, and though they went about their work only when full dark came, it was wise not to invite disaster, even in the glare of noon.

Negroes were no strangers to John Bottomley. Whenever he entered the quarters, however, an almost palpable emanation of strangeness seemed to rise and contain him on all sides. It was more than the disorderly appearance of the quarters—the scattered chicken feathers, the broken shoes and discarded rags, the bleached bones thrown long ago to the dogs—and more than the realization that he and Wilson were two white men among thirty-nine black people, two of the few white men anywhere in that part of the country. What caused the strangeness, John had come to believe, was that these people were somehow closer to man's original condition and to some earlier relation with the earth. There were naturally no duppies—a modern man could not believe in ghosts—but there was evil lurking everywhere, and the duppies gave reminder of evil, just as the veneration accorded the first sheaves of rice to come from the harvest gave contrary reminder of good, in a way that had been lost from the lives and imaginations of more civilized men.

But what was this, as Corwin Bottomley would remind him, except another way of saying that the Negroes were little more than savages? And those voodoo rites in the swamps, at which all kinds of obscenities were supposed to be celebrated; and the charms; and the whole rigid system of superstitions and taboos—were not these elements of savagery as well? John could not deny it. Even Professor Adam Sedgewick had been unable to deny it. "Yes, yes, Mr. Bottomley!" Professor Sedgewick had said impatiently, pulling at his beard in a way he had. "A creature captured in the jungles of Africa and then sold into slavery is hardly qualified to hold down a chair of philosophy—of *course* he's a savage! But is not a savage a man? And a man born a savage —does that mean he was born to be a slave? I'm not an Abolitionist and I'm not a radical. I think the worst thing that ever happened to this country was to make slavery a political issue. But I will tell you this, Mr. Bottomley—in so far as the Abolitionists and radicals hold that a slave is a man, and by that token heir to man's natural aspirations, then, sir, to that extent the Abolitionists and radicals are more enlightened than your Mr. John Calhoun, who finds good—*positive* good, mind you—in your peculiar institution. Has it ever occurred to you, Mr. Bottomley, what slavery has really done to your section?"

"Done, sir?" John replied. "What do you mean? I don't think I understand."

Professor Sedgewick pulled at his beard again. His beard and hair were white, but a youthful vigor shone in his dark brown eyes. "No, I don't suppose you do," he said. "You're too close to it. All you Southern people are. As I see it, however, slavery has caused something like a wall of mountains to rise up and separate the South from the outside world. It's shut off. It's like Spain in that respect. And it has now reached the point, or will have soon, when it will demand to be shut off. For only by isolating itself from the rest of the world will it be able to maintain its and Mr. John Calhoun's illusions about a slave society—I'm not talking about such backward places as Brazil; I mean Europe; I mean the world in which slavery is understood to be a thing of the past. Do I make myself clear?"

"Yes sir. I think so."

"Think so?" Professor Sedgewick lifted his brows. "There should be no difficulty, Mr. Bottomley. All I am saying, in essence, is that the South has turned its back on the modern world—there has already been secession, in a very real way. And now the South has no choice

37

but to retreat further into the past—Mr. John Calhoun's ideal of a Greek republic, for example. Think how far back that takes us—a good two thousand years or more. But even here your eminent statesman is in error. He may believe he wishes to create a Greek republic, but what he actually hopes to construct is one of the old feudal kingdoms. You are already a feudal people, Mr. Bottomley. You have built up a feudal society on a feudal base. The dukes of Burgundy would be more at home among you than Plato or Aristophanes. The South is the last great fief, and your Mr. John Calhoun is the last of the great minnesingers."

Though John could not quite remember what a minnesinger was, he felt obliged to defend Mr. Calhoun. But he was naturally no match for Professor Sedgewick. "Come, come, Mr. Bottomley," Professor Sedgewick said at one point. "All you are doing is speaking a collection of prejudices. I will believe what you say about emancipation when the South begins to emancipate instead of doing everything in its power to extend slavery to the new territories that are being opened in the West. The plain truth of the matter—the one big truth to which the South is compelled to blind itself or else fall apart—is that slavery is an indefensible thing.

"You say that the Negro is close to being a savage. I say that even as a savage he is a man. But what I say, since I am a Northern man, is naturally suspect. I belong to the world from which the South has sealed itself off. Today it is the Northern view of slavery that has been called into question. Tomorrow it will be the Northern view on any subject whatsoever. Merely to label a thing 'Northern,' no matter what, will be to render it suspicious, and perhaps dangerous as well. It may seem unimportant. To my way of thinking, however, it is this, even more than slavery, that is dividing the South and the North into two hostile camps. I see it as one of the reefs on which the Republic is likely to founder and go to pieces. By nature I am a hopeful man, Mr. Bottomley. It depresses me to take such a gloomy view. Just wait, however, and see."

John waited and saw, and as he rode past the cabins toward the sick-house, with the small boy still running after him, he could honestly say he no more believed in slavery than Professor Sedgewick did. He actually had better reasons for not believing in it, reasons that involved him as a person, flesh-and-blood reasons that were never altogether out of his mind—yet he lived and profited by the work of slaves. Approach it how he may, nothing could alter the fact that by the sweat of their brows the Deerskin Negroes earned his bread.

Where, then, having come to this crossroad of conflict, did his true path lie? Away from any kind of identification with slavery, Professor Sedgewick would say: "Come join with us in the modern world." Yes, yes, all very well—but where in the modern world? Professor Sedgewick's World Opinion, if followed to its logical end, led straight to the camp of the Abolitionists. Was it with them that he must join, those angry men and women who saw the South as a new Carthage that, no less than Hannibal's, must be destroyed? How could he? To them it was Carthage, but to him it was home. This was his country and these were his people. Could he be expected to help put it and them to the sword? He did not think that one wrong could be righted by another. He did not believe in extremes.

The fat, though, was already in the fire. Only a few weeks ago, just before Christmas, his own state had seceded, and several other states were preparing for secession conventions. Some of them might already have left the Union for all he knew, away from everything as he was, and it seemed almost certain that all the Southern states, including Virginia, which wavered first one way and then the other, would declare for secession eventually. So in a sense an extreme position had already been forced upon him. It was only a matter of weeks, if not of days, before the Union would be gone. Soon there would be a constitutional convention somewhere and a new country would be formed. Hard though the idea was to get used to, he was not a United States man any longer. He was a Confederate man. When the band played "Hail Columbia," it would never again be for him.

John could not believe, however, that the end would be there—not with the Abolitionists on one side and men like Gup and Ules Monckton on the other. He did not know much about the Abolitionists except that he was offended by their literature, but he knew all about the Moncktons. The North had a name for men like them, fire-eaters, and it was as good a name as any. Everywhere in the South it was being said that the slave states desired no more than to be permitted to go in peace (Corwin Bottomley had made what was considered a magnificent speech on the subject at the last meeting of the Agricultural Society), but men like the Moncktons no more wanted a peaceful separation than did the Abolitionists. And if the Abolitionists and the Moncktons got what they were after, and war came——

At that point John Bottomley's mind always rebelled. A war between the sections was unthinkable. With the new engines of destruction that had been invented—repeating rifles, new and heavier artillery, explosives whose power was beyond anyone's comprehension —it would mean the most fearful conflict ever known. And it would also mean he must stand and declare himself. No middle position would be possible. He would have to choose between the Abolitionists and the Moncktons.

His only consolation was that the moment of choice had not yet arrived. It was still possible to hope in the reasonableness of men and trust that neither the Abolitionists nor the Moncktons would prevail. Meanwhile he had the sick to look after. Meanwhile he wished he could rid his mind of Lydia Stanhope. Meanwhile he had never felt so completely alone.

He pulled up his horse before the sick-house and dismounted. The small boy who had all this time been trailing the horse stopped running and looked at him. The boy was still grinning, though not so widely, and what was the whiter, his teeth or his eyes, John found it hard to say. He took the boy to be about seven—too young to understand that the master must not be bothered when he made his rounds, too young to comprehend either the meaning of his skin or his identity as a slave. John remembered Miss Clarissa Drew and Professor Adam Sedgewick, and the thought came to him that this was Slavery—this one small boy standing in the dust and the sunlight, too young to understand. John said, "Tell me, little cooter. Am I a bad man? Should I go against my people for you?" and gave the boy a hard slap on the behind. The boy jumped back, laughing wildly, and scampered away.

John tied his horse to the hitching post in front of the sick-house and walked up onto the porch. "And if Wilson is right," he thought, "that boy's father may be in a plot to murder me. His mother may also be in the plot. And old Aunt Mim. And all the rest of them." He began to wish he had not suggested Wilson take the afternoon off—if there was going to be trouble, he would prefer not to be alone. It dawned on him what he was thinking, and he cut himself short. The tension, he realized, was beginning to get on his nerves.

iii

There were four rooms in the sick-house, two on either side of a narrow hall. Three of the rooms had been turned into wards—one for men, one for women, and one for expectant mothers lying in—and the fourth was used to store medicinal supplies. The door here always had to be kept locked, since the Negroes had learned that some of the remedies had certain attractions over and above their therapeutic content—a whole gallon of Pittman's Ague Cure had once disappeared overnight.

John Bottomley often thought his entire ability as a physician had been distilled into Pittman's Ague Cure. The remedy was manufactured in Philadelphia, and occasionally he wondered if it had ever come to the attention of Miss Clarissa Drew. According to its label, it had been compounded as "A Speedy Cure for Intermittent Fever, Fever, or Ague, caused by the malaria of miasmatic countries, and from which arise such grave disorders as Neuralgia, Rheumatism, Headaches, Blindness, Tooth-Ache, Ear-Ache, Asthma, Colic, Palpitations, and Derangement of the Stomach." Corwin Bottomley swore by it, as did most of the other planters who played cards at the Light Infantry Club, and though John did not altogether share their enthusiasm, neither did he know how, without Pittman's, he would have been able to manage. Even so the sick-house was his largest source of worry.

It did not take him long to discover that it was in need of constant supervision. There were long passages of daydreaming in which he saw it being looked after by Lydia Stanhope (and once, in an actual dream, by Miss Clarissa Drew), but since a more dependable agent was required he placed it in charge of a tall, thin, middle-aged woman named Rosella. Her husband, Tom, was Wilson's head driver, which gave him the status of assistant overseer, and she and Tom had several grown children. The youngest of these, Glory, was the girl Wilson had mentioned earlier in the day as having reported sick with an injured arm. Glory was seventeen.

Wilson had objected to Rosella's being taken off the work list. He did not like the idea of losing one of his best hands among the women, and he was further annoyed when Rosella, with her new position, put on a new set of airs. She refused to take orders from anyone except the master and lorded it over her former companions in the fields. She tried to lord it over even Hester, the sixty-year-old woman who served as John's housekeeper. Here, however, she did not get far. Hester had been John's nurse when the family was living at Rosebank, before Corwin Bottomley built Indigo; and Rosella, in Hester's scale of things, was just a trashy, corn-hoeing woman who had no notion or appreciation of the subtler refinements and never would. "Where that woman belongs," Hester kept insisting, "is back in the fields!"

There were times when John agreed with her. Rosella seemed to feel that with responsibility went privileges. She developed a habit of leaving the sick-house to go fishing, hoping to return before her absence was noticed, and though she was always meek and submissive when reprimanded, her love of fried fish was too great a temptation to be resisted. On the whole, however, John was satisfied with her performance. She kept the sick-house reasonably clean, gave her patients more care than they would have had otherwise, and developed unusual ability as a midwife. For this John was especially grateful. He had learned how to manage with the men, but with the women he always felt the worst kind of intruder. Unless they were miserably ill, as often they were not, they greeted his appearance with so many giggles, eye-rollings, and tittered asides, and with such wild exhibitions of shrieking modesty, that he was glad to leave them to Rosella.

Immediately John entered the sick-house he knew Rosella had gone fishing again—were she anywhere around she would have met him at the door. He called her name twice, sharply, and opened the door to the storeroom. A shaft of sunlight slanted through the small, barred window, and the room had a closed, aromatic smell.

A quick glance told John nothing had been interfered with. He heard a murmur of voices from the room set apart for the men, threaded with the cluck of some indolent hen just outside the window, and his impatience with Rosella increased. He went to one of the shelves, all of which were papered with sheets taken from the *News*, and took down a quart bottle of Pittman's Ague Cure. It seemed to him that more could be done for the sick than simply dose them over and over again with this same old remedy, and where in hell was the jugging spoon! Time after time he had told Rosella to leave it next to the bottle of Pittman's, and time after time he had to search high and low for it. And once again she had sneaked off, deliberately disobeying orders! It was all very well for Professor Adam Sedgewick to have his lofty notions, and Miss Clarissa Drew too, but if they ever had to live with these people, trying to get them to behave like responsible beings and never being able to depend on them for anything, not anything, Professor Sedgewick and Miss Clarissa might want to change their tune. But this was the end! Rosella would be back in the fields by morning! Where *was* the spoon?

John turned from the shelf, thinking to call Rosella again, and for the first time noticed he was not alone. A young Negro woman in a flimsy white dress stood watching him from the doorway. How long she had been there he could not tell. Her feet were bare, and her dress was too short and tight for her, obviously some garment that she had long since outgrown, and when their eyes met she lowered her eyelids slightly, looking at him steadily for an instant and then looking away. He recognized her as Glory. He had seen her less than a fortnight before, at the annual distribution of Christmas gifts, and he remembered his present to her—four yards of woolen cloth, a plaid bandanna, and a bag of hard candy. He also remembered how she had curtsied to him, and his thinking that during the past year she had developed fully into a woman—soon they would have the problem of young men coming to court her from the neighboring plantations.

He didn't know how news of a marriageable girl managed to spread so fast, but it always did. He addressed her in a mixture of white man's talk and Gullah, the lingua franca of the low country.

"Oonuh Glory, aren't you? Where's yo ma?"

Glory raised her eyes to his. "Ma enty hyah, maussuh. She say fuh me say——"

"Say what! That she's looking after a sick calf or something? How often does she think she can use that same excuse! You tell her that if she doesn't stay here in the sick-house, the way she's supposed to, and that if she keeps fooling around with me, sneaking down to the river whenever my back is turned——"

But what was the use? This girl was not responsible for Rosella. He said:

"Mr. Wilson tells me you hurt your arm. How did it happen?"

Glory said she had fallen down.

"Yes, I know. Mr. Wilson told me. But how?"

Her mother asked her to catch a chicken, which was wanted for the master's supper, and she was chasing the chicken, and there was that big crooked root behind the cabin where she lived——

"So you tripped and fell. Does your arm hurt much?"

No, not much, except when she bent her elbow. Then it hurt bad. It hurt very bad. She had tried to hoe but couldn't. The buckra, Maussuh Wilson, he didn't think she was telling the truth, but then, when he saw she couldn't hoe——

"Where does your arm hurt exactly? Let me see."

Glory extended her left arm and touched a place just below the elbow, and John was struck by the grace of even her simplest movements. He had a sense of a most precariously balanced tension, as if at any moment, like some creature of the woods, she would break and dart away. He drew her into the shaft of sunlight and bent over her arm, the better to see. As he did so his cheek came within inches of her bosom—he caught a glimpse of her ankles and bare legs and could smell the odor of her person. He saw a slight swelling on her arm, but no discoloration, and a more pronounced swelling on the joint

44

of her elbow. He fingered it lightly. Glory, drawing in her breath, winced and pulled away.

"It does hurt, doesn't it?" John said, straightening himself. "It's not broken or anything, though."

She stood in the shaft of sunlight, watching him closely. The yellow light streamed down on her, giving her face a dusky copper tone and putting glints in her coarse black hair. Her features were finer than those of most of her people, and there was something about her carriage that gave a kind of proudness to the way she stood. The thought of Sheba crossed John's mind, of apes and peacocks and ivory thrones, and a great surge of passion rushed through him, pouring into his throat—he moved a step forward, conscious that he was trembling and that her eyes had widened ever so slightly, and what he saw on her face was the same hushed expression he felt on his. All barriers were gone, all differences, and as they stood looking at each other, she in the fall of yellow sunlight and he with his back to the rows of shelves, mastery passed swiftly from him to her. She looked at him steadily, with only the faintest tremor of her lips to disturb the dusky immobility of her face, and when he reached out and touched her cheek, all that he was, every sensation he possessed, every longing, every desire, streamed out through his fingers. A fleeting glimpse of Lydia Stanhope came before him, that fairness against this darkness, that constraint against this freedom, and in this free and joyous darkness there could be such a complete submerging that he need never think of Lydia again.

"Oonuh beautiful," he said. "Oonuh want to leave the fields?"

The movement of her lips may have been a smile. John drew her close, feeling the flick of her tongue in the hollow of his neck. She said huskily, close to his ear, "What Maussuh want? Maussuh want Glory be good to Maussuh?" and when he replied, "No, no, Glory. You must forget I am the master," the iron gates clanged shut again —how could she forget he was the master, and would he not be possessing himself of a chattel, and was not this what they had most in mind, North and South, whenever they spoke of slavery? There was the white man, and the black woman, and what always lay at

45

the bottom of their thoughts, as the ultimate essence of slavery, was the easy availability of the black woman's flesh. It was never mentioned, but there it was. There it was and here he was, and how he was going to put this girl aside he did not know. What caused him to, finally, as even in his agitation he was fully aware, had nothing to do with any moral code—where did they come from, those light-skinned pickaninnies who were to be seen everywhere, and was he to add another to that ambiguous brood, a son or a daughter, *his* son, *his* daughter, the slave children of a slave mother, and in their slavery no less his? He remembered a certain mulatto barber in Pompey's Head—his name never mentioned at Indigo; his existence ignored—and somehow he managed to disentangle himself from Glory's embrace, feeling her legs hard against his.

"No, Glory, no!"

Nor would it do to say, as for an instant he wanted to, that this girl was without morals or shame. He had tried to bribe her by saying she could leave the fields. He found it hard to look at her, and harder to speak. He said something about her finding her mother right away and his returning to the sick-house later on, and added, as an afterthought, that she must not use her arm until it was completely well.

He hurried off blindly, stumbling down the steps of the porch, and it seemed a gift from heaven that he was obliged to go to Pompey's Head for Cameron's engagement party and the Light Infantry Ball. When he mounted his horse his temptation was to ride as hard and fast as he could. He poured himself a large drink of whisky as soon as he reached home, and then a second, smaller one, and forced himself to bear patiently with Hester as she grumbled over his lack of appetite, shuffling to and from the kitchen in a pair of broken shoes, trailing her heavy smell. He ate only a few forkfuls of rice and pork gravy, which he washed down with several cups of coffee, and then, taking a tumbler, the bottle of whisky, and the mail and the copies of the *News* that had come up that morning on the *Serena Moore*, he went out on the porch. He read through the mail and looked to see what was in the *News*.

CHAPTER FOUR

He might have found better solace. Gup Monckton, having got secession, now wanted war, and even the advertisements in the *News* seemed to be straining in that direction. Ten thousand Smith & Wesson pistol cartridges had just been received by W. J. Knight on Bay Street, orders were being taken for military and fatigue hats by A. B. Cornish on the corner of Magnolia and Lafayette, and the Maynard Arms Company of Washington, D.C., a Southern concern, now offered its breech-loading military rifle at thirty-three dollars a gun, ammunition not included, in lots not less than thirty—single guns, forty dollars each.

John reached for his glass and took another swallow of whisky. One would imagine that Gup Monckton's warmongering would have provided him with enough excitement for one day, but no, he also had to put a murder in his paper—one of those recently arrived Irishmen had been found dead on River Street. His name was Shamus O'Connell and he lived somewhere along Frenchman Street, in what had become known, because so many of the newcomers had made their homes there, as the Irish Channel. The coroner's inquest established that O'Connell had come to his death at or about half-past eleven in the evening by means of a knife wound inflicted by some party or parties unknown. It was also established that the knife was the property of the deceased. The weapon had been identified by the dead man's father, Timothy O'Connell, who also claimed the body. Timothy could not account for his son's presence on River Street at that time of night, nor was he able to furnish any clue as to the identity of the murderer. The sheriff's office was continuing its investigation.

John Bottomley could not believe that the sheriff's office would concern itself overmuch with the incident. The Irish immigrants had become established as a class apart. This murder was not the first instance of violence among them. Eighteen months back there had been a previous killing, and life in the Channel had been marked by so many brawls, fist fights, and broken heads that the new arrivals had come to be regarded as a wild, roaring crowd into whose neighborhood it was unwise to venture.

But the quick-temperedness of the Irish might have been over-looked. What gave them their singularity was that they worked at labor beneath the dignity of a white man's skin. Too poor upon their arrival to establish themselves in trade, and unable to turn to the land, all the land having been brought into the large plantations, it became their lot to perform the dirty, backbreaking jobs made necessary by the growth of the city—digging ditches for the new waterworks, working on the spur line of the Atlantic & Central between Pompey's Head and Bugtown, and draining a shallow, scummy lake near the south end of town, a fever bed since the earliest days of the colony, that was known as Jennie's Basin.

One of John Bottomley's secrets, which he preferred not to share, was that he liked these rough strangers. And there was one young woman among them, a full-bosomed girl with deep blue eyes and pale skin and black, black hair, who had struck him as one of the most beautiful people he had ever seen. He had come upon her but once, when he chanced to watch the work at Jennie's Basin, and she apparently had walked from home to bring some food to one of the men, but he never thought of the Irish without also thinking of her, remembering exactly how she looked. Such beauty as hers wanted to be pampered and adored. Put her into one of Missy's dresses and she would be the rage of the Light Infantry Ball. In his sympathy for her it was not hard to feel a measure of sympathy for this Shamus O'Connell, mysteriously murdered on River Street.

It could be argued, however, that Shamus's was perhaps a lesser misfortune than that which had befallen a grocer named Joseph

Schmidt, who lived in the central part of the state. According to the *News*, Schmidt had been visited in the middle of the night by a vigilante committee. The charge against him was that he fraternized with Negroes and had been seen in conversation with a mysterious stranger passing through the neighborhood. Not wanting to be tarred and feathered, and having made it necessary for his callers to act in self-defense (so said the *News*), he had been set upon in such a way that it was unlikely he would recover.

John rose from the chair and walked to the end of the porch. The house was built on the highest point of the property, overlooking the river, and he could see both up and down the stream. This Joseph Schmidt—if it was his turn today, might it not be John Bottomley's turn tomorrow? He did not fraternize with Negroes, nor was it his habit to become intimate with strangers, but what about his having refused to mount guard at Deerskin? What about many other things? If conformity was the measure, might he not fall several inches short? He was a Bottomley, yes, but even as a Bottomley how much immunity did he have? Not much, he feared.

Frowning, John stared into the sun. If that was the kind of society in which he must live, he would rather go with the North: he would be compelled to go with the North. And it was at that moment, when in imagination all he cherished had been put behind—home, family, place, friends—that he saw his brother Cameron coming down the river in one of the long, narrow skiffs peculiar to that part of the country, rowed by a crew of Gullah boatmen.

Surprised to see his brother, whom he believed to be in Pompey's Head, and delighted at the prospect of company, John ran down to the landing. Cameron waved a greeting and the Gullah boatmen bent harder to their task. They chanted as they rowed, the four pairs of oars rising and falling as though ruled by a single set of muscles, and the skiff was soon at the landing. Cameron stepped onto the wooden wharf, wearing his old hunting clothes and a pair of muddy boots and a white shirt open at the throat, and it needed only his appearance to explain why the young ladies of Pompey's Head were supposed to be jealous of Kitty Williams.

"Welcome to Deerskin, bridegroom," John said. "What are you doing out here? I thought you were in town. What happened?"

Instantly he knew it had been an unfortunate thing to say—Cameron's face went strained and harrowed, and John knew something worse than usual must have gone wrong. His first thought was that Cameron and Kitty Williams had fallen out, and then he thought their father and Cameron had had a final rupture, but the look on his brother's face, the hint of panic that always showed itself whenever Cameron got hopelessly beyond his depth, made him understand that matters were even more serious than that. This was not going to be the visit he had hoped for. He said:

"Have you had dinner? I've just finished mine, but Hester can warm something up."

"I could better use a drink," Cameron replied. "I was afraid you might not be here. I thought maybe you'd gone duck shooting or something."

"Well, why don't we? A big new flight came over this morning. Stay the night. Let's have ourselves a time."

Cameron shook his head. "I'd like to, Johnny, but I can't. I have to get on downriver to town."

"Right away?"

"I wish I didn't, but I have to. Elizabeth Paxton is giving a party tonight, and I'm supposed to take Kitty to it, and——"

"Tonight. This party is tonight?"

"Yes. I'm going to be late as it is."

"Late! You're not going to get there at all. Even if your boys break their backs you won't reach Old Pompey till way past midnight. What's got into you? Don't you realize how embarrassing it's going to be for Kitty? You're supposed to be engaged to her, you know!"

Cameron's face took on a hostile expression. He said belligerently, "More and more you sound like Father! Realize this, realize that! It's not for one of your lectures I came!" and though John wanted to reply, "That's right. Start getting unpleasant. Fall into character," he said, instead:

"If you're supposed to be taking Kitty to a party tonight, what are you doing out here? Where have you been? Cornwall?"

"Where else?"

"But why? You cleared out over a month ago. I thought you were starting in at Thrall & Lockhart this week."

"I was supposed to, but I got it changed till after the ball. So many things were coming up——"

"You got it changed! Oh for God's sake, Cam! That's no way to do. Don't you realize——"

"Yes, yes, I *realize!*"

"Sometimes I wonder. And I still don't understand what took you to Cornwall. I'm mystified."

"You mystify too easy. I left some of my stuff at Cornwall—my guns and that Mexican saddle I won off Tolly Rhett, and most of my fishing tackle—and I wanted to get it before that new overseer took it into his mind that it was his."

"But that still doesn't explain why, if you're supposed to be escorting Kitty to a party tonight——"

"Hell-fire, Johnny! What difference does it make if I happen to miss one party? Kitty will understand."

John thought, "Yes, she probably will, and that's what's the matter with you. You've been understood too often," but there was something about Cameron's story that did not hang together. Careless as he was of the things he owned, it could not be believed he had left Pompey's Head at the height of the season merely to get his guns and some fishing tackle and a saddle he'd won in a poker game.

"How did you get to Cornwall?" John asked. "You weren't on the *Serena* when she came up the river this morning, were you?"

"Questions, questions, questions! Maybe you should have married that little Yankee Philadelphia girl. Maybe you should have been a Philadelphia lawyer. You'd have made a good one. No, I wasn't on the *Serena*. I rode up yesterday. I meant to get an early start this morning but I slept late. My stuff is in the skiff. Now, are you satisfied? If you are, you might start showing me some hospitality. Did you say something about a drink?"

"No, but I think you did. Let's go up to the house. Then you can tell me what you came for."

Cameron put on a look of exaggerated innocence. "Came for? Now, Johnny, you don't think for one moment, do you——?" And then, like a small boy discovered in some piece of mischief, he flashed his most winning smile. Somewhere in his childhood Cameron had discovered that he had a way with him, and now, at twenty-two, he was still using the same bag of tricks. Instead of being won over, John was annoyed.

"Climb down, Cam," he said. "The charm is wearing thin. And if it's money you want——"

"Money? Now who in the world said anything about money?"

"Nobody had to say. It is money, isn't it?"

"Well, Johnny, now that you've brought the ugly subject up——"

"Oh what the hell, Cam! Not again!"

"Wait a minute, Johnny."

"What for? You've said what you came for, haven't you?"

"Yes, but——"

"But nothing! I'm getting fed to the gills!"

"Listen, Johnny."

"To what? I'm tired of listening. That's all you seem to think I have to do!"

John felt put upon and irritated. He had been foolish to imagine Cameron had come to make him a visit. In the ten years he had lived at Deerskin, Cameron had come to see him exactly twelve times, and nine of those times he wanted money. He wasn't a brother to Cameron any longer. He was more like a country branch of the Merchants & Mechanics Bank.

"Don't be like that, Johnny," Cameron said. "Hear me out. All right, it *is* money. But that's not all I came for. I know what you're thinking, and I can't say I blame you, but if you'd only listen——"

John shut his ears to the note of urgency that had come into Cameron's voice. He wasn't going to be charmed and he wasn't going to be cajoled. Noticing that the Gullah boatmen were listening to every word, he said, "Let's not talk about it here. There's no point in letting the whole country in on it. Let's go up to the house," and though he told himself it was foolish to let his feelings be hurt, nothing was gained by pretending they weren't. He had come to the end of his rope with Cameron. He no longer cared.

ii

That, however, wasn't true. Walking up to the house, with Cameron keeping step beside him, John felt threatened with the same sense of loss, only a deeper loss, as when Wilson had turned his back on him—he did not want to do anything that would cut him off from his brother, nor did he want to lose a friend. He had only this one brother, and too few friends. But the thing worked both ways, damn it! He didn't ask much of Cameron, and never had, but it did seem Cameron might have at least remembered to say, "How are you, Johnny? How have you been getting along?" instead of holding out his hand the moment he stepped ashore. It would not have been much, but it would have been something.

"Let's have it, Cam," he said when finally they were settled on the porch, each with a drink. "What's the mess this time?"

It grated on his ears the moment he said it. He knew it was his hurt feelings that were speaking, and was tempted to apologize, but Cameron's face was already flushed with anger. He said, "Jug! If that's going to be your attitude, *mess*, stow it! If you've become so high and mighty that you can't even hear what I have to say, you don't have to! Oh sure, I know! According to you and Father, I'm a weak, trifling son-of-a-bitch who's fouled up everything all along the line! I fouled up my schooling, and I fouled up being a planter, and now I'm getting ready to foul up my marriage to Kitty!"

"You're saying that, Cam, not me."

"But it's what you're thinking, isn't it? Oh, I've heard it all from Father. *Mess!* You're quick to jump to conclusions, aren't you? Just because you don't give a damn about anything but seeing how big a turnout you can make each year, working like a nigger and piling up money in the bank——"

"You watch your tongue, Cam! Mind what you say!"

Cameron's face seemed to disintegrate all at once. His features were a refined, handsomer version of their father's—the cheekbones leaner and higher; the nose more delicately modeled; the mouth almost feminine in its full-lipped sensuality—and John had the impression that a younger, weaker Corwin Bottomley was sitting across from him, going to pieces before his eyes. And it was then, as he realized later, that he should have risen above pique and hurt feelings and given Cameron the help he must have come for.

That, though, was later. At the time he felt only more irritation. It was unseemly of Cameron to show so little control: his lack of manliness was embarrassing. For Cameron to be one of the young bucks of Pompey's Head was to be expected. Everything considered, it could hardly be otherwise. At the same time, however, he ought to be able to carry through. He shouldn't fall apart whenever he found himself in a tight place.

Not wanting to sound harsh and yet unable not to, John said, "I'd try to get control of myself if I were you. And it's not that I'm unwilling to listen. It's just that I don't see the use. You need money again and you want me to bail you out. Do you think it makes it any more entertaining to hear how you almost filled a straight or how you would have cleaned up on that sure thing at the Twin Oaks track if she hadn't been given such a bad ride? That's what I'm tired of. It isn't amusing any more."

"You know so jugging much, don't you?"

"I know all I need to know. How much are you in for this time?"

Cameron seemed ready to go to pieces again: some torment caused him to draw back his lips, baring his teeth, and he shook his head desperately. "It's not just the money, Johnny. Honest to God it isn't! If you'd stop knowing everything just for a minute and hear me out——"

"All right, Cam. Have it your own way. I'll hear you out."

It was weariness that dogged his voice, the worst kind of weariness, but to Cameron it must have sounded like indifference. "You're real interested, aren't you?" Cameron said. "You just can't wait to hear.

All right then! Since you're only interested in how much, I'll tell you how much! I'd like to borrow fifteen hundred dollars."

"Fifteen hundred dollars!"

"I'll pay you back. I'm due the rest of my money from Grandpa's estate when I get married, eleven thousand in cash——"

"But for God's sake, Cam! How long do you think that eleven thousand will last? It's supposed to help you get started on your marriage. If you squander it beforehand——"

"I'll pay you back. I swear I will. I owe you an even nine hundred already, and that, added to fifteen hundred——"

"That's not the point, Cam! It's the way you seem to think you can throw that money around. Don't you know it's all you have left? You've run through the five thousand you got when you were twenty, and God knows how much Mother has let you have on the side——"

"That's right! Be like Father again! Throw it up to me!"

"Does Father know how deep in you are?"

"No."

"Does Mr. Williams?"

"No."

"Does anybody?"

"How do I know? No, I don't think so. What difference does it make?"

"Do you have to ask? How much good do you think it will do you if it gets around town that you've been running through money you don't even have yet, money that was intended to start you on your marriage? How do you think it will sound at Thrall & Lockhart? How do you imagine it will set with Father? Or Mr. Williams? How do you think it will make Kitty feel? Don't you realize——"

"Realize, realize, realize! Realize *what!* That Thrall & Lockhart is taking me in only because Mr. Thrall doesn't want to lose the family's business? That I'll hardly be able to support Kitty on the salary I'll be making and that we couldn't afford to get married if Father wasn't going to let me have the income from Cornwall? What else do you want me to realize? That Mr. Williams doesn't think I'm good enough for Kitty? Maybe I'm not! Maybe I'm not good enough for

55

anybody! Maybe the best thing would be for me to go off somewhere and never bother anybody again!"

"Look, Cam. Just because you feel bad——"

"Well, wouldn't it?"

"No, it wouldn't. And your abusing yourself doesn't help any, either. You can have the money. I'll write you a check you can cash on Monday. But don't think I can afford it. I can't. When last year's books are balanced, Thrall & Lockhart and I will just about break even. Sometimes I think we planters work only to support our factors. You'll probably end up richer than any of us."

"If I end up at all."

"Oh, drop it, Cam! You've got the miseries, that's all. You'll feel better by morning."

"A lot you know!"

"I know enough to know that."

"Isn't it fine you think so!"

"If we're going to argue, let's argue about something important. One thing I'd like to make clear. This is the last time. You fry your own fish for a change. If it wasn't for Kitty——"

Cameron gave a snort. "Sure! Sure! As if I wasn't aware! If it wasn't for Kitty you'd send me packing. But it isn't really Kitty you're worrying about. You're thinking of Mr. Williams. What you mean is that you don't want to give him a chance to call off the marriage. That would upset everything, wouldn't it? Think of all the plans that would be spoiled!"

What Cameron was saying came so close to the truth that John did not know how to answer. Cameron took another swallow from his glass, shuddered, and curled his lip scornfully. "Don't worry, Johnny," he said. "Nothing will happen. What you're forgetting is that land should marry land. Mr. Williams holds to that as much as Father. There's Cornwall, and next to Cornwall there's Peachtree, and what is more natural than that Cornwall and Peachtree should march to the altar? It's all right, Johnny. Mr. Williams won't do anything rash. He has four daughters to marry off. He may not think I'm good enough for Kitty, but when you look at it from the acreage point of view, Cornwall is by far the better part of the bargain. You're too sentimental, Johnny. You ought to take a more practical view. How about passing me the bottle? I'd appreciate another drink."

John did not like the turn the conversation had taken. He had never heard Cameron talk in this vein before. It sounded as if he was being forced to marry Kitty Williams against his will. But it was he who had proposed to her, wasn't it? However much their father and Mr. Williams desired the marriage, each for his own reasons, they had not engineered that. Or had they? John often wondered.

"Nothing has gone wrong with you and Kitty, has it?"

Cameron sloshed some whisky into his glass and rested the bottle on the floor of the porch. "No, of course not," he said, and nearly drained the glass. "If that was all——" Then, thinking better of what he had been about to say, he drained the glass completely. "I told you not to worry," he said, apparently a little more in control of himself. "Everything is going to be all right. Did you hear about the outhouses?"

"What outhouses?"

"The ones that got burned down."

"What are you talking about?"

"The great outhouse fire of '61. Don't you ever hear anything back here in the country? Last Saturday night the Light Infantry had a meeting. Mr. Ules Monckton got some books called Hardee's *Tactics* that he wanted to hand out. He wants us to study them so we can all be generals. Even if we don't want to be. Why weren't you at that meeting?"

"I had work to do."

"You'll never get to be a general that way. What's the matter with you? Don't you want to be a general?"

"Not specially."

"That's no way to talk. Every true Southern man ought to want to be a general. That's what Mr. Ules Monckton says."

"He does, does he?"

"Give the man credit for practicing what he preaches, Johnny. He was bound to be elected captain of the Light Infantry—he put up all the money, didn't he?—but just being captain wasn't enough. So he's going to get himself elected colonel instead. That's one step closer to general. It's all fixed. Tony Blackford will be captain."

"And you?"

"Me?" Cameron paused a moment. "I don't think Mr. Monckton likes me. The way he looks at it, I don't want to be a general bad enough. Mr. Monckton, though, he won't rest till he is. He knows that tactics book frontways and back. He says we should all know it like he does. That way the Yankees won't stand a chance. One big licking, he says, and the Yankees are done for."

"What else does he say?"

"It would take too long to tell. He got up to make a few remarks and went on talking for over an hour—all about how there is a new empire that belongs to the South, and how the North gave the South a jugging down in Mexico and Nicaragua, and how the Abolitionists want to turn us all over to the niggers. He makes a good speech— that I have to hand to him—and after the meeting he spread us one of the best dinners you ever saw. He even brought out some French champagne. Six whole cases of it. That's how the outhouses happened to go up."

"I think I'm beginning to see."

Cameron thought a moment, looking more subdued. Then, in what struck John as a determined effort to be cheerful, "It was mostly Tony Blackford's idea about the outhouses," he said. "Gordy Carpenter and Jack Wendover pitched in, but it was Tony who thought it up. He said that most of the outhouses in Old Pompey were architectural monstrosities. I don't know where he picked it up about the architectural monstrosities, but that's what he said. He made those monstrosities sound like a civic disgrace."

"And so?"

"So Gordy Carpenter remembered about those secession torches that are stored in the club, the ones that were bought for the parade, and now there ain't a single architectural monstrosity left along the whole of Alwyn Street from Musgrove to St. Andrew's Square."

"A lot you fellows have to do!"

"Don't sound like that, Johnny. It was a real entertaining evening. You should have been there. Somebody got into the steeple of St. Paul's and started ringing the general fire alarm, and both volunteer companies rolled out their pumpers, and the windows in all the houses lit up like if the Yankees had arrived, and old Mr. Peter Pettibone with tears in his eyes ran out in his nightshirt and begged to have his outhouse spared."

John had to laugh. Nobody liked Mr. Peter Pettibone, who was known as the town skinflint, and there was something most amusing about his pleading for his outhouse with bare shanks showing—it sounded like an evening that would be remembered for a long time.

"You might have set the whole town on fire, you know."

"What do you mean, 'you'?" Cameron said. "I had no part of that ruckus. All I did was to help the constables try to restore law and order. It wasn't my fault that one of them got tied to the bell rope in the steeple of St. Paul's."

"I'm sure it wasn't. I'm only surprised that you weren't sound asleep in bed. How many damage suits have been filed? That's not why you need this fifteen hundred, is it?"

"No, that's not it," Cameron said, and his mood darkened again. "I just need it, that's all. How about writing that check? I'd best be getting along."

"Just remember what I told you, Cam. This is the last time."

"I'll remember."

"It will help us both if you do. Other than that, if I may say something about you and Kitty Williams——"

But Cameron was no longer listening. His attention had been caught by something in the front yard. Glancing to find out what it was, John saw Glory walking toward the rear of the house. She had on the same short, tight-fitting dress and was carrying a small basket full of eggs. She walked slowly, keeping her eyes fixed straight ahead, but there was something about the way she carried herself, the merest suggestion of a flaunting of her person, that made John understand she was aware of his presence on the porch.

Cameron, sitting with his mouth slightly open, followed her passage across the yard, and though John found time to ask himself if this might be why his brother needed fifteen hundred dollars—"There isn't some other girl mixed up in this, is there, not so close to his getting married?"—he was more uncomfortably aware that the look on Cameron's face was almost the same look that had been on his own face only a short time before. It was like catching his reflection in a mirror, a magical, terrifying glass that stripped away all the little concealments behind which we are accustomed to hide, and when Glory finally disappeared around a corner of the house and Cameron again looked in his direction—a different look: a look that implied, "So that's what you have stashed away for yourself out here in the swamps? No wonder you don't care about coming to town"—he found it hard to meet his brother's eyes.

"What were you saying?" Cameron asked.

"Nothing that needs repeating. You wait here. I'll write that check."

iii

Once Cameron had the check, he was in a hurry to be off. Standing on the wooden landing with the Gullah boatmen waiting on their oars, he said, "I'll see you in town. I'm obliged for the kindness," and stepped into the skiff. The boatmen got the skiff out into the middle of the river and sent it leaping along, chanting as they rowed. Each forward thrust of the craft was marked by a flash of sunlight on their oars, and as the skiff went round a bend in the river and the sound of the chanting became fainter and fainter, the wall of solitude that had been breached by Cameron's visit began to rise again.

John wished he too were going down the river. Restless, and not knowing what else to do with himself, he stepped into a cypress dugout that was tied to the landing and slipped it free. Taking up the paddle, he worked upstream against the current. He went past a few of his people who had taken advantage of their free afternoon to fish from the banks, past one rice field after the other, until, two miles or so upriver, he came to a small creek, barely wide enough to admit the dugout, that twisted its way through the tangled grasses of Little Pigeon Marsh.

He followed the creek until it widened into a large, shallow pond where a flock of mallards were feeding. The ducks took to the air upon his approach, the rush of their wings leaving a rippled shadow upon the surface of the pond, and he watched them skein out raggedly, heading for the river—a white heron, standing on one leg on the far side of the pond, continued its meditations undisturbed.

John grounded the dugout on the mud and grasses of the marsh and lit a cigar. Wilson, Glory, Cameron, the *News* and its growls for war—one thing went into another, a third thing entered, and there was so much thought that there was no thought: only the last rays of the sun, and the marsh a solid sweep of gold, and a gradual shrinking of himself in the enormous solitude, shrinking and shrinking to the self that he was. John smoked his cigar and watched the heron. When it stood on one leg, the gathered cluster of its other foot looked like a crumpled purple flower, and when it searched for food, stalking along the edge of the pond with its high, precise steps, it seemed a mincing old woman shrinking from the touch of water—there now: the fool thing's caught a frog.

At this time of year the sun dropped quickly. The sky changed from blue to purple, the marsh grew vague with shadow, and the dark came on in its first swift rush. John knew it was beautiful, but the beauty was beyond him. Too many things were in the way. Housed in his diminished self, he could not go out to it. He threw away what was left of his cigar, hearing it hiss as it hit the water, and reached for the paddle. The heron, possibly alarmed by the motion of his arm, lifted itself upon a ghostly haze of wings and flew deeper into the marsh. With it gone there was nothing but the silence, and in the silence the sound of his voice—Lydia, Lydia, he said.

He followed the creek back to the river, and when he reached the river it was night. A fish jumped close to the dugout, making a loud splash, and when he drew near the landing he could hear the Negroes singing. They often did, this hour of evening. Supper would be over, and they would be sitting in their doorways, talking and laughing, and then some one of them would start singing all alone, and the talking and laughing would drop to a hush and then cease entirely as one by one the others slowly joined in. John paddled closer to the shore. He steadied the dugout in a piece of quiet water and sat in the darkness, listening. One high female voice rose pure and clear above the massed lament of the others, speaking of sinners and sorrow and lost young lambs, and for an instant it all was one—the darkness of the river, the darkness of the voices, and the darkness of his heart. John felt better, however, for his excursion. He was hungry when he got home.

PART TWO

PART TWO

Cameron's visit to Deerskin was on a Saturday, the Williamses' party took place the evening of the following Tuesday, and by the night of the Light Infantry Ball on Friday, three days later, it was all over town that Cameron Bottomley had run out on Kitty Williams and was nowhere to be found. Even in a place as large as Charleston or Savannah it would have caused a consternation. In Pompey's Head it was a scandal of the first degree.

The Light Infantry Ball customarily began at ten o'clock. This year, however, because of the parade of secession torches beforehand, it was set for ten-thirty. A large crowd turned out to see the parade, and traffic moved slowly. The crush was especially great in the neighborhood of Caledonia Hall. The ball was to be held there, and Monmouth Square, upon which the hall fronted, had been selected as the place where the Light Infantry would disband after the parade. This was the older part of town, and the narrow streets leading to Monmouth Square were clogged with a line of vehicles backed up three blocks or more.

John Bottomley, sitting in the family carriage with his father and mother and his sister Missy, who looked strangely grown up with her curls piled high on her head in the new fashion and her arms and shoulders bare, was beginning to be restless. They had not moved fifteen yards in fifteen minutes. Leaning from the carriage to see what was responsible for the delay, and finding himself no wiser than before, John noticed that the carriage immediately ahead was that of the Christopher Lakes and that the one just behind belonged to the Robert Mannings.

One of the Manning girls, little Mary Elizabeth, had her head out the window, apparently in hopes of catching a glimpse of the parade, and Cordelia Lake, who was supposed to be secretly engaged to Tony Blackford, had her head out the window of her carriage too. The street was filled with the sounds of creaking harness, the commands and cajolings of the Negro coachmen, the rattle of wheels over the cobbles whenever the carriages were able to move forward a bit, and, farther up the street, toward Monmouth Square, the sound of many voices. "It's like a picnic," John thought, "a wholesale holiday. Don't they know how close to the edge we are?"

The street was lighted by gas lamps placed at regular intervals. Patches of shadow lay between them, but there was enough light for John to tell that Cordelia had done her hair like Missy's, that she was wearing the emerald necklace Mr. Lake had brought back from Austria when he was United States Minister there, and that Albert, the Lakes' coachman, had been fitted out in a new coat with brass buttons. Albert called out something to Dowdy, a grizzled, portly Negro who had been Corwin Bottomley's coachman for more than twenty years (and who would be feeling jealous and put upon because he didn't have a new coat like Albert's), and Cordelia, hearing the exchange, turned her head. Seeing John, she started to smile, the Lakes and the Bottomleys being the best of friends, and then, with the smile left unfinished, she nodded gravely and withdrew into the carriage—John could easily imagine her telling her parents that the Bottomleys were just behind.

Missy, who was sitting next to him, began to lose patience.

"Why don't we *move!* We're going to be late!"

It was not merely that Missy was eighteen and impatient. Cameron's disappearance had put them all under a strain. Corwin Bottomley lifted himself from a heavy silence to grumble something about the damned curiosity-seeking mob, holding the slender silver cane that was General Lafayette's gift to the Light Infantry and which, as grand marshal, he would tap on the floor three times to signal the beginning of the ball, and John's mother, looking very pale, stared from the carriage as if hoping by some miracle to spy Cameron among the hurrying passers-by.

"You stop having the fidgits," John said to Missy. "We have the grand marshal in tow. The ball can't begin until we get there."

"But when *will* we? Midnight?"

"What's the matter with midnight? You afraid of being sent back to your rags?"

"I wanted to see the parade. I promised Gordon and Tolliver and Jack and Julian——"

"What? Are you still using scatter shot? I thought you were drawing a bead."

"I don't know what you're talking about! The parade must be over by now!"

"No, it isn't. There wouldn't be that crowd ahead."

"But it's hateful just to sit! How long must we? Why did we have to come this way? If Dowdy had taken Constitution Street instead of Bullock——"

"You will compose yourself, young lady," Corwin Bottomley said. "If you're old enough to be presented to society, you ought to be old enough to conduct yourself properly," and Mrs. Bottomley, drawn from her search for a moment, said wearily, her mind still on Cameron, "Yes, Missy, please do be still. You'll have your pretty dress all in a muss."

It was Missy for whom John felt sorry. He was worried about his mother and troubled by the dejection his father had fallen into, but Missy pulled at his heart. There wasn't a girl who didn't dream about her first Light Infantry Ball, and now Cameron had spoiled everything. But not only Cameron. This might have been avoided had he listened to what Cameron wanted to say.

But what could have gone wrong? Something more serious than usual: something damaging enough to cause Cameron to break and run. But *what?* John's suspicions at Deerskin, that Cameron had been gambling, had already been proved wrong. Tolliver Rhett, who sat in a game almost every evening, told him that Cameron had not had a bad run of luck lately, and Jack Wendover, who owned a couple of horses at the Twin Oaks track, said that Cameron had been lucky out there too. So it wasn't to pay off his gambling debts that Cameron had asked for fifteen hundred dollars. He obviously wanted it to get out of town. Why, though? Was it because he decided at the last minute he didn't want to marry Kitty Williams? Some credence was lent that by his remarks about land marrying land and the bitter look on his face when he had talked about Cornwall and Peachtree going to the altar, and it was just possible that he could think of no other solution than to run away. Among other things, he would have been afraid to face their father.

John thought the solution almost fit—almost, but not quite. One large piece was missing from the puzzle, and that was Cameron's visit to Cornwall. John was no more able now to believe that his brother had gone to Cornwall to pick up his scattered gear than he had been when Cameron first offered it as an explanation. The only thing John could think of was that Cameron had wanted to hide out—give him one day to ride to Cornwall, leaving Pompey's Head before dawn, and the next day to return by way of the river, not getting back till long after midnight, and it could mean that for two days he preferred not to be seen in town. Just "could," however. There was no certainty anywhere. Then, to the extent that it had been possible for John to trace his brother's movements further, Cameron cashed the check first thing Monday morning, spent most of Monday at home in his room, came down to supper so disgracefully drunk that he and their father had a terrible scene, and then, late Tuesday afternoon, left Pompey's Head only a few hours before the Williamses' party, borrowing one of their father's horses and taking only a few belongings stuffed in a saddlebag. Two things seemed clear to John—one was that the closer Cameron came to his engagement party the greater became his panic, and the other was that whatever he was running away from, he wanted to run fast.

The carriage moved forward a little and then came to a halt.

"Petunia!" Missy said. "Are we going to have to sit again!"

"I don't think for long," John replied. "Things seem to be moving up ahead. And try not to say 'petunia,' will you? I don't mind, but other people may. You know how they are."

"Petunia's just a flower."

"Yes, but the way you say it, it doesn't always sound like a flower. I don't mind, as I say, but——"

"Oh, you're too stuffy, Johnny! There's nothing wrong with petunia."

"Everything's wrong with it!" Corwin Bottomley came storming from his silence. "It's nigger talk! It belongs in the kitchen! I do not propose to have it said of a daughter of mine that she knows no better than to use the language of a scullery maid!" and he worked himself into such a muffled rage that John could have bitten his tongue for having called attention to Missy's harmless remark.

It was not really Missy, however, at whom his father was railing. Cameron was the target. His father had been struck in his pride, disgraced, and instead of being able decently to hide his disgrace, as would have been his inclination, he must now pretend that the bolt had not fallen, and parade his humiliation at the Light Infantry Ball.

John knew better than to interrupt his father's tirade. He endured with Missy and his mother until it was over, wishing Dowdy would get the carriage moving—it was dismal to be closeted in this little cave with Cameron's forlorn ghost, almost as if the boy had died: no, worse than died: been strung from a tree for the foulest kind of crime. John reached for Missy's hand, and her fingers closed tight on his. He said:

"You remembered to save me a dance, I hope."

"Did you think I wouldn't? Yours is the second after the grand march. Gordy Carpenter has the first."

"Am I supposed to be surprised?"

Missy preferred not to answer that particular question. Gordon Carpenter was Dr. James Carpenter's son, a tall, plain-looking young man of twenty-one who, rather than be a planter (Dr. Carpenter, along with being Pompey's Head's favorite physician, owned Happy Chance Plantation), had gone into medicine.

"Did you remember to bring your card?" Missy asked.

"Yes, of course."

"Is it all filled out?"

"No, how could it be? I'm not one of your fortunate young men who can arrange their programs beforehand. I live back in the swamps, remember?"

"Don't you have any dances at all?"

"A lancers with you."

"Oh, Johnny, that's no way! You don't want just to stand around all night and watch, do you?"

"Would you feel humbled in the world's eyes?"

"No, but I wouldn't like it—for your sake, I mean. Besides, it's not as though you had cross eyes or squirrel teeth or something. A lot of young ladies would be proud to have you on their cards. And, Johnny——"

"Yes?"

"Arbell Stanhope's card isn't all filled out. She had the fourth dance with Tommy Vincent—that's a waltz—and last night Tommy came down with the mumps——"

"The mumps? At his age?"

Missy giggled. "Isn't it embarrassing? If it was me, I'd be mortified to tears. But Dr. Carpenter says that Tommy has to stay in bed, that he can't even move—why is that, Johnny? When I had the mumps——"

"Never mind, Missy."

"But why is it that I have to never mind? That's what Elnora said when she was helping me get dressed for the ball. 'You never mind 'bout Maussuh's Vincent's mumps,' she said. 'A young gentleman's mumps ain't respectable for no young lady to go round gossiping about.' But why isn't it respectable? If it's all right for me to talk about my mumps——"

"Missy!" Mrs. Bottomley rapped out. "You will please to change the subject!"

"But——"

"If you don't," Corwin Bottomley threatened, "and if you dare to bring it up again——"

"Yes, Mama. Yes, Papa. But how was I to know that a gentleman's mumps are too indelicate to mention? After all, when *I* had the mumps——"

Seeing that his father was about to lose his temper again, John interposed hurriedly, "Never *mind*, Missy! Just forget that you ever heard of Tommy Vincent's mumps. What was it you started to say?"

"Oh yes, about Arbell. Well, because of Tommy's mum—I mean Tommy's temporary indisposition—she has that waltz open and I told her to save it for you. What's the matter? Aren't you pleased?"

It wasn't a question of pleasure. What John was thinking was that Arbell Stanhope—Arabella, her real name was—was Lydia Stanhope's stepdaughter. Arabella was eighteen, and Lydia was twenty-seven, and there were rumors that they did not get along.

"Arbell likes you," Missy said. "She thinks you're handsome."

Arabella Stanhope, John wanted to say, is one of the silliest, most frivolous, harum-scarum girls in town.

"I just don't understand you," Missy said. "Why do you act so peculiar? You'd think that Arbell was the worst stick in town instead of the very prettiest. Don't you think she's pretty?"

"Yes, I suppose so."

"Suppose so! Who do you think is prettier than Arbell?"

"Would it be all right if I said you?"

Missy made a face. "Flattery, sir, will get you nowhere. You know I'm not as pretty as Arbell. Not nearly. Just her eyes, for instance. Sometimes they're blue, and sometimes they're green, and sometimes they're blue and green both. I wish I had eyes like that."

"Why? So you could bat them at every man you saw?"

"Oh, that's just Arbell's way. It doesn't mean anything."

"That's the trouble."

"What *is* the matter with you, Johnny? I've never known you to be like this. It's living at Deerskin that's done it. You didn't used to be so glum and serious."

"I didn't used to be so old."

"Petun—— I mean pshaw! You're not old. What's thirty? Do you know what Molly Carpenter says?"

"No, what does Molly Carpenter say?"

"She says that it's not until a man is thirty, or older, that he begins to get interesting. She says——" And then, as the carriage began to roll along briskly, Missy bounced and clapped her hands. "Look, Johnny! We're moving at last! I do hope we'll see the parade!"

ii

They got there just in time. The parade was coming down the street as Dowdy drew up before the hall. John helped his mother from the carriage, then Missy and his father, who was clutching the silver cane, and since they had not time to reach the balcony, where already a flutter of scarves and handkerchiefs was greeting an oncoming sound of drums, they found places on the steps of the hall with the other tardy arrivals. Missy, joining forces with Cordelia Lake and Mary Elizabeth Manning, added her handkerchief to the flutter, and a cheer went up as the first line of horsemen, riding four abreast, came clattering past.

John, standing next to his father in the rear, put names and faces together: Ules Monckton, Tony Blackford, Jack Wendover, Tolliver Rhett. They wore their new uniforms—slouch hats turned up on one side, cadet-gray frock coats with fire-gilt buttons and gold braid frogs, more gold braid on the collars, red sashes, a black stripe down the trouser legs—and Tony Blackford, who could be expected to go beyond regulations, had added a flowing blue cape with a scarlet lining. John saw Tony's eyes search the balcony and a worried look cross his face, and then, as he caught sight of Cordelia on the steps, he flashed her a fervent, unabashed glance and dug his spurs into his horse's flanks, turning off smartly into Monmouth Square.

A second line of horsemen came past—Julian and Randolph Fitzpatrick, Tom Ingram, Gordon Carpenter and his homely, earnest face going through the same misery as Tony Blackford's until he at last detected Missy—more cheers, then more horsemen, hoofs striking sparks on the cobbles and one alarmed animal rising in a perfect rear ("Lord," John thought, "how those fellows can ride!"), Mr. Wolfgang Weber, also in uniform, leading the Old Pompey Band, the band playing "The Light Infantry March," a special cheer for the band, and

then, drawing up the rear, the unmounted members of the outfit re-
cruited from among the town's less affluent citizens, and the dripping
flares, red and green and yellow and blue, that were called secession
torches—a single steady long cheer now, and the ladies' scarves and
handkerchiefs fluttering wildly, and the cheer overridden by a yell from
the men who were already massed in the square beneath the oaks
and magnolias, the yell rising higher and higher as it was taken up by
the still marching ranks, and if it reminded John Bottomley of a
holiday, a splendid fooling on the edge of war, these were his people
and this was his country, and he loved his country very much.

"Shall we go in now, Father?"

It did not surprise John that his father's eyes were moist: what
surprised him was how clearly he could read his father's thoughts:
all these splendid fellows, ready to lay down their lives if need be,
and his own two sons not among them: one gone off somewhere
like a thief in the night, and the other infected with doubt, indecision,
and Yankee notions—they who should be in the vanguard: they on
whom he had rested so many hopes!

"Mother and Missy are waiting, Father."

Corwin Bottomley seemed not to hear. John saw him grip hard on
the silver cane, his knuckles going white with the pressure, and then
deliberately set his back and chin. "They made a fine showing, didn't
they?" Corwin said at last, and when John replied, "Yes, Father, they
did," his father looked at him in such a beseeching way, hurt and
disappointed and at a loss to understand, that it was all he could do
to keep from lowering his eyes—he was grateful when Missy came
rushing up. "Wasn't it wonderful!" she cried. "Weren't they *handsome!* Petunia! I'll never forget tonight if I live to be a hundred!"
and though John expected his father to make at least one remark about
kitchen language and scullery maids, either he was too far away to
have heard or else it did not seem especially important any more.

CHAPTER SIX

By midnight the ball was in full swing. John Bottomley, standing with a number of other gentlemen against a side wall of the ballroom (it was a convention of the Light Infantry Ball that all gentlemen must stand), saw his sister Missy lose herself in a polka, her white dress shimmering among the uniforms and frilled shirt fronts and other white dresses (it was a second convention of the Light Infantry Ball that all ladies must wear white), and so was able to tell himself, seeing the transported look on Missy's face, that she at least was having a glorious time.

He could not say as much for himself. To stand all evening was tiresome and he often wondered why invitations to the Light Infantry Ball were so highly prized. It meant, of course, that one had passed through the armorial gates and been admitted to the inner circle, but even so it seemed a tedious distinction. It did not occur to John that his was an extremely privileged view, or that, having been born within the armorial gates, he could afford to be indifferent. He must therefore put it down to a shift in temperament. He had lived too long in the country. He was too out of touch with the social graces. He was getting too old.

Had it not been for Cameron, John's inclination would have been to forgo the ball entirely. With his brother gone, however, the obligations of pride could not be evaded. It was demanded that the whole Bottomley family show itself. They must appear, and by appearing say in no uncertain terms, "Here we are, ladies and gentlemen. Make something of it."

No one had dared, naturally. Corwin Bottomley was old and failing, and John Bottomley had yet to call out a man, but it must not be assumed that the age of the one or the sobriety of the other made either of them less dangerous.

With so much stress on the proprieties, there was bound to be a strain. The bright, overeager greeting of the ladies and the reserved, overcautious behavior of the gentlemen struck John as forced and unnatural. Much as he would have liked to let down his guard, he could not. He had been made to feel too self-conscious. Too many veiled glances were being sent his way.

Had it been only that, however, he believed he would have been able to manage. What he could not manage was Lydia Stanhope. She too was caught up in the polka, dancing with one of the uniforms. She wore a billowy white dress and long white gloves, and though John saw her in her full, graceful completeness—her soft blond hair drawn across her ears; her small straight nose; her confident blue eyes; the determined thrust of her chin (too bold a chin, it was sometimes said: too assertive for real beauty)—though this John saw, running the risk of a long, steady look, the beam of his attention was centered on the shadowy cleft of her bosom.

His face had lain there once, ever so briefly, and it did no good not to want to remember. The memory was there always, like a prayer so often recited that it becomes part of the articulation of the blood, and at the center of the memory was the sound of his voice. "I don't know what came over me, Miss Chadwick. I most humbly apologize. If you will say I have reason to hope——"

Sometimes it seemed ages past and sometimes only yesterday. Losing sight of Lydia, and aware that Arabella Stanhope had flashed him a quick, penetrating look as she went by in the arms of one of the Fitzpatrick twins, John found that this was one of the times when it seemed only yesterday.

The actual date, however, was Saturday, June 7, 1856. The young ladies of Huntington Hall, a boarding and day school attended by the daughters of the plantation families, were having their annual pageant and picnic. That year the picnic was held at Dr. Carpenter's Happy

Chance Plantation, and both John Bottomley and Lydia happened to be along, John at the insistence of his sister Missy, who was going to play the part of Flora in the pageant—Flora, Goddess of Flowers—and Lydia as the newest member of the teaching staff of Huntington Hall.

Though John had never met Lydia, he had often heard Missy speak of her. Missy said she was the dearest. However, since practically everything was the dearest to Missy at that particular time—the dearest dress, the dearest moon, the dearest beauty spot—John could not take it as quite the recommendation that was intended.

A temple of learning, Huntington Hall was also a fountain of gossip. For a few days, when it become known that Lydia had been added to the staff, her appointment found its way into almost every family conversation. John Bottomley was staying with his family at Indigo at the time. Absent for four years at Princeton, and having spent the last five at Deerskin, John could not remember having heard of this Miss Lydia Chadwick before. He gathered from his mother that she was the only child of a widowed lady who lived on Gunpowder Street, and from Corwin Bottomley that her father had been a grain merchant who had antagonized local opinion by opposing the annexation of Texas and the Mexican War. "One of those discontented, misfit fellows who are just as well off dead," Corwin Bottomley said.

A young woman, then, who stood neither within nor without the pale—neither quality, sand-hill white, nor Channel Irish. There were many such in Pompey's Head, and it was hard to know where to place them in the social scale. Unlike the sand-hill whites and outcast Irish, whose status was irrevocably fixed, they had a certain mobility. Let a man start out as a modest tradesman and prosper mightily, and his daughters could reasonably expect to marry into the plantation elite. Though it did not happen often, it happened often enough. The mother of the Fitzpatrick twins, born Emma Smith, could be pointed to as one example. By now it was convenient to forget that her father had started out in a one-room notions store on the corner of Bay and Constitution streets, where the new building of the Merchants &

Mechanics Bank now stood. An inheritance of three quarters of a million always made a difference. It was what they meant in the Light Infantry Club when they talked about taking in new blood. Only the cynical ever mentioned the desirability of taking in new money.

But the exact placement of Miss Chadwick would not cause anybody too much trouble, John thought, listening to the conversation at supper one evening. Instead of prospering, her father had not only died penniless but unshriven of the wrong political opinions. Instead of being able to claim even a remote kinship to any of the families that mattered, her mother had been the daughter of an itinerant Baptist clergyman, properly ordained but having no church of his own. It was Mrs. Bottomley who dropped this piece of information, and John was amazed that such intimate details should be known. He thought that Pompey's Head was not unlike those orchids that Dr. Carpenter was experimenting with at Happy Chance. Nourished by gossip, it seemed to absorb sustenance from the air.

Arabella Stanhope, who was spending the night at Indigo with Missy, said that Elizabeth Paxton said that Miss Chadwick was stuck-up. There was a moment of heavy silence. Arabella was forever intruding into the conversation like that, saying things that were best left unsaid, and it was no excuse that she was fourteen.

"Why did you say that?" John asked. "Do you always go around repeating everything you hear?"

Were Arabella like most of the children who trooped in and out of Indigo, she might have been intimidated. Instead, she merely looked at him across the table—not defiantly or disagreeably, but with a quiet, placid stillness that was at once too masked and too forthright to be a stare.

"Well, why did you?" John asked. "And how do you know what Miss Elizabeth said?"

Arabella held up her chin. "*Miss* Elizabeth," she said. "That old maid."

By a quick piece of arithmetic John calculated that Miss Elizabeth, who was two years younger than himself, would now be all of twenty-three. Perhaps she was getting to be an old maid. Even so, however,

Arabella should be taught to mind her tongue. He was glad his mother seemed to agree.

"It's not kind to say that about Miss Elizabeth, Arbell," Mrs. Bottomley remonstrated. "Besides, she's not much older than you and Missy."

"Not much older!" Missy opened her eyes wide. "Miss Elizabeth is years and years older than we are! And it's true what she said about Miss Chadwick. Arbell heard her."

"Oh she did, did she?" John said.

Arabella met his eyes again. She said, "It was last Sunday at my sister Christina's. Elizabeth came to see the baby. She said she couldn't understand why the Reverend Mr. Priss——"

Corwin Bottomley, who all this time had been busy with his food, lifted his head menacingly. He said, "See here, young woman! You are not to call the Reverend Mr. Pryse *Priss* again, do you understand? Not in my hearing. I'll not have it! His name is Pryse. I should hate to have to report you to your father."

A lot of good that will do, John thought. Senator Stanhope probably thinks it amusing, the names she makes up for her teachers— Professor Cleanwick instead of Cleenewerck; Miss Flesh instead of Floersh; Mlle. Quadraped instead of Queripel. And why doesn't somebody shut her up? Our trouble is that we are just as interested in hearing what she has to say as she is in saying it.

Arabella hesitated barely a moment. "Yes sir," she said. "Reverend Pryse, not Priss. I'll remember. Anyway, what Elizabeth said——"

"*Miss* Elizabeth, Arbell," Mrs. Bottomley said in her gentle, indecisive way. "Can't you remember?"

"Yes ma'am, Mrs. Bottomley, *Miss* Elizabeth. Anyway, what she said was that it was beyond her imagination to conceive why the Reverend Mr. Pryse engaged Miss Chadwick to teach English and Elocution at Huntington Hall. Miss Chadwick's proper subject, she said, would be Arrogant Deportment."

Another instant of silence. Corwin Bottomley went back to his supper, Mrs. Bottomley looked around in helpless dismay, Missy regarded her friend admiringly, and seventeen-year-old Cameron, who was sitting next to John, let out a short laugh. He said, "Arrogant Deportment. That's pretty good," and there was something in his voice, a barely perceptible thickness, that made John wonder if he had been sampling their father's liquor again.

"But of course," Arabella had gone on, addressing herself to Mrs. Bottomley, "of course the real reason that Elizabeth doesn't like Miss Chadwick is that she's jealous. Miss Chadwick is pretty, and Elizabeth is plain, and everyone knows how jealous Elizabeth is of anyone with looks. My father says that Miss Chadwick's skin alone would make her fortune."

John wanted to say, "For goodness sake, Arabella! Is there nothing you won't babble!" but instead, trying to pretend he had not heard, he asked his mother would she please ring for the rice. Senator Stanhope was fifty-eight, and Miss Chadwick probably not much more than twenty, and someday Arabella's impulse to see how far she could go was going to cause trouble. It was unfortunate that Elizabeth Paxton had such a sharp tongue. Most likely Arabella was right. If Miss Chadwick was pretty, this would not be the first time that Elizabeth had let herself be betrayed. But still, Arabella shouldn't go around repeating everything she heard. Miss Chadwick had been placed under a needless handicap. She should not be asked to live down more than she had to live down already. Arrogant Deportment. A skin that alone would make her fortune. John discovered that he was beginning to look forward to the picnic at Happy Chance.

ii

Pompey's Head could take even a picnic and turn it into a fête. More than a hundred guests strolled about the grounds at Happy Chance. Next to the Blackfords' Mulberry, Happy Chance was one of the handsomest country residences anywhere around. Even were he not a planter and thus unaware of the boom in rice and cotton, John Bottomley would have been able to tell that Dr. Carpenter had had several good years. Dr. Carpenter often said that if it weren't for his practice he couldn't afford to keep Happy Chance up. All one had to do, however, was to look around to know better. The square white house with its columns and wide porches was newly painted, the barns and stables were in perfect repair, the long stretch of lawn between the house and the river could not have been more beautifully tended, and behind the barns and the stables, not far from the small greenhouse in which Dr. Carpenter conducted the agricultural experiments that were his hobby, a new half-mile track had been laid down.

A constant stream of gentlemen walked to and from the house to admire the improvement. A pair of horses were being worked out on the track, ridden by Negro exercise boys, and several other horses, each surrounded by a group of admirers, were being groomed in front of the stables. The animals belonged to various owners—Mr. Blackford, Mr. Rhett, Mr. Wendover, Dr. Carpenter, Senator Stanhope—and already a hum of excitement had got into the air. Ostensibly given in honor of the young ladies who had just received their diplomas from Huntington Hall, the picnic had come to be second only to the Light Infantry Ball as a social occasion. The race was naturally being looked forward to as the most important sporting event, but in addition there were to be archery contests for ladies and gentlemen, croquet, various games for the children, and, in the evening, a formal dance.

As much as any of these entertainments, however, the event which was being awaited most eagerly was the annual Huntington Hall pageant. *Flora's Dial*, it was called this year, and word had long since been carried home, by the girls who had parts in it, that it had been written and directed by their new teacher of English and Elocution, Miss Chadwick. And now, at the picnic, Missy was coming forward with a composed, attractive young woman who could only be Miss Chadwick herself. Missy wore the glowing look that always came over her when she was happy and excited, and rushed through the introduction: "This is my brother John, Miss Chadwick. Johnny, may I present my new teacher, Miss Chadwick," and then, with a look so stricken that John thought she must have been overcome by one of those stomach-aches to which she was partial in moments of stress, she clapped her hands over her mouth. "Oh dear!" she said, dropping

81

her hands and looking up at Lydia. "I got it all backwards, didn't I? I should have asked you to permit me to present Johnny."

Lydia drew Missy to her, saying, "It's all right, my dear. I'm sure no one will mind," and John was able to take his first good look at her. She seemed deliberately to have gone out of her way to be a school-marm. Her ash-blond hair was pulled back straight over her ears, and she wore a drab-colored skirt and a white blouse buttoned high at the throat. Either she was supremely confident or else she didn't care. John couldn't believe she didn't care. The tilt of her head spoke contrary to that. And if what Elizabeth Paxton meant by Arrogant Deportment was the way she carried herself, the lift of her chin and her firm straight back and the uncompromising look in her clear blue eyes—if that was what Elizabeth meant, she might well do with some Arrogant Deportment herself, instead of criticizing it in others. He said:

"I'm delighted to make your acquaintance, Miss Chadwick."

"And I yours, Mr. Bottomley. I have been hearing about you from Missy."

"Not to my disadvantage, I trust."

"Quite the contrary, sir. Did I not want to spare Missy embarrassment, I might repeat some of the things I have heard."

"Don't, please. It is not only Missy who would be embarrassed. We are all looking forward to your pageant, Miss Chadwick."

"Mine? Why do you call it mine? It belongs to my girls."

"You are too modest."

"Ah, I hope not, sir. What is it the poet says? 'All men have their faults, too much modesty is his.' Should not all things be in their proper proportion?"

For an instant John was taken aback. Female modesty in Pompey's Head was valued hardly less than female chastity. It might be thought overbold of Miss Chadwick even to insinuate that modesty might be carried to excess. But what a delightful person she was! John thought he detected a liveliness of imagination that reminded him of Miss Clarissa Drew. An image of Miss Clarissa passed before him, and then, as he noticed that there were three pale, tiny freckles on the bridge of Miss Chadwick's nose and that the sun broke upon her small blond head like an actual shower of gold, he discovered that Miss Clarissa no longer mattered. And it must have been that, he often thought later—the sense of freedom he felt—that prompted him to ask Lydia to share their picnic baskets.

"But she can't!" Missy said, looking cross. "I've already asked her. She's promised to Arbell and the Senator."

"I'm sorry, Missy," Lydia said. "Some other time."

"You promise?"

"Yes, I promise."

"I hope that you have not given your promise too lightly, Miss Chadwick," John said. "I, for one, will see that you are held to it."

Lydia rewarded him with a smile. Though it lifted her lips and cheeks, he noticed it left her eyes unchanged. She said, "You are much too kind, Mr. Bottomley. But now, if we have your permission to leave, Missy and I must go. I told my charges that we would have a last rehearsal. We are late already."

The only time Pompey's Head ever had lunch was at the Huntington Hall picnic. Otherwise the afternoon meal was always dinner. After lunch, which was over by two o'clock, the guests began to assemble for the pageant. The big front porch of Happy Chance was used for the stage, hung with a pair of turkey-red curtains. The mechanics of the curtains had been arranged beforehand—rings and ropes and pulleys—and benches for the audience were set out on the lawn in front of the porch.

John sat with his family in the front row. He hoped the Reverend Mr. Daniel Pryse, the principal and director of Huntington Hall, would not take forever with his speech. Mr. Pryse was a tall, bald, nervous man with a long skull, pale blue eyes, and a habit of making clucking noises that once caused Corwin Bottomley to liken him to a broody hen. A token of applause greeted him as he stepped before the curtains. He spoke for not more than five minutes, but it seemed much longer. John entertained himself by watching a pair of redbirds worry each other about the lawn. The Reverend Mr. Pryse finally withdrew to a second token of applause, a little less restrained. The curtains were parted, and in the ensuing silence a woodpecker could be heard drumming in the woods, loud and clear, and the applause became genuine for the first time. "By God now!" John Bottomley heard his father exclaim. "There's a pretty thing!"

Twenty-four girls, seated, were grouped on the porch. They wore different-colored dresses and each had a wreath of flowers in her hair. Great masses of bloom covered the wall of the porch on either side of the door, which was hung with a white curtain pinned with roses to form the letters H H, and the rest of the porch was banked with ferns and potted palms. Missy Bottomley, wearing a pale yellow dress that had kept the household in an uproar for weeks, stood in the center of the circle. She wore a wreath of small yellow lilies and carried a gilded wand. After quiet was restored, she began to recite:

> *"I am Flora, mistress of the dial,*
> *Your favor, dear friends, we beg for a while.*
> *Here for your pleasure I've gathered my flowers,*
> *In lieu of a sundial, they'll tell you the hours."*

The plan of the pageant soon became apparent. It had been Lydia's inspiration to build it around a fanciful dial formed by those flowers that opened at certain hours of day or night. Turning to Mary Elizabeth Manning, who wore a blue dress and a circlet of blue flowers, Missy touched her with her wand. Mary Elizabeth rose, stepped forward, paused hesitantly, and finally remembered her lines:

> *"The sky is my color, Norway's my home,*
> *On my northern seas the fisher ships roam.*
> *At one in the morning, to Flora's low whistle,*
> *I rise from my sleep, the Scandinavian thistle."*

And so it went. Each of the girls rose in turn to the touch of Missy's wand and recited a double couplet that identified the flower she represented and its hour of wakening—goatsbeard at two, oxtongue at three, dandelion at four, poppy at five, hawkweed at six—until the clock had been twice circled and midnight was reached. Midnight was Arabella Stanhope as night-blooming catchfly. It was plain that Arabella didn't like being night-blooming catchfly. The repressed half-smiles that crossed the faces of the other girls were enough to suggest that Miss Chadwick, and most probably Senator Stanhope, had had to do a lot of cajoling.

There were smiles in the audience too. Everyone knew Arabella and what a handful she was, and it was entertaining to hear her describe herself as a shy, hidden flower that loved the dark. Arabella looked so enchanting, however, in a forest-green dress and a wreath of small pointed leaves woven into her thick, reddish-brown hair that a murmur of appreciation rose from the company. Even John Bottomley had to join in. Much as Arabella aggravated him, there was no denying that she was growing into one of the prettiest girls to come along in years.

Then Missy again, bringing the pageant to a close:

> "And now, dear friends, parents, and neighbors,
> My flowers and I go back to our labors.
> Where'er you should find us, in sun or in shade,
> Should we give you joy, our lives are repaid."

Missy lifted her wand, the girls held their places, the curtains were drawn, and the applause was tremendous. Corwin Bottomley astonished John by raising a loud cheer. "By God, sir!" he said to his son. "That ought to be on the London stage!" The London stage was somehow more respectable in Pompey's Head than the New York stage, and had been even before New York had come to be associated with immigration, high interest rates, and the abolitionist tendencies of such newspapers as the *Tribune*. Old Mr. Robertson, who was sitting next to Corwin, appeared to share his opinion. "Fit for the Queen!" he exclaimed, and John Bottomley knew that the president of the Agricultural Society meant precisely what he said. Mr. Robertson regarded the separation of the colonies from the Crown as one of history's tragic errors. It was his program that the Southern states should restore themselves to the mother country. "Worthy of a court presentation!" Mr. Robertson let it be known, and then, in response to the audience's undiminished approval, the curtains parted

85

again. All the girls stood smiling and happy and flushed with success —all save Arabella Stanhope, who from the look on her face still didn't like being night-blooming catchfly—and as the applause rose higher, Miss Chadwick was discovered behind the bank of ferns and palms. Much as she seemed opposed to it, she had to come forward for an ovation.

"A true daughter of the muse!" Mr. Robertson said, peering out from the crook of his venerable, past-eighty back. "A handsome little thing, too! What did you say her name was?"

Although John Bottomley had wanted a victory for Miss Chadwick, he had not dared hope for a triumph. It was a good fifteen minutes before he could offer his congratulations. To some extent, however, he purposely lingered, hoping to be able to engage Miss Chadwick in private conversation. He stood to one side of the benches, watching the girls in their bright costumes and flowered headdresses scatter among the crowd, which was now beginning to drift off toward Dr. Carpenter's new half-mile track, and several times exchanged a few words with some of the ladies and gentlemen who passed near him. It was a pleasant gathering of friends and neighbors, and he was glad to be there.

All the while, though, he kept one eye on Miss Chadwick. Her conduct interested him. She was becomingly appreciative, but at no time did she fall into the agitated overpoliteness that John associated with nearly all the other teachers at Huntington Hall. What she was saying, John decided, was that though she was aware of her position and understood that she moved only on the far edge of the plantation world, with no more standing than a seamstress or milliner in some eyes, she knew her own value.

One of the last to go up to her was Senator Stanhope, and John sensed that he had also been biding his time. The Senator, who looked much younger than fifty-eight, was said to be vain of his personal appearance. Even Corwin Bottomley, one of his best friends, sometimes complained about it. Though the Senator now lived all year round in Pompey's Head except for the hot midsummer months, which he spent with Arabella at the Virginia springs, he still busied himself with his plantations, and years of being in the open had kept him lean and trim. Without being much above the average height, he gave the impression of tallness. The lines in his face had begun to deepen, and his hair was turning white, but seen from behind, with his hat on, he might easily be taken for a much younger man.

But he *was* fifty-eight. Nothing could alter that. As he engaged Miss Chadwick in conversation it was not so much the hang of his body that gave him away, or his white hair, but a sort of hesitant behavior that could only be put down as shyness. Miss Chadwick was younger than his middle daughter, Christina, who was already married and had just given birth to her first child, and he was bound to be seeing himself through Miss Chadwick's eyes, hoping that the sum of six decades was not too apparent and that she was not thinking of him in grandfatherly terms. John Bottomley was glad not to be so heavily handicapped. He wasn't fifty-eight, he was twenty-five, and if he wanted to be attentive to Miss Chadwick he could be. There would naturally be talk, since there always was no matter what you did, but at least his age couldn't be held against him.

Turned inward though his thoughts were, John was made to realize he must have been staring. Both Senator Stanhope and Miss Chadwick looked in his direction. The Senator beckoned him to join them, and Miss Chadwick watched him in a grave, speculative manner that caused him to be somewhat disconcerted—young women of good breeding were not supposed to indulge in such straightforward appraisals.

Senator Stanhope shook John's hand warmly. "I was just expressing my appreciation to Miss Chadwick," he said. "Did you ever witness anything more delightful than today's entertainment?"

John couldn't say yes—not after he had seen *The Gladiators* in Philadelphia and *The Broker of Bogota* in New York—and certainly he couldn't say no.

"I thought it was charming," he said. "My congratulations, Miss Chadwick."

"Did you know we had a poetess in our midst?" Senator Stanhope asked. "I was saying to Miss Chadwick that she ought to spread her wings in print. Don't you agree?"

"Miss Chadwick is wonderfully clever," John said, and from her changed expression, an almost imperceptible shifting of the tiny muscles around her eyes, he gathered she would have preferred something less restrained. She said, "Please, gentlemen. Either you are making sport of me, which I should not like to think, or else you are seeing my poor verses through the grace and beauty of all those pretty girls."

"Nonsense, nonsense!" Senator Stanhope said. "Will you not grant me the privilege of recognizing genius when I see it?"

John began to wish he were elsewhere. The ardent look in the Senator's eyes meant more than a recognition of genius, and it came as a surprise that a man of fifty-eight could be so overcome. The Senator vowed that though he didn't set himself up as an authority he was prepared to argue that he knew poetry when he heard it—"That much, Miss Chadwick, I will have to insist on"—and he was so engrossed in his appreciation that when Arabella joined them, still wearing her dark green dress and crown of shining leaves, he had visibly to wrench himself back to the picnic at Happy Chance.

He smiled warmly at Arabella, the pleasure he always found in her showing on his face, but she didn't smile back—her eyes, more green today than blue, as if, chameleon-like, they had partaken of the color of her dress, had a smoky, rebellious look. She turned the look on Miss Chadwick, the green eyes and the blue ones meeting in what John interpreted as a mutual challenge, and though Miss Chadwick was a full head taller than Arabella, she a woman and Arabella still a child, John had the impression that it was the child, not the woman, who held the upper hand.

"I've been hunting all over," Arabella said to the Senator in a flat, aggrieved tone. "It's most time for the race. Blue Fly's being saddled. Aren't you coming?"

Senator Stanhope looked startled. "What? Already? Did Andrew find his whip? Where is he? He's to ride her my way today, not his. There are a few last things I want to tell him. I had no idea it was getting so late."

"Well, it is," Arabella said. "And if you want to talk to Andrew you'll have to hurry. Make him give Blue Fly a good ride today! Tell him you'll send him back to the fields if she doesn't win. She's *got* to!"

Senator Stanhope put his hand on her shoulder, and it was easy to see how fond he was of her. Whatever else was said about him—his notion that having served one term in Washington made him a statesman, his pompous imagining that he was cabinet material, his exaggerated interest in his personal appearance—whatever was said, never could it be held that he wasn't a good father to Arabella. Many men had it in them to be good fathers, but being a good father to Arabella was an entirely different proposition. He said:

"She'll win, my dear. It was only a fluke, her losing to Red Rover last year. And if she doesn't win——" He tightened his clasp on Arabella's shoulder and laughed. "Well, in that case, we may have to cut short our sojourn at the springs."

"Who cares about that old place?" Arabella said. "What I want is for Blue Fly to win. You make Andrew *make* her win, you hear!"

Senator Stanhope laughed again. He looked very handsome with his white hair and tanned face and strong straight frame. He said, "It could be, my dear, that I want her to win as much as you do," and he turned to John and Miss Chadwick. "If you will excuse me, Miss Chadwick, and you too, John, I'd best look after my horse. I hope you will be cheering my colors, Miss Chadwick. They'll be the red with white stars. You'll see our friend to the track, John, won't you? You couldn't be in better hands, Miss Chadwick. Come along, Arbell. Don't hang back after lecturing me."

Arabella was looking at John. "Aren't you coming with us?" she asked, and then, shifting her eyes to Miss Chadwick, "No, I don't suppose you can. Good afternoon, Miss Chadwick. I want to thank you again for letting me be night-blooming catchfly. I'm ever so grateful."

John had never imagined that Arabella could be so spiteful. Senator Stanhope said, "Arbell! I'm surprised!" and he would certainly have made her apologize had not Miss Chadwick intervened—John had reason to suspect, from the quiet, unperturbed tone of her voice, that

89

in the contest between her and Arabella, the advantage had now gone over to her side.

"We couldn't have managed without you, Arbell," Miss Chadwick said. "I've heard from any number of people that you spoke your lines better than anyone. And looked the prettiest too."

"There, now!" Senator Stanhope said hopefully. "You see?"

He looked worried, however, as though he couldn't decide whether to make Arabella apologize or not, and then, as a cheer rose from the track, he apparently concluded that it was his jockey's instructions more than his daughter's deportment that required his attention. Miss Chadwick glanced after them as they started for the track.

iii

"They make a handsome pair, do they not?" she said. "But I fear I have made an enemy of Arbell. I don't think she will ever forgive me for night-blooming catchfly."

"You mustn't mind Arabella," John said. "She's like that. You never know when she's going to fly off about something."

Miss Chadwick's expression, contradicting him, said she was well acquainted with Arabella's unpredictable behavior.

"All the girls couldn't be scarlet pimpernel," she explained. "Left to their own inclinations, they would have had our stage looking like the Battle of Little Pigeon Marsh. My problem was to suit the colors of the costumes to the coloring of the girls. Lucy Vincent was the obvious scarlet pimpernel, so brunette she is, and I thought Arbell would look best in forest green. Was I too far wrong, Mr. Bottomley? I thought she looked lovely today. Don't you agree?"

"Yes, certainly, Miss Chadwick. There's nothing the matter with Arabella's looks."

Costumes and coloring were beyond John's range. What he was thinking was that they should get to the track. The Huntington Hall race was the most important in the low country. The Agricultural Society had put up a cup for it, and to win possession of the cup for a year, with one's name and the name of one's horse engraved on it, was one of the highest honors any gentleman could aspire to. John didn't want to miss anything. Besides, he had three hundred dollars bet on Blue Fly. Miss Chadwick's thoughts, however, were apparently still centered on Arabella.

"I notice you never call her Arbell. Why?"

John hadn't ever thought why. "I find it hard to say, Miss Chadwick. I reckon it's because I like Arabella better than Arbell. Arbell sounds too childish."

"And she isn't a child?"

This was a variation of a gambit that John knew by heart. It was part of the technique of flirtation, and he was surprised Miss Chadwick should resort to it. Not that he minded. If it pleased her to pretend she imagined he had developed some interest in Arabella—an impossible notion on the face of it—it could be taken to mean that she had begun to develop an interest in him. He said:

"Yes, she's a child, all right, and a spoiled one, too, I'm afraid. That, though, isn't hard to understand. She's the last of the Senator's daughters to be living at home. I suppose it's only natural for him to let her have things pretty much her own way."

"She has two sisters, has she not?"

"Yes, Christina and Julie. Christina lives in town now, but next week she's moving to Columbia. Her husband, Charles Westover, Jack Westover's older brother, has just bought a cotton plantation not far from there. Julie lives out in the country near Georgetown. We hardly see her any more."

Miss Chadwick looked thoughtful. "It's seven years now that Senator Stanhope has been a widower, I understand."

"I believe it's seven, Miss Chadwick. Mrs. Stanhope died when they were in Washington. But perhaps we should be getting to the track. The race won't begin for another half hour, but I thought you might like to see the horses beforehand."

"Yes, I would. Very much. I see no reason why I shouldn't make a confession, Mr. Bottomley. I have never been to a race meeting before."

It was an open, honest thing to say, John thought, and more of a confession than she knew. A race meeting was what took place at the

Twin Oaks track: what they were having today was a race. Any plantation girl would have known the difference, but Miss Chadwick was not a plantation girl—the weight of her confession was that she was an unknowing little schoolteacher who lived on Gunpowder Street.

"In that case you will want to see everything," John said. "Let's begin with the horses."

Miss Chadwick took his arm and they started for the track. The others were already there. Dr. Carpenter had had a walk laid down, covered with crushed oyster shells and bordered with box, that went past his greenhouse and then to the track. The fragments of shell crunched softly underfoot. It was warm but not too warm. John thought there could not be a prettier afternoon.

"Tell me, Mr. Bottomley. Is Blue Fly going to win?"

She sounded so disingenuous that John wanted to laugh. "If I knew that, Miss Chadwick, I wouldn't have to go to my factors next year. I wouldn't even have to worry about raising a crop. My own money happens to be on Blue Fly. The Stanhopes are our neighbors in town, and we have come to think of Blue Fly as being practically in the family. Besides, life with Arabella wouldn't be worth living if I didn't back Blue Fly."

"You have a nice regard for sentiment."

"Not when I'm putting money on a horse, Miss Chadwick. Blue Fly can run. She's lazy, but she can run. It's my judgment I'm backing, not Arabella's enthusiasm—my judgment and Andrew's whip."

"You *think* she'll win, then."

Again John wanted to laugh. He sensed a busy, eager mind, anxious to get everything neat, tidy, and in place. He said:

"Yes, but others have different thoughts altogether. Today's favorite is Mr. Rhett's Red Rover. He's an ungainly-looking beast, but don't let that deceive you. He won the cup last year. Senator Stanhope likes to call it a fluke, but the truth of the matter is that Red Rover is an excellent horse. So is Dr. Carpenter's Happy Girl. I don't think the other two entries, Mr. Blackford's Skyrocket and Mr. Wendover's Arion, have much of a chance. Skyrocket runs like the wind for the first five eighths and then falters, and Arion has never finished better than third. Still, in a race like this——"

Miss Chadwick fell out of step for a moment. They had reached Dr. Carpenter's greenhouse, and John could see a tangle of leaves behind the whitewashed panes. Miss Chadwick said, "I was wrong in calling this a race meeting, wasn't I? It's simply a *race*," and John realized that her earnestness was not to be discounted.

"Were you not tempted to correct me?" she asked. "I would be grateful to have you as a mentor, Mr. Bottomley."

"A mentor, Miss Chadwick?"

"Would you mind?"

"How could I?"

"You will tell me all I need know, then?"

"There isn't much to tell, Miss Chadwick. I'm sure you know most of it already. The race is at a mile, which means that the horses will go twice around the track. Mr. Robertson will fire the starting gun—that's because he's president of the Agricultural Society—and after that anything can happen. The only prediction I'd care to venture would be that Blue Fly, up to the end of the first half mile, will probably be running last. That's when Andrew has been instructed to start using his whip. If I had any say in the matter I wouldn't have him wait that long."

"No?"

"As I see it, Skyrocket will break fast, the way he always does. He may well open up a lead of as much as two lengths over the first half mile. The other horses will be strung out behind, and Blue Fly, as I've said, will most likely be bringing up the rear."

"Does she always?"

"Always, Miss Chadwick. It never fails to happen. That's why she's such an exciting horse to watch. She always holds back, and she always comes up in a rush. It's Senator Stanhope's plan to have Andrew lay on the whip after they've reached the half-mile turn. He believes that the other horses may be a trifle discouraged by trying to catch Skyrocket. But the other gentlemen will have similar plans—suppose one of them decides to move his horse before the half-mile turn? What then? If Blue Fly is still loafing along, admiring the scenery—— But see here, Miss Chadwick! You shouldn't let me talk so much. I owe you an apology. I'm afraid I've been tiresome."

"How can you believe that? It is I who should be afraid of being tiresome."

They looked at each other, and their eyes held, and all of a sudden they were moving on a different plane. They were standing near the greenhouse, and a murmur of voices rose from the track, where the colors of the ladies' dresses and parasols were bright splashes in the sun, but everything about them—the greenhouse, the voices, even the fall of the sun—was somehow pitched in a different key. John could feel the touch of her fingers on his sleeve, and he was again aware of the three tiny freckles on the bridge of her nose, and hard though it was to be sure about such things, it could have been the freckles as much as anything that touched off the trigger of another impulse.

"This is where Dr. Carpenter does his agricultural experiments," he said, indicating the greenhouse. "Dr. Carpenter is mostly interested in rice and cotton, but he likes to experiment with flowers too. Right now he's trying to keep alive some orchids that were sent him by a friend in South America. It was Mr. Lucius Ridgely, I believe, the one with the big red nose," and why he had brought the size and color of Mr. Lucius Ridgely's nose into it, he would never know. "Would you like to see them?"

"Do you think I might? I've often heard of South American orchids but have never seen one. Dr. Carpenter won't mind, will he?"

"Dr. Carpenter? Of course not."

What John most clearly remembered about the greenhouse was the warm stillness, the smell of earth long enclosed, and the shallow pans of seedling rice that stood on a narrow table made of rough pine slabs. Some of the shoots were longer and greener than others, and the water in the pans was covered with a light, sticky film. He found the orchids in a small gum sapling that Dr. Carpenter had had cut down, topped, and stripped of all but one of its lower branches. It was planted in the earth in one corner of the greenhouse. Round yellow wounds, still fresh, showed where the branches had been sawed off, and the orchids had been placed in the crotch formed by the trunk and the single remaining branch.

The orchids grew in a delicate spray; small white blossoms remindful of butterflies. John needed but one look at them to tell that Dr. Carpenter wasn't going to pull them through. A dingy grayness had discolored the blossoms, and the leaves of the plant were beginning to wilt. The pots of geraniums that stood at the base of the tree were much more impressive. John said so, and Miss Chadwick agreed.

"They're splendid," she said, glancing about the greenhouse and taking everything in. "I know most people regard geranium as common, a darky's flower, but I don't think so. I'm glad to see that Dr. Carpenter doesn't think so either. But I suppose that if one has money enough, and power enough, one is privileged to do what one likes even in regard to geraniums," and the detached, analytical tone of her voice struck John as being a reflection of the look in her eyes.

The relation of money to power was not a new equation to him. The whole structure of the plantation world was a constant reminder. And that Miss Chadwick should appreciate the value of money was not surprising—little as he knew about women, he knew most women did. The curious thing was her touching on power. Other women rarely went that far. He suspected it had something to do with Gunpowder Street. He was put off for a moment—why, he couldn't say— and he might have been more put off had she not turned and looked at him. Her face softened, and all he could think of was how wrong and unbecoming her costume was: that drab-colored skirt and high-collared shirtwaist. She said, "Thank you for showing me the orchids, Mr. Bottomley. Don't you think we should go?" and then, stepping toward the door, she tripped over one of the pots of geraniums.

John's left arm shot out to break her fall and in some way or other his fingers happened to slip between the buttons of her shirtwaist. He was aware of the buttons pulling free, and a cupped softness in his palm, and when she was restored to her balance and stood looking at him again, a look that wavered between vexation and amusement, her shirtwaist was partially open. He dropped his face to the curve of her bosom, moving his lips about until they found the opening in her shirtwaist, and what happened next was too chaotic to remember clearly. Soon, though, he was standing before her. His voice was trembling and so was he. "I don't know what came over me, Miss Chadwick. I most humbly apologize. If you will say I have reason to hope——"

He had expected to meet a look of dismay or disapproval, that much at least, but instead the calm, detached stillness was back in her eyes. She buttoned her shirtwaist and smoothed back a few stray locks of hair, and simply those feminine motions, with their implications of intimacy, were enough to put a new catch in his throat.

"Miss Chadwick, I hardly know what you are thinking——"

She rested her hand on his arm. "What I am thinking, Mr. Bottomley, is that your sister is right to be devoted to you. You must see, however, that we hardly know each other, that we have scarcely met."

"Yes, Miss Chadwick. But still——"

Her fingers tightened on his arm. "No, Mr. Bottomley. Let us not discuss it further. I do think we'd best be going."

He moved toward her, aching with her nearness, and would have taken her in his arms had she not put her palms against his chest, turning her face aside. "No, no, Mr. Bottomley. Do not destroy the respect I have for you. We must leave. We must! You will miss the race. Come! Perhaps together we can urge Blue Fly on to victory."

iv

They were too late to visit the stables. Old Mr. Robertson had taken up his position at the starting post, gun in hand, and the horses were being led onto the track. John Bottomley loved just the look of a horse, and these were five of the best horses in all the low country. He identified them for Miss Chadwick as they were led by their owners down the lane formed by the spectators—Arion, ridden by Jack Wendover in blue and white bars; Happy Girl with Dr. Carpenter's Negro jockey, Magnus, in yellow and white; the Blackfords' Skyrocket with Tony Blackford in solid scarlet (a hum of interest at this, since Tony had never ridden Skyrocket in a race before); Red Rover with young Charlie Rhett up, wearing green silks; and finally Blue Fly, ridden by Andrew, a small wrinkled Negro well past forty, in white stars on a red background. Senator Stanhope was leading Blue Fly, and Arabella, still in her green dress and crown of leaves, walked beside her father. John added his voice to those of Blue Fly's well-wishers.

"Good luck, Senator! And don't go along just for the ride, Andrew! Keep awake, both of you!"

Andrew turned in his saddle and made a show of displaying his whip. Senator Stanhope's face brightened when he saw Miss Chadwick, and Arabella's clouded. John felt himself getting impatient with her. She had no cause to look at Miss Chadwick in that dark, sullen way, and he didn't relish being looked at like that either. But he had other things to think about. The horses were out on the track, and two of the gentlemen of the Agricultural Society, Mr. Fitzpatrick and Mr. Waites, were preparing to stretch the long hemp rope behind which the horses were to line up. Old Mr. Robertson stood with his starting gun, giving directions in a cracked, tyrannical voice, and the three judges, one of whom was Corwin Bottomley, had taken their positions at the finish line. The silver Agricultural Cup stood on a table that was covered with the same white cloth used ever since the Huntington Hall race had its first running thirty-eight years before.

John, moving to the rail with Miss Chadwick, found himself standing next to his friend, Jeremiah Lake. Jeremiah's sister, Cordelia, was with him. John and Jeremiah had gone to Dr. Themistocles Prince's Classical Academy in Pompey's Head and were graduated from the same class, Jeremiah leaving for the Naval Academy the same year John entered the College of New Jersey. He was now a lieutenant aboard the U.S.S. *Powhatan.* Home on leave, he was wearing civilian clothes. John had seen him only the night before at the Light Infantry Club. The *Powhatan* had been for ten months in European waters, and Jeremiah had confided that he was disturbed by the vehemence of the secession talk he heard. "I don't like it," he said. "How can sane

97

men speak of splitting the Union? We are one country, one people. Secession would make it a damn hard choice for the Lakes."

John could appreciate his friend's position. Jeremiah's grandfather had been a justice of the Supreme Court, his father had been Minister to Austria during the Tyler administration, and he himself was looking forward to a career in the Navy. The Lakes were known in Pompey's Head as Union men, and though it used not to make any difference, now it was beginning to. John introduced his friend to Miss Chadwick. Jeremiah observed the necessary formalities, presented his sister to Miss Chadwick, and then said that he had recently spoken to a cousin of hers.

"A cousin?" Miss Chadwick seemed almost startled. "Of mine?"

"It was at the telegraph office," Jeremiah explained. "He said his name was Morris. George Morris. He operates the key. My parents are in Virginia and I had to send a message. In it I said that Cordelia and I would be coming to the picnic today, and Mr. Morris happened to mention that he had a cousin who taught English and Elocution at Huntington Hall. He expressed great pride in you, Miss Chadwick, I might add."

"Oh yes," she said finally. "Mr. George Morris. He is a distant connection of my mother's. I have not seen him in years."

John realized that for all her seeming confidence she walked on treacherous ground. He was glad Cordelia Lake's attention had been occupied elsewhere. He knew he could count on Jeremiah not to mention the incident, nor was he actually worried about Cordelia, who was one of the kindest people imaginable. It was just as well, though, that she had been too busy to notice—this way she couldn't let it slip that Miss Chadwick had been ashamed to acknowledge a cousin who worked at the telegraph office. He saw Tony Blackford, hunched up on Skyrocket, shoot Cordelia a longing glance as he and his mount passed only a few feet away—Cordelia pretended not to notice, but she had.

"What's Tony Blackford doing out there?" John asked Jeremiah. "Titus sick or something?"

"Sick with chagrin, I suspect," Jeremiah replied. "Tony persuaded

Mr. Blackford to unsaddle Titus and let him ride Skyrocket instead. Hadn't you heard?"

"I heard, but I didn't believe it. Does Tony think he can give Skyrocket an extra boot—better than Titus, I mean—or is there some young lady he wants to impress?"

Jeremiah avoided looking in the direction of his sister. He said, "You will have to seek that answer elsewhere. I wouldn't know," and there was no time for further conversation. The horses were finally got into position, Mr. Robertson fired his gun, Mr. Fitzpatrick and Mr. Waites dropped the rope, and the horses were off—down along the rail near the finish line, standing with her father, Arabella Stanhope let out a yell like a wild red Indian.

"Can you see, Miss Chadwick?" John asked.

"Yes, thank you, but I can't tell the horses one from another. Where is Blue Fly?"

"Just where she might be expected to be."

"And the others?"

"Skyrocket has taken the lead, Arion is running second by a length, Happy Girl is third, and Red Rover is on Happy Girl's heels. Blue Fly, as usual, is sound asleep."

John did not think that Miss Chadwick sounded particularly interested. He imagined her mind was still on her cousin, the telegraph operator—it had been foolish for her to get so upset: follow the ramifications of cousinship far enough, and there was no telling who or what might turn up.

"Look at Happy Girl!" Jeremiah Lake cried out. "She's caught Arion and is pressing Skyrocket for the lead!"

Red Rover came storming up. He passed Happy Girl and gained on Skyrocket. The three horses were bunched together, not an inch of light showing between them, and then Red Rover, faltering, was passed by Happy Girl, Arion, and Blue Fly. Happy Girl took the lead from Skyrocket, Skyrocket gave way to Arion, Arion tried to catch Happy Girl and failed, and Skyrocket, with Tony Blackford using the whip, regained the lead as they came into the second half mile.

"Skyrocket's never been given a ride like this," John Bottomley

99

heard himself saying to no one in particular. "Tony may bring him home in front after all."

The horses swept past again. There was one tremulous instant when the whole confused scene was contained in the field of John's vision —the huge staring eyes of the horses, the strain of their muscles, Tony Blackford clenching his teeth, Charlie Rhett on Red Rover with his high cheekbones shining with sweat, Andrew's black wrinkled face working violently as he lashed Blue Fly, Magnus on Happy Girl moving his lips in the prayer he was known to repeat over and over during a race, little Jack Wendover leaning so far forward that Arion's mane seemed to be blowing across his eyes—and then it was Blue Fly's turn to bid for the lead.

Arabella Stanhope's wild Indian yell cut across the noises of the crowd.

"Blue Fly! Blue Fly! Blue Fly!"

But John Bottomley knew it wasn't going to be easy. The race was still wide open and any horse could win. The big surprise was Jack Wendover and Arion. If Tony Blackford was giving Skyrocket the ride of his life, Jack Wendover and Arion were also showing the crowd a thing or two. Blue Fly moved up to second, passing Red Rover and Happy Girl, and Arion, who on past performance should have run himself into the ground by now, found a new burst of speed. Bringing his horse up on the outside and then cutting in toward the rail in a way that could have meant his neck, Jack Wendover closed in on the leaders. Red Rover and Happy Girl fell behind, and a groan rose from their backers. Arion, Blue Fly, and Skyrocket ran neck and neck as they came into the final lap.

John Bottomley felt weak with excitement. He was aware that Miss Chadwick was standing remote and silent amid the tumult, that Cordelia Lake was giving the whole show away by calling out Tony Blackford's name instead of Skyrocket's, that Arabella Stanhope was screeching her head off, and that first one horse and then the other was forging into the lead. Arion pulled out inches ahead, Skyrocket took the lead from Arion, Blue Fly fell back to third, and it looked as though Skyrocket had the cup—but no, not yet!

The three horses crossed the finish line in practically a dead heat, but it was Blue Fly who had won—a last roar went up, and there was that drained moment that comes after a race, the queer giddy emptiness, and then Arabella Stanhope was tearing after Blue Fly in the still unsettled dust, and everybody stood talking and milling about until Mr. Robertson, climbing on a chair, announced the decision of the judges—Blue Fly first, Arion and Skyrocket tied for second, Happy Girl third, and Red Rover fourth.

"Here they come," John said to Miss Chadwick as Senator Stanhope and Arabella made their way through the crowd, the Senator leading Blue Fly, and Andrew still in the saddle. "Mr. Robertson will make a little speech and hand the Senator the cup. Later on it will be engraved and the Senator can keep it until the race next year."

John was lucky enough to find a place for Miss Chadwick and himself directly in front of the table where the presentation was to be made. The crowd gathered round. Senator Stanhope held Blue Fly by her bridle, Arabella looked rather dusty and bedraggled after her turn on the track, having somewhere lost her crown of leaves, and Andrew's big toothy grin crisscrossed his old wrinkles with various new ones stretching from ear to ear. Mr. Robertson made his speech, getting in his customary allusions to gallantry, chivalry, and his own long tenure as president of the Agricultural Society, and turned to Senator Stanhope with the cup.

Instead of accepting it, the Senator prompted Arabella to step forward. A deep flush spread over her cheeks as she received the trophy from Mr. Robertson. She tried to curtsy, went off balance with the weight of the cup, and along with the applause there was an undertone of friendly, indulgent laughter. Senator Stanhope reached for the cup and put it back on the table. A Negro stableboy led Blue Fly away, and the crowd began to disperse. Senator Stanhope saw Miss Chadwick. He came forward with a happy, excited look on his face, saying, "Ah, Miss Chadwick! How good to see you!" and his eyes were swimming again.

"Congratulations, Senator," John said. "Your horse ran quite a race."

"Didn't she though!" Senator Stanhope exclaimed. "I was sure for a moment that the cup belonged to Skyrocket, but the old girl never lost heart! Not for a moment! Did you ever see anything like that finish! And you, Miss Chadwick? Did you enjoy the race?"

"Oh yes, Senator Stanhope. May I offer my congratulations also?"

"Offer them? You may even drink them, Miss Chadwick. Dr. Carpenter has invited us to gather round the punch bowl. I would be delighted if you would accompany me. And you too, John."

"Thank you, Senator. But right now I want to look up Tony Blackford and Jack Wendover. They ran us the best race in years and I'd like to tell them so. I'll see you both at the house."

He didn't mind Miss Chadwick's leaving with the Senator. The Senator was fifty-eight, and he was twenty-five, and he could afford to be generous. Arabella, he noticed, had lagged behind.

"Where's Missy?" she asked.

"She's around somewhere. I saw her just a few minutes ago. She was with some of the other girls. They may have gone to play croquet."

There was a smudge of dust on Arabella's nose, and the excitement of the race seemed to have left her spent.

"What's the matter? Don't you feel well?"

"I'm all right."

"You don't look all right. Do you want to go up to the house and lie down? I'll find Missy and she'll sit with you."

Arabella's eyes flared. "You don't have to put yourself out for me, John Bottomley!"

"Now see here, Arabella——"

"I'm sorry, Johnny. I didn't mean to speak like that. Please forgive me."

"What in the world are you so cross about? Blue Fly won, didn't she?"

"Yes, Blue Fly won."

"Aren't you glad?"

"Yes, I'm glad."

"You don't look very glad."

"Oh, who cares *how* I look! Who cares about me or Blue Fly or anything!" and before John could answer she started running toward the stables.

"Arabella! Wait!"

If she heard, she didn't want to hear. John started to follow her and then decided not to—it wasn't his responsibility to cope with Arabella Stanhope in one of her moods. He looked for Jack Wendover and Tony Blackford, and then, not finding them anywhere around the track, he went up to the house. The curtains and decorations had been removed from the porch, where a punch bowl and glasses had been set out, and Senator Stanhope was still receiving congratulations. John was able to have a moment with Miss Chadwick alone.

"I hope I will be able to see you again, Miss Chadwick."

"It is kind of you to say so, Mr. Bottomley."

"Will you be in town throughout the summer?"

"Yes, I have no other plans."

There were many times when John wished he had had wit enough to let it end there—if only, when Senator Stanhope reclaimed her, he had let her walk out of his life forever. He did not like to remember the two evenings he called on her that summer. Nearly everyone had left Pompey's Head to get away from the heat, and it wasn't hard to manage, but what a fool he had been! For if he had known that Senator Stanhope was looking in her direction, trusting to money and position to compensate for an oversupply of years, certainly she knew it too. He should have understood that she scorned being a schoolteacher, dressing and acting the part only because of some stubborn, perverse pride, and that the liveliness of imagination that had so pleased him was in no small part the alertness of ambition. He should have sensed that those cool blue eyes of hers were already taking stock, adding this, subtracting that, and that his own prospects, measured against Senator Stanhope's huge fortune, must have seemed paltry.

But even if he had known—known beyond question—he was sure he would have refused to credit it. How could he have, when already he was in love with her? He knew now, didn't he? What good did it do? Was he any less in bondage? Five long years. All those days and nights at Deerskin. The knowing now what he did not know then, and the bitter, hateful realization that it made no difference. Fool! Fool! he said under his breath, watching the swirl of the polka on the floor, and then, as the music stopped and a cloud of applause rose to the ceiling, it was time to look up Arabella Stanhope for that waltz Missy had got him into.

CHAPTER SEVEN

John Bottomley found Arabella in a bank of uniforms. Her white gown blossomed among the fire-gilt buttons and scarlet sashes. She wore a narrow black velvet ribbon around her throat, hung with a single jewel, and her thick hair, caught in a knot at the base of her neck, had taken on a bright and coppery sheen in the glow of the chandeliers. She stood laughing and chatting with the uniforms, first one and then another, occasionally sweeping them all with a single glance. All over town the next morning it would be said that Arabella Stanhope had had another success and that she had not cared how she purchased it—just as she was the first beauty of her generation, so was she its most unprincipled flirt.

"Ah, John!" she cried, catching sight of him. "I thought I'd been deserted. Have you come to rescue me?"

The uniforms returned his bow. They were worn by Julian and Randolph Fitzpatrick, Charles Rhett, Jack Wendover, and Neville Monckton. With the exception of Neville Monckton, they were all old friends. It was Cameron's disappearance, more than what might be regarded as his own lukewarmness to the cause, that was responsible for their reserved behavior. He could count on their tolerance until the first shot was fired. Arabella's laugh came less readily, conversation languished, and one by one the uniforms took their leave. Neville Monckton was the last to go.

"I shall claim you later, Miss Arabella," he said. "Mine is the third waltz from now, I believe."

It was hard for John to adjust to Neville Monckton's name being on Arabella's card. Up to this evening he had been seen only on the fringes of society. Had it not been for his oldest brother, Ules, who out of his own pocket had put up fifteen thousand dollars to transform the Light Infantry from a social organization to a military unit, Neville would never have been admitted into its ranks. Somewhere John had read that war was the first engine of revolution, and in Neville Monckton's presence at the Light Infantry Ball the first stirrings of revolution might be seen.

"I shall be looking forward to our waltz, Mr. Monckton," Arabella said, and the slow way she looked at Neville and the equally slow way he looked back caused John to think maliciously that it was a contest of beauties—much as he disliked Neville, it was impossible to deny that the youngest of the Monckton brothers had been favored with extraordinary good looks. Nearly six feet tall, he had wavy brown hair, a fine profile, a small golden mustache, and a sort of bored, languid grace. In a world essentially Tory, willing to forgive almost any vice in a man provided he be manly, Neville Monckton ran the risk of seeming effeminate. It was only the glint in his pale blue eyes that saved him, saying what his more intimate companions already knew—that he would not shrink from a fight, that he knew how to shoot, that he could handle a horse, and that he fancied himself, not without cause, as a devil of a fellow with women.

Neville bowed and withdrew. The fiddles began tuning up. Arabella turned and smiled.

"I'm pleased to see you, John."

"And I you, Arabella. May I say that you're looking extremely well this evening?"

"Why, John! You've paid me a compliment!"

"You've been visiting Christina, I hear."

Arabella looked at him with pretended surprise. "But what an astonishment that you should have paid any attention to my whereabouts! I should have imagined that I might have been in China for all the difference it would make to you."

John began to feel the stirrings of the annoyance Arabella always roused in him. He hadn't seen her in nearly a year, and though she looked older and taller than he remembered, she hadn't changed. She still thought it necessary to run through the finger exercises that she seemed to have memorized from some handbook of flirtation.

"How is Christina?"

Arabella shook her head in a despairing, artificial way. "Bored, I fear. It's dull as ditchwater on a plantation. But you don't find it so, do you?"

"Sometimes."

"Why do you bury yourself on Deerskin, then? Why don't you marry? I'm told that there are any number of young ladies who would be pleased to brighten up your life for you," and then, seeing how discomfited he was, she swallowed a smile. "Don't look so glum, John. Have I not a right to interest myself in your welfare? We're hardly strangers, you know."

John wondered. Having never been able to understand Arabella, he did not understand her now.

"And what do you hear from Julie?"

"Only that she couldn't get to the ball. How do my poor sisters stand it? They spend all their time with the drudgery of a plantation, looking after a hundred different things, and what thanks do they get? It's the men who have the fun. Me, I'd just as soon be in the dreadful place as to live in those tiresome swamps!"

According to Missy Bottomley, who kept John acquainted with the comings and goings of Pompey's Head, it was Lydia who was responsible for Arabella's prolonged absences from home. The ladies of the Wednesday Afternoon Ladies Society went further. They said Lydia and Arabella were finding it increasingly difficult to get along—but then, in all fairness, it had to be remembered that it was not easy for the ladies of the Wednesday Afternoon Ladies Society to speak kindly of Lydia. She had committed two unforgivable sins. The first was her marrying Senator Stanhope, and the second her exemplary behavior. By all rights the Senator should by now have been made to regret his impulsive wooing of a schoolteacher nobody, and, had justice prevailed, the arrows of regret should have been loosed from her bow. Senator Stanhope, however, presented the appearance of a completely happy man—much as the ladies of the Wednesday After-noon Ladies Society felt cheated by not having it proved that there was no fool like an old fool, the gentlemen of the Light Infantry Club envied him his good fortune.

John led Arabella to the floor. The waltz was "Bohemian Girl," and as they started dancing Arabella began humming under her breath. Humming while dancing was considered an error in deportment, against which the young ladies of Huntington Hall were specifically warned. Arabella kept on humming, however, dancing happily, and when Missy and Gordon Carpenter waltzed past, Missy looking gravely earnest and Gordon's homely face transfigured as by some soft, inner light, John thought that Arabella's humming must be on the same plane as Missy's saying petunia.

Arabella caught sight of Missy and stopped humming.

"How entrancing she is!" she said. "I've always envied her her looks. Those black, black eyes and light hair—could anything be more striking? Tell me. Is she going to marry Gordy Carpenter?"

"I don't know, Arabella. Do you?"

It was what all the girls in Missy's and Arabella's set were thinking, who was going to marry whom, and it was hard for John to get used to the fact that they were both of marriageable age. Actually, since they would soon be nineteen, it wouldn't be too long before it would be wondered if they were going to wither on the vine. A number of the girls in their group already had husbands, and, among those who hadn't, a number of pairings, besides Missy and Gordon Carpenter, had been struck off—Cordelia Lake and Tony Blackford, Mary Eliza-beth Manning and Tom Ingram, Lucy Fitzpatrick and Charles Rhett.

But with Arabella it was otherwise. No sooner was her name linked with that of some admirer than the link parted. For a time it would be Clay Vincent, then Tony Blackford's slightly older brother Rob-ert, then one of the Fitzpatrick twins, and then somebody from Charleston, Savannah, Port Royal, Beaufort, Georgetown, Columbia, or wherever it was she had recently been visiting—it was reported that Miss Elizabeth Paxton said that what Arabella really wanted was a harem, but that, naturally, was much too shocking to be believed.

"A penny, John."

"What?"

"Poor man!" Arabella shook her head. "You'd much rather be talking rice and cotton with the other gentlemen, wouldn't you?"

"Of course not."

"Alas, you don't sound very convincing. Promise me that you won't be cross with Missy for getting you into this waltz."

"Cross?"

"Oh, John, how solemn you've become! You didn't used to be. It must be living at Deerskin that's responsible."

John remembered Missy using practically the same words. Perhaps it was true: most likely he had changed. But what did they expect, these frivolous young girls? Of course he was solemn—he had things to be solemn about.

Arabella's thoughts seemed to have run along with his. "Don't be annoyed with me, Johnny. It's Cameron you're worried about, isn't it?" and for a few seconds he lost time to the music—the mention of his brother's name, so purposefully avoided all evening, took him that much by surprise.

"Yes, Arabella," he said. "Naturally I'm worried. You don't know anything about this that I wouldn't know, do you?"

"How could I? I just came from Christina's day before yesterday. I was bewildered when I heard. Have you no idea where Cameron may have gone to or why?"

"Unfortunately no."

"What do you propose to do?"

"I don't quite know. Try to find him, I guess."

"Dear John. So good you are. Promise you'll always be my friend."

Over Arabella's shoulder John saw Lydia dancing with Mr. Wingfield Manning, the new president of the Agricultural Society. Old Mr. Robertson, at eighty-seven, had finally taken his hierarchical notions to the severest hierarchy of all. Lydia's dancing with Mr. Manning seemed innocent enough, and yet John knew that she had let herself in for further criticism. It always amused him that the worst indictment the ladies of the Wednesday Afternoon Ladies Society could find to bring against Lydia was that she was too ambitious. The several counts of the indictment stemmed from a common root—who had rekindled Senator Stanhope's interest in politics; who would have urged him to stand for the Senate again were there still a Senate to stand for; who nourished his ambition to become a cabinet officer when a confederation of the Southern states was formed? Nor were the ladies of the Wednesday Afternoon Ladies Society inclined to believe that Lydia was thinking only of the Senator. They wrapped the whole of their animosity in a final question—she's his wife, isn't she?

Seen in this light, Lydia's dancing with Mr. Wingfield Manning took on more than a social meaning. Mr. Manning was a most influential man. The Agricultural Society, like all the other agricultural societies in the South, was a potent political organization. And besides being its president, which in itself would have made him someone to reckon with, Mr. Manning was the most powerful member of the state legislature. It was a certainty that he would be one of those called upon to attend the constitutional convention of any new government that might be formed, and although he alone could not put Senator Stanhope in the cabinet, he could help him take a long step in that direction.

John wondered if Missy was right about Lydia's being responsible for Arabella's frequent absences from home. It wasn't that Lydia was mean to Arbell, Missy said, or that she had caused the Senator to stop being nice to her. That wasn't it. It was hard to say just what it was exactly, since Arbell was too proud ever to admit that anything was wrong, but there were a lot of little things that anyone could see— things like the Senator's never taking Arbell to the springs after he married Lydia, and his selling Blue Fly to Mr. Rhett when he found out that Lydia didn't like racing, and Lydia's always giving parties for a lot of political people with whom Arbell felt out of place. What she thought it was, Missy said, was that Arbell had come to feel that she wasn't necessary to her father any more—almost any girl would feel like that, especially if she had been as close to her father as Arbell used to be, and while Lydia couldn't exactly be blamed, or the Senator either, it was his marrying Lydia that caused the change.

"Will you be home for long, Arabella?"

"I can't rightly say, John. The DeVeres have asked me to Savannah, and Julie wants me to come back to Georgetown, and I promised Cordelia Lake that if she went to visit her cousins in Charleston——"

Just then Lydia and Mr. Wingfield Manning came by again. Mr. Manning's face was aglow, and he was waltzing with a sort of portly abandon, and John thought that if it depended on Mr. Manning alone, Senator Stanhope was as good as in the cabinet. Lydia's eyes met John's and she pressed her lips together in what could be taken for a smile. He inclined his head in a slight nod, and as some slight change of expression crossed her face—amusement? disinterest? speculation? what?—he again found himself at odds with the music. He said, "I'm sorry, Arabella. I don't know what's the matter with me this evening," and then, as Lydia's eyes traveled from him to Arabella in the same aloof, detached glance that he remembered from the greenhouse at Happy Chance, Arabella seemed to be dancing less gracefully than before.

"Yes, Arabella. You were saying?"

"Have you forgotten so soon?"

"Of course I haven't forgotten. You were saying that you might be going away again. Why do you? We miss you."

"Do you now, Mr. Bottomley? That's most interesting to hear." She gave a little malicious laugh. "You missed me all last summer, I suppose?"

"Well, Arabella, last summer was a busy time. A lot of my people were sick, and we had to help with the work at Cornwall, and besides that——"

"Cornwall my foot! I never see you any more from one year to the next. Miss me! Avoid me, or avoid *somebody*, would seem to be more like it. Miss me indeed! What a clumsy piece of flattery!"

John felt that he had enough to put up with without one of Arabella's fits of bad temper. "Look, Arabella," he said, "if it pleases you to be angry," and then the waltz ended, Arabella made an elaborate, mocking curtsy—it was bound to be noticed, and all over town the next morning it too would be added to the talk. She said, "I *so* enjoyed our waltz, Mr. Bottomley. Thank you most kindly, sir. Don't waste away with missing me," and he was not sorry when the uniforms converged on her again.

Neville Monckton was not among them. He was standing with Constance Pettibone, waiting for the next dance. Out of a corner of his eye John saw him look at Arabella in an open, almost insolent way, and more directly he saw her cast Neville a long, sideways glance. Much as John was annoyed with her, he wished she wouldn't encourage Neville Monckton. Let him get it into his head that an invitation was extended, and he would be restrained by none of those gentlemanly considerations that she took for granted.

Handing Arabella over to Jack Wendover, who was next on her card, John made his way across the floor. He felt in need of a drink and a cigar. Walking toward the door of the ballroom, and having in mind a small room set aside for those who, like himself, might feel in need of a drink and a cigar, he saw Ules Monckton absorbed in conversation with Lydia Stanhope.

Ules Monckton was wearing one of the new uniforms. There was a hint of the schoolmaster in his appearance, a longness of skull and a balding bookishness that suggested the Reverend Mr. Daniel Pryse of Huntington Hall, and he wore his uniform poorly. His body had not yet molded the cloth to its shape, and even when it did he would be too gangly, too loose-jointed, and too stoop-shouldered ever to seem anything but a civilian stray. John remembered what Cameron had said about Ules's ambition to assume command of the Light Infantry, and he had picked up enough information to know the matter was all but settled. Ules's putting up the money needed to activate the Light Infantry had been a master stroke. It would not be forgotten that he had dug down into his own pocket while older men like Corwin Bottomley and Senator Stanhope were still debating the politics of secession.

Though Corwin and his planter friends did not want for influence, they no longer had absolute political power. Theirs was the day when the South had ruled Washington almost as completely as it ruled Richmond, New Orleans, Charleston, and Mobile. With them, as with most Southern spokesmen of their generation, secession was more a threat than a program. They had not really wanted the South to leave the Union. They wanted the Union to accommodate the South on its own terms. Often as they threatened secession, it was doubtful they believed the threat would have to be carried out. And now that it had and a new nation was in the making, they were no longer able to control the forces they had helped unloose. New times meant new men, intolerant of compromise, determined to act, and Ules Monckton was one of the new men.

Though Ules was too complicated to be read easily, it was apparent he enjoyed being in Lydia's company. His face, however, had none of the bubbly pleasure that had diffused that of Mr. Wingfield Manning. It wore an expression of intense concentration, and Lydia's countenance, as she listened to him, had taken on a matching intensity of its own. They gave the impression of forming a unit, of being somehow joined together, and it struck John Bottomley that the bond between them was not hard to discover. It was power that Lydia wanted, and so did Ules Monckton want power, and the hard ruthless drive of the one was matched by the quite different and yet no less forceful determination of the other. And there was another bond between them, hardly less meaningful. Lydia Chadwick, who only a few years ago had been a little schoolteacher living on Gunpowder Street, was now Mrs. Senator Stanhope, and Ules Monckton, who used to be a struggling lawyer in a one-room office over a harness shop, was but a few days away from assuming command of the Light Infantry. They had both come a long way, following almost parallel lines, and it intrigued John to recall that he had been privileged to know them at the beginnings of their careers.

CHAPTER EIGHT

The first time John Bottomley had seen Ules Monckton was at a meeting of the Agricultural Society on the evening of Thursday, September 7, 1854. John had come down the river on the *Serena Moore* especially to attend the meeting. He had just been elected to the Agricultural Society, and it was the first of its sessions he was privileged to attend.

The Agricultural Society met in a square, high-ceilinged room on the second floor of Mechanics Hall, a small brick building of early republican architecture that stood on the corner of Bullis and Hightower streets. A number of glass cases stood against the walls, full of stuffed birds, Indian relics, blue ribbons that members of the society had won at various fairs, and displays of rice, cotton, peas, corn, and other agricultural products.

Old Mr. Robertson presided over the meeting, and about forty members were present. John recognized most of them. All were plantation owners, and some, like his father and Senator Stanhope, had held political office. According to its charter, which hung framed on one of the walls, the Agricultural Society had been founded "to aid and assist in the development of soil and animal husbandry with special attention to the cultivation of rice and cotton." Over the years, however, it had taken on an increasingly political coloration. The reading of two papers was on the program—"A Consideration of the Merits of Island Guano from Jarvis and Baker Islands in the South Pacific Ocean," by Dr. James Carpenter, and "Our Southern Destiny," by Mr. Ules Monckton.

Dr. Carpenter's paper was listened to attentively. Large deposits of guano had been discovered on Jarvis and Baker islands in the Pacific, and it was being advertised as being superior and as much as fifteen dollars a ton cheaper than the Peruvian guano that most planters used. It had interested Dr. Carpenter to conduct some experiments at Happy Chance, and these were his findings—while not as nutritive as Peruvian guano, and here Dr. Carpenter gave some yields per acre of sweet potatoes, the Jarvis and Baker variety, because it appeared not to stimulate root growth to excess, would seem to hold less danger of killing off plants during a dry season, as Peruvian guano was known to do. Dr. Carpenter then read more figures and concluded by saying that the members of the society might find the Jarvis and Baker guano suitable for cane, peanuts, and sweet potatoes, and less suitable for corn and cotton—always remembering, he would like to repeat, that there would probably be less yield per acre.

The appreciative applause that followed Dr. Carpenter's remarks was followed by a hum of voices as the members discussed his paper, twisting and turning in their seats. After a reasonable time Mr. Robertson rapped for order. He thanked Dr. Carpenter for a most constructive and interesting contribution and introduced the next speaker— "Our fellow member, Mr. Ules Monckton, will address us on the subject of 'Our Southern Destiny.' Sir, the floor is yours."

Though Ules Monckton's name had often entered the family conversation at Indigo, John Bottomley had never seen him before. Watching him walk to the lectern at one end of the room and then stand facing his audience, John felt rather disappointed. Without having a sinister reputation, neither had Ules a conventional one, and John had not expected to be reminded of one of those tutors, so often of Yankee extraction, who had charge of the young people on the more isolated plantations. Ules's gangly frame, his thin growth of sandy hair, his slightly bulbous forehead, his long nose, and his loose, large mouth, half concealed by a scraggly red mustache, all added up to what most people would call a common, ordinary, undistinguished sort of man.

All John knew about the Moncktons was what he had heard, and most of what he had heard came from his father. Corwin Bottomley called them climbers. What he meant was that none of their people had ever been of the planter class. Of the three brothers, Ules, a lawyer by profession, was the oldest. He was forty-one. Gup was thirty-nine and Neville twenty. Two Monckton daughters had intervened between Gup and Neville, but they no longer lived in Pompey's Head. One was married to a merchant in Camden, the other to a druggist somewhere in the upcountry. Having thus taken themselves beyond the pale, they were never heard of again.

Details such as these, however, might be part of any number of personal histories. What made the Moncktons remarkable was that their name wasn't Monckton at all. It was Simpson. One of the favorite stories of Pompey's Head was how the three Simpson brothers, seven years before, had marched under Ules's leadership to the county courthouse and petitioned that their name be changed from their father's to their maternal grandmother's. Beyond the grandmother, in some forgotten pocket of time, there once lived a Frederick Monckton distantly connected with that Miles Monckton who, at the Battle of Little Pigeon Marsh, had ridden to a hero's death and legendary fame. There was consequently some claim to status in Monckton, whereas Simpson was too intimately associated with the debt-ridden, snuff-dipping lawyer who was remembered in Pompey's Head, when he was remembered at all, for his extraordinary bouts with the bottle.

At the time of the march on the courthouse, John Bottomley was in his first year at Princeton. He heard about it in a letter from his father. "I need not tell you the entertainment it has provided," Corwin wrote. "What these Simpson-Moncktons or Monckton-Simpsons hope to gain by such a move I cannot imagine. It is like taking a gray mare and painting her brown and then trying to pass her off as a chestnut. As the saying goes, 'It won't wash.' I returned home yesterday from a short trip to our properties on Little River, and if I heard the story of the Simpson-Moncktons Monckton-Simpsons once, I must have heard it twenty times. Could anything be more fantastical?"

Though Corwin had no way of knowing it at the time, the answer was yes. Two years later Ules Monckton married the childless widow

Jackson, whose plantation, Oak Hill, was not far from Dr. Carpenter's Happy Chance. The widow Jackson, *née* Minerva Pryor, belonged to one of the long-established plantation families. It came as a surprise that she and Ules Monckton were even acquainted. People like the Rhetts and the Mannings suddenly found themselves related to Ules by marriage. Calls had to be made and invitations extended. It was obligatory to admit Ules into the Agricultural Society, and though some of the members found it hard to swallow, there was no way of excluding him, because of the Rhetts and Mannings, from the Light Infantry Club.

Tongues were bound to wag. Corwin Bottomley grumbled that Ules Monckton was worse than a Vermont Yankee in his desire to get ahead, and Mrs. Percy Wyeth Blackford II, who at seventy-nine was old enough to say what she pleased, told the Wednesday Afternoon Ladies Society that Minerva Pryor was one of those women who would do anything to keep from getting into bed all by herself on a cold winter night. On the whole, however, Ules's marriage was not held too much against him. Not too much. A good alliance was understood to be one of the ways by which a man might better himself, and the widow Jackson had been notorious for her plainness. A number of coarse remarks were passed across the card tables of the Light Infantry Club, and most opinion in that quarter came to agree that whatever that Monckton fellow had got, it wasn't altogether a bargain—being hitched to that kind of plow, it was observed, must be damned uphill work.

In 1852, three years after Ules's marriage, Pompey's Head was swept by one of the worst epidemics of yellow fever the low country had ever known. More than a hundred people died in and around the city, and among the unfortunates was the widow Jackson. The end of the epidemic left Ules the sole proprietor of Oak Hill and four other plantations, a slave owner and man of property. That he did not try to press his advantage was held in his favor. He continued in the law, regretted the few invitations that came his way, and remained in mourning for exactly a year.

But then, in the autumn of 1853, Ules served notice that his ambition went beyond being a plantation owner with a sideline in law. He sold one of his lesser plantations and bought the *News*. As editor he installed his brother Gup, the head bookkeeper for the wholesale hardware company of Murdoch & Brown. Gup, however, was more than a bookkeeper. He was also Publicus, a frequent contributor to the correspondence columns of the *News*, where his lively intelligence ranged over a host of such interrelated subjects as slavery, secession, and the supremacy of cotton as a weapon against the North —it was Publicus, so far as Pompey's Head was concerned, who coined the maxim that cotton was king. He had ability and would serve Ules well.

What, though, did Ules want? On the evening of Thursday, September 7, 1854, as he rose to address the Agricultural Society, the question was not yet answered. A silence fell across the room as he prepared to speak.

ii

Dr. Carpenter had read his paper, but Ules Monckton, John saw, was going to speak from memory. John noticed that his father, who was sitting to his right, had stiffened in his chair, half scowling, hunching forward a little, and that Mr. Blackford, who sat to his left, had half turned his head so that his right ear, the good one, was held in the direction of the speaker. New though John was to the Agricultural Society, he understood what was happening—this was the first time Ules Monckton had been invited to address the members, and he was still very much on trial.

"You know what I think?" Corwin Bottomley said one night in John's presence at the Light Infantry Club, shortly after Ules had bought the *News*. "What I think is that that fellow would like to sweep us all from the board. You take a fellow like that, coming up out of nowhere, and he's obliged to be more royalist than the King. Dammit, he'd like to *be* King! You think it's fantastical, eh? Well, all I can say is that I'm glad there ain't a throne and that I ain't the one who stands in his way. I don't like the look in his eye. I've seen the look of a dead sheepshead that I've liked better. I wouldn't trust him from here to that spittoon!"

How far the other members of the Agricultural Society would be willing to trust Ules Monckton, John had no way of knowing. But a long way from completely, he imagined. Ules had no close friends. He kept to himself and invited no confidences. The gregarious gentlemen of the Agricultural Society were not used to that kind of self-sufficiency. The looks on their faces made it easy to see that they were more interested in him and what he might be up to than they were in the merits of guano from Jarvis and Baker islands in the Pacific Ocean.

Ules Monckton started in the usual way, "Mr. President, Fellow Members, Guests of the Society," and went on to observe that the South stood at the dawn of a new era in the history of civilization. It must be plain to his listeners that the federal Union could not maintain itself much longer. He would pass over the state of thralldom in which the South found itself. The ambition of the North to crush every Southern aspiration was too well known for him to dwell upon. But that the South would meekly continue in its present condition, slandered, vilified, ground down by the tariff, the very keystone of its social and economic structure under endless attack—surely it was time, long past time, for the South to serve notice that the end of its patience had come!

A number of voices said, "Hear, Hear," some in an undertone, others more audibly, and John Bottomley, reflecting with one part of his mind that this was the first openly defiant secession speech he had ever heard, marveled with another at the change that had come over Ules Monckton. No one would ever mistake him for a plantation tutor now. He spoke in a ringing, splendid voice, and the loose hang of his gangly, stoop-shouldered frame was braced with confidence and authority. It was his eyes, however, that most caught John's attention. They were of a curious slate-colored shade, and before he started to speak, as he stood behind the lectern, they had seemed to be filmed with a dull, flat inertia that gave more an impression of secrecy than of sight. But now the flatness was gone. The slate-colored inertia had given way to a feverish brightness. It seemed to reflect banked, hidden fires. It might even be thought a little mad.

"How often do they cry out the sacredness of the Union, our enemies in the North! But is not the true burden of their cry the sacredness of their right to pillage and plunder the South? Let us hesitate no longer! Let us put forth the proposition that if the time has come for either the South or the Union to pass from the scene, it is the South, not the Union, that must endure! The Union belongs to the past. The South is in league with the future!"

It was treason Ules Monckton was speaking, John realized, and yet he knew it expressed no more than the extreme Southern point of view. It was what followed that left him stunned. Ules said the Union was a jerry-built thing. He said that it had been founded on a philosophical error and that Thomas Jefferson and most of the other leading statesmen of his time were wrong—worse than wrong: incapable of understanding one of nature's profoundest laws: betrayed by sentimentality into the worst kind of error.

John found it hard to believe that any man could be so audacious. He noticed that his father was looking unfriendlier than ever, that Mr. Blackford had leaned forward and cupped his ear, as was his habit when he believed he had not heard correctly, and that Senator Stanhope, who had been fingering an unlighted cigar, was sitting bolt upright and pressing the cigar all out of shape. Along with the other gentlemen of the Agricultural Society, they were used to hearing diatribes against the North. Pompey's Head had come to depend upon such outbursts for some of its best entertainment. But this was more than a diatribe, an entirely different departure. Their faces were full of distrust.

"Why am I emboldened to say that Jefferson and most of the other statesmen of his time were wrong?" Ules Monckton asked. "Because they *were* wrong! Let not reverence blind us to the fact. And why were they wrong? Because they ignored the proper status of the Negro. Jefferson's ideas of government rested upon the assumption of the equality of races. This was an error, a misreading of all of nature's laws.

"The Negro by nature, or by the curse against Canaan, is fitted for that condition which he occupies in our society. It is, indeed, in conformity with the laws of the Creator, and the great objects of humanity are best attained in conformance to His decrees. Let us be guided by these laws, ridding ourselves of the errors of the past, and soon the other nations of the world, recognizing the wisdom of our course, will follow where we lead. The stone of slavery, rejected by the builders of the Union, must become the cornerstone of our new edifice. Let us delay no longer! Let the work begin!"

A cheer came from the rear of the room, followed by another, and then Ules Monckton was receiving an ovation. Even Corwin Bottomley and the other members of the old guard were moved to join in. This wasn't as bad as they had anticipated. If what this Monckton fellow meant was that Thomas Jefferson had been wrong because he didn't see that the niggers had to be kept in their place, why of course Jefferson had been wrong! That had been their way of thinking all along. It just hadn't occurred to them that, with a little tinkering here and there, their sentiments could be built into a philosophy. Maybe this fellow had some good stuff in him after all.

John Bottomley watched Ules Monckton with new attention. He was beginning to suspect that Ules was no ordinary man and that most of the things he had heard about him were wrong. For one thing, it was a mistake to call him a climber. He could hardly be more indifferent to the success he was having. Popularity was unimportant to him. Perhaps nothing was important to him except his vision of the future.

But what most interested John was that the moment Ules stopped speaking his eyes became flat and dull again, heavy-lidded, as though only the articulation of his thought had power enough to make them come alive. Ules sipped from a glass of water and waited for quiet. He put down the glass, and his eyes remained fixed in their hooded, secret look, and then he began speaking again.

The South, he said, had an empire to claim. It lay in the direction of the equator, beyond the Gulf of Mexico. Did the gentlemen of the Agricultural Society recall the heroic exploits of William Walker? He was confident they did, since Mr. Walker's bold enterprise had been fully reported in the *News*. He would like, however, to go further into the matter. Most of all he wished to impress upon his listeners that Mr. Walker was no mere adventurer. That was simply another piece of slander on the part of the Northern press. There was reason for the slander. It so happened that Mr. Walker was one of the most devoted partisans of the South.

The name of William Walker was unfamiliar to John Bottomley at first, but then he remembered having read about him in the *News* —a Tennessee man who had been a doctor, lawyer, editor, and more recently the leader of a filibustering expedition to Mexico. "A plain damn fool!" Corwin Bottomley had said at breakfast at Indigo one morning, glowering over the *News*. "He couldn't make a living no place else, so now he wants to make himself president of Mexico. And here's Gup Monckton calling him a great man. Great man, my behind! A damn-fool crackpot, that's what he is!"

But no, Ules Monckton said—a man of bold, inspiring imagination. Let the gentlemen of the Agricultural Society pause to consider what Mr. Walker's attempt to establish himself in Mexico meant in relation to the South. And let it be remembered that had it not been for the machinations of the federal government, which had stepped in to prevent supplies and reinforcements from reaching Mr. Walker, he would have succeeded in his aim. Mr. Walker's cause, it would be recalled, had at first been attended with success. Having invaded Mexico, he had proclaimed Lower California and the neighboring state of Sonora an independent republic, with himself at its head. And such might be the present state of affairs had it not been for the interference of the federal government. And what was the reason for such interference? Why had the federal government put every obstacle in Mr. Walker's way?

"What is not generally known about Mr. Walker," Ules Monckton said, "is that he is a slavery man. One of his first acts, had he been able to maintain his position in Mexico, would have been to abolish the laws forbidding slavery.

"Think of what that would have meant to our cause!

"And think, also, had the South been free to act, as the independent

123

nation it should be, how we could have assisted Mr. Walker. With men, with arms, with money. And consider the results that might have been accomplished! Mr. Walker, having secured his base of operations in Sonora, would then have been able, through our aid, to march on to the conquest of all Mexico!

"For years we have expended our efforts in a vain political struggle to bring one new slave state into the Union. But what if, instead of a slave state, we had a slave country as an ally—nay, more than an ally: a *dependency!*

"What good to us are those stretches of barren desert in the West? Shall we think forever only in terms of how many congressional votes we can muster? Let the votes and the Union go! Our destiny lies to the South! Mexico awaits but the landing of a Southern army to become the first of our foreign possessions! We have an empire to claim!"

John Bottomley sat spellbound. He had heard of visionaries and read of men who believed they could bend the shape of history to their will, but never had he imagined that he would someday be sharing the same room with one and hearing a vision told out loud. For Mexico was but the beginning. After Mexico would come Nicaragua, then Honduras, and after Honduras Guatemala, followed by El Salvador and Costa Rica, and then across the Caribbean to Cuba and Santo Domingo—a golden circle of slave countries which would be under Southern control: truly an empire: a dazzlement of power and riches that would make the Confederacy one of the mightiest nations in the world.

But the vision was too intense. Absorbed in politics though they were, the gentlemen of the Agricultural Society were essentially planters. The world they envisioned, should it become necessary for the Southern states to leave the Union, was a world not too unlike their own plantations—domesticated, patriarchal, and orderly. And the Southern heartland, stretching from the Potomac to the Gulf of Mexico and from the Rio Grande to the Atlantic, was empire enough.

Ules Monckton said, "Think of the prospect, gentlemen. Let your imaginations extend a hundred years into the future," but the imaginations of the gentlemen of the Agricultural Society were not that expansive. Ules lost his audience. His success went down to failure. He ended as he began, a man too intense for comfort, an outsider, a probationer who, having had his chance, had missed his opportunity.

John knew that Ules was too shrewd not to sense what was happening. He persisted to the end, however, his voice ringing out as though he believed he was still in control, and when finally he finished, standing slack and stoop-shouldered, his dull eyes staring into failure, something in the stiff, mechanical way he bowed to the grudging, slightly embarrassed applause made John understand that he cared even less for the gentlemen of the Agricultural Society than they cared for him. The South could not depend on them and their kind much longer. He was willing to bide his time.

That was seven years ago, and on this evening of the Light Infantry Ball, as he stood conversing with Lydia Stanhope, Ules Monckton could say his time had come. John doubted, however, that he thought in those terms. That was what made him so puzzling, and why the gentlemen of the Light Infantry Club were still asking what did he want. Part of the answer was known—he wanted power; but the larger part of the answer—power for what?—was as much a mystery as ever. John had heard a number of speculations put forward—Ules Monckton wanted to be governor; he hoped to become a general; he wished to be made minister to one of the foreign powers—but John felt that what he wanted was both larger and lesser than any of these. The gentlemen of the Light Infantry Club fell into the error of concreteness: they were unable to understand ambition that did not turn on personal gain. John did not think that what Ules Monckton wanted was so mysterious. All one had to do was to read the editorials in the *News*. If Ules confided in no man, he did not mind confessing to the world. And what he wanted was no more than he wanted the night he addressed the Agricultural Society. He wanted to see his vision come true.

CHAPTER NINE

When John Bottomley entered the room that had been set aside for those who might want to relax for a few moments over a drink or a cigar, he found it warm, crowded, and full of smoke. Some of the gentlemen were refreshing themselves from a silver punch bowl, others had flung themselves into armchairs, and still others were grouped about this or that topic of conversation, striving to make themselves heard.

"Once that baboon from Illinois is in the White House, we'll have no choice. If he tries to reinforce the forts——"

"I'm not worried about Virginia. Let the other states join in and Virginia will join too. My wife had a letter from a cousin in Lynchburg, and he says——"

"Biggest damn buck you ever saw! He came busting out of the swamps like he was carrying a rocking chair on his head, his spread was that large. You remember the buck that Ransom Truett got two years ago? Well, this one——"

"Look at it this way. If I have to pay the bank twelve per cent, and if my factors will carry me for eleven——"

"What will the North do without our cotton?"

"What will England do?"

"And France? Don't forget France."

"It was in the third race at the Twin Oaks track. If that damn nigger jockey hadn't lost a stirrup——"

"Yes, and if a bullfrog had wings——"

"What I say is that there ought to be an oath! And any man who won't sign it, swearing he's ready to stand with the South, no matter what, then by God he ought to be tarred and feathered and run out of town!"

It was Clay Vincent speaking, and as he unburdened himself he happened to notice John Bottomley. Clay was in uniform, dark and handsome, as all the Vincents were, and though there was no reason for John to believe Clay had had him in mind, he began to feel uncomfortable. Clay's stern expression neither hardened nor relaxed.

"Good evening, John."

"How are you, Clay?"

Clay had been directing his remarks to Jeremiah Lake and Robert Blackford, and John hesitated before he joined them—had it not been that he did not want openly to acknowledge the separateness he felt, he would not have. Neither Jeremiah nor Robert was in uniform, but John knew that their evening clothes, unlike his own, would not be held against them. Jeremiah had resigned his commission in the Navy, and Robert, who only a few days ago had returned from London, where he had gone to look after some family affairs, had not had time to have a uniform made.

"You have a good time in London, Rob?" John asked.

"Not unless you can call freezing to death a good time. Our English cousins ought to be introduced to the advantages of lightwood and pitch pine. If there's anything I hate, it's a cold climate."

"And you, Jeremiah? I'd ask after your new bride, except that there's no reason to. If I have your permission to say so, she looks radiant this evening. You must have left quite a wake of despair in Mobile, carrying off such a prize."

Jeremiah fingered the small blond mustache he had lately grown. "If I say yes I stand convicted of arrogance, and if I say no I seem unappreciative of my good fortune. You make it hard for me, John. But I'll tell Molly what you said. She'll be pleased."

This, though, was forced conversation. What they wanted to talk about was the trouble with the North, and John knew his presence interfered. Clay Vincent could be seen getting increasingly restive. Things had fallen silent for a moment, and it was part of Clay's vitality not to be happy with silence. He understood the proprieties and wanted to respect them, but he looked like a man struggling in quicksand. Finally the struggle was too much: another moment and he would have gone under. He turned to John and said:

"Now that we may be at war with the North most any minute, do you still think we can't win?"

It was Clay's right to ask: he and John had grown up together. What sounded like a question, however, was actually a challenge. John saw that Jeremiah's and Robert's face had taken on the same expression, a look that hovered midway between solicitude and alarm, and two thoughts ran side by side in his mind—that Jeremiah and Robert were afraid things might get out of hand and that there were pleasanter things than having to face the disagreeableness of a man who used to be one of your best friends. He said, as much to Jeremiah and Robert as to Clay:

"I'm not aware, Clay, that we have ever discussed this particular matter before. You pretend to ask what I think, when actually you're assuming you know. Why not make sure of your ground before jumping to conclusions?"

Clay looked less confident. "All right then!" he said. "Maybe we haven't talked about it, not in so many words. But didn't I hear you say——"

"Look, you fellows," Robert Blackford interposed. "Why don't we have a drink? That's a specially noble batch of punch that's been brewed up for tonight, and I'm ready for another glass."

But Clay Vincent was not going to be diverted. Looking straight into John's eyes, and with his heavy black brows bunched over his own, he said, "Exactly what *do* you think? How am I wrong? It seems to me that I heard you say at the club, five or six months back, that you couldn't agree that the South was bound to win over the North. Ain't that what you said?"

Clay Vincent had never been one to keep his voice down. His demanding "Ain't that what you said?" cut across the room. The various conversations crumbled about their edges and fell into an apprehensive silence. This was how trouble started these days. One word led to another, tempers flared, and there was no way of telling how things would end. Aware that he and Clay had become the center of attention, and with some still disengaged part of his mind identifying the music that drifted from the ballroom as another waltz, "Evening Star," John said:

"You're right, Clay. I did say that I don't think the South is bound to win. I don't agree that once we go to war the North will fold up in a month or two. Instead of being a short war, it may well turn out to be a long one, and I believe we must consider the possibility that the South may lose. Once we get into a war——"

Clay Vincent gave an irritated snort. "Hell, how can we lose! How could the North last out a war? What will the North do without our cotton, just for one thing?" and the tension in the room began to ease. The punch bowl was remembered, conversation was resumed, and John was able to feel that while he may not have won any general approval, neither had he aroused any particular hostility. Clay Vincent said, "With our cotton, we hold the trump hand! Once we start holding back our cotton, the North will start caving in," and he began repeating a set of arguments that John remembered from an editorial in the *News*—without Southern cotton, the trade and commerce of the North would come to a standstill; its ships would rot at the wharves; its looms would stand idle; its other factories would have to shut down; its laboring classes would roam the streets, crying for bread.

"The North couldn't last out a month!" Clay Vincent insisted. "That ain't the point, though. What we have to do is to give the North a licking! That's what it's been asking for, and that, by God, is what it ought to get! Ain't I right, Rob? Don't you agree, Jeremiah?"

Jeremiah Lake looked grave for a moment, and John awaited his reply. It hadn't been easy for Jeremiah to leave the Navy—as he had said the day of the picnic at Happy Chance, secession had made it a hard choice for the Lakes. It had been less than a month since he handed in his resignation, and the strain he had been under still lined his face. He said:

"All that I'm inclined to agree about right now is that I'd like another drink. My wife has been generous enough to save me a dance and I don't have much time. But there's one thing, Clay, I feel that I'm obliged to say—if, that is, you promise not to start spouting like a wounded whale again."

"All right. I promise. What is it?"

"Just this. What John here was saying makes more sense than you seem to imagine. It could be a long war, a very long war, and we'd be foolish to be overconfident—— No, you promised not to start spouting. I don't want to get into an argument. Let's have that drink, shall we?"

"Wait just a minute!" Clay said. "There's one question I'd like to ask. Seeing as how you're a Navy man, then how do you figure——"

Robert Blackford took Clay by the arm. There was a strain of shortness in the Blackford line, and Robert, like his younger brother Tony, was an inch or so below the average height. His head came just above Clay's shoulder. It was he, however, who stood in command. He said, "I want a drink, Clay Vincent. I've been wanting a drink for the past five minutes. Besides, I'm tired of hearing you carry on. A stranger coming in, he would figure you're the only Southern man in this room. And you ain't. Remember that. You ain't! Now, dammit, let's have that drink!"

And that was where the evening should have ended, John often thought later—Clay Vincent's animosity had been turned, Robert Blackford and Jeremiah Lake had gone out of their way to show they were his friends, and for the first time, as they stood around the punch bowl, he enjoyed being at the ball. It was just his bad luck that Ules Monckton picked that moment to appear. He was listening to Robert tell about the streets of London, and Jeremiah the Italian ports, when Clay Vincent, turning away from the punch bowl, said in a voice full of admiration, "Ah, Mr. Monckton, sir. Won't you join us? You know my friends, don't you?"

Ules Monckton said it was his good fortune to have that pleasure, and John could feel his good spirits begin to drain away. He understood that he need expect no consideration from Ules Monckton. Ules would be remembering that he had not attended any of the recent meetings of the Light Infantry, that he had shown a huge indifference to Hardee's *Tactics*, and that, if gossip was to be believed, he was the only man present whose loyalties might be questioned.

"We've been discussing how long the war is going to last," Clay Vincent said to Ules. "I agree with you, sir, that it will all be over with one fight, but Jeremiah and John here, they feel that the war could turn into a long one. Tell them what you said at our last meeting, sir."

But that too had been in the *News*—read the *News*, John thought, and what you had was a running account of what was going on in Ules Monckton's mind. John was more interested in him than in his opinion that the war could be decided by a single battle. Ules had aged considerably since the night he addressed the Agricultural Society. Forty-one then, he was forty-eight now. He looked much older, however. His thin growth of sandy hair had receded beyond the middle of his scalp, a tier of oxbow wrinkles creased his forehead, and there were several gray patches in his ragged red mustache. He was thinner, too, but he looked not so much thin as wasted. John was reminded of a remark credited to old Mr. Robertson just before he died. Mr. Robertson was spending the evening at the Light Infantry Club, playing whist, and the talk got around to Ules Monckton. It was shortly after Ules bought the *News*. "The trouble with that fellow," Mr. Robertson said, "is that he's too much like that other fellow in Shakespeare, the one that thinks too much. Thinking's all right, up to a point, but after that it starts clogging up the stomach, and there ain't nothing like stomach trouble for eating a man away. I don't hold with that kind of thinking myself. What good does it do?"

Were Ules Monckton less formidable, one might feel sorry for him. No matter how significantly he triumphed, he would never belong. Old Mr. Robertson was dead, but there would always be other Mr. Robertsons. Nothing had changed since the night of the Agricultural Society meeting. He was still too intense for comfort. Watching him, John was reminded of someone he knew or used to know. He couldn't place who it was at first, and then, when Ules Monckton, rousing himself, said, "I think it most improbable that the war will be a long one. Let us consider for a moment what might be called the philosophical differences between the two sections," it came as a surprise to discover that it was Professor Adam Sedgewick. The two could not be more unlike, nor live more emphatically at opposite poles, and yet there was an affinity. They were joined by what Mr. Robertson had held to be a fault. It could be said of them that they both thought too much, and what good did that kind of thinking do?

Ules Monckton said that the difference between North and South might be seen in part as the difference between Puritan and Cavalier. And though the analogy could easily be carried beyond the point of usefulness, it helped explain some of the things that separated the two sections. "The North," he observed, "has a civilian outlook. We, on the other hand, are a military people. We always have been. Why, in this county alone there could be raised a force of cavalry that would do credit to the finest army in Europe. Our boys ride like Arabs. And as for marksmen, give me a company of low-country deer shooters and I'll promise to hold any regiment of the Regular Army at bay."

"And so it is your opinion that we hold a decided advantage," Jeremiah Lake said. "You believe that because of our skill with horses and arms, a Southern army, meeting the Northern forces for the first time, would be bound to carry the day. Is that it?"

"Yes sir, it is," Ules Monckton replied. "But we hold an even greater advantage. Our courage. A Southern man is bred to courage. He would consider himself disgraced if he turned away from a fight. A man in the North takes a different view. He is less bold, less individualistic. Used to living in crowds, he has become a crowd creature. It has made him timid and cautious. An army cannot be created from the urban masses, especially when, as has happened in the North, they have been swollen by hordes of immigrants—an armed mob, yes, but not an army."

"You see what I told you!" Clay Vincent said. "One good fight and the North will be done for! We'll have Washington in no time at all! Ain't that right, sir?"

"Such is my belief," Ules answered. "But only if our leadership does not hesitate or falter. We must drive on relentlessly—a decisive victory, a march on Washington, and the absolute destruction of the

133

North as a political power. Only then can the South feel secure. Only then will we be able to accomplish our historic mission."

The vision, John thought, the huge dazzling dream, and a gesture on Ules's part brought his attention to the older man's hands. They were big hands, covered with a thick mat of coarse, almost colorless hair, and something about them—John couldn't say what—gave off a suggestion of cruelty. Ules wanted nothing for himself, only to see his vision come true, but in the service of his vision he would stop at nothing. John had never before thought of him as a fanatic, but now he did.

"Let me see if I understand you," Robert Blackford ventured to inquire. "You're not arguing if there's going to be a war. What you're saying is there *has* to be one. Is that correct?"

"Yes sir, it is," Ules answered. "Without a war, we stand as we are. And as long as the North exists as a political unit, we have an enemy at our backs. Our leaders are foolish to seek a peaceful separation. They are even more foolish to believe that a slave South can exist side by side with a free North. The Northern President-elect sees the situation far more clearly. Criminal though he is, I am forced to agree with him. He is right to believe that this country cannot endure half slave and half free. It must be the one or the other. Our task is greater than our leaders seem to realize. It is not enough for us to maintain a slave South. We must direct our energies to the creation of a slave nation."

Once again, as on the night he had listened to Ules Monckton at the Agricultural Society, John Bottomley found it hard to believe his ears. "A slave nation?" he said. "The whole country?" and instantly he regretted having spoken. Ules Monckton looked at him, his eyes gone blank for the instant, filled with a kind of spectral emptiness, and it needed only that to make John understand he stood beyond the limits of toleration. Ules Monckton knew all about him, and all he knew he held in contempt.

"You seem astonished, Mr. Bottomley," Ules said, and his voice hardened. "Does the concept of a slave nation seem fantastic to you?"

Unlike Clay Vincent, Ules Monckton knew how to keep his voice down. What he was saying, however, was being carefully listened to —a scrap here and a scrap there: that was how Pompey's Head learned about Ules Monckton. For the second time since he entered the room, John found himself at the center of attention. Conversation dropped down to nothing, and the music from the ballroom, a schottische this time, again could plainly be heard. John recognized the schottische as "La Fête des Gondoliers." He followed the tune for a moment or two, recalling that Missy had been playing it lately on the piano, and then it was time to say if the concept of a slave nation seemed fantastic to him. The whole room was waiting.

"Yes sir," he said. "It does."

Though he knew it was only his imagination, the walls seemed to shiver and then stand still. Ules Monckton said, "So I had an inkling, Mr. Bottomley," and the tone of his voice could not have been more maddeningly disdainful. "I must apologize, sir, for having brought up what must have been a most unwelcome subject. But I am sorry that you are not with us. The South needs all her sons."

It stung like a slap. John felt a hot stain spreading across his cheeks. He had not said he was not with the South. He had said only that the concept of a slave nation seemed fantastic to him. But still he had been made to appear the worst kind of traitor. A black spout of anger spewed up in him, blurring his eyes. He said, "You will please not to take it upon yourself to judge me, sir. I find it offensive," and though he tried hard to get hold of himself he could not. "And let me say this, sir!" he heard his loud, unnatural voice go on. "Whatever I do, whatever I say, is done and said in my own right and under my own name. There is at least one gentleman in this room who cannot claim as much!"

Who was more shocked, himself or Ules Monckton, John would have found it hard to say. Ules's face went ashen and his eyes absolutely dead, and though John could see that what he had been driven to do was now accomplished ("He'll now think twice before he insults me again, by God!"), actually had it been worth it? For what he had done was monstrous: this was a slash that cut through the bare quivering tissues of a man's pride, down to the naked bone. And now that the damage was done—this thing that could never be undone—John was able to understand what he might have comprehended all along. As clearly as if there had been an open confession, he realized that Ules Monckton had long since come to regret that march on the courthouse. For years now he must have been aware that what had been achieved as Monckton could just as well have been attained as Simpson, and in a sense more honorably. It must have been the only time he had let himself be persuaded into a set of values not his own, when some frustrated hankering to assert his equality with the plantation elite had got the upper hand, and when, foolishly, he had let himself be betrayed into believing that by assuming a distant connection's name he might cloak his worth, as yet unproved, in the importance he knew it deserved. "This time I've truly done it," John thought. "He'll want me dead for sure," and even as the words were forming in his mind, Ules Monckton hit him in the face. He reeled with the blow, falling against Clay Vincent, and when he regained his balance Ules Monckton's fist was still clenched. Ules said:

"Doubtless, sir, you will require satisfaction. Should you, I will be at your disposal."

John thought it was rather like a nightmare. The last thing he wanted was to lift a pistol and fire at Ules Monckton, and even less did he want Ules Monckton lifting a pistol and firing at him. It couldn't be true, yet obviously it was true, and there was only one thing to say.

"Thank you, Mr. Monckton. I will see that matters are arranged."

He hoped he had got it right, since there were certain formalities to be observed, but still it was like a nightmare. He noticed that Ules Monckton was excusing himself and that most of the other gentlemen were finding it necessary to hurry off to the ballroom, and then, without quite being able to remember what had happened in between, he found himself back at the punch bowl with Robert Blackford and Clay Vincent and Jeremiah Lake, having another drink. He heard Clay say, "Don't forget you'll need a second," and Robert, "I'll be glad to arrange the details if you want me to," and Jeremiah, "He gave you no choice, John. You had to stand up to him," and a chill ran down his back. He thought that it was most probably the punch. The committee in charge of refreshments liked to have it icy cold.

CHAPTER TEN

That he must fight a duel with Ules Monckton was still unreal to John Bottomley, but as he made his way to the stables behind his father's house on the morning after the Light Infantry Ball, no longer did he feel that he was moving quite so completely in a nightmare. He did not doubt that Ules Monckton would want him dead, since it would take years for that much hatred to spend itself, but at the same time he could not believe that Ules would actually try to kill him. Prone as man was to violence, there were all sorts of barriers that society had erected against violence, and murder was still murder, even when accomplished in a duel.

His own mind was made up. He would fire into the air and let it go at that. And if by any chance Ules Monckton had other ideas and truly intended to kill him—well, in that case it was best not to think of it. Calm gave way to the most loathsome kind of fear. He had been through that once, when for more than an hour in the middle of the night he would have been willing to endure the most humiliating debasement in order not to die, and he would not permit himself to go through anything that squalid again. If he could not meet death bravely, at least he could pretend to. He owed that much to pride.

It might have been easier, however. Never had earth or morning seemed so fair. Each blade of grass stood out, each shrub, each tree, and when he entered the stable, where the sheltered shapes of darkness were just beginning to take on form and definition in the dim half-light that filtered through the small square windows, and the sleepy noises of the horses rose into the warm smells of hay and manure, there was such a containment of wonder and so much to love and live for that he had to stand still for a moment, wanting to bow his head.

Sensing his presence, the horses began to move about more purposefully. John spoke to them as he walked along the row of stalls, stopping once to pat an ancient mare named Delilah who had been foaling since he was a boy, and when eventually he went into the tackroom to get his saddle he was startled by the curled-up shape of a full-grown Negro boy snoring gently on the floor.

In his sleep, lying on one side with his knees drawn up and his head cradled in the crook of an arm, the boy looked like a bundle of rags. His name was Simon. There was no reason for him not to be where he was, since Corwin Bottomley would no more leave his stable unguarded than he would his house, but neither need he be asleep on the floor. A good cot had been set up for him in an empty stall. He had simply gone to sleep where sleep had overcome him. You were always coming across them like that, sometimes in the most unlikely places, and how was it possible not to despair? Give them a cot and warm blankets, and still they would sleep on the floor. Do all you could to get them to keep their cabins and their persons clean, and it was as hopeless as if you never tried. Trust them enough not to lock them up at curfew, and half the compound would go sneaking off for a night of voodoo in the swamps. Cast in the shapes of men, they seemed almost determined to prove themselves less than men. Was slavery all they were fit for? Sometimes you had to think so.

But there was the ragged Simon, snoring on the floor. John's boot hit against the door of the tackroom, and suddenly the boy awoke. He jumped to his feet, instantly and wholly alert, and his shape was the shape of a human being—no matter where you began, you always came back to that: try as you might to avoid it, it forever blocked your path. Simon said, "Morning, maussuh. Who you going to ride today? Old Nellie?" and what the trouble was, the largest of all the troubles, was that you could never see them plain. Slavery was like a curtain, you on your side and they on theirs, and because of the curtain you were eternally separated.

John waited for Simon to saddle up, admiring his dexterity, and just before he mounted he reached in his pocket and gave the boy a silver dollar. The richness of the reward left Simon dumfounded: his entire person shivered with delight. But what Simon did not know, what he could not know, was that it was not so much a gift as an impulsive offering to the gods and, beyond that, an effort to find a way through the curtain.

But nothing helped. You hoped to be kind and ended by being cruel. It availed nothing to pretend otherwise. Giving a silver dollar to Simon was no more than giving a bucket of oats to old Delilah—except that Delilah had the nicer smell—and what could be crueler than that? Or more depressing? He could be going to meet his Maker, since there was no way of telling what Ules Monckton had in store for him, and there might have been a better preparation.

ii

John was to meet Jeremiah Lake and Robert Blackford behind the Blackfords' barn and to get there had to ride past the Stanhope residence. Standing on a tract of thirty-three and a third acres, as did the other two houses—the Bottomleys' and the Blackfords'—it was separated from Indigo first by a stand of magnolias, then by an oak-lined avenue that all three families used to gain access to a wide dirt road that led to the more thickly settled parts of Pompey's Head, and finally by a sweep of gardens and lawn.

Though town houses, all three dwellings looked like country residences. Each was built in the shape of a square, each had a big front porch behind a line of columns, and the general effect of their barns, stables, servants' quarters, and other outbuildings was that of three small, compact, adjoining plantations. Of the three, however, it was Indigo that was the prize. Intended as a monument, it fulfilled its purpose. Corwin Bottomley wanted a big house. Expense did not matter. Indigo was the biggest house anywhere around. Its exquisite proportions saved it from bulkiness, however, and the six slender columns that supported the roof of the porch, which was actually an extension of the roof of the house itself, gave it a grace and lightness that justified its reputation as one of the handsomest residences anywhere in the country.

Coming to Indigo from his own crude dwelling at Deerskin was one of the happiest pleasures John knew. But not so much as formerly. Everything was different since Lydia had married Senator Stanhope. The first time John visited Indigo after her wedding was agony. He soon discovered that he must cast out the images that raged through his mind, lest they destroy him. He no longer permitted them to rise to the surface of consciousness but he knew they were there. Turning his mind in another direction, he soon was at the Blackfords'. Robert and Jeremiah were waiting on their horses, and Robert carried a shallow, highly polished case under one arm.

"Good morning, you fellows," John said. "I hope you got more sleep than I did. I spent most of the night drawing up my will."

"Rich as you are, I'm not surprised," Jeremiah said. "You remembered me generously, I hope."

"Don't sound so eager," John replied. "You'll make me think you don't value me for myself," and he nodded toward the case Robert Blackford was carrying. "What's in the box, Rob? Cigars?"

Robert gave a grunt. "Damn if you ain't a real comedian this morning. You ought to arrange to get yourself called out every day. It makes you a sight more entertaining than generally you are," and John's spirits brightened immeasurably. It simply wasn't possible that Ules Monckton would try to kill him: no man would want that kind of blood on his hands—soon they would be having breakfast, and this all would be something to laugh about.

"Well, let's don't keep the quality waiting," he said. "The man's mad enough at me as it is. Which way are we going to ride? Through town or through the woods?"

They decided on the shorter route of the woods. If they followed the path for a little over a mile and then took another that veered off sharply in the direction of town, they would emerge only a few blocks from Colonial Square, one of a number of squares laid out during the earliest days of the colony and the official dueling ground of Pompey's Head. Not that all differences were settled so formally. What was more likely to happen (though it did not happen often) was a blaze of gun-fire on the street. It was often said that if two gentlemen agreed to meet in Colonial Square it meant they wanted only to go through the motions. On more than one occasion, however, things took a dead-lier turn. There were three headstones in the cemetery bearing the names of the deceased and beneath the names the chiseled reminder that they had been KILLED IN A DUEL by so-and-so. Nor was it true, as was sometimes believed, outside the South, that killing a man in-volved no penalties. The families of the victorious duelists had lived in the shadow of those somber triumphs ever since. Murder was mur-der, no matter if accomplished in a duel, and even this hot-tempered society could not altogether condone it. John Bottomley hoped that Ules Monckton would remember.

iii

A ten-minute ride brought the horsemen to the place where the woods ended at the eastern outskirts of Pompey's Head, two blocks from Colonial Square. At this early hour the streets were deserted. There was such a feeling of dawn, of beds still being slept in and hushed, unawakened rooms, that John Bottomley was more than a little surprised to hear the sound of voices moving toward them.

The voices had a ready explanation. They belonged to a gang of Irishmen on their way to work. The men came into view just as John and his companions reached the intersection of one of the side streets. They carried a varied assortment of tools—spades, crowbars, pickaxes —and though they were of all ages, shapes, and sizes, they were given a sort of regimental alikeness by their faded blue shirts, heavy brogans, and the compounded compactness of their hard muscularity. The fin-gers of the older men went automatically to their caps and there was a mutual exchange of good mornings (one always exchanged good mornings in Pompey's Head), but John noticed that the younger members of the gang kept their free hands at their sides and that one of them, blue-eyed and black-haired and somewhere in his twenties, was staring at him with a kind of deliberate stoniness.

It was John who first averted his eyes. More than stoniness had entered the young laborer's eyes—a shaft of pure hatred—and John felt he had enough hate to deal with this morning, without inviting any more. As he and his friends rode on, approaching Colonial Square, he saw two men standing beneath the trees, and a pair of horses nibbling at a patch of grass. He did not recognize the shorter and bulkier of the two men, but the other, unmistakably, was Ules Monckton. His throat tightened and there was a small sick feeling at the pit of his stomach, and an old, almost forgotten sequence of words tumbled into his mind, speaking themselves aloud. He turned his head to listen, picking up the words in the middle as one picks up the count of a clock that has already begun to strike, and he recognized them as the prayer he used to say as a child before Missy was born: *God bless Mama and God bless Papa and God bless my little brother Cameron and God bless Moon and Zeke and Ellie May and all our other people and make me a good boy. Amen.*

He braced his shoulders as he reined up in the square and held them braced as he dismounted, and though it couldn't be true it was true, and as bad a nightmare as ever. There were bows and introductions all around. The man with Ules Monckton turned out to be his brother Gup, and it was a measure of Ules's solitariness that he had only his brother to act for him, and off at the far end of the square, standing all alone, there was someone who was plainly Gordon Carpenter, but what was Gordon Carpenter doing there, holding a small black satchel? Jeremiah Lake drew Gup Monckton off to one side, and the way they stood there with their heads together, speaking in subdued tones, reminded John of a pair of conspirators he had seen in a play one evening in Philadelphia when he attended the theatre with Miss Clarissa Drew—*The Gladiators*, it was called. Edwin Forrest was in it, and Jeremiah Lake and Gup Monckton might well be figures on a stage.

JEREMIAH LAKE: *I believe, sir, that were it urged strongly enough, an apology might be arranged. But only, of course, if we are assured of an apology in return.*

GUP MONCKTON (frowning): *I am afraid that we would be wast-*

ing our time, sir. *There are some occasions when an apology will
not suffice. This is one of them.*

JEREMIAH LAKE: *You take a strong position, Mr. Monckton. Am
I to understand that our offer has been declined?*

GUP MONCKTON (stiffly): *I have been given a set of instructions,
sir. I have no authority to go beyond them.*

JEREMIAH LAKE: *Your answer is final?*

GUP MONCKTON: *Yes sir, it is.*

JEREMIAH LAKE: *In that case, we'd best pass on to the details.
Would thirty paces be satisfactory to your principal?*

GUP MONCKTON: *It would.*

JEREMIAH LAKE: *And shall we agree to a simultaneous firing at
the moment of turning?*

GUP MONCKTON: *No, I think not, Mr. Lake. I believe that according to the rules we have the choice in that regard. Our
preference is for a count of five.*

JEREMIAH LAKE (after a pause): *Very well, sir. As you say, the
choice is yours. Would it be satisfactory if Mr. Blackford does
the counting?*

GUP MONCKTON: *Yes sir, it would.*

JEREMIAH LAKE: *That takes care of everything, does it not?*

GUP MONCKTON: *I believe it does.*

JEREMIAH LAKE: *My compliments to your brother, Mr. Monckton.*

GUP MONCKTON: *And mine to your friend, Mr. Lake.*

Gup Monckton bowed, and Jeremiah Lake bowed in return, and
John thought that more than ever it was like *The Gladiators.* "I
couldn't arrange an apology, John," Jeremiah Lake said. "Our offer
was declined. And the way it's to be worked is this—you and Mr.
Monckton will step off thirty paces, turn, take aim, and wait until
Robert counts up to five before you fire. Is everything clear?"

John nodded, because it was clear, but not nearly so clear as *The Gladiators*, Miss Clarissa Drew, and the painted arches of the Colosseum. Jeremiah Lake withdrew, Robert Blackford stepped forward, and John found himself facing Ules Monckton across the handsomest pair of pistols he had ever seen, the long barrels smooth as satin and the graceful curves of the handles sheathed in mother-of-pearl. The floor of the case was lined with wine-colored velvet, and a small label was pasted inside the cover. The weapons must have cost a fortune, and John wondered where Robert had got them.

"Mr. Monckton," Robert said.

John saw Ules Monckton's right hand reach out and take up one of the pistols—the thick growth of curly hair that covered the backs of his hands looked coarse and lifeless in the dull morning light.

"Mr. Bottomley," Robert said. "Mr. Bottomley."

What Robert wanted him to do was to take the second pistol, as well he knew, and he started to explain that if his attention had seemed to stray it was because it had been drawn to the label on the inside of the cover—"HALL & FARRADAY," it said, "5 Whitefriars Street, London, Detonation on the Latest Principle," and he realized that Robert must have bought the pistols on his recent trip to London.

"Mr. Bottomley," Robert repeated. "Mr. Bottomley."

It dawned on him that he was standing as though stupefied, which wasn't at all true, since his senses couldn't have been keener, and he picked up the pistol. Thirty paces, Jeremiah Lake said. He must remember to keep accurate count. He could ill afford to turn around at twenty-eight or twenty-nine paces while Ules Monckton was still striding in the opposite direction. They would never let him forget it at the club. He could imagine the sort of joke they would be cracking at his expense—"Some fellows are quick on the draw, but Bottomley here, he's quick on the turn."

Robert Blackford said, "Please remember, gentlemen, that you are not to fire until I reach the count of five," and what John found most curious, as he and Ules Monckton took up their places back to back (*my little brother Cameron and Moon and Zeke and Ellie May and all our other people*), was that he could see Ules's face just as plain as if they were looking at each other. It was on the tip of his tongue to say, "Good hunting, Mr. Monckton. Don't get buck fever," and perhaps he would have, if only to show how calm he was, but there wasn't enough time. Robert Blackford said, "Are you ready, gentlemen? Prepare to step off your paces," and then he was obliged to keep his mind on the count—one, two, three, four, five, six, seven, eight—and he had never realized how much moss there was in the trees of the square (*and make me a good boy. Amen*).

At the count of thirty he turned. Ules Monckton turned also and raised his pistol, and even at that distance John could see the flat, empty look in his eyes. "One," Robert Blackford's voice said, "two," and when John sighted Ules Monckton's forehead along the barrel he knew that all he need do was to squeeze the trigger and Ules was a dead man—you could nearly always tell when you were going to shoot well, and this was one of the times, and with a pistol like this he could hit a pine cone at thirty paces, much less Ules Monckton.

The nightmare took on a new, more frightening dimension—a squeeze of the finger and Ules Monckton would be a dead man. "Three," Robert Blackford's voice said, "four," and John relaxed his arm so that he could swing the pistol upward and discharge the bullet into the air. Robert Blackford's voice said, "Five!" and the two charges exploded at almost the same instant, rocketing across the square. John felt a thud of pain centering in a core of numbness where his right elbow used to be, and what happened, he realized, was that his head had been aimed at and that the bullet, going slightly wide of the mark, had found a target in his elbow, which had been momentarily left exposed when he raised his arm to fire. "He wanted to kill me," he thought. "He really did," and the small sick feeling at the pit of his stomach became a larger sick feeling, which turned into terror, and the terror was so agonizing that he wanted to turn and run before Ules Monckton could shoot him again.

Waves of dizziness danced before his eyes. He saw Ules Monckton turn on his heel ("I think he's pleased. He got a lucky hit and still he's pleased!") and suddenly the terror was no more. After so much fear he did not think he would ever be fearful again. He reached for his elbow with his free hand. It came away smeared with blood, and as he stared at it, unable to do anything to alter the dazed expression on his face ("He's ruined my arm. I'll be a cripple. I'll be useless if war comes"), the years of doubt and uncertainty were over. He would have to stand with the South. His involvement was too intense. He now knew where he stood, irrevocably, and he supposed he had Ules Monckton to thank for it.

It must have been then that he fainted. He could not have been unconscious for long, however, for soon someone was trying to get him to swallow from a flask of brandy. He recognized it as brandy by the smell.

"I believe he's coming to," a voice said. "How bad is it?"

"Bad enough," a second voice replied. "Look at those splinters of bone. This is a compound fracture if ever I saw one. We have to get him to the office."

John recognized the first voice as Robert Blackford's and the second as Gordon Carpenter's, and what Gordon was doing there, as he might have known all along, was simply to be on hand should a physician happen to be needed. "What do you think, Gordon?" he heard Jeremiah Lake say. "Should I borrow a carriage somewhere?" and much as he wanted to explain that he was quite capable of riding his horse and please not to bother anyone at this inhumane hour, he couldn't get out the words. He managed to swallow some of the brandy, but it went down the wrong way and made him cough. It was the cough, as much as the brandy, that brought him to.

"What's in the bottle?" he said. "Coal oil and lye? Is that the best you can do for a dying man?"

"Well!" Robert Blackford said. "Our comedian is back with us again."

Robert and Jeremiah helped him to his feet, and he found that although he was a little unsteady and dizzy he was able to stand. He might have been dead, however, and it was Ules Monckton who had wanted to kill him, and for a moment he thought he was going to faint again. He waited for it to happen, and then, when it did not, he noticed that the sun had risen. That was the big thing. The glorious thing. The sun had risen and he was there to see it. He could tell it was going to be a fine, bright day.

PART THREE

CHAPTER ELEVEN

"Johnny, you're back!" Missy cried, gathering up her skirts and running into John's bedroom. "Did you find out anything about Cameron? And your arm? How is it? Oh, I'm so glad to see you."

It was past midnight and nearly two weeks after John's duel. Though he still had to carry his arm in a sling, he could move about fairly comfortably. For six days he had been on a trip to Deerskin and Cornwall plantations, returning to Pompey's Head late that evening on the *Serena Moore*, and Missy had just come in from a dance given by the Palmetto Rifles. She gave him a quick hug, taking care not to press against his sling. "Tell me about your trip," she said, looking around for a place to sit. "What happened? Did you learn anything at Cornwall?"

John's excuse for leaving Pompey's Head had been that he wanted to look after the neglected affairs of Deerskin. Missy, however, knew better. She understood his real reason had been to visit Cornwall. Needing someone to talk to about Cameron, John had taken her into his confidence. Their father refused to mention Cameron's name, and kindness suggested that their mother best not hear it. Grief and anxiety had proved too much for her. Dr. Carpenter had prescribed laudanum and ordered her to remain in bed. That left Missy. She might not be able to help, but at least she could listen.

One night after supper she had come into the library, where John was trying to read by the fire. It was five days after his duel. John's book was *The Mill on the Floss*, a new novel by an Englishwoman named George Eliot. The author's private life had recently blown like a storm through the meetings of the Wednesday Afternoon Ladies Society. The word was that she had formed an alliance with a man not her husband. According to Missy, some of the ladies refused to read her any longer. Six states had left the Union, and a constitutional convention was about to be held in the city of Montgomery, Alabama, but it was George Eliot's unnerving alliance that caused stitches to be dropped and set teacups to rattling in their saucers.

John could not keep his mind on the book. With six states having seceded, it could no longer be hoped that the Union would stand. "We'll die first!" the mood now was. "Ask us to submit to anything, any tyranny, any despotism, but do not ask us to rejoin the Union!" The sentiment, if not the language, seemed everywhere the same. If there were any voices of moderation left, they no longer were heard. The line between moderation and treason was drawn very fine. Only that morning the *News* had carried an account of a commercial traveler who had narrowly missed being hanged as a spy. It turned out he was a St. Louis man who had been overheard to say in the lobby of the Commercial Hotel that he was sorry to see the old Union go. The *News* noted approvingly that he had been hustled out of town.

John closed *The Mill on the Floss* and looked into the fire. What was he going to do with himself if war broke out, and what about Cameron? Somehow his brother had to be found. A man simply doesn't disappear, he told himself. Cameron was bound to have left some trace, some clue. How, though, to find it? It seemed an impossible task.

A large piece of coal fell apart in the fire, sending out ribbons of flame, and John decided he had best make a trip to Cornwall. A search of Cameron's room had yielded nothing but a batch of unpaid bills and several empty whisky bottles hidden in a bureau drawer. Though Cameron had lately been spending most of his time in town, Cornwall was where he had lived. Something more revealing might be turned up there.

John had just resolved to go upriver on the *Serena Moore* when Missy walked into the library. The Mannings were having an evening of amateur theatricals, and she was going there with Gordon Carpenter. Her face was clouded and there was a tired expression around her eyes. "Mama's asleep and Papa's gone to the club," she said. "I wish I didn't have to leave you alone. You've been sitting here thinking about Cameron, haven't you?"

John was momentarily astonished that Missy was so well able to read his thoughts, and then he found no reason to be—ask anyone in the Bottomley family these days what he was thinking about, and the answer was almost certain to be Cameron.

"Could you sit a minute?" he said. "There are a few questions I'd like to ask."

"About Cam?"

"Yes, about Cam. And don't say it like that. It's foolish of us to shy away from speaking of him. We can't evade what's happened forever. And another thing. We might as well face the fact that wherever he has gone to he isn't going to return. If he was, he would have by now."

"It's too horrible, Johnny. What are we going to do?"

"There's only one thing we can do. Try to find him."

"How?"

"I don't know. I wish I did. What I'm hoping is that we can learn what made him run away. My idea is that since we have to begin somewhere that's the place."

"It's hopeless."

"Possibly. But still we have to try."

"Does your arm hurt?"

"Some, but we're not talking about my arm."

"I hate that man."

"No, you don't hate anyone. It was more my fault than his."

"*Your* fault!"

"Yes, Missy. I lost my temper and said something I shouldn't have. There were other things I might have said—better things, actually— but some low meanness in me made me seize on that. What I was after, I suppose, without really knowing it, was to destroy a man's pride. Under those circumstances, it was not too unnatural for him to want to destroy me. So you don't hate anybody. There's enough of that around."

Missy gave him a still, affectionate look. "Your trouble is that you're too good. Everything is always your fault, never anybody else's. But I love you for being the way you are. It's just like Arbell says."

"Must you always bring her into everything?"

"This isn't everything. What she said was that there's nobody as good as you. And brave, too. She says she can't imagine anyone being as brave as you were when you had your duel. Isn't that nice?"

"It's Cam we're talking about, not Arabella. Did he and Kitty have a quarrel? Did anything go wrong there?"

"I don't think so."

"Are you sure?"

"As sure as anyone can be of a thing like that. Of course they could have had a quarrel without letting onto it, but I don't think so. They would have been almost bound to give it away."

"Yes, I suppose so. You don't know anything else that might have gone wrong with Cam, do you?"

Missy shook her head. "No, Johnny, no one thing in particular. He was drinking too much, and he always seemed to need money, but you know more about that than I do. That day he stopped off to see you at Deerskin—he asked you for money then, didn't he?"

"How did you know?"

"Do I have to say?"

"I wish you would."

"He asked me for money. That was before he went to Cornwall."

"How much did you give him?"

"Do I have to say again?"

"Well, since you've gone this far——"

"All right. It was eighteen dollars. I had it left over from Christmas."

"Did that happen often?"

"What?"

"His asking you for money."

"No, not often. But Mama, though——"

"Yes, what about Mama?"

Missy glanced toward the door. "You won't tell her I told you, will you? Or Papa? He'd be furious."

"About what?"

"Mama's rent money from the Channel. You know those houses she owns there? Sometimes she'd let Cam collect the rent money and keep it."

"But what about Mr. Roundtree? He's her rent collector. How did they get around him?"

"Mr. Roundtree has been sick on and off the past three years. Cam would collect the rent in his place. Since it was Mama's money, Papa never knew."

Except as a reminder of Cameron's indifference as to how he got hold of money, so long as he got hold of it, John did not think it sounded particularly important. "I can't see it tells us anything about Cam we don't already know. What I'm trying to get at is this—what was it that went wrong with Cam and when did it happen?"

"I don't know, Johnny. It's hopeless, I tell you. We're not detectives."

"No, that we surely aren't. I told Father that we ought to call in a detective, a good one, even if we had to hire him from up North somewhere, but it only made him angry. What I think is that he's afraid of what a detective might turn up."

"Is it that bad?"

"How do I know? On the face of it, it would seem bad enough. Why else would Cam want to run away? Let me ask you this. Did you notice anything special about his behavior after he returned from Cornwall? Did it seem peculiar in any way?"

"What?"

"Weren't you listening?"

"Yes, but I was thinking how bad you need a haircut. You ought to go to the barber."

"For heaven's sake, Missy! What difference does my needing a haircut make? What I asked was did you notice anything peculiar about Cam's behavior when he returned from Cornwall? The next day, for instance. That would have been a Sunday."

"A Sunday? Wasn't that when the Blackfords had their picnic?"

"Was it?"

"Yes, that's when it was."

"Was Cam there?"

"At the picnic? Yes, he brought Kitty."

"How did he seem?"

"Very nice. A little quiet, maybe even a little sad, but nice. He was specially nice to Kitty."

"Wasn't he always?"

Missy hesitated an instant. "No, Johnny, not always. Not that he was ever deliberately unkind to her. I don't mean that. It was more that he was—well, thoughtless. You know how he is."

"Oh yes. I know how he is all right!"

"Don't say it like that, Johnny. You sound like Papa. And there's nothing mean about Cam. He doesn't realize it when he's being thoughtless. You know that."

It was the same old story all over again, John thought. No matter what Cameron's transgressions, there would always be someone to find excuses for him. And it wasn't true what Missy said about Cameron's not being mean—he could be as mean as anyone and, when the mood was on him, meaner than most. John said, "Let's get back to where we were. You say he seemed all right at the Blackfords' picnic. What about that night? Did he stay out late?"

"No, he didn't," Missy said. "That much I'm positive of, and the reason I'm positive is that after the picnic he and Kitty came back here. Mrs. Williams and Gordon were here too. We all came home in the same carriage. Elnora made some coffee and brought us the rest of the fruitcake Aunt Mary Nesbitt sent for Christmas."

"And then?"

"Then Cam drove Kitty and Mrs. Williams home. Gordon left with them. I was still downstairs when Cam got back. He couldn't have been gone more than fifteen minutes. We finished the last of the fruitcake."

"It sounds like a nice day."

"It was. When I think of those hateful Yankees and how they want to come down here and ruin everything——"

"Like what? All-day picnics and Aunt Mary Nesbitt's fruitcake? Let's not get off on the Yankees."

"Tell me something, Johnny. What is it about you and the Yankees? Nearly everybody else gets so mad they can't see straight, but you never seem to lose your temper even a little. Is it because of that girl in Philadelphia? Are you still in love with her?"

"No, I'm not still in love with her, and it's because of a lot of things. It would be more profitable if we went back to the fruitcake. Because of it and the Blackfords' picnic, Sunday seems accounted for. That brings us to Monday. I know something about what happened on Monday already. Cam cashed my check first thing in the morning——"

"So it was a check you gave him."

"Yes."

"Was it for a lot?"

"For me it was. But try to follow what I'm saying. Cam cashed my check first thing Monday morning, came back here, and spent most of the day in his room. And it was that evening, when he came down to supper—rather the worse for wear, I gather—that he and Father ran head on into each other. As best you can remember, did Cam say anything that might have indicated——"

Missy sat up straighter. "Don't make me talk about it, Johnny. I wish I hadn't been there. It's bad enough when you see someone you don't know who's drunk, some stranger on the streets, but when it's your own brother, and drunker than you ever dreamed anyone could be——"

"It's all right, Missy. You don't have to put yourself through that again. I think it's fairly clear."

"What is?"

"That whatever Cam got into, he got into before he went to Cornwall. I suspected as much already. He was in rather bad shape when I saw him at Deerskin. I should have known that something was wrong. And if only——"

"Yes? If only?"

"If only I had had sense enough to realize he was in trouble. That, though, is water under the bridge. Let's see where we are. Cam stopped off at Deerskin on a Saturday. He'd gone to Cornwall the day before, which was a Friday, and that was the Friday before the Light Infantry Ball. The ball was on the eighteenth, so a week before that would make it the eleventh. January eleventh. Whatever happened would then seem to have happened before January eleventh. It doesn't tell us much, but it tells us something."

"I wish I could think as straight as you."

"It isn't hard, I promise. Put it down to keeping a set of plantation books for ten years—if I'm really thinking straight, that is. Can you remember as far back as January eleventh?"

"I can try."

"All right, then. If we are on the right track and what happened to Cam happened before January eleventh, some kind of change must have come over him. *After* the eleventh. At some point or other he must have seemed not himself. Moody, disconsolate, worried about something. Can you remember anything about that?"

Missy thought a moment and shook her head. "No, Johnny, I can't. The truth is that I was too busy to pay much mind to Cam. The ball was coming up, and there were a lot of other parties, and Mama and I were having some new dresses made, and I just didn't pay much mind to him, that's all. Perhaps if I hadn't been so selfish——"

"Don't be foolish. Why go out of your way to borrow blame? Let's try to get at it another way. If you can't remember Cameron's seeming moody or depressed, perhaps you can remember when it was he last seemed in especially good spirits. You know what I mean, don't you? Particularly gay. Helling around with that crowd of his. Can you remember?"

"Let me see." Missy drew her brows together, thinking hard, and then her face brightened. "Yes! I know now! It was the night he and Gordon and Tony Blackford and some of the others—— Didn't you hear about it?"

"Hear about what?"

"What they did. You must have heard about the fires."

"Fires? What fires?" And then John remembered. "You mean the night they burned down the outhouses? Truly, Missy, I think you're old enough to mention outhouses in front of your own brother."

"Well, I don't know. When I think of all the trouble I got into because of Tommy Vincent's mumps——"

"Tommy Vincent's mumps were a different matter entirely."

"You see! You make me tired!"

"That I don't doubt. Having your innocence protected must be a great trial at times."

"Innocence my foot!"

"Take that attitude toward innocence, my child, and you'll end up like those Yankee women who are said to believe in free love."

"Johnny!"

"Just don't say you weren't warned, that's all. When was the night of the great conflagration?"

"I have to think. I remember I was spending the night with Arbell and went to early Sunday service with her next morning. That would make it Saturday, wouldn't it? Yes, that's when it was. The Saturday two weeks before the ball."

"And the Saturday, then, before the eleventh. If the eleventh fell on a Friday, the Saturday before that would have been the fourth. No, the fifth. January fifth. That gives us from the fifth to the eleventh. Certainly nothing seemed to be bothering Cam the night of the fifth, and on the morning of the eleventh he left for Cornwall. That leaves us the five days from the sixth through the tenth."

Missy gave him another affectionate look. "I think you're wonderful. Papa's right. We don't need a detective. No detective could be any better than you. What are you going to do now?"

ii

It was then John confided his decision to go to Cornwall. Two days later he left Pompey's Head on the *Serena Moore*, and now, back at Indigo after his six-day absence, Missy was asking did he find out anything about Cameron.

John did not know what to tell her. He might have learned something about his brother, and he might not have—a crumpled sheet of foolscap on which Cameron had apparently been trying to cast up some accounts and on which he had printed either the letter M or W several times amid a nest of whorls, spirals, and other scratchings; the same letter, looking more like an M than a W this time, inscribed more elaborately on the back of an envelope; and a bundle of rough, coarse clothes, almost new, that had been thrown into the corner of a closet—possibly it might mean something, and again it mightn't.

Missy's disappointed look made him sorry he felt obliged to shut her out. The letter M or W, however, urged him to be cautious. Missy's instinctive response, were he to mention it, would be to see it as the first letter of some girl's name. Once let her get that idea and nothing could keep her from launching an investigation of her own. Which meant she would start asking questions and talk the whole thing over with Arabella Stanhope, and in less than twenty-four hours it would be all over town that Cameron had thrown over Kitty Williams and run off with some mysterious, unknown girl.

"Didn't you find out anything?" Missy asked. "Anything at all?"

Other than the sheet of foolscap and the envelope, there was only the bundle of clothes—cheap woolen pants, a blue cotton shirt, a cloth cap, and a pair of heavy brogans.

"You're keeping something from me," Missy said. "I can tell."

"No, I'm not. I was thinking of some clothes I found in Cam's closet."

"Clothes? What kind of clothes?"

"Those on the chair by the bed. I brought them back with me."

He crossed the room and held up the garments one by one.

"Did you ever see these before?"

"They look like some darky's to me."

"That's what I thought. But I found them in Cam's closet, the one in his bedroom."

"Those aren't Cam's. He wouldn't be caught dead in them. And that's all you found?"

"Just about."

Turning, John hit his wounded elbow against one of the bedposts. The pain made him grit his teeth.

"Your poor arm," Missy said. "Does it hurt?"

"When I give it a crack like that it does. What do you say we go to sleep? It must be nearly one."

"Oh, it's way past one. I didn't get home till quarter after."

"Don't be so proud about it. All the more reason you should be asleep."

"Oh, stop it, Johnny! Don't try to sound like Papa. I'm not afraid of that big deep voice of yours."

"I don't ask you to be. All I ask is that you let us get to sleep."

"Nothing could be further from my mind," Missy said. "I'm going to stay and talk with you some more, and then I'll wake Elnora and have her fix me something to eat with my milk, and then I'll write pages and pages in my diary. It will be daylight before I close my devastating eyes. Did you know I have devastating eyes?"

She blinked several times, enjoying her own silliness, and John imagined that if you were almost nineteen and remarkably pretty, with wheat-colored hair and a turned-up nose and bright, dark eyes, it was probably difficult to stay unhappy for long. He said, "Your devastating eyes, eh? That's not Gordon Carpenter, I'm sure. Are you playing him false already?"

"Don't be impertinent, silly. All I'm doing is to make him a little jealous. He mustn't think he's the only one in love with me. Do you want to hear about the dance?"

"Not specially."

"Good! I knew you would. Do you want to hear it from the beginning, or shall I just tell about my great success?"

"You're a small idiot. You know that, don't you?"

"Only in your eyes, my dear brother. I can think of at least four or five gentlemen who would be pleased to disagree with you."

"So! At least four or five. Is Gordon still speaking to you?"

"Speaking to me? Only now is he beginning to appreciate me!" Her face lighted up and she gave herself a hug. "Oh, I'm so happy,

Johnny! Is it wrong of me? With Cameron gone and all our other troubles, I mean? Is it?"

"Don't be an even worse idiot. Tell me more about the dance."

"You didn't think I was through, did you? And you didn't get a haircut, either."

"No, I didn't have time."

"Well, you'd best soon. A few more days and you'll be able to wear braids like our noble ancestor Chief Tupichichi. Why is it that Papa always calls him noble?"

"He was the head man around here at one time, wasn't he?"

"But did that make him noble? Really, I mean. If he was anything like those Indians who used to trap in the swamps near Rosebank, I'll bet he smelled."

"You'd best not express that opinion to your father."

"Am I mad? How far away from being Indian are we, Johnny? Seven generations?"

"Yes, why?"

"No reason. It just happened to cross my mind, that's all. I hardly ever think of Tupichichi's being in the family, or Mary, his daughter, the one who ran around without too many clothes on, or about our having Indian blood. And none of us look Indiany, do we? Except maybe you when you let your hair grow so long."

"Come on, Missy. Stop your chattering. Let's go to sleep."

"But it's true! You *do* look a little Indiany, even with your nice gray eyes. My big, bold, Indian-chief brother Johnny!"

"And my little, giddy, harum-scarum sister Missy. You do have an intelligence, I know, but sometimes it reminds me of a bird with a broken wing."

"I like that! Oh, what an ugly thing to say! If I weren't so fond of you I'd start despising you this instant! And I'm not at all sure I would like you in braids. Why is it you always look so shaggy? Even at the ball you did. Don't you like going to the barber?"

"Right now I'd rather go to bed. I've had a long day."

"No, Johnny, not yet! Please. I haven't told you the most important thing. Guess who was with Arbell at the dance tonight."

"Look, Missy! I had to get up at dawn this morning, and the *Serena* broke down twice. We didn't tie up until almost midnight. If you imagine that all I have to do is to guess who was with Arabella at the dance tonight——"

"But wait, Johnny! It's not what you think. Arbell was with a gentleman from New Orleans—a Mr. Livingston Hall."

"Was she now? I will admit New Orleans is a long way off, and it's interesting to know she has widened her range of operations, but I can't say I'm impressed. Does Mr. Livingston Hall know that his has been added to the largest collection of scalps this side the Great Plains?"

Missy looked hurt. "I knew it! I just knew you'd say something like that! That isn't like you, Johnny. It really isn't. You've no cause to talk that way about Arbell. Just let me mention her name, and right away you start getting ugly and mean. Besides, it's not what you think. Mr. Hall is most as old as Senator Stanhope. He didn't take Arbell to the dance. He was just *with* her. Julian Fitzpatrick took her to the dance. Mr. Hall is visiting the Stanhopes on business."

"What kind of business?"

"He owns a huge cotton plantation somewhere above New Orleans, and Senator Stanhope is buying it. They say it's going to cost him nearly a quarter of a million dollars."

John's interest began to pick up. Though he had heard the Senator was thinking of investing in the fertile cotton lands along the lower Mississippi (urged on by Lydia, it was said), this was the first definite word he had of it. Any number of planters had put large sums of money into cotton plantations farther west. Corwin Bottomley was one of the few who resisted the trend. His was the earlier low-country belief, almost mystic, that a planter's proper crop was rice. Cotton might be admitted were it of the sea-island variety grown on the chain of islands that stretched along the coast. Cotton farther west, however, in the Yazoo-Mississippi delta and elsewhere, meant a crowd of pushing, get-rich-quick fellows who made the mistake of believing that new money had the same value and status as old.

"You see!" Missy said. "I told you it wasn't what you thought! Aren't you sorry you said all those mean things about Arbell?"

"Yes, if you want me to be. Who told you that this plantation is costing the Senator nearly a quarter million?"

"Selph Lockhart."

"Since Mr. Lockhart is the Senator's factor, Selph ought to know. It's probably nowhere near a quarter million, not by fifty thousand or so, but even at that it isn't petty cash. Where is the Senator getting the money?"

Missy was eager to tell. "He's selling a lot of stocks and bonds he owns up North, and also a tract of woodland. The rest he's going to borrow. Selph told me that too."

"You and Selph must have had a nice statistical evening. When did he get it in about your devastating eyes?"

"How do you——"

"It's all right. I won't tell Gordon. And I suppose the Senator knows what he's doing. It seems to be a good deal of money to be putting into cotton land, though, especially at a time like this."

"But everybody says——"

"Indeed they do. Didn't you read the editorial in yesterday's *News*? Already king, cotton will soon be czar. Lowell, Massachusetts, has to have six hundred thousand bales a year. Leeds and Manchester in England are absolutely dependent on it. Let the South hold back its cotton for only two or three months, and prices will go soaring to as much as fifteen cents a pound."

"Is that a lot?"

"That, Missy, is beyond man's wildest dreams of avarice. You don't think the Senator is going into cotton as a hobby, do you? You should read Gup Monckton more carefully. The estimated value of our annual cotton crop is two hundred million dollars. On this the North makes at least ten million by advances, interest, and other financial transactions. But all this money, from now on, instead of lining foreign pockets——"

"Oh petunia, Johnny! Who cares about all that stuff?"

"You'd be astonished."

"Well, I don't. It makes my head swim. Do you want something to eat? There's some ham and cold turkey, and I think a peach pie. I'll get Elnora to fix it in the library. We can have it by the fire."

"Must you wake Elnora?"

"She'll be cross as two sticks if I don't. You know that."

Missy's old nurse, Elnora was now her maid, confidante, and watchdog. She slept in a small bedroom adjoining Missy's. She was fat, jealous, privileged, domineering, wildly superstitious, and apt to be bad-tempered with everyone but her charge.

"It's all right about Elnora," Missy said. "I'll have to wake her to help me undress anyway. Besides, she'll want to hear about the dance. Would you like her to make some coffee?"

"Well," John said, "if you're going to bribe me with coffee," and that was as far as he got—a scream ripped through the house, followed by another. Missy turned white as death. She jumped to her feet and moved swiftly toward the door.

"Dear God it's Mama again!" she said. "What is it this time?"

John's parents slept on the second floor of Indigo, the others on the third. John hastened from his bedroom and started running toward the stairway at the end of the hall. Missy came flying after him, and behind her he could hear Elnora calling out something in a frightened, unintelligible voice that, as past experience reminded him, would in another instant also be a scream—there it came now, wild and piercing, and as often as this had happened, much as it was part of the life of Indigo, it never failed to make his blood run cold.

"Another one of Mama's spells," they would call it in the morning, folding it into the recollection of her other spells—the time she thought the soup was poisoned, the time she heard someone crawling on the roof, the several times she detected prowlers on the lawn, and the who could say how many times she spied a black midnight face on a ladder by the window. "Poor Mama," they would say in the morning. "It's too bad she has these spells."

But it was many hours till morning: at times like this, one wondered if morning would ever come—as John raced down the stairs, with Missy a step behind, the house drew back from another scream.

"Smoke! Smoke! It's them! Help! They've set the house on fire! Help!"

Missy dodged past John as they reached the hall on the second floor. She almost upset a lamp that stood on a table against the wall, burning with a low wick. "We're coming, Mama, we're coming," she called, and the agitated flutter of her skirts, disturbing the air, caused the flame in the lamp to tremble in its clear glass chimney. John saw that the door of his mother's bedroom was open and that a frightened face was peering out—Septima's, one of the house girls who was sleeping on a cot in his mother's bedroom now that she was ill. When he reached the door Missy was already bending over their mother and taking her into her arms. "It's all right, Mama," Missy was saying. "We're here. It's all right," and John was compelled to turn away. It hurt too much to see.

iii

Corwin Bottomley, holding a candle, stood in his bare feet and nightshirt in the doorway of his bedroom across the hall. The light from the candle fell mostly on the lower part of his face, leaving the rest in partial shadow. It deepened the wrinkles that ran from each side of his nose to the corners of his mouth, and made the wide fleshy base of his nose seem larger than it was. He sniffed the air suspiciously.

"I don't smell any smoke," he said. "Do you?"

"No, Father," John replied. "There's no smoke. You know that."

Corwin Bottomley raised the candle higher and began to sniff again. He hunched his head forward and turned it first one way and then the other. He said, "No, I reckon not. But still we'd better look. I'll go downstairs. You look around here and up on the third floor. It won't hurt to make sure."

John's spirits could not have been lower as he started on his rounds. There was no smoke in the house and both he and his father knew it. There was no smoke just as there had been no poison in the soup, no climber on the roof, no prowlers on the lawn, no faces by the window. But still we'd better look. It won't hurt to make sure.

Taking the lamp from the hall table, John went into all the

rooms on the second floor except his mother's. There was no sign of smoke anywhere. He climbed the stairs to the third floor, and there was no sign of smoke anywhere up there either, and when he looked in on Elnora, thinking to get her to go to Missy, since Septima was one of those stupid girls who could only polish and clean, he found the old Negro woman kneeling by her bed, moaning deep in her throat and, at the same time, saying her prayers. She had been sleeping fully dressed, as was her habit when Missy stayed out late, and her skirts had slipped up across her bare, fat legs, exposing the ends of her drawers. Her snowy turban was pushed slightly to one side, permitting an escape of frizzly gray hair, and as she knelt there, moaning and praying, she seemed taken by a trance.

John touched her shoulder, saying, "Get up, Elnora. Missy needs you," and then gave up. He looked down at her, and by some release of self saw himself looking down at her, a fat Negro woman kneeling with the ends of her drawers showing, muttering some primitive jargon he could not understand, and he remembered the stableboy Simon asleep on the tackroom floor—giving a silver dollar to Simon had been like giving a bucket of oats to old Delilah, and Elnora might be back in the jungles under some witch doctor's spell.

The images of Elnora and the boy Simon hung side by side for an instant, and various other images joined them—ancient Aunt Mim at Deerskin, Rosella who would persist in going fishing instead of taking care of the sick, Dowdy the coachman, Esau the butler, William the houseboy, little stupid Septima who could only polish and clean— and behind these faces, the accustomed and familiar, there stretched a denser and more ambiguous convocation of other faces, hundreds, thousands, an endless multitude, still and impassive as masks. And of course we trust our people! We could not trust them more. But though we trust and do not fear them, knowing their loyalty and devotion— aye, their actual love—once more his mother had waked up screaming, and he and his father were searching the house for smoke they knew was not there.

Leaving Elnora, he joined his father downstairs in the double parlor they called the drawing room. And as if to see what he was unable to smell, Corwin had lighted the candles in the sconces. The soft light fell on the piano in the corner, the harp nearby, the portrait of John's grandmother Nesbitt above the mantel, the sofas and tables and chairs, the brocades at the windows, the thick carpet with its design of repeated sheaves of rice, and the heavy, sagging figure of Corwin Bottomley in his rumpled nightshirt and bare feet. John rarely saw him so. He looked tired and vulnerable.

"I couldn't find anything," Corwin grumbled. "Did you?"

"No, Father. Of course not. There wasn't anything to find. You know that," and what riveted his attention, causing him to wonder did he see correctly, was that his father was holding the silver cane that General Lafayette had presented the Light Infantry after his visit to Pompey's Head in 1825. It was known as the Lafayette Cane, and as grand marshal of the Light Infantry Ball, it was Corwin's right to have it in his possession, the cane being handed down from one grand marshal to the other.

John looked to make sure it was the cane, hardly trusting his eyes, and then glanced across the room at the narrow case in which the cane was kept. The case rested on a small stand that stood between the piano and the harp, and in it was a red velvet cushion worked with silver thread, the nap of the velvet bearing the imprint of the cane. John felt he would remember this scene always, the handsome room and the unhandsome man in his bare feet and nightshirt, and though he knew that someday he would want to laugh at it (Cameron gone, his mother ill, Missy's evening ruined, he with a wounded arm, war likely to break out at any moment, and the Lafayette Cane the most important thing in the house to be saved!), he also knew that his laughter would never be harsh or cruel.

"You'd best get back to bed, Father," he said. "It's cold down here."

Corwin glanced about aimlessly.

"You have a good trip?" he asked.

"Yes, Father, pretty good."

"I didn't hear you come in. What time was it?"

"Almost midnight."

"The *Serena* break down again?"

"Yes sir, it did."

"The trouble is those boilers of hers. They're damn near rusted out. I remember when the *Serena* was new. That was before you were born. How's your arm?"

"Much better."

"I don't reckon you can bend it yet."

"No sir, not quite."

"But you can move your fingers, can't you?"

"Yes sir, there's never been any trouble with my fingers."

Corwin looked at the cane absent-mindedly and polished it on the sleeve of his nightshirt.

"I saw Ules Monckton today."

"Did you?"

"He was out drilling some of the men. He takes his job like he was Napoleon himself. My notion is that those fellows are going to regret electing him colonel before it's over. Would you mind letting me onto something?"

"Of course not, Father."

"Why didn't you shoot him?"

"I couldn't have, sir. It just wasn't in me."

Corwin nodded slowly. "That's what I figured. And what you did was the right thing. It must be hard to live with, having a man's blood on your hands. But he could have killed you. It seems like he wanted to. If that had happened, old as I am——"

"I know, Father. Thank you."

"What's there to thank me for I'd like to ask? The *Serena* have a big crowd?"

"No sir. Not more than four or five passengers in all."

"Anybody we know?"

"Only Mr. Waites's overseer."

"Oh, that fellow." Corwin went to the stand and put the cane in its case. "He's going back up North. He comes from up there somewhere. His leaving will go hard with Waites, I reckon, but maybe it's a good thing. If we're in for trouble with the Yankees, well, I dunno——" He closed the top of the case and shrugged off the rest of his thought. "Everything in good shape at Deerskin?"

"Yes sir, more or less."

"Plowing all done?"

"Just about."

"Wilson keeping on his toes?"

"Yes sir, I think so."

Corwin tried the top of the case to make certain it was secure.

"You go to bed, Father," John said. "You'll take cold."

"Yes, I reckon I'd better. I'll leave you to blow out the candles."

Corwin took a step toward the door and then turned around. "Be sure you snuff the wicks out good. We don't want your mother imagining she smells anything else." He half shook his head and let his shoulders go slack. "Let's hope she'll be all right in the morning. It's too bad she has these spells."

CHAPTER TWELVE

Perhaps because of his late prowling, or perhaps because he had gone to a turkey shoot several days before and stood for hours in a misty rain, Corwin Bottomley awoke next morning with a cold. When Dr. Carpenter came to call on Mrs. Bottomley, for whom he prescribed a double dose of laudanum every six hours, he told Corwin to get back to bed, saying that a cold like this could mean the beginning of pleurisy. Corwin grumbled but did as he was told. He didn't feel too well anyway.

After a late breakfast John went upstairs to his father's room. There was an unaccustomed silence in the house, as though it were still recoiling from the experience of the night before. Even the rays of sunlight slanting through the windows seemed wary and cautious. John mounted the stairs to the second floor as quietly as possible, not wanting to disturb his mother, who was in a drugged sleep induced by the laudanum, and rapped on his father's door. "Come in! Come in!" Corwin said, and John was not surprised to find him restless and irritable.

Corwin lay propped against a pile of pillows, working over a daybook. A stack of ledgers stood on the bed table, and a scatter of bills, letters, and other papers were strewn across the quilt.

"I'm laid up, dammit!" he complained. "Carpenter says I may be getting pleurisy. And I can't afford it! I don't have time to be sick! I had a meeting at Thrall & Lockhart this morning about that flour mill and wharf that's up for sale, and I was going upriver tomorrow. Here's a letter from Belden, the new man at Cornwall. He says some of those fields were plowed too deep last year, so that they're already full of alum spots, which means he might just as well not have planted for all the rice he'll get, and he tells me that some of those ditches and sluice gates haven't been looked after in two or three years. That's no way to do with land! If you want it to look after you, you have to look after it. That's the only way. Dammit, if somebody had been *running* Cornwall——"

But that brought him too close to Cameron: let him continue and he would have to mention Cameron's name. Picking up another letter, he said, "And that ain't the worst of it! We're having trouble at Nightingale too. Listen to this from Coxey. He says more than a third of the gang is down with some kind of sickness or other, that he lost a boy from lockjaw, and that he's most run out of Pittman's. And on top of all that, he tells me the hogs are dying off. Dammit, no plantation man ought to let himself run out of Pittman's, and it's part of his business to tell a sickness when he sees it. He says it's not the fever, but if it's not the fever what is it? And if the hogs are dying, why don't he move them to a different piece of land and burn over the piece they're now on? There's that whole old cane field he could use. It would be easier for me to go up there and straighten things out than all this writing back and forth. Hand me that toddy, will you? How much did you get for the last rice you sold?"

"A barrel? Around eighteen dollars and seventy-five cents. Why?"

Corwin gulped down the rest of the toddy and put the glass on the bed table, atop the pile of ledgers. He reached under the pillows for a handkerchief and blew his nose. "You sold too cheap, that's why. You should have told Lockhart to hold it back till later, even if you had to pay storage on it. That's what I'm doing. Three-four months from now number-one rice will be up to twenty-two dollars, maybe even more. Where's the letter from that Stevens fellow in New York? He's the one in the bank up there, the one with the Georgia wife. He writes that, because of all the war talk, commodity prices are bound to go up, rice and cotton especially. You hear about Stanhope? It's more of the cotton fever, but maybe he made a good move. Stevens says cotton is bound to go to fifteen cents a pound or more. It's those cotton fellows who are going to get rich out of this, you mark my word. According to Stevens, all the big people up North are on our side. They don't relish that Illinois fellow any more than we do. That letter of his must be here somewhere. Never mind. It don't matter. Here's one that came for you. It got mixed in with my mail."

John recognized the handwriting on the envelope instantly. The slanting characters and heavy downward strokes could only belong to Professor Adam Sedgewick. He had not had a letter from Professor Sedgewick in over seven years, but the handwriting was unmistakable.

So now you people have had your way! You are going to form a new government in Montgomery, I hear. Your Mr. John Calhoun must be grinning down from on high. But I wonder! I should not like to believe that his voyage to the Hereafter left him as shortsighted as he was during his stay on earth. Surely he must now see that his cause is lost. Grinning, did I say? Or does he weep?

Yes, yes, my dear Bottomley! I too am acquainted with what is being said in your newspapers, and with the prevailing Southern belief that cotton starvation will soon bring the North to heel. Nonsense! And have you considered that there are starvations more dangerous than an industrial need for cotton? The question is not how will the North survive without cotton but how will the South survive without the manifold requirements of the modern state?

Your whole population constitutes no more than nine millions, of which three millions are slaves. The population of the North is twenty millions. Where are your army and navy, your machine shops and manufactories? How can you supply the armies needed for war on a large scale? Look at your map. See what a country of scattered agricultural communities you are. You will be cut off by the blockade, and there can be but one issue. The South must lose. But do not think it gives me pleasure to say so. The tragedy we face is that we must all lose, North as well as South, the whole nation. Let others find joy in the coming conflict. I cannot.

You will have surmised from the address in the heading that I have retired from Princeton. This Massachusetts village is where I was born.

I have been putting some of my papers in order and happened to come across a copy of the address you made before the Whig Society in '49. It was then your position, you may recall, that the South would rid itself of slavery by gradual emancipation, and I fear I may have offended you by some of the things I said in disagreement. At my age one begins to regret such intemperateness. It is the opinion of my wife and two sisters, however, that remorse over past errors does not improve my present conduct.

I would like to hear from you again. I enjoyed the correspondence begun after your graduation and have often regretted its having lapsed. I am now in my seventy-seventh year. Though somewhat infirm in my lower limbs, I enjoy reasonably good health. It is hard for me to realize that this calamity has befallen us. I was born in the light of the old Revolution, and now my last years must be spent in the shadow of this new one. No truer thing was ever said than Heraclitus's πάντα ῥεῖ, οὐδὲν μένει, *but I do not find it hard to wish it were otherwise. Can you still read Greek? I doubt it. What did you learn from me, Bottomley? Anything?*

The last few lines of the letter were so like Professor Sedgewick that John wanted to smile. At the same time, however, he felt resentful over what had been said about the South's inevitable defeat. It was one thing to have such forebodings of one's own and quite another to have them hurled down like lightning bolts from somewhere up in Massachusetts. And all that marshaling of comparisons. It made one think of those itinerant wrestlers who appeared at county fairs, flexing their muscles and offering to take on all comers. Except, of course, that Professor Sedgewick hadn't meant it that way; so in the end John smiled. He was sure Professor Sedgewick's wife and sisters were right. He couldn't imagine that old man as being anything but tart, irascible, and sharp of tongue.

"What's so entertaining?" Corwin Bottomley asked, looking up from some bills he was checking. "Or is it a secret?"

"No sir, it's no secret. It's this letter from one of my old professors at Princeton. He wants to know can I still read Greek."

"Can you?"

"No sir, I'm afraid not. I never could very well. But I can read the quotation he sent. It's from Heraclitus: 'All is flux, nothing is stationary.'"

"So that's where that comes from, eh? I always thought it was one of the Romans who said that—what's that fellow's name? Plautus?" Corwin reached for his handkerchief and blew his nose again. "Dammit, I'm most stopped up as a crawfish hole that's been stepped on. You going downtown this morning? If so, I wish you would stop in at Thrall & Lockhart and tell them I'm laid up and for Tom Thrall to come here. I'm supposed to tell him what I want to do about that flour mill and wharf that's up for sale. They want $18,900. It seems around three thousand dollars too high to me."

Corwin sniffed hard, trying to clear his nose, and then went on. "What I'm thinking is this—if we bought a couple of lighters and had a wharf to tie them to, we could save the money we now spend on lightering and wharf fees. All that money could be put into land. They tell me that the Fitzpatricks are considering selling that Oak Grove property on Little Pigeon Creek, and I'd like to have it. But $18,900 is too high. If they'll knock off three thousand dollars, I'm ready to buy it. It's only the wharf I'm after, and we can always sell the mill. What do you think?"

It was a new experience for John to be asked by his father what he thought. He started to reply, "I don't know, Father. That's for you to decide," but since something more emphatic would be expected and since he did not want to appear disinterested, he said, "Offhand it sounds like a good idea. Lightering gets more and more expensive, and it would be wonderfully convenient to own a wharf," but what he really thought was that while all is flux and nothing is stationary his father would give it a more practical turn—what a man had to do was to take the flux at high tide; he had to look to the future; there was no sense in paying lightering charges if you could find a way out of it, and if you had a chance to buy more land the thing to do was to buy, even on the eve of war. Land was land, rice was rice, and maybe

177

there wouldn't be a war—all is flux and nothing is stationary only up to a point. A man had to keep his head.

"You didn't say if you were going downtown," Corwin said. "I can send William if you're not."

"I'll deliver the message. I have to see Mr. Lockhart about ordering some stores, and I thought I'd get a haircut. Even Mother got after me about it this morning."

"You need one, all right," Corwin said, and whether or not some slight change of expression crossed his face, John found it impossible to say. "What's that joke I heard at the club? Either get yourself a haircut or hire out as Samson. I thought it was pretty good."

Corwin picked up another batch of bills and began going through them. "You need salt pork at Deerskin?"

"Yes sir. Some."

"Buy yourself more than some. Tell Lockhart to lay you in a year's supply. Those Nightingale hogs are not the only ones that are ailing. Something's got into the hogs all over. Salt pork's cheap right now, but it won't be for long. You can save yourself a nice piece of money by buying ahead."

"Thank you for the advice, Father. Sometimes you make me wonder if Tupichichi could have been a Mohawk."

"A what?"

"A Yankee Indian."

"I don't know what the hell you're talking about. Tupichichi was a Creek. You know that."

"Yes, Father. I was just trying to make a poor joke. Can I do anything else for you downtown?"

"Not that I can think of. You see the paper yet?"

"No sir. Esau said you had it. What's the news?"

"There's too much news. A man would have to spend all his time keeping up. It looks like the convention in Montgomery will be getting under way most any day now. The way I hear it, those cotton fellows are going to run the show. If Virginia was in, we'd have a better chance."

"How so?"

"We could make common cause. Our state and Virginia could stand together. This way, those cotton fellows will be in the saddle. By all rights one of our men ought to be President—who took the lead in this thing? I'd like to ask—but without Virginia we won't have enough support. I'm not looking forward to what's going to happen. I know those cotton fellows from the time I was governor, and what's wrong with them, the big thing, is that they've come up too fast. All that cotton money has given them the notion that they're bigger than they are."

"Politically, you mean?"

"Not only politically but *especially* politically. You take the way it's been in Washington. When did we last have a man in one of the big cabinet jobs? Not since Tyler? That's the way it's been in Washington, and that's the way it's going to be in Montgomery. Let the cotton crowd have their way, and we'll be left out in the cold."

Corwin stopped long enough to blow his nose and then went on. "By all rights one of our men should be President, as I've said, but there's no chance of that. The way I hear it, that Mississippi fellow is going to have it offered him on a silver platter. He's in hand and glove with the cotton crowd and has been for years. So it will go, right on down the line. The cotton crowd will look after their own. Where we'll come in, I don't know. It all depends on Manning and what he can do for Stanhope."

"The Senator?"

Corwin nodded. "Don't sound so surprised. You know what he's after as well as I do. And we can't be left out of it entirely! We're the only state that's really back of this thing all the way down. We have to have some consideration. What's on your mind?"

Too many things were on John's mind for him to reply. He was thinking not so much of Senator Stanhope as of Lydia. It would please her to be the wife of an important personage in the Confederacy. Gunpowder Street and Huntington Hall would be left that much farther behind.

"Fix me another toddy, will you?" Corwin said. "You'll find the whisky and the sugar in the cabinet. Don't sweeten it too much."

John went to the cabinet, opened it, and began mixing a toddy.

"What's the Senator in line for?" he asked.

"That all depends. Manning has more influence than most people realize. He wants to be governor someday, as most likely he will, but, more than that, he's been attending these Agricultural Society conventions all over the South. That in itself don't mean much, but when you add it to the way he's been cultivating the cotton crowd, it does. Manning has a long head on his shoulders. If we form a new government down here and get our own country going —don't you see? What Manning is thinking about is ten or fifteen years from now. You don't think he aims to stop at being governor, do you? You look surprised."

"I am," John said, handing his father the toddy. "Here we are with the new government not even formed yet, and perhaps a war in the offing, and you tell me that Mr. Manning is looking forward to the day when he will be running for high national office. Or high Southern office. How can I not be surprised?"

"Politics ain't like rice," Corwin observed. "What you plant today, you don't figure on reaping tomorrow. A man in politics has to take the long view. It's no use otherwise. Anyway, Manning's having worked along with the cotton crowd makes it all the better for Stanhope. If Virginia was in and backing us up, Manning might be able to get him something big—nothing as big as the presidency, or even the vice-presidency, but maybe the Navy or the Treasury."

"Has the Senator ability enough for that?"

Corwin looked at John keenly. "What is said in this room stays in this room," he said. "Let there be no mistake," and from the tone of his voice, as well as the look on his face, John understood his father had decided he had finally come of age. It was another tribute to his wounded arm. He had been frightened beyond all belief, and at one point so taken by panic that he wanted to turn and run, but by letting himself get shot at and, even more, by stopping a bullet, he had passed the test.

Corwin looked at John an instant longer. He said, "The answer to what you just asked is no. It was said in this room and it stays in this room. But you as good as knew before you asked, didn't you?" He paused, snuffling, and then went on. "Stanhope's a gentleman, and he couldn't be a better neighbor, but the plain truth of the matter is that he's mostly—what do you call it?—façade."

He looked away from John, reflecting. "Maybe, to explain what I mean, I have to go back to your great-grandfather, the first Corwin, and the men of that time. They had something to do and they did it. And they looked after their land. That was the big thing. They were planters. A man like Stanhope, he's a gentleman planter. It's being a gentleman that comes first. You see the difference?"

John need look only at his father to have the difference drawn. He said, "Yes sir. I see," and Corwin finished his toddy.

"You take the run of the men at the club," he said. "They're nice fellows, and they're not all lacking in brains, but something's run down. They don't give you much confidence. They're fine for a spurt, but they make you wonder about the long haul. And except for five or six, there's not one of them who can call himself his own man. They're owned by their factors. Every penny they take in is pledged in advance.

"And that's another thing about Stanhope. A man can't make a move around here without the whole town's knowing it, and what they say is that he's getting in over his head. That little schoolteacher wife of his has been something of a luxury, and that Arbell girl isn't exactly what you'd call an economy, either. But that's neither here nor there. Where were we? I seem to have run off the track."

"I asked you if the Senator had ability enough for one of those big jobs you mentioned."

"And I said no. But now I want to back up a little. There's more than one way of looking at it. How good is that Mississippi fellow? How much ability does he have? Enough to be President? Some say yes and some say no, and the way I hear it the noes are in the majority. So what you have to do is not measure Stanhope against the big men of the past, but against the men they are talking about for the new government. By that scale he doesn't show up too bad. He won't get the Navy or the Treasury—there's no chance of that—but he may end up with something a little further down the line. They can't leave us out entirely."

Out in the hall a clock struck ten. It was a slow strike, solemn and portentous. John said, "If I'm to get to Thrall & Lockhart before everybody starts going home to dinner, I'd best be on my way. I'm to tell Mr. Thrall that you'd like him to come here. Is there anything else?"

Corwin glanced at a bill, studying it for a moment. He looked up and said, "Yes, there is. This thing we're in, this likelihood of trouble with the North—have you made up your mind what you're going to do?"

It was such a simple question, and had been such a long time coming. And that it had been asked, John understood, was also due to his wounded arm. Man to man he and his father could now discuss such things. He shook his head as he spoke.

"No, Father, I haven't. It's something I'm trying to decide."

"You could get a commission. You know that, don't you?"

"No sir, I wasn't quite that certain."

"Don't be a damn fool! All you have to do is ask!"

"Well, perhaps I will. Right now, though——" And what he wanted to say was that right now he felt an obligation to find his brother. A letter that could be either M or W, and a bundle of workingman's clothes. It wasn't much to go on.

"What's the matter?" Corwin said. "Is it because you want to raise a company of your own? If that's it——"

"No, Father. I have no ambitions to have my own company. And a commission isn't especially important, either. I'd just as soon go into the Light Infantry as a private."

"Under Monckton!"

"Yes, Father."

Corwin Bottomley began to look outraged. "Don't be a damn fool again! You know who was second-in-command when the Light Infantry fought at Little Pigeon Marsh after General Carvell was killed? Your great-grandfather Corwin. You know who led the Light Infantry when it went to Mexico? Your grandfather Nesbitt on your mother's side. And now you tell me you'd as soon be a private!"

What Corwin did not say, and what he meant, was that John, not Ules Monckton, should be at the head of the Light Infantry—its command, like the Lafayette Cane, belonged in the family.

"I can't make heads or tails of you," Corwin said. "I've been trying to, but I can't."

"Perhaps it's because I've taken one of your lessons too much to heart."

Corwin shot him a suspicious look.

"What do you mean by that?"

"Nothing alarming, I hope. I'm a planter, Father. Left to myself, I could go on being a planter for the rest of my days. I don't like what's happening. I don't believe this war will be the short, swift affair that some people are predicting. And the longer it lasts, the more the odds will be against us."

It could have been Professor Sedgewick's letter that was prompting him to say these things, but John didn't think so. Hold back what you feel and believe long enough, and eventually it must come out. He was glad to be able to unburden himself at last.

"I love the South," he said. "I'm proud of belonging here and of being who I am. That's why, if war comes, I couldn't stay behind. I would have to stand by my state. It would be my way of saying who I am. But that's all it would be. I can't pretend otherwise. If we are fighting to save slavery, I don't believe in slavery, and if we are fighting for the right to extend slavery wherever we please, even to Mexico and Central America, as Ules Monckton says, I believe in that even less. But most of all I don't believe in this war. I'm sorry to disappoint you, Father. I know this isn't what you wanted to hear."

Corwin looked at him, saying nothing, and John wished that he could have done less damage—one son brought to mind a second son, and neither had turned out the way a man had hoped. A man could lie in bed with a stopped-up nose and see the crumbling of all his hopes.

"If you're going to fetch Tom Thrall for me," Corwin said, "you don't have much time. I want to see him before dinner and I've wasted enough of the morning as it is. Now you get. I've got work to do."

CHAPTER THIRTEEN

River Street, where the offices of Thrall & Lockhart were located, was the financial and commercial center of Pompey's Head. Poorly lit and deserted at night, and too near the Irish Channel and a mean side street of sailors' bars and rooming houses to invite the late pedestrian, it was during the daylight hours the busiest part of the city. Cobbled, and having a plank sidewalk, it ran along the river front for seven blocks.

The offices of Thrall & Lockhart were housed in a two-story brick building. Mr. Henry Lockhart, the senior member of the firm, conducted his affairs from a room on the second floor, overlooking the wharves. He and John Bottomley had just concluded their business. Opening the bottom drawer of his desk, Mr. Lockhart brought out a bottle of whisky and two tumblers. All his movements were massive. He was six feet four inches tall and weighed two hundred and eighty pounds. He poured a drink for himself and one for John.

"Health and prosperity," he said. "The Governor isn't bad sick, is he?"

"No sir, Mr. Lockhart," John replied. "At least I don't think he is. He seems only to have a heavy cold."

"You get him to take care of himself. A cold can lead to anything. You've heard about the Light Infantry, I suppose?"

"What is there to hear? I've been upriver for a few days, as I explained."

Mr. Lockhart looked across the desk at John, as if savoring what he was about to impart. He said, "The Light Infantry marched out of town this morning," and waited long enough for it to sink in. "It was a few hours after that dance given by the Palmetto Rifles. The whole thing was kept a secret. I only heard about it when I came to work. My boy Selph didn't let on a thing. He came home for a few minutes after the dance, to get some gear he needed, and then left without anybody's knowing it. He tells me he saw your sister at the dance."

One thing you had to say about Pompey's Head, John thought— it wasted no time keeping up with who had been where. He wondered if Mr. Lockhart had heard about Missy's devastating eyes.

"Yes sir, Mr. Lockhart," he said. "My sister was at the dance. But tell me more about the Light Infantry. What happened?"

Mr. Lockhart's desk was strewn with samples of rice and cotton. He noticed a piece of lint clinging to the sleeve of his coat and plucked it off.

"It's hard to be sure exactly what happened," he said. "Nobody seems to know. My understanding is that the Light Infantry had a meeting three nights ago. The way it's being told around town is that Ules Monckton made a speech and that it was all decided then."

"What was?"

Mr. Lockhart dramatically lifted his bushy eyebrows. "To march to the mouth of the river and make camp near the forts. The Light Infantry is already there. Except, if the truth be told, it didn't exactly march. They went down the river on the *Serena*."

"Last night?"

Mr. Lockhart nodded. "Or early this morning, whichever way you want to put it. Didn't you say you came back on the *Serena*? That must have been an hour or so before the Light Infantry began going aboard. Captain Bostwick was in on it too."

"So I'm beginning to see."

"The Light Infantry even took those two brass cannon with them," Mr. Lockhart went on, "the ones they use in the Fourth of July parade. That Monckton fellow doesn't let any grass grow under his feet, does he?"

As a member of the old guard, Mr. Lockhart could not altogether approve of Ules Monckton—Ules had come too fast out of nowhere and showed too little respect for the proprieties. But still there was a note of admiration in Mr. Lockhart's voice. One wouldn't think of inviting Ules Monckton to dinner, and there was something in the way he looked at you that didn't sit too well, but at the same time it was a real smart move for him to get hold of the *Serena*—you might not like him, but you had to admit he had enterprise.

Mr. Lockhart reached across his desk and picked up a sample of cotton. He pulled it apart and held it out to John.

"You want to see something pretty?" he said. "It's from Mr. Charles Montague's crop on Mungo Island. Damn if I ever saw sea-island cotton like this in all my life. Everything must have gone just right on Mungo this year. Long staple always has to sell for twice as much as short to pay for itself—you have to figure on extra costs adding around ten cents a pound—but cotton like this will bring twenty-seven cents anywhere. And if we start holding back our cotton, just to teach the North where to head in, there's no telling how high the price will go. I don't mean to offend your loyalties, John, but it looks as though rice is going to have to take a back seat. The big money is in cotton these days."

Letting the sample fall from his fingers, he said, "I see by today's paper that the proceedings in Montgomery are about to start," and went on to repeat Corwin Bottomley's grievance that the constitutional convention would be controlled largely by men from the cotton states. "What they ought to call this new government is the Cotton Confederacy," he said. "And another thing. Why didn't they hold that convention here? Or in Charleston? Why did they pick Montgomery? Fifty years ago there was no Montgomery. There was no Alabama either, for that matter, or any Mississippi, Louisiana, Florida, or Texas. Not as states, that is. But if you listen to the cotton crowd, you'd think they're the ones who provided the statesmanship from the very beginning, not us and Virginia. I don't like that gang."

Nodding at the proper intervals and putting in a few words when occasion demanded, John permitted his attention to wander. It could be argued that more important than what was happening in Montgomery was what had happened here in Pompey's Head. For months Gup Monckton and the *News* had been clamoring for the capture of the two forts at the mouth of the Cassava River, and now the Light Infantry was camped somewhere near them. If Ules Monckton should move against the forts or, rather, against Fort Signal, since Lookout hadn't really been a fort for years——

"They owe it to our state to put one of our men somewhere near the top," Mr. Lockhart said. "That's what the Governor said at the club the other night, and I agree with him. If you read between the lines in the *News* it's easy to see that Gup Monckton thinks he ought to be the one, which means that Ules thinks so too, but who's going to go along with that? Have you heard about these notions of Gup's?"

"A little. I didn't pay much attention."

"No sane man would," Mr. Lockhart asserted. "But did you see his editorial this morning? Fresh, aggressive leadership is what will be needed in the new government, he said, and he couldn't have more pointed a finger at himself than if he'd printed his own picture and then under it, in big black letters, HERE IT IS. But whatever our other worries, we don't have to worry about that."

"Yes sir," John said, thinking of the forts. "I suppose so."

"I'm a Stanhope man myself," Mr. Lockhart went on. "He did all right for us when he was in Washington, regardless of what they say, and what if he did want to get in the cabinet? What's wrong with that? He would have been better than some of those fellows we've had to take. More than any of that, though, Stanhope's a gentleman. We'll need a few gentlemen to balance off the cotton crowd."

"Yes sir," John said.

"The way I see it," Mr. Lockhart continued, "Stanhope has a good chance. Better than good. I agree with the Governor there too. Wingfield Manning knows what he's doing, and they can't leave our state out entirely. You've heard about the Senator's buying that cotton plantation in Louisiana, I suppose?"

John said yes, he had, and hoped Mr. Lockhart wasn't going to get started on the subject of cotton again. The day was approaching noon and River Street was at its busiest. A steady procession of wheels rattled across the cobbles, rising above the brisker sound of many heels striking the plank sidewalk, and now and then, through the open window, one could hear the voices of the Negroes working on the wharves, hired out by their masters by the day.

"Excuse me a minute, will you, John?" Mr. Lockhart said. "I'll get one of the clerks to figure out what your order comes to. You'd like to know, I suppose."

"If it isn't too much trouble."

"No trouble at all. Are you sure you want that much salt pork?"

"Yes sir, I think so."

Mr. Lockhart looked at him sharply, as if trying to discover what it was he knew about salt pork that no one else knew, and rose from his desk—it was only when he stood that one realized how vast he was. And his mind was plainly rooted on salt pork. John had the feeling that the size of his order had already raised the price to future purchasers by at least two cents a pound.

"I'll be right back," Mr. Lockhart said. "Have a cigar. Help yourself to another drink while I'm gone."

John lit the cigar and went to the window. Though it was the first day in February, the morning was soft as spring. From the window John had a view of the cobbled street, the wooden wharves, the ships at their moorings, and the muddy, slow-moving waters of the Cassava River.

Sixteen miles downstream were the forts. One, Lookout, was a small block relic of colonial times. It had been twice strengthened and enlarged—first during the Revolution and again during the War of 1812. Since then, though still identified as a fort on the sailing charts pertaining to these waters, it had been slowly taken over by a dense invasion of vines, creepers, and scrub palmetto. Its only garrison was hundreds of gulls.

The second fort, Signal, was a more formidable affair. Intended to replace Fort Lookout, it stood on a long, narrow, marshy island about a quarter mile farther downstream. The distance from it to the nearest point of the shore was several hundred yards. It could be reached, from the shoreside, only by small boat. The arm of the river separating it from the shore, a salt-water creek actually, was one of the favorite haunts of the Negroes who fished for the market. They sold part of their catch to the men and officers of the fort, and also peddled the fruit and vegetables their masters allowed them to grow.

Built of brick, the fort took the shape of an irregular pentagon. Its walls were six feet thick. There were emplacements for ninety guns, but only thirty were in position. The garrison also was below full strength. Though upward of two hundred men would be required to man it properly, its present complement consisted of three officers and twenty-six men. All the coastal defenses were undermanned.

But three officers and twenty-six men, backed up by six-foot-thick walls and thirty guns, might be expected successfully to maintain their position against all but a full-fledged expeditionary force. And whatever the Light Infantry was, it was not that. If Mr. Lockhart was correct and Ules Monckton had got the whole outfit aboard the *Serena*, it meant he had around one hundred men at his disposal—one hundred men, eager but green, and two brass napoleons that hadn't been fired in years.

Were it not so serious it might be entertaining—all this secrecy, night marching, and military play. But let just one of those young hotheads take a single pot shot at the fort and be unlucky enough to hit somebody, and the North might well consider it a cause for war. The balance was that precarious.

Smoking his cigar at the window, John Bottomley could not remember ever having seen the harbor more crowded with shipping. An ocean-going steamer was berthed directly opposite, a big side-wheeler was tied up next to her, and a line of other craft followed the curve of the wharves—river packets, another transatlantic steamer, schooners in the coastal trade, two- and three-masters that had resisted the advent of steam, and a grimy old scow stacked with fresh yellow lumber from one of the waterfront mills.

Easing his arm in its sling, John turned his attention to the vessel lying closest. Her name was *Falcon*. Flying the British flag, she was taking on cargo. A line of low, flat carts drawn by mules and piled with cotton rattled up to her side, where a gang of stevedores worked at getting the bales aboard. A thin Negro woman in a purple dress crossed the street with a basket on her head, a horse-drawn omnibus lumbered past, the one that ran from Marlborough Square to the Irish Channel, and a Negro coachman guided a pair of matched chestnuts through the confusion. Stopping on the wharf side of the street, the omnibus discharged two of its passengers—a young man and woman approximately the same age, he in the rough dark trousers and blue cotton shirt that were practically the Channel uniform, and she, smaller, slighter, wearing a severe dress of coarse gray wool and a kerchief round her head.

It was she John first recognized—that incredibly beautiful Irish girl he had seen when he stopped to watch the work at Jennie's Basin. Even at this distance he could see how white her skin was, and he remembered the deep dark blue of her eyes, and what he thought now was what he had thought then—put her into one of Missy's party dresses and she would be the rage of the Light Infantry Ball.

Something, however, was different. Her grave expression, the quiet thoughtfulness, had become a look of sorrow. Her whole lovely face was lost in grief. She and her companion began to cross the street, hurrying along a diagonal line that would bring them to the sidewalk below Mr. Lockhart's window, and what most joined them was not so much an unmistakable family resemblance, for they could only be brother and sister, but rather some half-repressed antagonism that put a scowl on the young man's face, she the offender and he the sullen unforgiving one.

John's gaze must have been intenser than he knew. The girl looked up as she neared the sidewalk (it could have been the white patch of his sling that caught her attention), and for the briefest of instants their glances held. The girl looked quickly away, as much in fright as haste, and it was only then, as John met the cold hard stare of her companion, that he remembered him as the young workman whose unconcealed dislike he had had to turn away from on the morning of the duel.

Mr. Lockhart strode heavily into the office. The girl and her brother were lost from view. Mr. Lockhart said:

"What's so fascinating out there? You see a pretty woman?"

"No," John wanted to reply, "a beautiful one, beautiful and sad and full of trouble," but instead, nodding toward the *Falcon*, "Is she taking nothing but cotton aboard?" he asked.

"That's all," Mr. Lockhart said. "This may be one of the biggest cotton weeks in history. I wouldn't be surprised if we shipped out thirteen thousand bales."

John could still see the girl's face. No one should be that unhappy. He said:

"What's the stampede? Are people afraid of the blockade?"

Mr. Lockhart snorted. "What blockade? All the way from the Capes to the Rio Grande? England and France together don't have enough ships for that, much less the North," and he would certainly have gone into a long elaboration had not the *Falcon's* whistle intervened— the loud blast, thrice repeated, rattled the panes of the window.

"It must be getting on to noon," Mr. Lockhart said. "That's when she's scheduled to sail. She was supposed to leave yesterday, but she wasn't finished loading yet. We could use another hundred men on the wharves." He looked out the window for a moment, a few minutes longer, and then turned back to John. "Here's your account. It comes to a little over eight hundred dollars. All that salt pork sort of ran it up."

Mr. Lockhart's attention was back on salt pork. If there was anything to know about salt pork, he ought to know it. Caught between his curiosity and the rule of conduct which said no gentleman must ask another gentleman a too direct question about his personal affairs, there was something volcanic about his submerged rumblings.

John was not unwilling to explain that the salt pork had been his father's idea. That, however, was prohibited. It would be implying that his father was shrewder than Mr. Lockhart. So in the end he decided that this was as good a time as any to take his leave.

"What's your hurry?" Mr. Lockhart said. "Stay and visit. Why don't you come to dinner? Mrs. Lockhart was asking about you just the other day. She'd be glad to see you."

"Thank you, Mr. Lockhart, but today I can't. I have some business at the bank and I want to get a haircut. I've been putting it off for weeks."

He need not have explained about the haircut. He stole a glance at Mr. Lockhart's face, but all he could see was a spreading look of joviality. Mr. Lockhart's splendid stomach strained against the buttons of his vest. His watch chain jiggled. He began to chuckle.

"What's that joke I heard at the club?" he said. "Either get yourself a haircut or hire out as Samson. I thought it was pretty good."

CHAPTER FOURTEEN

By all rights the barbershop should have been crowded since this was the busiest time of day. Instead, two of the three chairs stood empty. When John Bottomley walked in from the sun, Allbright, the mulatto proprietor, sprang to attention. Seeing him, John wished he were elsewhere. He would have preferred to have his hair cut by one of the apprentices; now he would be obliged to sit in Allbright's chair. Allbright bowed to him, far more elaborately than was necessary, and John was barely able to conceal the irritation which, much as he fought against it, never failed to spring up in him whenever he laid eyes on the short, stout mulatto whose airy high-tonedness was one of the jokes of Pompey's Head.

Allbright's shop was in a two-story, two-room frame building on Bay Street, a valuable piece of property that he owned outright. A free Negro in his late fifties, he had been emancipated when he was eighteen. Five years later, after he learned his trade from a barber in Georgetown and established himself in Pompey's Head, four of the leading citizens of Marlborough County petitioned the state legislature to remove the restrictions that still handicapped him as a free man of color. He was permitted to acquire property, to travel outside the state, to own slaves, to marry without permission, and to walk the streets after curfew. He could not vote, join the militia, or serve on a jury. These were ironclad regulations that no petition could void.

That four of the leading citizens of Marlborough County should interest themselves in the welfare of a mulatto youth was not quite so remarkable as it sounded. Slaves were being set free all the time, and it nearly always followed that they were granted certain civil privileges. The most recent instance was Mr. Blackford's jockey, Titus, and Titus's young son, Luke. It was Mr. Blackford's way of rewarding his jockey for having finally won the Huntington Cup on Skyrocket. Titus and Luke were given their freedom, and Skyrocket was retired.

But it was nonetheless inevitable, when the notice of Allbright's petition was advertised in the *News*, as required by law, that some people should surmise that one of the interested gentlemen must have been his father. Gossip, however, was no certification of parentage. If ever the identity of Allbright's father had been known, the passing of more than a half century had long since drawn a veil. He had been a free Negro for forty years, the most expert barber in Pompey's Head and a man of considerable property. He owned a small cottage at the far end of Liberty Street, a seventy-two-acre scrub farm he took in on a mortgage, and his two-story, two-room building on Bay Street. The room on the ground floor housed his shop. He made his home in the room above.

Allbright was also a moneylender in a small way. Things always got around in Pompey's Head, and everyone knew that the young men of the town often went to him for twenty-five, fifty, and even a hundred dollars. He charged them three per cent interest. The curious thing was that when he made a loan to someone more responsible, like old Mr. Van Horn who kept a saddle shop a few doors down the street, his interest doubled.

The accepted explanation was that Allbright liked to identify himself with the ruling class. No man was more conscious of status. As a freeman, he looked down on slaves. Unmarried, he associated only with other free Negroes, always on his own terms, and insisted his apprentices be light in color. He wore a waistcoat on weekdays, a silk hat on Sunday, and a heavy gold tiepin engraved with a set of ornate initials all the time.

Tony Blackford, Tolliver Rhett, Jack Wendover, and other members of the let's-go-and-burn-down-an-outhouse set had all been on Allbright's books at some time or other. Cameron Bottomley was perhaps his steadiest client. One of John's worst quarrels with his brother was caused by Cameron's coming to him for money which, he learned later, had gone in part to clear up a debt to Allbright. "A fine thing," he said to Cameron, "coming to me for money to pay him off!" Furthermore, if Cameron was so anxious to clean up his debts, why didn't he begin at home? And another thing—why did he have to hang around that barbershop so much? Didn't he realize how it looked?

"Realize, realize!" Cameron said. "Jesus God Almighty! Is that the only word you know?"

John started to explain that it wasn't merely the money, that what he resented was Allbright's having a claim on any member of the Bottomley family, no matter how slight, and then thought better of it. "Why not?" Cameron would ask. "What does that have to do with it?" and some kind of answer would have to be made.

"Jug!" Cameron said. "Why shouldn't I visit with the other fellows in his shop? It's entertaining. And one reason it's entertaining is that I don't get any lectures! Nobody's always asking do I *realize!*

"You say you don't trust him. All right! That's your business. But don't ask me not to trust him just on your say-so! Why shouldn't I? What's he ever done to cause me not to? Lend me money? Charge me three per cent? That's less than the bank charges, or those robbers Thrall & Lockhart! And not once has he ever pressed me! Not once has he ever said no. You may not trust him, but I do! That yellow nigger is one of the best friends I have."

"A better friend than me, I suppose," John thought, and the thought hurt deeper than he cared to admit. But when he entered the barbershop, to be greeted by Allbright's bow, a bow that would have been more in place in a minstrel show, he hoped what Cameron said was true. For a best friend might know why Cameron had run away and where he was. John doubted, however, that Allbright would care to confide in him. They were on too touchy terms. Unlike Cameron, he had no wish to claim the barber as a best friend, nor was he inclined to invite any intimacies. He admitted no obligation but civility, and even civility had its price.

Allbright at last emerged from his bow. John tried to read his face, without quite knowing what he hoped to find there, but all he could see was Allbright's heavy round head, his thick neck, his coarse features, his yellow skin with a big liver spot on one cheek, and his hopeful, eager look, straining like a hound on a leash—it was the look more than anything that set John's teeth on edge.

The barber's change of expression indicated he sensed John's mood. He said cautiously, "Good morning, Mr. John. It's been a long time. You must have been hibernating yourself in the country. Could I relieve you of your hat, sir?" and John's irritation at last had something tangible on which to seize—*hibernating yourself in the country: relieve you of your hat!* It was straight out of a minstrel show, and Allbright's name might just as well be Pork Chops or Ham Gravy.

"Good morning, Allbright," John said. "How are you?"

The barber's hopeful look began to strain on the leash again. He said, "I is impeccable, sir. A day like this inspirits a man. Like the Good Book says, the winter is done over with and gone. Leastwise I hope so. You is looking well, Mr. John. I understand that you had a misfortunate accident to your arm. You is recovering nicely, I hope."

Allbright's voice could have been imagined to have a note of sincere concern, and John was halfway ashamed of the impulse that made him want to drive the barber off—take him at face value, and what was he asking but a normal amount of human consideration? John dropped his guard an inch or so.

"It's kind of you to ask, Allbright. My arm is coming along."

"That's fine, sir. Yes sir, that's mighty fine for sure."

Allbright bobbed his head up and down, looking genuinely pleased. John turned over his hat to him and sat in the hard, upright wooden chair nearest the door. The chair next to it was empty, and in the third, the last in line, a tall, red-haired man with a freckled forehead was getting a shave. John nodded to him and said good morning. The man replied good morning and said wasn't it a beautiful day, and from his flat accent and the way he used the word "beautiful," John knew he was from somewhere up in the hills—days were pretty, not beautiful, in Pompey's Head.

Allbright spoke sharply to his unoccupied apprentice. "Boy! Get me a cloth for Mr. John! You want to keep me waiting all day like the no-account you is!" and that was something else about him that John did not like. Allbright was hateful to his help. He kept a strap handy and often used it. "That wretchified Charles!" John once heard him complain of an apprentice who was later discharged. "He is a Negro pure and simple, in heart and in action. He might as well not be part white at all. Three times running he's been caught at it, cuddling a low black wench, and I refuse to have that kind of repugnation in my shop! I gave him a good whipping, but I don't expect it to do no good. Butter will run in suitable weather, and like-feathered birds will flock together. Oh, what a set!"

Allbright shook out the cloth that the apprentice hastened to bring him, and John braced himself against his touch. It was having to submit to Allbright's ministrations that he could hardly bear. He held himself stiff and his emotions stiffer, looking at Allbright's gold tiepin. It was fastened to the barber's shirt front in the center of the V made by the lapels of his clean linen jacket.

"There now!" Allbright said cheerfully. "The usual, I suppose, Mr. John? An all-around trim? Yes sir. You make yourself comfortable and let old Allbright take care of you. Boy! Bring Mr. John the morning paper! Here you are, Mr. John. I see that cotton is selling for nine and a half cents a pound today. Mr. N. N. Jones came in for a shave a while back this morning, and he said that in his ascertainment cotton will go up six points or more. What do you think, Mr. John?"

What Mr. John thought was that Pork Chops/Ham Gravy was never more exasperating than when he attempted the role of man of affairs. The tall, red-haired stranger introduced himself into the conversation. "I'd allow that six points is lenient," he said, addressing John by way of the mirror on the wall. "I don't buy cotton or sell it, my business is mules, but I'd venture to say that we'll be seeing cotton at seventeen cents or more before the new crop comes in. My name is Morgan, sir, Robert M. Morgan, the M standing for Macdonald. I live up Greenville way. And you, sir, I take it, are an Old Pompey man."

"Yes, I am," John said. "My name is Bottomley."

The red-haired man was impressed. He said, "Here that can mean

199

only one thing. You must be of the Governor's family. Am I correct?"

"Yes sir, you are. The Governor is my father."

The red-haired man inclined his head in a bow. "I'm pleased to make your acquaintance, sir. I was proud to support the Governor and I'd be proud to support him again. We could use a man like him at the head of things right now. He made us the best governor this state ever had. Yes sir, I've always said so, and I always will."

The attentions of the apprentice who was shaving him drove him into silence. Allbright began trimming John's hair. Every time John felt the touch of his fingers he wanted to draw away. "I'm here on business," the red-haired man said, taking advantage of the first opportunity to resume the conversation. "I have a drove of mules to sell, twenty-eight in all. I'm showing them in the square behind the courthouse. I don't reckon I could interest you in a pair of sound Kentuckys, could I, sir, guaranteed to be out of thoroughbred trotters by an imported Andalusian jack?"

"No, I think not."

"You can't go wrong, sir, not with these animals. Three-four months from now, once the war starts, you won't be able to buy them at half the price. That's a fact. I don't know if you've heard the news, but Northern agents are all over the middle states, buying up every mule they can. They're thick as the locusts of Egypt. They don't show no sign of slacking off, either, and it won't be long before we'll start feeling the pinch."

He looked at John in the mirror and shook his head dolefully. "There is just so many mules in the world, sir. That's a fact. Let the North corner the mule market, and where will we be? Where will cotton be? You can have the land and you can have the seed, but unless you have mules you can't make a crop. Cotton, sir, depends on mules. Even niggers is secondary."

The apprentice's razor, squaring off his sideburns, hampered his flow of talk. But not for long. He said, "You know what I think, sir? I think the day is coming when niggers will be cheaper than mules. That don't seem sensible, I know, but I took in a couple of nigger auctions lately—only this morning I took in one: it was down the street a piece—and already the price of niggers is beginning to go soft. You weren't at that auction by any chance, were you, sir?"

"No, I was not!"

John Bottomley spoke sharply, provoked that it should even be imagined he would be seen with those down-at-the-heel loafers who went to slave auctions for free entertainment, but the mule dealer gave no sign of having noticed. Allbright's scissors, however, rustling nervously, seemed to have been thrown off stride.

"It's my business to keep up with the price of stock," the mule dealer resumed, "and that means the price of niggers as well. Now you take that auction I was telling about. The highest bid run up was nine hundred dollars, and that was for a good, sound, number-one hand. The auctioneer had to sweat getting that much, too. He looked kind of down at the mouth about it, and I don't blame him. Many's the time I've seen a hand less good than that one bring twelve hundred dollars or more. And not too far back, either. No sir, there's no two ways about it. The price of niggers is getting cheap."

The rustle of Allbright's scissors stopped completely. Ill at ease himself, John expected the barber to be ill at ease also. He looked for a sign of resentment or at least a show of displeasure, and what he saw was one of Allbright's fawning, servile smiles. Turning to the mule dealer, whose shave was over and who was rising from the chair, smelling of bay rum and talcum, Allbright said ingratiatingly:

"Nine hundred dollars, eh? That's the most recessional transaction I've heard of in a long time. Why, just three weeks ago that whole gang of Mr. Edward Montague's went for eleven hundred a head. That means a deficiency of two hundred dollars in less than a month. What you say is correct, sir. The price of niggers *is* getting cheap. Yes sir, it surely is."

At that moment, could John have eliminated Allbright's existence by wishing him out of it, the barber would have dropped through the floor. Vowing that he would never set foot in Allbright's shop again, that this was the end, absolutely, he noticed that the mule dealer was looking at Allbright with his mouth half open—he could not have been more confounded had one of his beasts found voice.

A stranger in Pompey's Head, the mule dealer naturally knew nothing of Allbright's history. All he saw, as John also was able to see, peering through those pale astonished eyes, was a yellow nigger barber who had talked out of turn. A hard look showed on his face. It said he had no use for niggers to begin with and that it would be dangerous to push him too far. But Allbright, who could not have missed the look, became more ingratiating, not less. "You have yourself a nice visit, sir," he said, bowing the mule dealer to the door. "You come back to see us, sir," and John sat in the chair, fuming, clamping his jaw down hard. Allbright turned from the door, his face still creased with the wrinkles of the last smile he sent after the mule dealer, and merely the sight of him was offensive.

"Well, now," Allbright said. "That Mr. Morgan was an interesting gentleman, wasn't he? I expect he's staying down the street at the Commercial Hotel. Trade is kind of slack there this week, I hear. Well, that's the way trade is. Sometimes it blows one way and sometimes it blows the other. Fame and riches reward the bold, but a silver dollar is hard to hold. Turn your head a little the other way, will you, Mr. John? Thank you, sir. Boy! Ready me the lather! Can't you see that I'll be needing it soon? You need the strap to make you step?"

John forced himself to scan the columns of the *News*—Northern manufacturers had refused to fill any more orders for Colt revolvers that came from the South; pilots in Pensacola had been notified not to bring any more United States vessels into their harbor. It was not until he heard a voice say, "Here's your saddle, Maussuh Allbright. Maussuh Van Horn says hit's all fixed. Where you want hit put?" that he looked up.

A Negro boy of around twelve was wrestling with a saddle, much too big for him and full of silver trappings. John thought he recognized the saddle and then was sure he did, and the instant of recognition froze where it stood. The saddle belonged to Cameron. He had had it in his skiff the day he stopped at Deerskin.

"Can't you see I is busy?" Allbright said to the boy. "And ain't you ever been told to wait until you is spoken to, instead of just busting in? Put the saddle in the corner over yonder. Put it and get out of here!"

The boy did as he was told, easing the saddle to the floor. He dawdled for a few moments, as if hoping to be rewarded with a penny or two, and then left the shop. Allbright said, "These young ones! They ain't got no more manners than a billy goat!" and he might have gone on, making an oration of it, had he not seen John looking at the saddle. He started to smile, checked himself, and avoided John's glance. John felt he stood close to danger. He would not put it past Allbright to wish the Bottomleys harm. There was Cameron's saddle, and he was gone, and if he had done some bad or foolish or wicked thing and Allbright knew what it was——

"May I respectfully inquire into the healthfulness of your family, Mr. John?" Allbright said. "The Governor and his lady is well, I hope. And your sister Miss Margaret? She is well too, I trust."

Nothing could have sounded more innocent than Allbright's expression of interest. "I do declare if I don't see a little bit of gray around your temples, Mr. John," he continued. "Yes sir, I do believe that the first touch of frost has arrived. Not that you have any cause to mind. No sir! It'll just help to distinguish your appearance that much more," and so cheerful he appeared, so warmhearted and friendly, that John was almost led into believing it was absurd to imagine that this pompous, foolish man could be an agent of disaster.

"It sure is a pretty day, ain't it, Mr. John?" Allbright said cheerily. "Yes sir, it looks like old man winter has done gone and took hisself out the back door. I reckon you got more work to do in the country than you can shake a stick at, eh, Mr. John? It's no easy thing to make a turnout of rice. Most anybody can grow cotton that has a mind to, but rice, that's something else again. All you hear around town these days is cotton, nothing but cotton, but what I say is that there ain't but one crop for a gentleman, and that's rice. Cotton is to try to get rich on. Rice, though, rice *means* something. Ain't that the truth, Mr. John?"

John wanted to shake him. What made his chatter especially infuriating was that it summoned up a distorted image of Corwin Bottomley. For he too would say that cotton was to try to get rich on and that a gentleman's proper crop was rice. It was as though Corwin had been inveigled into minstrel-show dress. John said, weighing his words, "I doubt that anything means what it used to, Allbright, rice included. But tell me this. That saddle that Mr. Van Horn's boy brought in. Haven't I seen it somewhere before?"

Allbright, soaping John's neck from a bowl of lather, took longer than necessary to reply. "What's that, sir? You say something, Mr. John?"

"Yes, Allbright. I said haven't I seen that saddle before?"

"That saddle, sir? Has you seen it somewheres before? Well, sir, that's something I can't rightly say. There's a lot of saddles in Old Pompey."

"Yes," John agreed, "but not many like that. Does it belong to anybody I know?"

"Excuse me, Mr. John." Allbright placed the bowl of lather on a shelf near the mirror. "And now, sir, if you don't mind, I want you to sit still a minute. I'll be using the razor for a little bit, and we don't want to have no accidents. No sir, that we don't. There now! That takes care of that. Thank you, sir. What was it you was saying, Mr. John?"

"I asked if that saddle belonged to anybody I know."

Allbright wiped and folded his razor. "Oh, that saddle. Yes sir, I reckon you could say it do. That old saddle belongs to me."

"To you?"

"Yes sir, that's right. It's a gift, you might say. A couple of times I admired that saddle when the young gentleman to who we is referring came in to get a haircut, and he said he wanted me to have it. Wasn't that handsome and generous of him?"

John said, "Yes, very," and Allbright's cleverness amazed him—no young gentleman had been referred to, and yet Allbright had all but mentioned Cameron's name.

"It's a valuable saddle. That young gentleman must think a lot of you."

Allbright's voice changed tone. "Ah, yes sir. That young gentleman does me the honor of saying that I is one of his best friends. I'd do anything for that young gentleman, anything at all."

John was at a loss. It would have been impossible for anyone to sound more affectionate or sincere, and the look on Allbright's face, his thoughts turned inward for the instant, was that of a kindly, benevolent uncle.

"The young gentleman who gave you the saddle," John said. "Have you seen him lately?"

Something in his manner of speaking must have put Allbright off, an overeagerness perhaps, a too close coming to grips, or it could have been that Allbright, rehearsing his words beforehand, wanted time to think. The barber stepped back from the chair to examine his handiwork, glancing obliquely at John in the mirror, and in the mirror, with its suggestion of a piece of still water, it was as though they were two swimmers, fully clothed, who were grappling with each other at the bottom of a pool. Allbright said, "What's that, Mr. John? What did you say, sir?" and John came close to the end of his patience. He said, repressing his irritation, "It was merely an idle question, Allbright. What I asked was have you seen that young gentleman lately?" and Allbright, picking up his scissors to make a few last snips, seemed more at ease.

"Lately, Mr. John? Well, sir, that all depends on what you mean by lately. Midnight for Jim is morning for Jack, and a skinny man's door is a fat man's crack. Lemme see now. The last time I seen that young gentleman was maybe two weeks ago. That was when he came and brung me the saddle. It could have been a day less than two weeks, or maybe a day more, but that in general was when it was."

John tried to put things in order—two weeks ago, more or less, was when Cameron had disappeared. That much was in order. But if Allbright was telling the truth, why had Cameron gone out of his way to make him a present? And this in the midst of his panic? There was a large gap somewhere. John began to doubt that the saddle was a present at all. A likelier explanation would seem to be that Cameron had tried to buy Allbright off with it. It was not too much to imagine that part of his fifteen hundred dollars had gone toward the same end. He said, offhand as possible:

"I understand that the young gentleman we are talking about has gone away. Would you know anything about that?"

Allbright's fleshy face creased itself into a set of earnest wrinkles. "No sir," he said, "that I don't. I *hear* that that young gentleman has gone away, that much I do, but it ain't nothing that I can *say*, sir, not for sure."

"Perhaps you can tell me this, then. The day that that young gentleman came to give you the saddle. Did he say anything about going away then?"

Allbright reached for the bay rum, and John knew beforehand that they were going off on a different tack. "Oh, sir," Allbright said, "that young gentleman was *always* talking about going away."

"Always?"

"Well, sir, maybe not exactly always. But enough to make it *seem* like always. That young gentleman was sort of uncontented around here."

"Was he?"

"Yes sir, I do believe he was. And that's the curious thing, once you stop to think of it. A young gentleman like that, being who he was and all. Now why should he be uncontented? That's what I used to ax myself time after time."

"Did you ever ask him?"

"Me, sir?" Allbright made a cup of one palm and filled it with bay rum. "Now what would I be doing axing a young gentleman like him a question like that? No sir, Mr. John. I never axed him anything."

"But you say he used to talk to you about wanting to go away."

"Yes sir, that he did."

"Did he ever say why?"

Having applied the bay rum, Allbright began to comb John's hair.

"*Why*, sir?" he said. "Well, Mr. John, that's kind of hard to say. You know these young gentlemen. Some little old thing goes wrong with them, something that don't amount to a hill of beans, or else they just up and lose their tempers, and right away it's off to Texas or Mexico or even South America. You know how they is."

Texas, Mexico, or South America—John wondered if Allbright was hinting that Cameron must be searched for in those parts. He was finding it harder and harder to control his exasperation. Let Allbright keep up this evasiveness and the sheriff would have to be called in. Even as the threat crossed his mind, however, he knew what an empty threat it was. To call in the sheriff would be to make the whole thing public property and, worse, perhaps to bring down on their heads the very harm he hoped to avoid. But more than that, there stood himself. He could never hand Allbright over to the sheriff, knowing the sheriff's methods, and Allbright must be aware of it. Pork Chops/Ham Gravy seemed to hold the advantage at every turn.

"This young gentleman," John said. "Not once did he tell you why he wanted to leave Old Pompey. Is that it? Not ever?"

Allbright said, "Yes sir, Mr. John. That's right. Not ever," and the lie was so manifest that his every muscle gave it away. He put away the comb and brush, and began to unpin the cloth around John's neck. He said, "That young gentleman just used to talk about going away, that's all. He especially talked about it in the last two-three months or so. Some kind of change come over him. A big change."

John tried not to let his mounting resentment show. He could feel the same antagonism building up in him as when, having boated an eel while fishing, he had to contend with the slippery creature—in the end there was nothing to do but bash in its head.

"You say a change came over him? I wonder why."

Allbright did not have to wonder why. He knew why. Nothing could have been any plainer. He went through some kind of conflict with himself, seemingly pulled first one way and then the other, and John was ready to believe that he stood on the verge of telling whatever it was he knew. John waited, hoping that the shock was not going to be more than he could bear, and when Allbright, in his Pork Chops/Ham

Gravy inflection, said, "What's that again, Mr. John? What was it you asked?" it was impossible to hold back his anger any longer.

"I want you to stop beating around the bush, Allbright!" he said. "What has happened to my brother? I insist you tell me!" and all the while he knew he was taking unfair advantage—he was John Bottomley, the master of Deerskin, and Allbright was a mulatto barber, and he might as well be standing over him with a whip. "I warn you, Allbright! Either you tell me what you know or I will take measures to make you tell! I want to know what has happened to my brother!"

Allbright's face had paled to a sick, grayish color. "Your brother, Mr. John? You mean Mr. Cameron? Now surely, Mr. John——"

"I told you to stop beating around the bush, Allbright!"

"But Mr. John!"

"Where is my brother!"

Allbright tried to arrange his features into a look of innocence, buttressed by what was intended to be a cajoling smile. "Could I tell you where Mr. Cameron has gone to I would, Mr. John, but that ain't to be. I don't know nothing about Mr. Cameron. Oh, yes sir, I *heard* he went away, that I did, sir, but as far as me knowing——"

John held onto his temper hard. "I'm at the end of my patience, Allbright! Either you tell me the truth about this or I'll have the sheriff in here before the hour is out! You don't think you have any special immunity, do you? If so, I'll damn well teach you otherwise!"

Allbright felt the crack of the whip. A bleak look came into his eyes. "Well, sir," he said quietly, "if you want to call in the sheriff there's nothing I can do, no sir, that I can't," and this was one of the few times in his life that John Bottomley detested himself. "You tell the sheriff to do something and he'll do it," Allbright continued. "I know that, sir, and I know it will go hard with me. But there ain't nothing I can tell the sheriff, any more than I can tell you," and John, thoroughly unsettled, sensing that Allbright was both lying and telling the truth, knew that his outburst had cost him the game.

"So you don't know where my brother has gone?"

"No sir, Mr. John."

"Or why he went away?"

"No sir, Mr. John."

"Or anything at all?"

"No sir, Mr. John."

John was swept by a spasm of rage. It could have been the wooden monotony of Allbright's replies that set it off, or it could have been his own sense of shame. "You listen to me, Allbright! You're a liar, the damnedest liar I know! I'm not through with you yet!" and he might have gone on, heedless of the shame he felt, had not a sudden commotion boiled up in the street.

Several horsemen in uniform swept past the door of Allbright's shop, trailing a wake of cheers in a wake of dust. A crowd began to gather on the sidewalk amid a mounting accumulation of voices, and almost immediately a bald, middle-aged man in shirt sleeves darted into the shop. "The forts are taken!" he cried. "The Light Infantry has taken the forts!" and then sped on to spread the news elsewhere.

John Bottomley glared at Allbright, trying to find excuses for himself, saying that despite his occasional offenses he had never turned his back on the man, not once, and did he not deserve better than these evasions, these subterfuges, these lies?—and then, with anger once more turning into rage, against himself, against Allbright, against the involvement that had placed him in this harsh position, he turned and left the shop.

It was not until he was halfway down the next block, nearing the Commercial Hotel, that he regained enough control to remember he hadn't settled for the haircut. The Commercial Hotel was caught up in some special excitement. The state flag had been run out on the flagpole that jutted across the sidewalk, there was much shouting and cheering, and some young fool of a horseman, having ridden a big gray horse up the wide wooden steps of the hotel, was causing his mount to rear on the porch, pawing wildly and baring its teeth.

John recognized the horseman as Tony Blackford, streaked with dust and sweat, and it fell into place that he was one of the riders who had dashed past Allbright's shop, galloping back from the forts. John thought of returning to pay for the haircut and decided it could wait. He could not free his mind of the thought that Allbright, because of Cameron, had been placed in a position to do the Bottomleys some dangerous, vengeful harm. He strode through the noise and excitement, wondering what to do.

CHAPTER FIFTEEN

Pompey's Head had always had a fondness for celebration. Corwin Bottomley once said that all a man needed to start a parade was a sick mule and a sour bass drum. Within a half hour of the arrival of the news that the Light Infantry had taken the forts, all ordinary business came to an end. Crowds of cheering, singing men swarmed through the downtown district, the bars and restaurants were thronged to the doors, Mayor Josephus Warren delivered three speeches from the steps of City Hall, store fronts were decorated with bunting and streamers, firecrackers were set off, guns and revolvers were fired into the air, steamboat whistles were tied down, six runaway carriages turned over, Boykin's livery stable burned to the ground when a spark from a bonfire ignited a pile of hay, and the four young men who had ridden to town with the news were so patriotically roughed up that they were forced to take refuge in the Light Infantry Club, where thirty gallons of Light Infantry punch had been hastily brewed—never had the world seen such brave lads, never so brilliant a victory: it was a combined Waterloo and Solferino, and bloodless, besides.

By three o'clock the *News* was on the street with an extra. It said that a splendid triumph had been won, that not a life was lost, that only one man was injured, and that Ules Monckton, by this one stroke, had proved himself a commander of surpassing genius.

At five o'clock a second extra appeared with a longer and more factual account of the action. John Bottomley was in the Light Infantry Club at the time. Nearly the whole membership was present, except for those who were with the colors ("with the colors" was a

211

new expression, sprung up in recent weeks), and the thirty gallons of Light Infantry punch were running out fast. Tony Blackford stood on the billiard table leading a songfest—the cloth would have to be replaced, but what, at a time like this, was a piece of felt?

The quietest place in the club was the library on the second floor. It had come to be established, by a sort of squatter's right, as the fief of the older members, who found it a pleasant place to doze. John brought the *News* into the library to read. When he entered he saw that eighty-two-year-old Mr. Montague Vincent, Clay's father, was fast asleep near a marble bust of General Lafayette, that Thaddeus, the oldest of the Negro stewards, was standing in his usual place in one of the corners, half asleep himself, and that Mr. Robert Ransome and Mr. George Pruett, who were rather like stripling members of the library sub-club, being only in their seventies, were conversing in subdued tones on a low, worn couch before the empty hearth. They nodded respectfully to John, who ordinarily would no more have ventured into the library than he would have clapped Mr. Vincent on the back, the old irascible terror, and John was able to detect another tribute to his wounded arm. His not being in uniform was no longer held against him and by letting himself get shot he had somehow certified, along with his courage, his loyalty to the South.

Having already had a firsthand account of the incident from Tony Blackford before his songfest phase, John was curious to see what Gup Monckton had made of it. "At about seven o'clock this morning Forts Signal and Lookout surrendered to the officers and men of the Pompey's Head Light Infantry, under the leadership of Colonel Ules Monckton. Colonel Monckton, with a shrewdness that would have won the admiration of that earlier low-country hero, Francis Marion, the Swamp Fox, engineered a maneuver that history must surely record as one of the most brilliant in the annals of warfare. Not a single man was lost, and only one injured. Private Neville Monckton, a brother of the colonel, suffered a severe powder burn to his right hand and arm when a field gun exploded at the breech."

The remainder of the account, which ran to two full columns, went into a detailed explanation of the plan that Ules Monckton had proposed to put into effect. All the fishermen's skiffs in the neighborhood, eighteen in all, were commandeered. Each had room for at least six men. Deserted Fort Lookout presented no problem. Fort Signal was the target. The assault was planned to begin at dawn. Twenty members of the Light Infantry shed their uniforms, put on old clothes, and blacked their hands and faces. Under the pretense of being Negro fishermen, they were to approach Fort Signal by way of its creek side, pretending they had fish, berries, and garden produce to sell.

On the basis of the known routine of the fort, the *News* went on, as carefully studied by Colonel Monckton over a period of several months, it was expected that twelve men, in two skiffs, would contrive to be admitted into the fort. These were placed under the command of Colonel Monckton and Captain Anthony Blackford. Once inside the fortifications, this vanguard was to overcome the sentries as quietly as possible. The other skiff-loads would instantly effect a landing, render such aid as might be necessary, and seize the guns. The third wave of the Light Infantry, which all this time would have been lying concealed ashore, would leap into the remaining skiffs, join their comrades, and take final possession of the fort.

"Not a single detail was overlooked, nor anything left to chance," Gup Monckton commented, and it was not until one came almost to the end of the account that one discovered that chance had played at least a small part in the proceedings.

What happened was that twenty members of the fort's twenty-nine-man complement had gone ashore shortly after daybreak on a wood-cutting detail. The commanding officer, a Major Granby, was still asleep. Whatever his dreams were, it was unlikely they were dreams of danger. Undermanned Fort Signal lay at the end of nowhere. Last month's pay was still owing Major Granby's men, and his stores were almost gone. The national administration appeared to have forgotten Fort Signal's existence. Major Granby was a disgruntled, frustrated man.

Possibly Ules Monckton's plan would have succeeded even had all the members of the fort's garrison been present: certainly it was aided by the laxness that prevailed. The counterfeit Negroes of the Light

Infantry were not even challenged. They simply beached their skiffs and walked into the fort. The nine men left on the premises instantly surrendered. So did the woodcutting detail. Not a shot was fired. Everything was conducted in the friendliest manner. Major Granby was permitted to shave and dress before his meeting with Ules Monckton. It was understood that his sensibilities would be offended did he have to hand over his sword in his underwear.

The only loud noise that attended the operation was caused by the firing of one of the brass napoleons. It was Neville Monckton's way of celebrating the victory. He fed the weapon enough powder for a piece twice its size. The gun burst at the breech, and Neville was burned on the right hand and forearm. "His is the distinction of sustaining the first injury suffered in the cause," Gup Monckton meditated. "His wounds are the envy of every patroit and will do him honor the rest of his days."

Though John Bottomley was able to smile at Gup Monckton's fraternal enthusiasm—it was even touching, in a way—he understood that what he was reading was the unveiling of a hero. Wounds maketh the man. Neville's languid handsomeness would go well with a sling. He could count on more successes. Additional credit would be extended. The shady patches in his background would be forgotten. Thanks to an ignorance of explosives, the youngest of the Monckton brothers had finally arrived.

ii

But Pompey's Head could also be said to have arrived. The beam of the nation's attention swung from the forts in Charleston Harbor to the forts at the mouth of the Cassava River. It was not until several days later, when some of the out-of-town newspapers were received, that Pompey's Head began to understand how completely it occupied the center of the stage. The North had been served notice. Defiance had been hurled. The fame of the Light Infantry, ringing round the country, would soon ring round the world.

More than a spontaneous celebration was called for. Mayor Josephus Warren issued a proclamation declaring a holiday, and the *News* published the order of events—the return of the Light Infantry aboard the *Serena Moore* at 11 A.M. (all save a small detachment that would be left behind to hold the forts), followed by the presentation of a bouquet of red roses to Colonel Ules Monckton by six-year-old Miss Marybelle Wendover, and then a parade from the Bay Street wharf to City Hall by way of Bay, Magnolia, and Alwyn streets with the following units in the line of march—two grand marshals on horseback, the Always Ready Fire Brigade, the Marlborough County Brass Band, the six surviving members of the War of 1812 riding in open carriages, two more grand marshals, Colonel Ules Monckton and Mayor Warren in another open carriage, the officers and men of the Light Infantry, the Old Pompey Band under the direction of Major Wolfgang Weber, and, bringing up the rear, the Never Asleep Fire Brigade and its Protect Your Property Brass Band.

The parade was scheduled to file past the reviewing stands that had been erected before City Hall at approximately 12 noon. At 12:30 P.M., following a few remarks by Mayor Warren, there was to be an address by Colonel Ules Monckton, after which the remainder of the day would be devoted to rest and recovery. At 10 P.M. a display of fireworks would be set off from two barges anchored midstream in the Cassava River, and at 11 P.M., after the fireworks, there was to be a ball in honor of the Light Infantry, to which Major Granby, the vanquished commander of Fort Signal, had also been invited—the *News,* in a separate paragraph, explained that Major Granby would depart for the North by railroad the following morning and that Mayor Warren was planning to escort him to the station.

CHAPTER SIXTEEN

John Bottomley, having promised his sister Missy he would take her to the parade, began to grumble when he learned she had invited Arabella Stanhope along. "Oh, don't be like that, Johnny!" Missy said. "Arbell hasn't an escort. Everybody's in the parade, even the Senator. He's one of the grand marshals. Arbell won't be any trouble. She'll just be riding in our carriage and sitting with us, that's all."

Cards for seats in the reviewing stand had been sent to the Bottomleys as a matter of right. John's mother was still confined to her bed, and though Corwin Bottomley hadn't fully recovered from his cold, he decided to attend the ceremonies anyway. As a former governor his presence would be expected: how would it look if he didn't appear? Beneath the requirements of propriety, however, there ran the stronger pull of curiosity. John understood that his father's real reason for deciding to attend the ceremonies was the same as his own—they both wanted to have another look at Ules Monckton.

No longer was Ules a purely local figure. Extras telling of his exploit had appeared in every city North and South. A special correspondent of *The Times* of London telegraphed Mayor Warren, explaining that he was en route to Pompey's Head to write a series of articles and asking the mayor's help in arranging an interview. The Mobile *Advertiser* urged Ules's appointment as commander-in-chief of the Southern armies. The New Orleans *Picayune* proposed him for President. The Vicksburg *Daily Citizen*, in an editorial that Gup Monckton saw fit to reprint on the first page of the *News*, warned the members of the constitutional convention meeting in Montgomery not to fail to take the fall of Fort Signal into consideration—Colonel Monckton, the members were reminded, was the foremost man in the South.

"And dammit, it's true!" Corwin Bottomley said to John, sitting in the reviewing stand before City Hall. "I can't stomach the fellow, and all this hoorah ain't making it any easier for me, but you have to give credit where credit is due. He went out and did it. He showed the North where to head in. But the big thing, the way it said in the paper, is how this will affect those fellows in Montgomery. They'll hem and they'll haw, the way they always do, and the cotton crowd will be out to grab all it can, which won't be hard, seeing as how they've got everything rigged their own way, but this fellow's taking the forts is bound to make a difference. He's given Wingfield Manning a trump card. The cotton crowd can't afford to ignore us now. Manning has been put in a position to get something big for Stanhope. The odds have gone over to his side."

"But what about our friend Gup?" John asked, seeing the editor of the *News* in the front row of the stand. "How will he take it?"

"Take what?"

"What you said about the Senator. Isn't Gup hoping to be made a member of the cabinet? More than hoping? Expecting? Hasn't he as much as come right out and said so?"

"What difference does that make?"

"I can imagine its making a lot of difference. Won't he feel that he should be the one to reap the rewards, not Senator Stanhope?"

"Well, what of it?"

What of it was easy, John thought—should Senator Stanhope actually be named to the cabinet, Gup Monckton was not likely to take it gracefully. Having cast himself as an important member of the new Confederate government (and why not? was he not recognized as perhaps the most brilliant spokesman of the secessionist South?), and then to see the plum fall into another man's lap, largely as the result of his own brother's enterprise——

"It seems to me," John said, "that Senator Stanhope is going to have an enemy on his hands."

Corwin Bottomley shrugged. "Any man who don't want to make

enemies had best stay away from politics. All you're saying is that
Gup Monckton will be rubbed the wrong way. What do you want
me to do? Take up a collection? Do you think that if a fellow happens to run a newspaper and says that he ought to be President or
Vice-President or even Secretary in Charge of Exterminating the
Wild Red Indians—do you think that that's all there is to it and that
he's going to be obliged? Things don't work out that way."

"I never thought they did."

"Maybe not, but you gave that impression. The thing is, in politics
you have to have friends at court. And they have to have friends *in*
court. That's where Wingfield Manning counts. Maybe our people
aren't as strong as they used to be, but Manning knows his way around.
We ain't ready for the boneyard yet. We still have more of a say-so
than maybe you think. We made up our minds a long time ago that
we weren't going to be left out of the new government, and we picked
Stanhope as our man."

"We? I didn't know you had a hand in it."

"Well, now you do."

"Is Gup aware of this?"

"I wouldn't be surprised. There's always bound to be a leak somewhere. But what if he is? What can he do except write something
else about how the new government will need new leadership and new
faces and new enterprise? Him in the cabinet? Don't be a fool! If
we're so close to the bottom of the barrel that all we can come up
with is some fellow who is always hanging onto his brother's coat-
tails——"

"Not so loud, Father. He'll hear you."

Gup Monckton was dressed to the nines. His position as editor of
the *News* would have placed him up front in any case, and his being
Ules's brother added to his prestige. He sat with an open notebook
on his knee, wearing the constrained look of one who, though full of
his own importance, was trying hard, unsuccessfully, not to let it appear. "Let him hear!" Corwin said. "He looks like a wax dummy, don't
he?" but John noticed that his father paid Gup the tribute of lowering his voice considerably. Most of the men in the stands belonged

to Corwin's generation—gray heads, bald pates, and wrinkled cheeks predominated. None of them liked Ules Monckton and they would never forget, as long as they lived, that Gup, before Ules's emergence as landowner and newspaper proprietor, was nothing but a book-keeper. But there Gup was, sitting in the front row, and here they were, waiting, theoretically, to pay tribute to Ules—it was not hard to see them as the aging, disgruntled patricians stripped of most of their prestige and power by younger, more energetic, more ambitious men.

The seats assigned to the Bottomleys were in one of the forward rows, not far from the speakers' platform. A large crowd had gathered on both sides of the street, and Alwyn Square, opposite the stands, was filled to overflowing. The raw lumber of the stands was hung with bunting, a more elaborate display was draped across the face of City Hall, and a large state flag was wrapped like a skirt around the speakers' platform. John sat between his father and Missy, and next to Missy sat Arabella Stanhope. Arabella wore a dark green dress and a little plumed hat. The sun caught the ends of her reddish-brown hair, putting bronze highlights in it, and John was reminded of the time she was night-blooming catchfly in the pageant at Happy Chance.

"What time is it?" Corwin Bottomley asked. "Do they expect us to wear out our behinds all afternoon?"

"It's just a little past twelve, Father. How do you feel?"

"I feel fine."

"Are you sure?"

"Yes, I'm sure! Stop pestering me, dammit! I'm a long way from having to spend the rest of my life in bed."

"Nobody said anything about that."

"And I said I was feeling fine! Ain't that enough for you? I see that Stanhope's wife is sitting with Mrs. Mayor Warren. One thing you have to say for her—if Stanhope don't get in the cabinet it won't be her fault."

John had noticed Lydia the moment he arrived—he was deliberately not looking in her direction. She sat in a place of honor with Mayor Warren's short, dumpy wife and must have had her seamstress run up a new gown for the occasion, white, with long full sleeves, the bodice embroidered with the sheaf of rice that was part of the state emblem, worked into a circle of small blue stars. In place of a bonnet she wore a rosette of gray, blue, and scarlet ribbon. Missy called it a secession cockade.

Lydia's manner toward Mrs. Mayor Warren, John thought, was too cordial and affectionate. It was bound to be chalked up against her as another black mark by the ladies of the Wednesday Afternoon Ladies Society. Mrs. Mayor Warren was overdressed and underbred. She talked too loud. She wore too many rings. She was one of the commonest women in town.

The ladies of the Wednesday Afternoon Ladies Society, however, were no longer important to Lydia Stanhope. In the Tory world of the Light Infantry Club, where all the important decisions were made, hers were the invitations most highly prized. Where else in Pompey's Head could one meet a delicious little French actress, or that delightful contralto who sang at the Marlborough Theatre a few weeks back, and who else would have thought of hiring a band of traveling acrobats, accompanied by an ape, a troupe of trained dogs, and a Chinese magician, to perform in her garden after dark, with torches on the lawn and flambeaux in the trees?

Outnumbered and outflanked, Lydia had beaten the ladies of the Wednesday Afternoon Ladies Society at their own game. When visiting dignitaries stopped off at Pompey's Head—old friends of Senator Stanhope from Washington; a famous English author; a Danish merchant prince—it was Lydia who first entertained them. Already, with the help of Mrs. Warren, she had snared the correspondent of *The Times* of London. She would be giving a little supper for him tomorrow night. And if by some chance it should happen to be mentioned in *The Times* that Senator Robert Stanhope was eminently fitted for high office in the new Confederate government—well then, could she be blamed?

A sound of music rose beyond the square, coming from the direction of the river and riding above a more muffled sound of cheers. Looking away from Lydia, John saw Arabella Stanhope watching him intently. Her face wore a bemused, speculative expression, and her eyes, more gray today than green, were wide and still. John's thoughts were so close to the surface that he felt he must be as transparent as glass. Arabella's look persisted, meeting his directly, and then, with the barest flicker of a smile acknowledging the exchange—not mocking, not scornful, merely a smile—she turned her attention elsewhere.

"Damnation!" Corwin Bottomley said. "There's no excuse for this! Why can't these things ever begin on time?"

"I don't think we'll have to wait much longer, Father. Can't you hear the music?"

"No, I can't! And don't imply I'm getting deaf!"

John knew the signs. Boredom was making his father cross, and deeper than boredom was the worry they felt about Cameron—though his father had elected not to discuss Cameron's disappearance, thereby implying that he had washed his hands of him, it could not be imagined he was immune from the strain. John said without thinking, "You're not getting tired, are you, Father?" and Corwin let him have it full blast. "I told you to stop pestering me, goddammit! Can't you find anything better to do? Flirt with the girls, look at the crowd, say your prayers! But stop clucking over me!"

"I'm not clucking, Father."

"Well, that's what it sounds like!"

"I didn't mean to annoy you."

"Now who said anything about being annoyed! Why are you so touchy?"

Silence, at a time like this, was the safest refuge. Looking at the crowd, John judged that half the population of Pompey's Head had collected in the neighborhood of City Hall. Whole families had turned out, and many of the country people, picnicking under the trees in the square, were making a day of it in town. "I don't see how you can say a thing like that," John heard Missy say to Arabella Stanhope. "I suppose he can be called handsome, if you like his kind of looks, but I doubt that he's sincere."

"Fiddle!" Arabella said. "That's Constance Pettibone speaking, not you! Any man she makes eyes at and who doesn't swoon at her feet, overcome, why then he's not sincere! She set her cap for him from the very beginning. Didn't you see her the night of the ball?"

"Well, if you mean——"

"*If* I mean! Don't play Little Miss Innocent with me! You know what I mean. Constance Pettibone all but threw herself at his head. No wonder she finds him insincere! I would too had I been royally snubbed as that."

"The way you talk, Arbell! It almost sounds as if you were in love with him."

"Dear, dear, does it now? Constance Pettibone's tongue clacks away, hinged in the middle and loose at both ends, the *insincerest* tongue in town, and if one finds her tiresome and says so, then naturally one has to be in love."

John felt unaccountably dejected—did they ever think of anything else, those two? They had been prattling of love almost from the time they had been able to prattle at all. He stole a glance at Lydia, who was leaning toward Mrs. Mayor Warren in a way that caused her face to be seen slightly from above, its most appealing angle, and what love was, was an odious, festering, degrading wound. *And for what!* Corwin Bottomley said, squinting, "Ain't that Peter McIntosh over there by the lamppost, the one that keeps the forge in Bugtown?" and John looked at his father closely—Peter McIntosh had been in his grave for five years, as Corwin Bottomley knew, or should have known, since out of some impulse of affection or loyalty he had attended the old smith's funeral. John was prompted to remind his father of Peter McIntosh's demise, only to decide, as Corwin went on squinting, that it was kinder not to. He heard Arabella Stanhope say acidly, "And now, since he's been wounded and all, she'll probably make a worse spectacle of herself than ever," and it dawned on him that it was Neville Monckton who was being debated. It couldn't be true what Missy had implied, that Arabella was in love with him (whatever soft, sleazy thing they meant by love), and yet given Neville's looks, his uniform, and his romantic emergence as a hero——

A burst of music came from down the street, much closer, and the crowd pressed forward to get a better look. The first rank of spectators was separated from the stands by only the width of the street. John saw a horse-faced countryman who even from this distance bespoke the smell of chewing tobacco and manure; another man, a town dweller by his dress, who had hoisted a towheaded boy to his shoulders; a phalanx of youths in the blue work shirts and heavy brogans of the Irish Channel, and, looking fixedly toward the stands, the stolid, imperturbable figure of Allbright.

Ever since the episode in Allbright's shop, three days before, the image of the mulatto barber had been somewhere in John's mind. He would open his eyes in the morning, aware that something was nagging him, as might some pain or ache partially numbed by sleep, and gradually, as the disorderly landscape of night gave way to the more dependable geography of day and one by one he lifted his burdens and strapped them to his back—Cameron, his mother's illness, what to do with himself if war came, his infatuation with Lydia Stanhope —gradually he would remember what the undertow was, and that it was Allbright.

Watching the barber from the stands, and unable to keep his eyes from him, John felt weighed down with misgivings. Allbright was dressed in his broadcloth best, sporting a high silk hat and a gold-headed cane. His large head seemed set lower than usual between his heavy shoulders, hunched forward in a way that was remindful of Corwin Bottomley when his attention was riveted on something, and despite the jostling of the crowd, pushing this way and that, he gave the impression of standing aside, withdrawn and superior. "Petunia!" Missy said. "What's holding up the parade? It ought to be here by now!" and it was then, when John's spirits could not have been lower, that Allbright caught sight of him. The barber's face lit up, the eager look came into his eyes, hopeful and straining, and he lifted his hat —then, unable to leave well enough alone, drawn into one of those implications of intimacy that John abhorred, he lifted his hat higher and bowed. He couldn't have called attention to himself more had he stood on his head.

"Who's that fellow?" Corwin Bottomley asked. "You know him?" and Corwin was not the only person in the stands whose curiosity was aroused. Had Allbright been coal-black and garbed in ragged hand-me-downs, his exaggerated gentility might have been laughable —as it was, light of skin and expensively dressed, he came too close to home for comfort. It could be suspected that a criticism was implied, and the criticism was disquieting. Embarrassed that Allbright had presumed to this public display, almost as equal to equal, John said to his father, seeing no way out of it, "That's that mulatto barber, Allbright," and though he looked searchingly at Corwin, who was squinting at Allbright with his blunt, fleshy nose crisscrossed with wrinkles, he could detect only an impassive detachment. "He sure thinks a lot of himself, don't he?" Corwin said. "That's the trouble with these free niggers, especially if they're half white. They act like they own the place," and there was hardly any difference between Corwin's tone and that of the red-haired stranger in Allbright's shop comparing niggers and mules.

There was a nearer crash of music, and the first units of the parade came into view. The parade was headed by two grand marshals on horseback, Senator Stanhope and Mr. Endymion Waites, and next in line, stepping lively, dressed in red shirts, black trousers, and white helmets, came the Always Ready Fire Brigade. Some of its members were pulling their brand-new pumper, a shiny white-and-gold machine with the name EXCELSIOR lettered in gold on both sides, and immediately behind the firemen marched the twenty-two-piece Marlborough County Brass Band playing "The Light Infantry March." The crowd broke ranks, a flutter of scarves and handkerchiefs livened the stands, and in the excitement John lost track of Allbright. The damage, however, was done. John found it hard to interest himself, after the parade, in Ules Monckton's address.

ii

Mayor Warren, in his introduction, threatened to go on forever. When eventually he delivered up the crowd to Ules Monckton, it was ready for anything he had to offer. John watched him rise from his seat, step to the rail of the speakers' platform, and wait for the cheering to cease. His uniform was wrinkled, his boots wanted polishing, and either he had shaved early that morning, before the Light Infantry boarded the *Serena Moore*, or else it had slipped his mind. He seemed indifferent to the crowd's acclaim, even bored, and his eyes had the dull, empty look that could be taken as an oblique reflection of his gangly stance.

Eventually the crowd quieted down. Remembering the night Ules had addressed the Agricultural Society and how transformed he was once he started speaking, John waited for a similar change to occur. But not at all. Ules said he appreciated this reception by his fellow citizens, that he wished to express the thanks of the Light Infantry, and that his only wish was to serve his country in the field. And then, with that clumsy bow of his, he sat down. Charity would have said that he was too weary to make a speech, but charity was precluded. The impression he gave was that of one who had nothing to say to the crowd, who did not intend to pander, and who cared not a whit for the crowd's affection.

The gathering sensed that something was wrong. A murmur of disbelief rose as Ules returned to his seat. Ready to be lashed into a frenzy, the crowd felt disappointed and let down. It had its own image of a hero, and Ules's indifference was not to its liking.

But even less was it to the liking of the audience in the stands. Indifference to the crowd might be passed over: what could not be overlooked was indifference to them. "It was damn near an insult," Corwin Bottomley said, riding back to Indigo. "You'd think that he'd let all this hoorah go to his head. There he was with a chance to show he knew how to behave, and make a few friends for himself, and what does he do but act like he thought he was God Almighty!" and while that was one way of looking at it, John thought that another, no less tenable, was that the man on the platform was the same man who had addressed the Agricultural Society. It was not his duty to court popularity. His task was to make his vision come true. Seizing the forts was the first move in that direction. There would be others in time.

PART FOUR

CHAPTER SEVENTEEN

"I knew this would happen," John Bottomley said to his father, glancing up from the latest edition of the *News*. "I said as much the day of the parade. Remember?"

Corwin Bottomley was sick in bed again, propped up amid the usual clutter of ledgers, daybooks, bills, and letters. He said, "Yes, I remember. What do you want me to do? Order you a medal?" and more than irritation over being laid up showed in his voice. Though his new ailment was that combination of loose bowels, random aches, and other small miseries known as the colic—nothing in itself to be alarmed about—John didn't like the way he looked. His color was bad, there were pouches under his eyes, and his cheeks hung down flabbily. "All the same, though," Corwin said, "it's a feather in our cap. Wingfield Manning did all right for us. Stanhope's in. That's what counts. You expect me to lose any sleep over what that bookkeeper says in the *News*?"

John had another look at the newspaper. A DISASTROUS SELECTION, a headline announced, running across a front-page editorial that dealt with the appointment, just revealed, of Senator Stanhope as one of the secretaries of the new government. He was to be in charge, primarily, of what was described as the country's internal defenses.

Two weeks and three days had passed since the parade welcoming the Light Infantry back to Pompey's Head. The Montgomery convention had met and disbanded, the representatives of the cotton states had proved Corwin's astuteness as a prophet by getting hold of nearly all the more important offices, and John Bottomley, who had left for

Deerskin the day after the parade, had just that morning returned to Pompey's Head, summoned by his father through Captain Bostwick, the master of the *Serena Moore*—"The Governor sent that boy of his, Esau, with word for you," Captain Bostwick had explained. "He says for you to stop what it is you're doing and come home right away."

John Bottomley knew a command when he heard one. He boarded the *Serena* on her night trip down, wondering what the hurry was and if it might be related to Cameron. The *Serena* developed boiler trouble and was four and a half hours late. Due to arrive in Pompey's Head at six in the morning, she tied up at the Bay Street wharf at half-past ten. Esau was waiting in a carriage, and John drove to Indigo.

"You sure took your time getting here," Corwin said. "What did you do? Swim?"

"I might have made better time had I. The *Serena*——"

"I know! You don't have to tell me. She broke down again! Dammit, I'm going to get after Bostwick one of these days! The money I've paid him in freightage alone would be enough to buy a new set of boilers twenty times over. You sleep on deck?"

"Yes, Father, and well. How do you feel?"

"Feel? How do you think I feel? I feel like a man with the colic. You been in to see your mother yet?"

"Yes sir, I just left her room."

"How did she seem?"

"I couldn't very well tell. She was asleep. What does Dr. Carpenter say?"

Corwin's tone was a mixture of exasperation and despair. "He says what he always says, that she ought to rest her nerves. All he does is to give her opium. I don't know. Maybe she ought to go away. She and your sister could visit the springs. She won't hear of it, though, and Carpenter says that she's not well enough to make the trip. But just giving her opium ain't going to make her well. I'm no doctor, but I know that much." He stared past John for a moment, brooding. "We had another one of her spells the other night."

"No, Father. Not again!"

Corwin drew in a long breath and expelled it slowly. "This time

it was the stables. She was sure she smelled smoke, just like before. We had to call out everybody and make a search. And in the rain,
at two o'clock in the morning. We had a time with her, I'll tell you.
It must have been daylight before your sister could get her quieted
down. If only there was some way——"

But it was futile even to hope. "She spoils them!" Corwin said re-
sentfully, wrinkling his brow into a scowl. "That's the whole trouble!
She makes up to them, she gives them presents, she lets them feed
half the yard from the kitchen. And all the time she's afraid of them!
It's been like that from the beginning. It goes back to when she was
a little girl. They had some trouble near your grandfather Nesbitt's
place—two of them ran amok and tried to butcher up a family: there
was nothing to do but shoot them down—and it must have left
some kind of mark on her mind. We had one of her spells the night I
brought her to Rosebank."

"I'm sorry, Father. I know it hasn't been easy for you."

Corwin gave one of his grunts. "Live as long as I have and you'll
find nothing is easy. But that's not why I asked you to come to
town, to complain about your mother. It's not her fault. She can't be
blamed. She's not the only one who's afraid of them. Let the truth be
known, and it might come out that we all are, in some way or other."
He stared past John again, his mouth half open. "It must be easy for
them in the North, telling John Brown to come down here and slit
our throats in Christ's name. It don't cost them anything to be pious.
They sit up there a thousand miles away, writing books like that Uncle
Tom woman's, and never coming within sight or smell of one of them.
But we ain't that lucky. Half the time we might as well be African
missionaries. And what thanks do we get, except to have it preached
that all we deserve is to have our throats slit in this world and suffer
eternal damnation in the next?"

"I know, Father. They don't always understand."

"Always? They don't even try to understand! But maybe they can't.
Maybe that Uncle Tom woman is the best they can do. Me, I'm a
cruel slave owner. I feed them, I clothe them, and I look after them.
But still I'm a cruel slave owner. And why?" Anger darkened his face

and gave his voice a harsher tone. "Because I let my overseers use the whip if they have to? Because I don't believe in being soft and easy like your mother? Because if it wasn't for me and men like me the whole black tide would come pouring in?"

Since no answer was expected, John did not reply. Corwin's teeth were clenched and his breathing was heavier than usual. He said, "Do they think we *like* it this way, by God? Let that Uncle Tom woman come down here and live with them, just for a week, and she'd be quick to change her tune. They look human, they act human, but way down at the bottom they *ain't* human! That's the whole plain truth of it! Maybe they have souls, like some of the preachers say, but maybe horses and mules have souls too. Until I believe the one, I can't believe the other. And if that makes me a cruel slave owner, there's nothing I can do. That's the way it stands."

John Bottomley thought of the boy Simon asleep on the stable floor. Giving a silver dollar to Simon had been like giving a bucket of oats to the mare Delilah, and who was he to sit in judgment? Corwin reached under the bedclothes, pulled down his nightshirt, and shifted his position against the pillows. He said, "But that ain't why I asked you to come to town, either, to blow off steam against the Yankees. Let them keep to their side of the fence, and we'll keep to ours. How did you leave things at Deerskin?"

There was never a time that John Bottomley came to Pompey's Head without his father's asking him how things had been left at Deerskin, but this time the question had some new and special importance. Again suspecting that Cameron was involved, which would account for his father's reluctance to broach the subject, John said, "Except for those fields nearest the marsh, most of the planting is done. I'm having a little alum trouble, but not enough to speak of. Why, Father? Why do you ask?"

His father seemed not to know how to proceed. "What about Wilson?" he said. "Suppose—well, suppose you had to leave Deerskin for a time? Could Wilson manage?"

It was bound to be Cameron, John thought. What had happened, what could have happened, was that Cameron's whereabouts had been located, that he was sick somewhere or in more trouble, and now his father was trying to ask could he go and bring him home. Wanting to give himself up to the relief he felt, and yet afraid to, John said, "Yes, Father, I think Wilson can manage. He's the one who really runs Deerskin. You know that," and he waited for his father to say what was on his mind. "Is there something you want me to do? Can I help in any way?"

"Yes and no," Corwin said. "Sometime while you're here, today or tomorrow, I'd like for you to go and look at one of those houses your mother owns in the Channel. Roundtree's sick and I'm laid up, and those people are complaining about a leak in the roof. Their name's O'Connell. But that's not why I sent for you, either. I wouldn't want to take you away from planting just for a thing like that. Your mother would be wise to sell those houses. Peter Pettibone wants to buy them, and for once he's willing to pay a decent price. I don't like having that kind of property in the family."

"Neither do I. But you still haven't said why you sent for me. What is it you want me to do?"

Corwin rubbed the end of his nose. "You're putting it the wrong way," he said. "It's not what I want you to do. It's more on the order of something you might want to do for yourself."

"But what is it, Father? Why don't you say? If only you'd come out with it——"

Corwin bridled, sitting up straight. "Now you hold your horses! There are some things that can't be spilled out all at once! Have you heard the news about Stanhope?"

"No sir, I haven't."

"Here then! Read it for yourself. It just came out this morning. You'll find it on the front page."

So it wasn't Cameron, then. Having permitted himself to hope, John felt his spirits sag. He reached for the copy of the *News* his father held out to him. A DISASTROUS SELECTION, the heading of a front-page editorial said, and in the editorial Gup Monckton trained his guns on Senator Stanhope. Sawdust statesman. Proved incompetent. Weakest link in a chain of weak links. A mistake that cried out to be rectified. And it was then, glancing up from the newspaper, that John said he knew this would happen and was asked by his father did he expect him to lose any sleep over what that bookkeeper said in the *News.*

"No, I don't," John said. "You'll sleep all right, I reckon. This is what you wanted, isn't it? You must be feeling pretty good."

"With the colic? And with all the work I have to do? I have to admit, though, that I'm pleased with the way things turned out. We couldn't let the cotton crowd steal the whole show. What's puzzling you?"

"Our friends the Moncktons," John said. "According to Gup, the new constitution is practically identical with the one we've been living under. He is especially outraged over the article forbidding the importing of slaves. It was put in, he says, to mollify the North. Listen to this. 'What is there in this new constitution to prevent the Union from being reconstructed? We will have run a round circle, and end where we started.' "

"All right!" Corwin hunched forward belligerently. "So the bookkeeper's nose is out of joint! It's too bad, ain't it?"

John thought it might be. Gup's dissatisfaction was probably not too important, but what about Ules? Piece together some of his remarks before the Agricultural Society and some of his conversation at the Light Infantry Ball, and it was not too much to suspect that the attack on the new government was as much his doing as Gup's.

"I don't believe we've seen the end of this," John said. "Gup may have written the editorial, but I have an idea it was Ules who held the pen. Gup's being passed over in favor of Senator Stanhope probably angers him, but his real anger is against the new government."

Corwin had not relaxed his belligerent pose. "Suppose it is. Does he think he can rule the roost!"

"That I don't know. I wouldn't be too surprised, though, if he wouldn't like to. And there's one thing you forget. He's still the hero of the hour. Should he come out in the open and continue these attacks——"

But Corwin had had enough. He said, "Now you listen to me! What

234

do you think three quarters of politics is, except attacks? Don't you try to teach me my A B C's! There's no way of pleasing everybody, and there will always be those who know how to do things better than you. But that's neither here nor there! I've decided to buy that wharf, and Tom Thrall's coming here with the papers for me to sign. I can't waste all morning talking to you. Let's get down to why I sent for you. How would you like to be on Stanhope's staff?"

It came so suddenly that John's mind went blank. He stared at his father dumfoundedly. He said weakly, "Me?"

Corwin gave a sort of lurch beneath the sheets. "Yes, dammit, you. You'll have the rank of captain. It'll put you at the center of things. What do you say?"

Beneath his dumfoundedness John thought he was going to laugh —the cunning of this man who was his father, sick in bed with the colic! He could imagine the scene between him and Senator Stanhope. "I'll get behind you," he would have said, "and I'll work to get the others behind you, including Wingfield Manning. What do I want out of it? I'll lay the cards on the table. What I want out of it, if the thing comes off, is a place for my son. Not any old place. Somewhere close to the top, on your staff. Is it agreed?" Looking at Corwin, who was hunched forward from the waist and watching him intently, John could not restrain a chuckle—the old, devious, bald-headed scoundrel!

"You're closer to Tupichichi than I imagined," he said. "And now I'm sure he was a Yankee Indian. What did Senator Stanhope say when you told him I was part of the deal?"

"What deal?" Corwin looked indignant. "You must be crazy. There was no deal. This was Stanhope's idea, not mine."

Corwin said that in his opinion John could do worse than accept the offer. "You may be able to make a real contribution," he added. "The way it stands now, with the cotton crowd running things, the danger is that the new government will be filled up with riffraff. Well, practically. And who knows? You say that all you want is to be a planter, but maybe later on, ten or twelve years from now, you may change your mind and decide to go into politics. This kind of experience won't hurt you any. Wingfield Manning is going to be our

235

next governor, that much is certain, but Manning doesn't intend to
stop at being governor, and maybe someday, if the idea appeals to
you——"

John hardly listened. He was thinking he had no choice, that the
debate over what he was going to do with himself had gone on long
enough, and that he could not ask his father to bear another disappointment. And also he was thinking of Lydia Stanhope. There would
be many times when, as a member of the Senator's official family, he
would find himself in her presence. What gain he hoped for, he could
not say. The promise of proximity was enough.

"I'll be glad to accept," he said. "When am I supposed to give an
answer?"

"Today. Stanhope is waiting for you to call."

"Have you any idea what my duties will be?"

"No, not exactly. Stanhope won't be able to tell you much about
that, either. He doesn't know his own yet. Internal defenses. That
could mean anything they want it to mean, from transportation to
currency. My notion is that you'll probably be working close to the
War Department, but that's only a guess. Did I tell you that you
would be an under-secretary?"

"No, you didn't. You must have driven a hard bargain."

Corwin began to look irritated. "I told you once, didn't I, that
there was no bargain and that this whole thing was Stanhope's
idea. Now you get over to his place. He's leaving in the morning and
wants to talk to you."

"In the morning? I can't get ready by then."

"Stanhope understands that. You'll have at least a week to arrange
your affairs. And don't you worry about Deerskin. I'm thinking of
throwing it and Cornwall into one. I'll put Wilson in charge and let
that new overseer at Cornwall work under him. I'm disappointed in
that fellow. The work seems more than he can handle. He writes that
he's not finished repairing those dikes yet and is going to be late with
some of his planting. That, though, ain't his fault altogether. If your
brother Cameron had done what he should have done at Cornwall,
instead of letting it go to rack and ruin——"

He cut himself short, startled, caught in the predicament of having mentioned Cameron's name. Outside, in one of the trees, a redbird began singing, stopped, and started singing again. Made uneasy by his father's embarrassment, and wanting to rescue him from it, John said, speaking the first thing that came into his mind, "Don't be too hard on Cameron, Father. Something went wrong somewhere. Perhaps if he hadn't been forced into being a planter——"

"Forced!" Corwin sat straight up, his eyes blazing. "That's what your mother says. Listen to her and it's all my fault! Is that what you think too? *Forced!* By God, when I look back on all the things I've done for him, the money I've spent and the chances he's had, and now to have him sneak off like some damn chicken thief——"

John put out his hand. "Please don't get angry, Father. I don't like what's happened any more than you do. But can't we talk about it calmly and quietly? Getting this excited isn't good for you."

Corwin looked at John sternly, his brows bunched above his nose, and then, as if the tensions caused by Cameron's disappearance had suddenly given way, his whole body went tired and slack. "All right," he said. "Let's talk about it. You've been playing detective, haven't you? Why did he run away?"

"I don't know."

"Do you know where he is?"

"No sir, I don't."

"So you haven't been able to find out anything. Is that it?"

A bundle of workingman's clothes, a letter that could be either M or W, and Cameron's saddle in Allbright's shop—"Yes, Father," John said, "that's it," and though he did not like to lie it seemed better to lie, at least for the moment, than to spread out these scattered fragments that might not even be part of the same puzzle. Looking through the window, John rested his eyes upon the dark green stillness of one of the trees. The branches spread close to the window, hung with moss. "May I ask you a question, Father? Do you know why he ran away?"

Resting for the moment against the pillows, Corwin did not move. "Because he's a coward," he said. "Because he's never been man

237

enough to stand up to anything. Because he's in some kind of trouble that's too big to hide behind your mother's skirts. Because he's turned into a common, ordinary, down-in-the-gutter drunk."

"Why say these things, Father? Why hurt yourself?"

"Hurt myself?" Corwin's voice became strained. "How? By not making excuses for him the way your mother does? What do you want me to do? Pretend that he's the kind of decent, honorable son a man can be proud of? What am I, a fool?" He looked straight into John's eyes. "If you take my advice you'll forget him. Say that it's good riddance to bad rubbish. Now that he's gone away, pray that he stays away."

John thought it was anger speaking, along with disappointment and hurt pride, but as he saw the coldness on his father's face and the hard lines of the jaw beneath the flabby cheeks, he realized that his father meant every word. Corwin said, dropping his voice, "I no longer recognize him as my son. He is not to enter this house again," and when John replied, protesting, "Don't say that, Father. Think of Mother," Corwin's eyes began to blaze again. He said, "You are not to give me instructions, you understand! This is my house and I am still the master here! I say he is not my son!"

"But Father——"

"I remind you not to give me instructions. He is not my son, and if you take my advice you will forget he is your brother. You will be wise not to make any further inquiries. Leave bad enough alone. Are you so free of trouble that you have to borrow more? Sometimes I think it's a habit you have. But this time, if you know what's good for you——"

A knock sounded on the door, interrupting him, and both he and John turned their heads in the door's direction. The door opened a crack, and Missy's voice said, "May I come in, Father? Is Johnny with you?" Corwin raised his arms and dropped them on the littered bedclothes in a gesture of despair. He said, "All right, come in! Let's have a damn reception!" and Missy, opening the door, ran to John and gave him a hug. "I've been downtown," she said. "Esau just told me you were here. Have you had breakfast?"

"No, I haven't. The *Serena* was hours late."

"Why didn't you say you hadn't eaten?" Corwin asked. "How was I to know? Go with your sister and let her feed you, and then get over to Stanhope's. I told him you'd be there before dinnertime."

John, leaving the room with Missy, stopped near the door.

"Thank you, Father," he said. "I appreciate all you did for me."

Corwin looked irritated. "How many times do I have to tell you——" And then, reaching for a sheaf of unopened letters, "All right!" he said. "If you want to be bullheaded, be bullheaded! Go get some breakfast and leave me alone. You two may be able to trifle, but I have work to do."

CHAPTER EIGHTEEN

John ate a second helping of ham and hominy and drank a third cup of coffee. Missy, sitting at the dining-room table with him, said, "You were hungry, weren't you? I wish you'd take care of yourself. You look thin. It's not good for you to live all alone at Deerskin."

John started to say didn't she know he wouldn't be living at Deerskin much longer, and caught himself just in time. Missy's not having mentioned his going into the government meant it was still a secret. She would be bubbling over if she knew. He said:

"If I'm thin, I'm glad. I needed to lose some weight."

"Lose any more and you'll be a beanpole. You must have lost ten pounds. What made you come to town? You and Papa didn't have a fight, did you?"

"Of course not. What gave you that idea?"

"Papa's voice, I guess. I could hear him through the door and I thought he sounded angry. Was it about Cam?"

"Yes, in part."

Missy looked tired and pale. "Poor Cam. I thought it was bad before, with him and Papa fighting all the time, but this is even worse. Where is he, Johnny? Haven't you found out anything at all?"

John shook his head. "Tell me about you. How's Gordon? What's the news?"

Missy looked at him soberly. There were faint blue circles under her eyes, John noticed, and the eyes themselves, which he always thought of as bright and lively, were dull and troubled, not far from tears. Reaching for her hand, John said, "Something's wrong. What

241

is it? Tell me," and Missy, shrugging her shoulders, said, "It's—oh, I don't know. *Everything!* Cam's gone, Papa's sick and getting more and more bad-tempered all the time, just because he's sick and worried and has too much to do, and then these spells of Mama's on top of it all——" She stopped abruptly, giving him a guarded glance. "Did Papa tell you about the other night?"

"Yes, he did."

Missy touched her fingers to her eyes. "It was awful, Johnny. Mama's had bad spells before, but never one like that. She didn't even know me. All the time she kept weeping and screaming, saying they were trying to burn us up and had murdered Cam somewhere in the woods. She's so *afraid* of them, Johnny, even little Septima. Just last night she said that Septima was trying to poison her and that she could taste something bitter in a glass of water."

The tears, so valiantly restrained, could be held back no longer. Through them, and with her head raised higher, as if trying to rise above the humiliation they imposed, Missy said, "I'm frightened, Johnny. I don't know what to do. Papa doesn't seem to realize it, and neither does Dr. Carpenter, but I'm afraid Mama is losing her mind."

John reached for her hand again. "You get hold of yourself. If you start imagining things——"

"I'm *not* imagining things!" Missy said. "Listen to me, Johnny! Don't treat me the way Papa does, as if I didn't have sense enough to fill a thimble. I mean what I say! Mama's not herself any more. She hasn't been since Cam went away. Do you know what she said this morning when I went in to see her after breakfast? She said, 'Why do you have on your best dress?'—this old thing, she meant. 'Have you not been told that it is unseemly for a young lady to wear her best clothes to school?' You see what I mean, Johnny? You *see!* She thinks I'm still at Huntington Hall."

Two big, slow tears rolled down Missy's cheeks. "Here, use this," John said, and after she wiped her eyes with his handkerchief and sniffed discreetly, he said, "That's no way to blow a nose. It won't come off," but Missy was beyond cheering. "She's losing her mind, Johnny. I know she is. What are we going to do?"

"I'll have to think. Have you discussed this with Father?"

"Yes, but not really," Missy said. "I tried to, but he wouldn't listen. You know the way he is when he shuts his mind. He says it's all because of Mama's nerves and that she ought to go to the springs. But when she doesn't even *know* me, Johnny, and thinks I'm still at Huntington Hall——"

"Perhaps it's the laudanum," John said. "You know what it is, don't you? A derivative of opium. It could be, if Mother has been taking too much of it——"

Missy's eyes opened wider. She said, "Do you really think so? Yes, that *could* be it, couldn't it?" and her face so shone with relief that John wished he had not floated such a frail, perilous straw. "That's just a guess on my part, you understand," he said. "I don't want to build up any false hopes. And perhaps Father is right. It could be only her nerves."

"Oh, Johnny, you know better than that! You know as well as I do——"

"I'll talk it over with Dr. Carpenter," John said. "Meanwhile there's one thing I've made up my mind about. We'll have to get someone to stay with you. This is too much for you to handle alone. What about Aunt Mary Nesbitt? She's been wanting to make a visit, and now seems like a good time."

"No, Johnny, absolutely no." Missy sat up straight. "Aunt Mary Nesbitt is seventy-five years old and so crippled with rheumatism she can hardly move. Besides, she's almost as bad about them as Mama, except that she's able to hide it better. I don't need Aunt Mary Nesbitt. What I wish, though——"

"Yes?"

"Oh, it's no use. You wouldn't."

"Wouldn't what?"

Missy looked at him steadily. "Come here to live. You don't have to bury yourself at Deerskin. You could look after it from town just as well. That's what Papa does with his properties. Why can't you?"

Though it wasn't as simple as Missy made it sound, with a few rearrangements it could be managed. Except that it was impossible.

Matters had been taken out of his hands and he wasn't going to be a planter any longer. Not for some time, anyway.

"Won't you, Johnny?" Missy said. "It would be good for everybody. You're the only one Papa will listen to, even a little, and I know that Mama, if you came to live with us——"

"I can't, Missy. I'm going away."

Missy stared at him. "Going away? Where? Do you have to?"

Of course he didn't have to. For him to refuse Senator Stanhope's offer would disappoint his father, but by any sensible measure his place was here. Except that it was still impossible. The matter was settled and he was glad to have it settled. He said:

"You mustn't say anything about this, not yet, but Senator Stanhope has been named to the cabinet of the new government. I'm to be on his staff."

He expected Missy's face to light up and a rush of excitement to come, and it suddenly struck him as she looked at him quietly, saying nothing, that this wasn't quite the same Missy any more. He said:

"Now that you know that much, you might as well know the rest of it. Father more or less took things into his own hands. He helped line up support for Senator Stanhope, and now the Senator is paying off his debt. It seems that I was made part of the deal."

"That's not true," Missy said. "Senator Stanhope wanted you from the very beginning. Arbell told me."

"*Arbell* told you?"

Missy's face brightened somewhat. "All these great big secrets," she said. "But you're wrong in thinking it was Father's idea. Senator Stanhope's the one who brought it up, weeks and weeks ago. Arbell heard him talking about it to Lydia. He said he would rather have you on his staff than anyone he knew. His wanting you may have caused Father to help him, that's true enough, but it was the Senator who thought of it first."

Perhaps, John thought; just perhaps. He and Senator Stanhope had been on purely formal terms since the Senator's marriage to Lydia—in all that time he had set foot in the Stanhope house but twice, once for a New Year's Eve party he could not get out of, and once when Lydia had that English author in tow. Why, then, out of the blue, should the Senator want him on his staff? Apparently his father had been truthful in saying it had been Senator Stanhope's idea, and he could feel he wasn't completely a pawn, but something, somewhere, was left unexplained.

"So you knew all about it?"

"I knew that much," Missy said, "what I told you. But I didn't know if it was just talk, or what, and certainly I didn't know the Senator had got what he was after. Or what Lydia was after. By all rights, she's the one who should be in the cabinet."

"Why do you say that?"

"You know why," Missy said, "you know perfectly well why," and there might have been the faintest trace of sarcasm in her voice. "Why do you want to pretend?" she asked. "Lydia is possessed to *be* somebody. You know that. Arbell says she won't be content until the Senator is President."

John wished he could change the subject: there were too many pitfalls. He said, "Does she now? That's very interesting. And she still talks too much, I see."

"No, not really. Just to me."

"Let's not get off on Arabella. Do you understand why I can't come here to live, much as I'd like to?"

Missy watched him closely, grave and composed. "Yes, Johnny, I understand. And don't worry about me. I'll be able to manage. But tell me. Is this what you want to do, being on the Senator's staff?"

John needed time to think. "That's a hard question. There's most likely to be a war, since so many people are insisting on it——"

"And you don't want to be left behind. Is that it? I wouldn't either, if I were a man."

"That's one way of putting it."

"You feel you have to do something, and it might as well be this. It hasn't been easy for you, has it, Johnny?"

"What hasn't?"

"This whole thing."

"No, it hasn't, now that you ask. But now, if you'll excuse me, I must be going. I enjoyed my breakfast."

"You ought to eat a good breakfast every morning. I don't like seeing you this thin. Would you like another cup of coffee?"

"No, three is enough. Besides, I'm due at the Stanhopes'. It may be that Father had nothing to do with this, as you ask me to believe, but he hasn't been above taking care of a few odds and ends."

"Like what?"

"Like arranging this appointment with the Senator."

"Don't blame him, Johnny. He can't help it. Do you think you'll be seeing Arbell?"

"Seeing her wasn't part of my plan."

"Now there you go again. You never give her a chance. You don't even try. Not even a little. I wish you'd be nicer to her."

"Now there *you* go again."

Missy shook her head. "No, this time it's different. It really is. I'm worried about her. She's all upset. She says she doesn't know what will happen to her when the Senator goes away."

"What are you talking about, she doesn't know what will happen to her? You make it sound as though she were going to be homeless."

Missy frowned. "You don't understand about Arbell. You don't want to. Everything's been different for her since the Senator married again. In a way, she might just as well be homeless right now."

"How can you ask me to believe anything like that? It's too ridiculous!"

"That's what you think. You don't know how hard it is for two women to live under the same roof. Lydia's made Arbell feel she gets in the way."

"Are you sure you know what you're talking about? This sounds like the Wednesday Afternoon Ladies Society to me."

"Does it? And have you ever stopped to consider that some of the things said at the Wednesday Afternoon Ladies Society may be true?"

"And is this true? Is that what you're saying?"

"Yes."

"How do you know?"

"Because I've seen it happen."

"Seen it happen?"

"Yes, with my own eyes. Little snubs and little impolitenesses. What you don't seem to realize is that that isn't Senator Stanhope's house any more. It's Lydia's. You always seemed inclined to take up for Lydia—why, I don't know——"

"Take up for her? What gave you that idea?"

"Lots of things, Johnny. You mustn't mind my saying so. And it's not true that I don't know why. You've been on her side from the very beginning. I could see it happening. You think she has been unfairly treated because of who she was, coming from Gunpowder Street and all, and so naturally——"

That he should be brought to confusion by Missy was a new experience for John. He said, "You credit me with too much charity. Someday you'll find out better. It's true that I think Mrs. Stanhope has been unfairly treated——"

"Mrs. Stanhope," Missy said.

"All right then, Lydia. It's true I think she has been unfairly treated, but I'm astonished I ever let it show. It's not that important to me. But you were saying that Arabella is upset over what will happen when the Senator leaves. Why? You're not implying that Lydia is trying to turn her out, are you?"

"Now who said anything silly as that? Even if things were that bad, as they aren't, Lydia wouldn't go that far. She wouldn't want to offend the Senator, just for one thing."

"What's the problem then? I don't understand."

"Well, the thing is that Arbell——"

But John was beginning to get bored. "Do you want a prediction? Your friend Arabella will move to the capital with the Senator, she will open up a whole new field of operations, and when things begin to get too dull for her, as apparently they are now, she will blow up another storm. I'm afraid I can't feel sorry for Arabella Stanhope."

"Sometimes you make me tired," Missy said. "You're getting more and more like Papa every day. You don't approve of Arbell and never have, and so everything she does is wrong. But that doesn't mean that everything Lydia does is right. I used to like her when she taught at Huntington Hall, but I don't any more. And she isn't kind to Arbell. That's the plain simple truth of it. I'm not saying it's all Lydia's fault or that Arbell isn't partially to blame, but things are getting to the point—— Oh, never mind! It doesn't matter. You're not interested a fig."

"That I can't wholly deny," John said. "But apparently it does matter, at least to you. What can I do about it, though? Be reasonable."

"You're right," Missy said. "There's nothing anyone can do. I just thought that if you saw Arbell you might try to be nice to her. Just for my sake. Will you?" and she went into her trick of fluttering her eyelids. "And do you want to know something else about Arbell?" she asked. "Something that will really make you mad? I think she's falling in love with Neville Monckton," and then, seeing the look on his face, "You see!" she said. "I knew you'd get mad. I'm sorry I told you. I should have let you find out from somebody else."

John rose from the table. He said, "Trust her to make a mess of things!" and Missy gave him an unhappy, pleading look. "Don't be too hard on her, Johnny," she said. "I shouldn't have told you. Besides, I don't know if it's really serious or not," and John came to the end of his patience.

"Of course it isn't serious!" he said. "When has anything been serious with her? Neville Monckton fools around with a fieldpiece and comes back a hero——"

"That's what I think too," Missy said. "That's it exactly. It all started at the ball the night of the parade, the one you wouldn't go to. Neville was there, wearing a brand-new uniform and with his arm in a sling, and Constance Pettibone was making a fool of herself, just as Arbell said she would——"

"Spare me the details," John said. "Constance Pettibone takes a shine to the handsome hero, and Arbella says, 'No, you can't have him. I'll show you who's boss,' and so, out of nothing but vanity——"

"That's not fair," Missy broke in. "I know Arabella gives some people that impression because of all the admirers she has, but it's not her fault. Can she be blamed for being so attractive?"

John started for the door. "Look, Missy. Defending Arabella is a waste of time. She's run through all the eligible men in town, and so now, with time on her hands——"

"You really don't like her, do you?" Missy said. "I used to think you merely pretended you didn't, and enjoyed being gruff, but now I know better. It's funny. Arbell says mean things about you sometimes, that you've turned into an old disagreeable hermit and things like that, but still, in all the years I've known her——"

"I have to go, Missy. I've wasted enough time as it is."

Missy pushed back her chair. "You're all upset about Arbell, aren't you?" she said, rising. "Is it because you think she shouldn't be having anything to do with Neville Monckton? Is that it? People say——"

"People will always say," John interrupted. "That's one of the basic laws. But this time your friend Arabella has truly given them something to chew on. Have you seen this morning's editorial in the *News*?"

"You know I hate editorials. What was it about?"

"It was about—what it was about was that Senator Stanhope no more belongs in the cabinet than my dog Tray, and that Arabella, as his daughter, should have more sense than to get involved with Neville Monckton."

"You're making it up. It didn't say that, did it?"

"Read it for yourself. People who hate editorials should be left to stew in their own ignorance. And now I'm going. Do you want to ride over to the Stanhopes' with me?"

"I have to stay with Mama. Dr. Carpenter hasn't come yet this morning, and I want to be here when he calls. And, Johnny——"

"Yes?"

"Promise me one thing."

"What?"

"That you don't worry about me. I'll be able to manage when you go away. I promise. You won't worry, will you?"

A year ago, six months ago, he would have said, "Worry? Of course I'll worry. How can I not?" but during the past few weeks some line had been crossed, some forward step taken, and this wasn't the same Missy any more. He said, "No, I won't worry," and bent down and kissed her cheek.

"What's that for?" Missy asked.

"For just this once. Don't get any notions."

"Never fear," Missy said. "I won't."

ii

It was a sign of Lydia's influence in the Stanhope household that the butler was in full plum-colored livery, with white silk stockings, and square silver buckles on his shoes. No other establishment in Pompey's Head went quite that far. Full livery was for high occasions only. The butler's finery—Amos, his name was—could be taken as another example of Lydia's increasing confidence. Amos answered John's knock, took his hat, showed him to the double parlor, asked him please to wait, and went off to find the Senator.

Left alone, John looked about the room. The curtains were looped back from the windows, and the bright sunlight, falling through a smell of wax and polish, splashed across the floor. The room, recently done over, looked different to John. He remembered it as more crowded, cluttered to the point of fussiness, and he noticed that the ancestral portraits were gone, the Senator's family tree. Missy was right: this wasn't the Senator's house any longer, it was Lydia's—her broom had swept clean, making it her own.

John's thoughts were interrupted by the strike of a clock on the mantel, starting the count of twelve. A second clock took up the strike in the hall, deeper and slower, and the returning silence, when finally the clocks were quiet, seemed heavier than before. A woman's voice broke into it, coming angry and muffled from somewhere on the upper floor. "Why must you object . . . everything I want to do . . . not accountable . . . if you imagine . . ." A quieter, firmer voice responded, less distinct ". . . your father . . . sense of obligation . . . not asking that you be accountable . . ." For a few moments, like the striking of the clocks, the two voices were merged in a heated argument that for an instant became markedly louder—"Always my father! Will you ever stop using him as an excuse!"—and was then ended abruptly by the slamming of a door.

Footsteps raced down the stairs, and John caught a glimpse of Arabella, in a dark brown riding habit, sweeping past the door. She must have caught sight of him at the last instant. She stopped, turned around, and entered the room.

"The master of Deerskin," she said. "Or should I say the hermit? To what, dear sir, do we owe this pleasure?"

"I'm calling on your father," John said, conscious too late of how wooden he sounded. "Amos has gone to say I'm here. I suspect the Senator must be in his office in the garden. Had I known——"

"And deprive us of this visit?" Arabella tilted her head slightly to one side. "We see you all too rarely as it is. How long has it been since you favored us with your presence? A year? Two? Truly, Mr. Bottomley, what a delicious surprise!"

John knew these moods and the meaning of this stilted language— Arabella, in a fit of temper, was taking it out on him. Uncomfortable at having been surprised in the role of eavesdropper, he said:

"Let's don't fight, Arabella. How have you been?"

Arabella held up her head and looked down her nose. "My health is excellent, Mr. Bottomley. How kind of you to ask," and then, in a sudden change of mood and with a gentler look in her eyes, "Oh, I'm all right, Johnny," she said. "And I didn't mean to be disagreeable. It's just that I never see you any more, and then, when I do, the first thing you say is that you're here only to call on Papa. You might have at least said good morning."

"You didn't give me a chance. The first thing you said was what was I doing here. I can think of more hospitable greetings."

Arabella began to smile. "Not only am I graceless, I'm bad-tempered. Let's start all over. I'll see what I can remember from my lessons in deportment. Good morning, Mr. Bottomley. How happy I am to see you. Won't you sit down? And have we not been having a delightful spell of weather lately?"

"Yes, we have," John said. "We were able to get nearly all our planting done," and Arabella, after a moment of trying not to, broke into a laugh. She said, "I never put much faith in what I was told about using the weather to begin a conversation, but apparently I should. So you were able to get nearly all your planting done, were you? How interesting! Tell me more, Mr. Bottomley. How many acres do you have under cultivation this year?"

John could feel himself getting angry—only Arabella could make him feel so completely a clod. Taking advantage of the years they had known each other, he said, "Aren't you ever going to grow up?" and Arabella forced back another laugh.

"Ah, Johnny, that's a grievous problem. I must work at it harder. Will you help me? Say the word and I'll place myself entirely in your hands."

She tilted her head to one side again, and apparently decided she had gone too far. She said, "How's Missy? It's too bad she couldn't come riding this morning. Please sit down. Amos moves like cold molasses these days, slower, even——"

At the sound of footsteps her eyes darted toward the stairs. In a moment Lydia appeared in the doorway. She wore a silk gown of palest blue, and her light blond hair, drawn back across her ears so that only their tips were showing, was caught in a bun at the nape of her neck. She glanced from John to Arabella and back again to John. Arabella looked at her more forthrightly, pressing her lips together, and in the contrast of her dark brown riding habit and Lydia's pale blue gown, her high coloring and Lydia's blondness, it was Lydia who looked the more virginly innocent. She held out her hand to John, saying, "Mr. Bottomley. I had no idea you were here. Does the Senator know?" and Arabella said disdainfully, "That's to be wondered. Amos is supposed to be telling Papa, but I wouldn't be surprised if he wasn't making the rounds of the yard, showing off his pretty new suit. Did you notice it, John? Plum, it seems, is the height of fashion."

John was confounded by the deliberateness of the cut. His mind went back to the picnic at Happy Chance, when Arabella had said to Lydia, "Thank you again for letting me be night-blooming catch-fly, Miss Chadwick. I'm ever so grateful," and he had the sense of a door being thrown wide open and of looking into a stale, closed-off room strewn with the debris of a hundred bitter quarrels dragged across the years.

But not for a moment did Lydia lose her poise. She gave Arabella what might be taken as a tolerant, even affectionate smile. She said, "In that case, my dear, since I know your father would not want to keep Mr. Bottomley waiting, you might make sure that Amos isn't dawdling around the yard, as you say. You don't mind, do you?" and though she could not have spoken in a kindlier voice, John wanted to interpose himself between it and Arabella—Arabella had asked for this rebuke (more than asked: gone out of her way to insist on it), but the contest was too unequal.

A deep flush spread across Arabella's cheeks—not to mind was not to mind having been sent packing like a servant. She said, "I'm afraid Mr. Bottomley will have to depend on Amos. I promised Mary Montague and some of the others that I would join them for a ride, and I don't want to keep them waiting," and though she tried to make the best of it, holding up her head in a stiff, unnatural fashion, her rout was complete. "Good-by, Johnny," she said. "Come back to see us again, without its being just to call on Papa," and as she left the room, sweeping her eyes past Lydia, it came as a surprise to John that he could feel so drawn to her—granted the bad manners of her wanting to make a show of crossing swords with Lydia, for whatever sulky reason, it seemed a larger offense on Lydia's part to have brought her to such humiliation.

Arabella's departure did nothing to lessen the embarrassment in the room. As though addressing herself to it, Lydia said, "I'm afraid that Arbell isn't herself today. It's not like her to be in such a temper," and though the implication was one of kindliness, of tolerant, affectionate sympathy, it was actually a wholesale lie—Arabella was as much herself as ever she was, it *was* like her to be in such a temper, and now, under the guise of tolerance and sympathy, a last volley was being sent in her direction.

Lydia's eyes wandered about the room in an abstracted, far-off fashion, as though her thoughts were still trailing after Arabella, and for a moment John thought he was about to be free of her at last.

A mist began to lift, and through its partial dissolution, as though gazing upon some tranquil landscape, he saw how blessed it might be—the solace, the emancipation, the unspeakable relief.

Lydia turned to him. "How good it is to see you, Mr. Bottomley. Won't you make yourself comfortable?" and though she spoke merely the conventions of courtesy, the goodwife seeing to it that a visitor was made to feel at home, there was a warmth in her voice, a note of intimacy lightly struck, that he was not prepared for. She rested her fingers on his arm, saying, "Come, Mr. Bottomley. Do sit down," seemingly unaware of the movement of her hand, and when he looked into her clear blue eyes, noticing that the three tiny pale freckles on the bridge of her nose were still there, he knew how wrong he had been to imagine, even for an instant, that he had escaped her or that he wanted to.

Composing herself on a sofa and arranging the folds of her skirts, Lydia motioned him to a nearby chair. She said, "I can't imagine what's keeping the Senator, unless it's another office seeker. It was only this morning that it became known that he is in the cabinet, but already he is being besieged," and that Senator Stanhope was in the cabinet, from the way she spoke, was in no way to be remarked upon but rather to be taken as the most natural thing in the world. John recalled her saying, at the picnic at Happy Chance, "I was wrong in calling this a race meeting, wasn't I? It's simply a race," and once again, as on that earlier occasion, he was impressed by how fast she learned—yesterday she was Mrs. Senator Stanhope, with a courtesy title only, and today she was the wife of a cabinet member, yet if she was gratified by her swift advance or pleased with this latest flowering of her ambition, in no way did she permit it to show. Success would seem to have softened her: she appeared self-effacing to the point of meekness: the ladies of the Wednesday Afternoon Ladies Society would be confounded again. John said:

"I would like to offer my congratulations, Mrs. Stanhope. The Senator has brought distinction to us all."

"It's generous of you to say so," Lydia said. "I fear, however, that

not everyone will agree. You saw the editorial in the *News* this morning, I suppose."

"Yes, I did. But I question its being an editorial. I'd say it was
more a case of sour grapes."

Lydia looked at him gravely. "Yes, perhaps so. But that makes it
none the easier to bear. What is it the poet says? The fangs that wildly
strike are no less venomed in their sting—is that it? I can't remember.
I haven't had quite as much time for poetry since I left Huntington
Hall."

Her reference to Huntington Hall took John by surprise. What was
she trying to say?—that she was now so secure that she might boldly
refer to her former status? That though she was aware how some people had used it against her, she depended on his larger understanding? Or was it her way of hinting, most delicately, that she too remembered the picnic at Happy Chance? The silence would have become
uncomfortable had not she spoken again.

"Tell me, Mr. Bottomley. Do you think we will be able to effect a
peaceful separation, or must we have a war? I have seen so little of
you that I have not had the chance to hear your views. I would value
them greatly."

She turned her grave look on him again, waiting attentively, and
he did not discount that it could be flattery. He was sure there were
other views she had valued greatly. He said:

"My views? I doubt they're worth discussing."

"I hear otherwise."

"In that case, I'm afraid you hear wrong. I shouldn't even call them
views. Sentiments would be nearer the mark."

"Very well then. Your sentiments."

It became for an instant a little unreal. Mrs. Senator Stanhope she
might be, the wife of a cabinet minister, but at the same time she
was also Lydia Chadwick, whose breasts had yielded to his kisses, and
not so long ago that she could have possibly forgotten. The room
seemed suddenly to grow warm and close, still and airless as the hush
of the greenhouse, and why were they sitting here, she the lady of

the manor and he the gentleman caller, making this forced conversation? He said:

"My sentiments are these—that the chances of war are greater than the chances of peace, and that we are mistaken to believe we are bound to win if war comes. Beyond that, I have not thought, nor much cared to think."

"Beyond that, I do not see how anyone can think," Lydia said. "But do you not paint a gloomy picture, Mr. Bottomley? Follow your trepidations to the end and see us defeated, and will we not all be ruined?"

She lowered her eyes, gazing at the floor, and John thought it was as if she had heard the distant tolling of a bell, solemn as curfew across the swamps. "Lydia's possessed to be somebody," little Missy had said, but now little Missy only in the sense that she came barely to his chin on tiptoe, older and wiser and nobody's fool. Lydia was possessed to be somebody, and the possessed was in possession at last—house, barns, stables, chattels, rice fields, cotton lands. But if war came, and with war defeat——

Lydia shook her head. "We left the North because our tempers were such that we could no longer live under the same roof. We were divorced for reasons of incompatibility. Must a war be waged to force us back into a union that was found so disagreeable on both sides? Shall the poor South suffer further?"

But not only the poor South. The poor South and poor Lydia. The poor possessor dispossessed. Her eyes, meeting his, begged for comfort—war might still be avoided: should it come, the South might win with one bold stroke: all would be then as it was now, but sounder and more secure: why raise the hobgoblin specter of ruin?

John permitted himself a repressed smile—this appealing blond presence, this air of virginal innocence, this promise of ecstasy, and at bottom the soul of a greedy clerk—how could he imagine himself in love with such a woman? Having for once the upper hand, he was not inclined to show any mercy. He said:

"*Delenda est Carthago.* They planted it with salt, you will remember, and there are many elder Catos in the North. To them we are the new Carthage, fit only to be destroyed as the old one was. They have not hesitated to say so. They have even mentioned the planting of salt."

But Lydia was being pressed too far. "Abolitionists!" she said. "How I hate them!" and some instinct must have told her that John had been deliberately turning the screws. Her voice changed tone, becoming higher and more metallic. "I do believe you are trying to frighten me, Mr. Bottomley. If not, yours is too dark a picture. And my own inclination is to be much more hopeful. The Senator has insisted from the first that we shall be able to go our way in peace, without a war, and, until it is proved otherwise, I must follow his way of thinking."

"I would not wish to question the Senator's opinion," John said, "nor would I want to argue the correctness of my own. I grant I may be too pessimistic. You would not be the first to find me so. I regret I cannot be more sanguine."

Lydia meditated a moment. "Is it completely a matter of sanguineness?" she asked. "Must we not rely on faith and courage? Is it well to admit defeat before the issue is joined?" and though he had not impugned the value of faith or courage, nor admitted defeat, John was too preoccupied to answer—what she was saying was in its essence what Ules Monckton had said in the final moments of the conversation that led to the duel: "I am sorry you are not with us, sir. The South needs all its sons."

John was surprised how little the rebuke meant to him. More interesting was the problem it posed. Was he to take Lydia's remarks to mean she disapproved of him, and, if so, why had he been offered a place on Senator Stanhope's staff? Her slightest show of opposition would have caused him to drop the idea immediately. Though he knew that there had to be an explanation, John could not imagine what it was. He said:

"Faith and courage never hurt anyone yet. I am not sure, however, in this particular instance, if I understand what is meant by faith."

"Faith in our cause," Lydia said, "faith that right and justness must prevail," and she might have gone on to elaborate, warming to her rhetoric, had not Senator Stanhope come striding into the room. "Ah, John," he said. "Welcome, welcome!" and his voice reminded John of a ripe, juicy peach—it was a new way of speaking for the Senator, and there was something new about his appearance also. Fifty-eight when he married Lydia, he was now sixty-three. Time was beginning to creep up on him—the lines in his face deeper; his frame considerably heavier, especially around the waist; his hair gone completely white and beginning noticeably to thin—but the change went beyond these unkind corrosions of advanced middle age. "I'm sorry I was detained," he said. "I had to listen to a hard-luck story from a man who wants a government job. He's the fifth this morning. You would think my pockets are lined with plums," and what the change was, John decided, was that his face was diffused by a glow of self-satisfaction that appeared to have enlarged all his features by the minutest fraction of an inch.

"This applicant?" Lydia asked. "Who was he?"

"Man named Ransome," the Senator replied. "He claims kinship to those Ransomes on Little River. Says he used to work in the ordnance department in Washington, but I wouldn't be surprised if he was stringing a long bow."

"You got rid of him, I hope."

"I most certainly did," the Senator said emphatically. "I told him I couldn't do anything for him now, since the department isn't organized yet, but that if he was so minded he could come see me in the capital."

"Was that a good idea?" Lydia asked. "Will he not take it as a promise? If you let your kindness sway you, and are not firm with them, you will have your hands full."

"Now don't you worry about me, my dear," the Senator said. "I've had some experience in these matters before, remember," and though he spoke confidently in that new rich voice of his, it was clear he was afraid he had risked Lydia's displeasure. "Besides," he said, "it's one of the penalties of public office. One has to make oneself available to petitioners. It's a bore and a nuisance, but it has to be done." He smiled benignly, first at Lydia and then at John, and it was not hard to understand why he had acquired his reputation for pomposity when he was in Washington.

"I'm glad it's you who has to put up with them," Lydia said. "I'm afraid I'd lack the patience."

"Yes, my dear, I daresay you would," the Senator said, laughing. "But you leave these matters to me. It's enough I have to be bothered, without their bothering you."

"They don't bother me," Lydia said. "I just don't want you to be badgered to death, that's all."

"I won't be, you can depend on that." The Senator smiled complacently and turned to John. "Well sir! It's good to see you. How is the Governor this morning?"

"Cross as a bear. He's sick in bed again."

Senator Stanhope laughed again. Since John could find little that was amusing in his father's irritability, and even less in his being sick, he decided that the Senator, in his flush of well-being, just wanted to laugh. "The trouble with the Governor is that he won't admit to the ills that flesh is heir to, or to any ills at all. Instead of looking upon them as indispositions, he sees them as personal insults." He beamed at John, holding himself at his full height, and the exuberance he felt seemed actually to seep through his pores. He said, "But I'm not worried about the Governor. He'll live to be a hundred. Will you join me in a toddy? Dealing with office seekers always did give me a thirst," and John, who had noticed that Lydia was watching the Senator in a constrained, reined-in manner, with a tight expression around her eyes, began to feel edgy—Lydia glanced at him, and he was not quick enough to avoid her glance, and what she said in the masked exchange was that she knew he was embarrassed for her husband and that she was a little embarrassed too.

"And your mother, Mr. Bottomley?" she asked. "How is she? I hear she's not been well."

"My mother appears to be some better," John replied, knowing that she and the Senator were acquainted with every detail of the situation. "According to Dr. Carpenter, it's mostly nerves."

"Nerves can be a bad thing," the Senator said, lending himself to the game. "My own mother was troubled with them all her life. And she lived to the ripe old age of ninety-two." Mrs. Bottomley's illness, however, was too disturbing an element: the Senator had happier things to think about. He said, "Well sir, what about that toddy?" and then, to Lydia, "Could I pour you a glass of sherry, my dear?"

Lydia shook her head. "No, I think I will leave you two men to yourselves." She rose from the sofa and nodded to John. "Good-by, Mr. Bottomley. I hope your visits will be more frequent in the future."

"Of course they will!" Senator Stanhope said. "If he's here for the reason I hope he is, we will be seeing each other right along." He beamed another smile at John and brought it to bear on Lydia. "There's no reason for you to leave us, my dear. We have nothing to say that can't be said in your presence. Besides, we enjoy your company. Isn't that right, John?"

"Yes. Certainly."

"You see!" the Senator said. "Now you make yourself comfortable again and join us in our talk. John understands I have no secrets from you. Do you imagine he thinks you don't know why he's here or that we haven't been talking about him a great deal lately?"

"Senator!" Lydia said.

Just what the Senator's mistake had been, John couldn't understand. The sharpness and dryness of Lydia's voice, however, made him suspect that it was more than an error of overexuberance into which the Senator had been led by more toddies than he was accustomed to in the morning.

"What have I done now?" the Senator said, making a show of being baffled. "All I said, if I recall——"

"Never mind," Lydia said. "If Mr. Bottomley doesn't object to your saying how clever he is, neither should I. And now, Mr. Bottomley, if you will excuse me, I truly must go." She paused and looked at the Senator. "You haven't invited anybody to dinner without telling me, have you?"

"To dinner? No, of course not. But if John here——"

"No, thank you, Senator," John said hastily. "Much as I would like to, I can't. They're expecting me at home."

"Are you sure you're not able to join us?" Lydia asked.

"Some other time perhaps, if I may."

John bowed to her, and Lydia, her small back held rigid and straight, left the room. Senator Stanhope watched her depart, and with a half-humorous, half-baffled expression shook his head. "Women!" he said. "Damned if I'll ever be able to understand them. Expect them to jump one way, and they're bound to jump the other. It's a hopeless proposition." But not so hopeless, at that particular moment, as to cause him much concern. "Why don't we stop talking about that toddy and start mixing it? Then we can settle ourselves for a good long talk. You didn't come here to disappoint me, did you?"

"I hope not."

"So do I. Look here, John. Why don't we get it over with? We know each other well enough to dispense with the ceremonies. Are you going to accept?"

"Yes, Senator, I'm going to accept. That's what I came to say."

The Senator's hand shot out and clapped John on the shoulder. "That's what I was hoping. I'm delighted, delighted," and though he meant what he said and showed his delight unmistakably, it seemed to John that he was really delighting in himself. He gripped John's hand and pressed it firmly. "I can't tell you how pleased I am. Yes sir, this is all I needed to finish off my day. I've changed my mind about that toddy. Let's have a little celebration and open a bottle of wine instead." He became quite tipsy before John had to leave.

CHAPTER NINETEEN

"Pass me the sugar, will you, Johnny?" Missy said at breakfast a few mornings later, and then, as he handed her the bowl across the table, "Your arm's much better, isn't it?" she added. "I notice you aren't favoring it the way you used to. Does it hurt any more?"

"Only when it's cold or damp. Other than that, and except when I bend it too quickly, it bothers me hardly at all."

"I'm glad," Missy said. "But is that the best you can straighten it? Will it always hang a little crooked like that?"

"Yes, I'm afraid so," John said, flexing his arm. "And it's nice of you to call it a little. By actual measurement it's a good inch and a half shorter than the other."

"I'm so sorry. Do you mind?"

"Not much. Not any more. I'm getting used to it, and better this than a bullet through my brain."

Missy shuddered. "Don't say that. It makes my blood run cold."

"It doesn't exactly make mine run warm. How was the Wendovers' party last night?"

"All right, I reckon."

"Don't you know? What happened? Did you catch Gordon flirting?"

"Clever man," Missy said. "You should have been in *The Rivals* last night. You could have been Bob Acres—odds chiggers, blushes and blooms, and all the rest of those things he says."

"A blustering coward, eh?"

Missy put down her fork. "You know I didn't mean it that way. You can twist things around more than any man I know."

"Can I?" John smiled. "Let me twist something else around then. It isn't odds chiggers. It's odds *triggers*. Perhaps you should have been Mrs. Malaprop."

"Oh petunia," Missy said. "Chiggers or triggers, why bother? Besides, chiggers makes more sense. At least down here it does." She looked at him suspiciously. "Are you sure it isn't chiggers?"

"I'm sure," John said. "The man who wrote that play didn't have the benefit of knowing about our low-country insects. But why so glum? Has anything gone wrong?"

Missy stopped eating. "No, not exactly. I just feel blue. Everybody is going away. Arbell leaves this afternoon, and all the men have been ordered back to the forts. There's talk of most of them having to go to Virginia, should war break out. And in a few days, when you leave——"

"Cheer up," John said. "I don't think you'll be completely deserted. Those fellows will find ways of getting home from the forts, and even from a war. Tell me more about the party. Who was there?"

"The usual," Missy said. "The same old crowd." Sipping from a cup of coffee, she looked at him over the cup's rim. "Kitty Williams was there."

"Was she?"

Missy nodded. "It was the first party she's been to since Cam did what he did."

John Bottomley felt a drain of fatigue. Absent, Cameron had never been more present. Missy said, "Poor Kitty, I've never felt sorrier for anyone," and it seemed to John he had no choice—Allbright would have to be turned over to the sheriff. Cameron had been gone for more than a month and only Allbright might know where he was. John said:

"How is Kitty taking it?"

"How would you take it?" Missy said, putting down her cup. "It's been a terrible thing for her. She might as well have been left standing at the altar. She's been up to Flat Rock in the mountains, but I can't see that it did her much good. What's a few weeks? It will be months, years even, before she can forget what happened. If ever she does."

"I didn't know she'd gone to Flat Rock."

"I thought I told you," Missy said. "Mrs. Williams took her there a few days after it happened. The hardest thing last night was how dear Kitty was to me. It made me almost want to cry, seeing her try to join in the fun and pretending that nothing had happened. She's one of the dearest girls I know. Why did Cam do it? How *could* he?"

Not even her love for Cameron could quell her anger—Kitty Williams was one of the dearest girls she knew, a bosom friend, and for once Cameron could not be defended. "Haven't you been able to find out anything?" Missy asked. "Are you sure you aren't holding something back?" and John's margin of choice shrank to narrower proportions—it went against his every principle to turn Allbright over to the sheriff, and more sharply against every instinct, but what could he do? Time was running out. In less than a week he would be gone from Pompey's Head.

"You are holding something back, aren't you?" Missy said.

Cameron's saddle in Allbright's shop, a bundle of workingman's clothes, and a letter that could be either M or W—— John was forced to evade again. He said:

"I'm just as disappointed as you are. I'd hoped to learn something by now, but I haven't. I'm as much in the dark as ever."

Missy's thoughts were turned inward. She said solemnly, "Do you think we will ever see him again?" and the pause that followed her question pulled at John's heart—for what she was saying by her silence was that the breaking off of even the most casual relation is often a painful amputation, leaving torn, dangling tissues that want to be restored, and so how was one to adjust to the loss of a brother not taken by death, which by death's grace would have permitted death's grief and finality, but wandering homeless, no one knew where, across the face of the earth?

John said, "Yes, Missy, I think we'll see him again. It will come out all right in the end," and he hastened to change the subject. "Are you going to town this morning?" he asked. "I'll drive you in the buggy if you are. Father's asked me to have a look at one of those houses Mother owns in the Channel. Mr. Roundtree is sick again, and something's wrong with the roof."

He waited for Missy to answer, and, when she fell deeper into silence, he realized it had been a mistake to mention Mr. Roundtree and the Channel. It was Mr. Roundtree's frequent illnesses that gave Cameron an excuse to collect their mother's rent money, keeping it for himself. "Why don't you come to town with me?" John said, reaching for her hand. "It'll cheer you up. We'll go the long way, by way of the woods. The jasmine and honeysuckle ought to be coming out, warm as it is."

Missy watched the movement of his sleeve as he brought it back across the table. "I'm glad your arm's all right," she said. "I was afraid you'd be a cripple. I said my prayers."

"I said mine too. How about it? Are you coming with me?"

"How long will you be?"

"An hour or so."

Missy thought a few moments. "I'd like to, but I think I'd best stay home. Dr. Carpenter is coming to see Mama and I don't want to miss him. How did she seem to you this morning?"

John wished she hadn't asked. He had found his mother so pale and wasted that he did not see how she could endure much longer. Missy said, "I can't see she's any better, can you? Except that she knows who I am." She paused, looking off into space. "Do you remember how beautiful she used to be?" she asked. "You want to hear something funny?"

"What?"

"Do you know that ten-dollar gold piece I used to have?"

"No, I can't say I do."

"You wouldn't. It was a long time ago. You were at Princeton." Missy stared across the table, her eyes wide open. "Papa gave me the gold piece for my birthday. How old would I have been? Six? Seven? It doesn't matter. Papa gave it to me and it was fresh from the mint. I put it away in my box, and sometimes, when I wanted to do a very secret thing, I'd go to my room and look at it. The secret was how beautiful and shiny it was and that it was all my very own. You don't understand, do you?"

"Yes, I think I do."

"Not long after my birthday, the next week maybe, we moved from Rosebank and came here to Indigo. There was a big party. Mama had a new white dress, and because I'd had a birthday I was old enough to stand beside her when the guests arrived. Mama looked beautiful. Whenever I want to remember how beautiful she was, I close my eyes and think of her in her white dress. She *was* beautiful, wasn't she?"

"Yes," John said. "She was."

"I suppose you're wondering what this has to do with my ten-dollar gold piece," Missy said. "That's the next part. Because of its being such a special party I was allowed to stay up late. Past eight o'clock, I mean. And then, after Elnora undressed me and I was in bed, supposed to be asleep, I got up and opened my box with the ten-dollar gold piece, just to see if the secret was there and still mine. But the thing is that when I opened the box how beautiful Mama was was mine too, a brand-new secret. And when I put the gold piece back in the box, I put Mama in her white dress back in the box too. You don't understand, do you? I don't blame you." She was silent for a few moments. "Silly old me," she said. "I broke the box and spent the gold piece. And now Mama is the way she is." She shut off her thoughts and turned to him. "What did you say you were going to the Channel for?"

"To look at one of those houses of Mama's. There seems to be a leak in the roof. Are you sure you don't want to come to town with me? You can buy yourself a new hat."

"Without Papa's permission? The way he is these days? I wouldn't dare."

"I'll treat you."

"Not this morning, Johnny. I don't want to miss Dr. Carpenter. If I leave him to talk with Papa, all I'll get is that it's just Mama's nerves. Besides, I promised Arbell I'd go over to her house around noon for early dinner. She's leaving on the four o'clock train, you know. Have you told her good-by?"

"Why should I? I'll be seeing her in a week or so. You tell her good-by for me."

"All right, I will," Missy said. "It's going to be lonesome for me around here without Arbell. I'll miss her. I'll miss you too. I'll miss everybody."

"Poor Polly-sit-by-the-fire," John said. "Sorry though I am for you, it's time for me to be getting to town."

"Are you going to be here for dinner?"

John pondered a second. "I'll be eating all alone, won't I?"

"Yes, I'm afraid so. Unless you want a plate in Papa's room."

"That I could forgo. I stopped in to say good morning and we had a session that lasted for nearly an hour. And me without so much as a cup of coffee. Perhaps I'd better eat at the club."

"Yes," Missy agreed, "perhaps you'd better. And will you do something for me while you're in town, Johnny?"

"What?"

"Buy me a twist of thread at Mr. Kirkland's?"

"A twist of thread? For God's sake! Can't you send William or Esau?"

"I could, but if I sent one of them downtown just for that and Papa should happen to want him——"

John gave in. "All right. What kind of thread?"

"Green silk, number fifty. At Mr. Kirkland's."

"I'll try to remember."

"Green silk, number fifty," Missy repeated. "You're a dear to do it for me," and all of a sudden she began to laugh. "Something just struck me," she said, struggling to keep her face straight. "One of the under-secretaries of the new government buying a twist of green silk thread. Wait till I tell Arbell."

"You say anything and I'll——"

"I won't," Missy said, going through another struggle with her face. "She'd give you no peace. Before you knew it you would be under-secretary in charge of green silk thread. It's funny though. Don't you think it's funny?"

"What I think, you already know," John said. "That intelligence of yours still reminds me of a bird with a broken wing."

"Sticks and stones," Missy said. "I'll see you when you get home. Don't forget my thread."

ii

Driving to town in a buggy, John passed through the same woods he had traveled with Jeremiah Lake and Robert Blackford the morning he fought his duel with Ules Monckton. He could remember the woods from an earlier time, when Indigo was built. They were then a dense, virginal wilderness, splendid with game.

It had bothered Corwin Bottomley not to own the woods. The five thousand acres of Rosebank had affirmed a habit of privacy. A month after he moved his family to Indigo, Corwin bought the woods, and then, finding they were too much of a jungle for his sense of order to live with, he dispatched a gang of workmen to tidy them up. The men cleared away brush, sawed fallen timbers, built a narrow road that led to the outskirts of Pompey's Head, dug out a boggy place watered by several springs and transformed it into a pond, cut a network of bridle paths, and otherwise accomplished Corwin Bottomley's idea of what a proper woods should look like. The work took over a year. When it was completed Corwin announced that henceforward the woods were to be known as Bottomley Woods. Though it pleased him to think of himself in partnership with nature, it would have been unlike him not to establish who was senior partner. The name became part of local reference and the woods a favorite riding place. They also attracted poachers.

John rarely entered the tract, even if only for a short ride, without being rewarded with a sense of release and renewal. Today, however, as he guided the buggy along the narrow dirt road that wound its way to town, holding the reins loose and giving the horse its head, he hardly noticed his surroundings. Debate shut him off, the question of Allbright and the sheriff—if it had to be done, why wait any longer? Get Allbright to talk and the whole mystery of Cameron's disappearance might be solved within the hour. He had wavered long enough. Soon as he finished his business in the Channel he would drive to the sheriff's office and have Allbright brought in. Yet never had he felt more unsettled in his mind. The sheriff was not a man to waste much time, and Allbright was not the sort of man the sheriff would want to waste much time with. As much as his spirit, John's flesh rebelled.

A bright shaft of green, tree-top high, flashed across the road. His attention engaged, John brought the buggy to a halt. Searching the branches of a tree into which the dart of green had disappeared, he detected, moving along one of the lower limbs, a small green parrot with a yellow head. To see one of these little birds nowadays was an event. Slaughtered by the thousands for their plumage, they were becoming increasingly rare. The parrot began to preen itself, working its bill first under one wing and then the other, croaking softly and fluffing its feathers. A woodpecker rapped in another part of the woods, loud and clear, and the parrot, alerted, turned its head in a watchful, suspicious circle that made John smile. He lit a cigar and sat watching the parrot.

The problem of Allbright and the sheriff, however, weighed no less heavily on his mind. He could see the barber clearly, his thick coarse features, his heavy jowls, the big liver spot on one cheek, and though Allbright was wearing his most aggravating Pork Chops/Ham Gravy expression, with his head hunched forward and the dog-on-a-leash look in his eyes, there was such a show of hurt and accusation on his face that John involuntarily turned the other way.

The parrot croaked softly in the branches overhead. The woodpecker rapped again. A blue jay called. Some small animal scurried through the leaves. Shut off once more, John decided that the course to take, instead of calling in the sheriff, was to go to Allbright's shop and have another talk with him. It was his own anger that had caused things to get out of hand the other day. He must approach the barber on a friendlier basis. It would be acknowledging a defeat and in a sense appearing with cap in hand, but better that, and to persuade Allbright to tell what he knew, than the alternative of the sheriff.

His mind made up, and the parrot having flown deeper into the woods, John was about to signal the horse to move along, when some two hundred yards away, near a rise of land where he once jumped an enormous flock of wild turkeys, he caught sight of two still, stand-ing figures. They could not have been there long and must have come from around the farther side of the rise. John's first thought was that they were poachers. It was the furtive stillness of the figures that made him think so. The taller of the two broke his rigid pose, turning to his companion with an abrupt, throttled motion, and it was then, as John noticed a pair of horses standing near them and as the slighter of the figures, unmistakably a woman, tossed her head in an impatient gesture that he would have known anywhere, that he recognized them as Arabella Stanhope and Neville Monckton.

The first moment of astonishment over, John was not particularly surprised. It was no more than might have been predicted, the foolish girl risking her reputation by meeting Neville Monckton in these rela-tively sequestered woods. Besides, she was going away. She would not want to be deprived of the sweet sad ache of parting. Nor would Neville Monckton. He too was going away. The first rumble of the guns would bring him to the front. A soldier expects his farewells.

John sat motionless in the buggy, hoping he would not be observed. Suppose, however, someone else came along? Imagining Arabella surprised, John began to find excuses for her. Under the circumstances she had no choice but to meet Neville Monckton in secret, and if they were discovered she could always say she had gone for a ride in the woods and just happened to meet him.

But even so she was taking too big a gamble. John hated to think of the holiday Elizabeth Paxton and Constance Pettibone would fling themselves into if they had merely the barest inkling of this ren-dezvous. And why stop at Elizabeth Paxton and Constance Pettibone? Theirs were not the only furs Arabella had rubbed the wrong way. Half the young women in Pompey's Head would join in the fun. Headstrong though she was, Arabella was bound to understand the danger she ran. It began to appear that more than willfulness was in-volved, and no longer could it be assumed that this was simply an-other one of her flirtations.

The more John considered the possibility that she might be in love with Neville Monckton, the more distasteful it became—the one totally unacceptable man among the many men she had to choose from and, on top of it all, the brother of her father's two most determined enemies. Reminding himself that he was prejudiced against all the Moncktons—getting shot by one brother is apt to jaundice one's view of the others—John could not believe his prejudices mattered, nor that Neville Monckton, as hero, wounded and in uniform, was any different from the shady skipjack of the low dives and houses of ill fame at the far end of Liberty Street.

John chewed the end of his cigar. "Why don't you talk to her?" he could hear Missy saying, and if it was Missy's voice he heard rather than his own, it was because he was reluctant to speak in his own authority. Talk to her indeed! Having never listened to anyone, why should she listen to him? "But she might, Johnny," Missy's voice went on. "You never can tell," and he began to envision the scene it comforted him to imagine Missy had in mind—a quiet moment, a quiet corner, a quiet chat: "I know, Arabella, that this is no affair of mine and I don't like to intrude, but Neville Monckton isn't the sort of person you should encourage. Give him an inch and he's sure to try to take a yard. You mustn't let yourself be carried away by his uniform or that silly wound of his—despite the big thing that Gup has made of it, what was it but a powder burn? A man could get worse hurt with a firecracker. The point is that Neville Monckton simply isn't your kind of person. I have good reason for talking to you like this, believe me, and it's your own welfare I'm thinking of."

Finding a shred of tobacco on his tongue, John spat it out, and with it the notion of talking to Arabella—she would quite properly tell him to mind his own business, and he already felt restive in that avuncular role. Moreover, if Neville Monckton was that important to her——Ah, but it wouldn't work! It wasn't Neville Monckton she was attracted to—it was the damn-fool nonsense of his being a hero—and how could Neville see her as anything except another conquest? Even if one went so far as to imagine his marrying her, what would it be but his keeping his eye on the main chance—that, and a sort of pilgrim's sexual progress? One began in the cribs of Liberty Street and ended up in a bed in Stanhope Hall. The prospect was bound to please.

A further movement of the two figures caused John to break off his thoughts. Not wanting to look, and afraid to stir, he tried not to see by straining his eyes in another direction. He was able to glimpse enough, however, to tell that Neville had seized one of Arabella's hands and that she, pulling away in a sidelong motion, was trying halfheartedly to wrest it free.

As Neville stepped closer to her, John forgot his determination not to look. The wild notion came to him that Neville was about to trespass beyond all permissible bounds, but then, as Arabella quietly stood there, gazing into Neville's face, he anticipated a fervent embrace. "That's right," he said. "Be a fool. Do it up proper," and he didn't know whether to be relieved or disappointed when Arabella, shaking her head and freeing her hand with a steady, uncompromising tug, moved from Neville toward her horse. Helping her into the saddle, Neville voiced some final plea, the whole hang of his body taking on a petitioner's stance. Arabella again shook her head, slowly and gently, and turned her face the other way—see not, hear not, she seemed to be saying, and the only inference to be drawn was that she was afraid to look into Neville's eyes.

A woodpecker began to drum in a far-off part of the woods. The quick short spurts of sound, much less distinct than those that had alerted the parrot, seemed to be muffled by the dense hangings of moss that even on a sunny day gave the woods a dark, gloomy look. Neville Monckton, apparently unable to regain Arabella's attention, took a few short strides and swung himself into the saddle with a tall, easy motion (even a handsome motion, John was constrained to admit), but pulling at the bit so impatiently that John was able to hear the faint thin clink of it and the creaking of the saddle. Neville brought his horse alongside Arabella's, and John watched them ride across and beyond the rise of land, slowly, their shoulders almost touching.

Sitting in the buggy a time longer, John snubbed out the lighted end of his cigar and flung it away. The melancholy silence of the woods began to weigh down on him. Their mood was too close to his own. Restless, and pervaded with a deep sense of unease, he flicked the reins and got the buggy into motion—first his errand in the Channel and then a call on Allbright. Already he had wasted too much time.

CHAPTER TWENTY

Rattling across the cobblestones of River Street on his way to the Irish Channel, John noticed that the clock on the sidewalk before the Merchants & Mechanics Bank said quarter of one. Wondering what it was he had to do besides going to the Channel and then calling on Allbright, he was almost to the intersection of River and Frenchman streets, where the Channel began, before he remembered it was Missy's twist of green silk thread. He made a note not to forget it, observing that the harbor was so clogged with shipping that four British merchantmen were anchored midstream, awaiting berths, and then, after pulling up to let a train of cotton wagons go past, he turned into Frenchman Street, the Channel's principal thoroughfare.

Though John knew that Frenchman Street had formerly been known as Frenchman Road and that the Channel's first inhabitants were a handful of French immigrants who had settled there around the turn of the century, this was the first time he had visited it. Nothing had ever brought him to the Channel, not even curiosity, and up to now it was simply one of the various sections that made up Pompey's Head.

What he had expected to find, he couldn't say, but as he went down Frenchman Street, remembering the tales he had heard of the Channel, he felt almost let down. The scene presented by the weedy lots and small wooden cottages that lined both sides of the street, shaded by a dual row of chinaberry trees, was not unlike that in other parts of town. It was a pair of women who first caused him to feel he had crossed over into unfamiliar territory. Neighbors, they were scrubbing their steps. They were too old to be called young and too young to be called middle-aged. Each wore a loose cotton dress that showed dark splotches where the water from her bucket had splashed, each was on her knees, barelegged, and each wore her hair, jet black in one instance and light brown in the other, caught up in a knot on the top of her head. They chatted as they worked, speaking across the few feet that separated them, and though John could plainly hear their voices he was so unaccustomed to their manner of speaking that he could not understand a word.

But it was the women themselves, rather than the way they spoke, who made him conscious of his outsideness—in Pompey's Head white women did not get on their knees to scrub steps, wearing loose cotton garments splashed with soapy water, nor did they, especially when a stranger rode by, stop what they were doing to look at him with such unabashed curiosity. John glanced cautiously in their direction, tipping his hat, and brief though his look was he could see the half-curious, half-amused speculation in their eyes. They continued to watch him as he went past, and he heard one of the women say something to the other in a brash, lively voice that ran uninterruptedly into a laugh. There was nothing harsh or derisive about the laugh —it was quite gay, actually—and John could find no reason to believe it had been directed at him. Still it was a disagreeable experience.

With that much of his composure eroded, the rest soon followed. By the time he reached the third block of Frenchman Street and began to look for Number 304, where the O'Connells lived, several things had been made apparent—that life in the Channel was lived on the streets almost as openly as in a plantation compound, that the place was aswarm with children, that the few men he passed made no bones about appreciating the looks of his horse more than they did the looks of him, and that he had been a fool to come on this errand in his father's newest buggy and his own best clothes.

It pleased him to see that Number 304 was the best-kept cottage on the street—he was reminded of his father's adage that a man who owned property should either look after it or get rid of it. Set back from the street, and with a small front yard enclosed by a picket fence, the cottage had been painted recently enough to stand out from its neighbors, nearly all of which had the gray bleached look of raw lumber left to bake for years in the sun. There were flowers in the yard and more flowers in pots on the front porch, and it was not jumping to conclusions to assume that the O'Connells, even though they rented property instead of owning it, were the sort of people who could appreciate Corwin Bottomley's feelings about real estate.

As John pulled up and stepped from the buggy, five or six small boys, all shapes and sizes, came up to have a closer look. One clutched part of a broomstick, another chewed on a piece of licorice that had smeared his mouth and chin, and a third, to John's mild disgust, had a finger looped around a piece of dirty string tied to the feet of a stiff, dead redbird. John recognized the clump of feathers as an immature female, and the boy, as if in response to the disapproving glance sent his way, began to grin and twirl the bird around his head.

All up and down the street the scene was being observed. A short, stout woman stopped sweeping her porch a few cottages away, another stood watching from her door, and in the yard directly opposite, where a dog had begun to bark, a gaunt man with sunken cheeks, sitting in the sun in his undershirt, kept his beady gaze fixed on John and the boys. The dog's barking rang in the stillness, the stillness closed in, and from being an intruder John was transformed into being an invader, flaunting the divisions of class.

Pointedly ignoring the boy with the dead redbird, John tied his horse to one of the pickets of the O'Connells' fence. Rarely had he felt so uncomfortable. Had he known it was going to be like this, he would have dressed in those workingman's clothes he had found in Cameron's closet and come under cover of blackest darkness, riding the mangiest mule he could find.

The boy with the dead redbird inched a step closer, wearing an impudent smirk, and the spinning motion of the bird caused John's horse to skitter. "Easy, girl, easy," he said, and then, to the boy, "That's enough of that! Can't you see you're worrying the horse?" and he could hear the sound of his voice, which was louder than he meant it to be, rise above the barking of the dog. "You, Peter Higgins!" the woman who had been sweeping her porch called out. "You come home, do you hear!" and though her shrillness had theoretically been loosed against the boy, John sensed that the hard sharp edge of it, the bitterness honed fine, was more pointedly aimed at him.

Stung by the sound of the woman's voice, the boy let the string go slack. The redbird raised a puff of dust as it fell to the earth. "You, Peter Higgins!" the voice repeated. "You come home, do you hear! I'll not be asking you to mind me again!" and John, anxious to put an end to this awkward episode, opened the gate in the O'Connells' fence. When he knocked on the door he kept his back to the street. He knew he was being watched, however, every move, and it was a little like waiting to be bushwhacked. It seemed hours until the door opened. He was beginning to think it never would.

ii

John said, "I'm John Bottomley, Mrs. O'Connell. I've come to see about the roof. Mr. Roundtree is sick again," and Mrs. O'Connell, holding a large metal spoon, seemed hard put to understand. Her faded blue eyes wore an expression of strained anxiety, and there were deep, tired lines on her face. She said, "Ah yes, the roof. It's mostly the kitchen," and though she motioned with the spoon to the rear of the house, abstractedly, she still did not seem quite to understand.

Trouble dogged her face. It drained what was left of what must once have been a decided prettiness—the residue, John thought, was an echo of prettiness—and her features had a pinched, sharpened look. How old she was, John couldn't tell. But along with the echo of prettiness there was also an echo of youth, fainter, much farther away, worn down as much by work and worry as by time. She wore a faded gingham wrapper, patched here and there with pieces of other material, and her hair was turning gray. She said, bringing her anxious look to bear on John's face, "You say it's the roof you're wanting to see?" and he thought her eyes had filled with suspicion, holding him at a distance. "You're not wanting the rent?"

Her voice was suspicious too, crouched in a corner amid the recollections of many badgerings, since Mr. Roundtree would always have

been thinking of his own five per cent, and John was sorry he con-
sented to come on this mission. The landlord's agent walks in the
landlord's shoes. He said, "No, Mrs. O'Connell, I don't want the rent.
It's the roof I'm interested in. I understand it needs repairing," and
Mrs. O'Connell seemed less on guard. "It's mostly the kitchen," she
said, repeating the gesture with the spoon, and then, in a firmer tone,
"But it's more than repairing that will be needed this time. Bad enough
it was before that wild terrible wind we had, with the thunder so close
you could hear it rolling around the floor, and now there's no end to
the kettles we need every time it rains."

They were standing in the front room of the cottage. Seeing how
bare it was—a small iron bedstead, a table and chair, a brown crinkled
mirror, several hooks on the wall from which hung various pieces of
clothing—John tried not to be reminded of one of the cabins at Deerskin. The house was full of a thick, cabbagy smell, and the spoon in
Mrs. O'Connell's hand was enough to tell him he had interrupted
her in the midst of getting dinner. Not wanting to linger, he said,
"We'll do whatever has to be done, Mrs. O'Connell. Perhaps a whole
new roof is needed. You say it leaks most in the kitchen?"

"Aye, but not only in the kitchen," Mrs. O'Connell made it clear.
"There's also that place right above you, there, you can see the ugly
stain, and then there's that new leak over my Shamus's bed, poor boy,
though he'll never be sleeping in it again, more's the pity, and may
God rest his troubled soul."

Seeing that her eyes had become misty, John edged away. The last
thing he wanted was to be drawn into this woman's private affairs.
"We'll take care of everything, Mrs. O'Connell," he said. "I'm afraid
we didn't know the roof was that bad off," but Mrs. O'Connell had
gone too far away to hear. "My oldest, he was," she said. "A fine,
lovely boy. And unshriven he died. Left alone in the gutter to bleed
his poor heart out. Murdered."

The shock that fell on John Bottomley was not merely the shock
of a blood-drenched word—it was more that the word had been
spoken in this place by this woman, the unnatural oneness it shared

with the smell of cooking and the shapeless garments that hung from the hooks on the wall.

"Murdered?"

Mrs. O'Connell nodded. "Killed with his own knife on River Street. It happened not two months past, the tenth of January. And on his birthday, too." Pausing, she looked at John more intently. "Did you not see it in the paper?" she asked. "They had it on the front page."

It could not be that she was speaking pridefully, John thought—the changed tone of her voice must have some other meaning. What it was, he finally decided, was that she was able to find some shred of comfort in that her Shamus's violent passing had not gone altogether unnoticed in this hot, indifferent, alien land. "It was on the front page," Mrs. O'Connell said. "Did you not see it?" and John remembered that he had—the account was in the copy of the *News* he had been reading on the porch the day Cameron stopped off at Deerskin. He said, "Yes, Mrs. O'Connell, I did see it. It must have been a terrible thing."

"Terrible it was," she assented. "In his own bed I believed him to be, sound asleep, but instead, stealing off in the middle of the night, and for what reason God alone knows, he was set upon and murdered. And him who used to be such a grand, openhanded, bighearted fellow, without an ounce of meanness in him and always thinking of others."

"I'm sorry, Mrs. O'Connell. What does the sheriff say?"

"And what would he be saying after two months?" Mrs. O'Connell asked. "Would he even be remembering? Let some black man run away from his master, and then, ah yes, then there's no end to the commotion, but let a decent, God-fearing lad be murdered in the streets, and it's no more to the sheriff than if he never lived." Her voice trailed off and she looked at John distractedly. "Ah, sir, it's no offense I'm meaning, not to you personally, but it was a sad day when we left our own green land to take ourselves here. The old O'Connell was all against the emigration, and so was Father O'Brien, the dear good man, knowing the welcome we'd get from the Protestants, but my Tim had no thought but that we should better ourselves, stubborn as an ox, and he would no more listen to others than if he had been born deaf in both ears." She retreated into some melancholy distance, staring at the wall. "A fine betterment!" she said. "Shamus murdered, my old man laid up with a sprained back, and young Kevin left with all our mouths to feed. Betterment, they call it! A fine betterment indeed!"

She stood lost in thought, staring blankly, and though it was no offense she had meant, not to John Bottomley personally, a sense of responsibility began to close in on him. He said, "If you will show me where the other leaks are, Mrs. O'Connell, I won't trouble you any longer," and Mrs. O'Connell, discovering some element of humor he was unable to detect, made an effort to smile. She said:

"It's a gabbling old woman I am, and I don't blame you for wanting to be on your way. But you're not the one who generally comes, are you? You're a new one."

"I thought I explained," John said. "Mr. Roundtree is sick again."

Mrs. O'Connell sniffed disparagingly. "It's not the old Roundtree I'm speaking of. It's the other I have in mind, the young handsome one who comes in his place."

"Oh," John said. "You must mean my brother."

"Well now, so that's it!" Mrs. O'Connell appraised him intently. "I was beginning to think as much. There's a likeness about the mouth and eyes." She gave her astuteness an appreciative nod. "And how is the gay handsome young man? Not sick like the old Roundtree, I hope."

John thought two things—that even here Cameron had been able to profit by that way of his, and that he must remember to tread carefully. "No, Mrs. O'Connell," he said. "My brother's not sick. He's gone away."

"Off to the fighting, I suppose," Mrs. O'Connell said in a tone that might easily be mistaken for cheerfulness. "Ah, the pity and sorrow of it, all the fine young men going off to be killed." She shook her head dolefully, but her brightness of tone remained. "They say the warring will start any minute now and that there will be great huge warships steaming up the river to blow us all to the gates of heaven—those, that is to say, who have the right to be knocking on those blessed doors."

Puzzled by her manner of speech (one would think she was anticipating almost with relish the arrival of the great huge warships), John realized this was a new way of looking at the impending crisis. Unlike most of the people he knew, Mrs. O'Connell was not so complicatedly involved. What meant state rights, slave labor, and colonial exploitation to her? Though there might be a war, it was not her war. Not on those terms. She said, speaking her terms, "And war will also be a betterment, I suppose, all the shooting and the killing and the dying far away. It's the women who will be paying for it, just as they always do, and even now every evening my young Kevin is marching and drilling with our other good lads, they having the war fever no less than the others."

John had heard of this marching, drilling, and war fever before. It was a source of amusement at the Light Infantry Club that some of the young men of the Channel had banded together in what they called the Hibernian Guards.

"Is it for this that we came?" Mrs. O'Connell said. "For my Shamus to be murdered and Kevin killed in a war? Is that the betterment I'll be asked to endure? Both sons gone and only my daughter left? Betterment! I wish I never heard the word!"

A mixture of anger and anguish showed on her face, more anguish than anger, and the jokes that were making the rounds about the Hibernian Guards were not the least amusing. Hoping to bring the conversation back to the reason for his visit, John said, "If you will show me those leaks, Mrs. O'Connell," and got no farther—footsteps sounded in the rear of the house, apparently entering from the back yard.

"Ma! Where are you? Do you want me to give Pa his dinner?"

The footsteps came nearer—bare footsteps, from their sound—and then a girl entered the room. John looked at her, looked harder, and forgot it was incorrect to stare. She was that same incredibly beautiful girl he had seen twice before—once when he stopped to watch the work at Jennie's Basin, and a second time when he stood at the

window of Thrall & Lockhart, observing the activity on the wharves.
She wore a dark shapeless sack of a dress that yet somehow managed
to suggest a roundness of breast and sturdy legs and a small, strong,
appealing figure. Her brows were sooty black above her startled eyes,
staring at him as though she had seen a ghost.

"Dear God in heaven, the soup!" Mrs. O'Connell broke in. "Here
I was forgetting all about it, and my patient old man waiting to be
fed." She looked at John in her distracted way, nervously waving the
spoon. "If you will excuse me, sir, I have to be looking after him.
He's in the back yard, sitting in the sun to comfort his back. I want
to give him his dinner there so he won't have to drag himself into
the house, aching and miserable as he is. You'll not take it amiss if
my daughter shows you the leaks?"

"No, Mrs. O'Connell, of course not. And don't worry about the
roof. We'll have it fixed."

"Ah, it's a kind and understanding young gentleman you are," Mrs.
O'Connell said, glancing at him fondly. "And it's been a pleasure,
your visit. Better for us if you came always, instead of the old Roundtree, forever complaining about this and that and always making excuses. But here I am starting to gabble again instead of being about
my business." Turning to her daughter, she said, "Moira, you show the
gentleman the leaks in the roof. He's come in place of the Roundtree," and hurried from the room.

Left alone with the girl, John thought the same thing he had
thought those other times—put her into one of Missy's party dresses
and she would be the rage of the Light Infantry Ball. But why was
she looking at him like that, so frightened and deathly pale? He was
searching for something to say that might put her at her ease, conscious of the meanness of the room and the thick cabbagy smell that
filled the house, again thinking how much better it might have been
had he worn those workingman's clothes he had found in Cameron's
closet, and it must have been that—the recollection of those workingman's clothes—that was responsible for what happened next.

"Moira?" he said. "Is that your name? Moira?"

Wide as they were, the girl's eyes opened wider. John said, "What's wrong? I don't understand. I've just come to see about the leaks in the roof, you know," and then the mystery of Cameron was a mystery no longer—it may have been the look on the girl's face, or that he had been brought to a higher point of sensibility, but in any case he knew. The letter *M* or *W* had been revealed to be *M*, *M* stood for Moira, Moira was the girl before him, and Shamus, her brother, was a man Cameron had killed.

John even comprehended the explanation of those workingman's clothes in Cameron's closet. Cameron had made an engagement with this girl (engagement? assignation?) and the clothes were meant to add concealment to the dark. And then what? In some way or other the girl's brother had had his suspicions aroused. He had surprised them, there had been a struggle, and in the struggle Shamus was killed.

John steadied himself against the shock, and over a long benumbed instant the awareness congealed. A chill set in, horror's child, and then, as the girl stood watching him, seeming to cringe within the drab folds of her dress, John could feel himself plunging into panic—the fleshy face of Allbright loomed up before him, Pork Chops/Ham Gravy, and the meaning of the episode in Allbright's shop at last came clear. Allbright knew. Cameron was a murderer, Allbright knew, and they were all at his mercy.

As a man in a nightmare may try to shake it off, and thinking for a moment that this too must be a nightmare, John tried to break free. But he knew it was no nightmare. Too many things fitted together and fell into place—Shamus O'Connell had been killed on the night of January tenth, Cameron left Pompey's Head for Cornwall before dawn next morning, he appeared at Deerskin the following afternoon wanting fifteen hundred dollars, the next day he attended the Blackfords' picnic, all the day after that he stayed in his room, getting drunk, and late next afternoon he broke and ran. Cameron Bottomley was a murderer and Allbright knew.

All this time John had been aware of noises in the rear of the house—dishes rattling, the lid of a cookstove being moved about, the scrape of a spoon across the bottom of a pan. The noises subsided and he heard Mrs. O'Connell go into the back yard. He waited for the silence to settle. "How did it happen?" he said to the girl. "I have to know. He's my brother, do you understand?"

The girl could not or would not speak. John had a sense of tension drawn perilously fine, as if she were bringing every ounce of courage to bear against a desire to turn and flee, and in her bare feet and shapeless dress she reminded him of the slave girl Glory—he tried to resist the thought, and could not, that to the average eye there would be little to distinguish the two except the color of their skin. The mere thinking of it was a brutal injustice, trailing a wake of shame, but it must have been that way that Cameron had seen her, a tempting carnal convenience, just as Glory had been to him. So huge a burden of guilt fell down on him, the guilt of his brother, the guilt of himself, the guilt of them all, that he could feel his shoulders slumping.

"Please don't be alarmed," he said. "All I want is to help. There must be some way out of this evil thing."

But actually it was himself and his family he was thinking of, not the girl. The realization that they were all at Allbright's mercy was wedged like a spike in his mind. The barber need evolve no elaborate plan of revenge. Let him simply tell what he knew, and the deed would be done. John could see his mother in her pitiable condition brought to the grave, his father longing for the grave as a blessing, and Missy done a harm from which she might never recover.

"You must tell me what happened," he said to the girl. "We're in this together. Don't you understand?" and though seemingly no less alarmed, she appeared at least to have heard. "Please trust me," he said. "How did it happen? Did your brother find you and Cameron together? Was that it?"

Without moving a muscle the girl seemed to draw back. Seeing how close he had come to the mark, John pressed his advantage. He said, "That *was* what happened, wasn't it? Your brother followed you from the house, he found you and Cameron together, he and Cameron had a quarrel—a fight—and it was then that your brother was killed. Wasn't that it?"

"In God's name don't tell them!" the girl said, the words coming all in a rush. "They would perish of shame. And you don't know my father in his wrath. He would whip the flesh from my back if he knew! And Kevin! He'd never rest till he took his revenge."

Standing so close to terror, John began to be unnerved. "I won't tell them," he said. "Don't be frightened," and it was through the girl's terror that he began to glimpse a way out—if she could be counted on not to talk, and if Allbright was made not to talk either, then no one need ever know. Not until Cameron was brought home and given a chance to speak for himself. There would be a trial, and they would have to live through the humiliation of Cameron's being a prisoner in the dock, but he could enter a plea of self-defense and testify, depending on this girl as a witness, that Shamus O'Connell had drawn a knife on him.

"Wait a minute," he said. "It was your brother who started the quarrel, wasn't it? He attacked Cameron, pulling a knife, and it was with his own knife that he was killed. That much has already been proved. It was he who started the trouble, not Cameron. After all, you can't expect a man who is attacked with a knife not to defend himself——"

Caught up in fearfulness though she was, the girl shot him a burning look. John realized she was more durable than he had imagined. The product of a society in which only the softer female virtues were emphasized, a world in which there were no women, only ladies, he began to understand that this was a woman who stood before him, a woman and a person, making up in character and self-reliance what she lost by not being winsome and feminine, and not so helpless that she would not fight back.

"It's not that I mean to excuse my brother," John said. "I know the harm he has done. All I meant when I said he would have to plead self-defense——" And then he stopped again. The same look was back in the girl's eyes, and the way out he had envisioned began to seem much too easy. For if self-defense was the answer, why had Cameron run away? Cameron was bound to understand he would not be punished for protecting his own life. He would panic, since he always panicked under pressure, and he would be afraid of their father, but would he run away?

In the end John decided he would. Cameron's single thought would have been to get out. Distance would have been clothed in the illusion of safety. But still there were ominous gaps to be filled. Cameron had acted in self-defense, that much was plain, but what else was there, bringing that searing look into this girl's eyes?

"I wish you would trust me," he said. "You mustn't believe I want only to protect my brother. Won't you tell me what happened? From the beginning? If you care at all for my brother——"

"Care? I hate him."

Her earlier terror had been mastered, and she was fully in control. She stood in her bare feet and worn black dress, small and sturdy, unflinching, and John had the impression that for the instant she was engrossed by one thing only—to have back at the man who had done this to her, forgetting nothing and forgiving nothing, no pathetic maiden undone, a woman and a person, the obstinate implacable enduring female.

"Is there no way I can get you to trust me?" he said. "All I ask is that you tell me what happened. It's not only you that my brother has used ill. It's all of us," and he could see her face begin to soften. "Let me speak frankly," he said, knowing that time was growing short and Mrs. O'Connell wouldn't be staying in the back yard forever. "My brother has gone away, as perhaps you know," and when the girl replied coldly, "Aye, that he would, thinking only of his own skin," he comprehended that she did not know, that her animus had been sharpened, and that he had lost what little ground he had gained.

"Yes, I suppose you're right," he said. "Much as I'd like to deny it, I don't see how I can. But still he's my brother. I can't desert him completely. I don't know where he is or if we will ever see him again, but I'm trying to hope we will. For if he should come back and face up to what he has done, especially to you——"

"Him?" the girl said. "Him?"

John began to doubt that he could ever reach her. "Are you really that bitter?" he asked. "What was it my brother did? Besides what happened, I mean. Under the circumstances, knowing he had to protect himself, I believe you might have been able to forgive him. I believe you must have loved him even enough for that. But there was something else, wasn't there, something you can't forgive him for? What was it? What else did he do?"

For a moment John was ready to believe he had reached her at last. But only for a moment. Her eyes grew hostile and she pressed her lips into an uncompromising line. She said, "More? Shamus O'Connell in his grave, my own brother, and you ask what more? Is not my brother's life enough for you? What more would you have, fine gentleman?"

It was the "fine gentleman" that did it—John winced and gave up. The wise thing would be to leave her, praying she would keep silent. On that score, however, he was not alarmed. With her the secret was safe. Not because she was truly fearful of having the flesh whipped from her back, since that was merely her manner of speaking (and would she not submit to the punishment willingly could it make amends?), but because she too was aware of the family context and wanted to spare those who lived with her in this house. She would live with her agony and she would endure. He said, "Someday I'll find my brother, Miss O'Connell, and then, when I do——" But since he had no idea of what he would do, nor any hope of finding his brother in the few days left before he went away, his thoughts fell apart and he started to leave.

His unhappiness must have showed on his face. The girl looked at him in a kinder, gentler way. "It was a wicked thing I did," she said, "calling you names in your trouble. It's your forgiveness I'd like to ask," and John was so taken by surprise that he was rooted where he stood. "You had every right, every right," he said. "And tell your mother not to worry about the roof. I'll see that the house gets a new one."

The girl watched him quietly, the gentle expression still on her face, and he hoped she would not believe he was offering a paltry trade—a roof in exchange for her silence, a thousand cypress shingles for her brother's life. "Good-by, Miss O'Connell," he said. "I wish——" And then, not knowing what he wished, no beginning to it, no middle or end, he left the room and walked out into the street.

This being the dinner hour, the street lay empty and dead quiet, not a sound or movement anywhere except for a rooster who in some foolish confusion elected this moment to crow, strutting amid the weeds of one of the vacant lots. The sun beat down, the rows of chinaberry trees cast patches of shade, and in one of the patches a hen was sitting in a scooped-out hollow of dust, her wings half spread and her eyes half closed. Everything seemed different to John—the houses, the ruts and potholes in the street, even the look of the sky. When he got into the buggy and started back to the center of town, his mind racing ahead to his meeting with Allbright, he knew exactly what he intended to do.

CHAPTER TWENTY-ONE

Half hour later, as John Bottomley left the small cluttered room above Allbright's shop where he had surprised the barber at his midday meal, he fought to bring himself under some sort of control. The notion was on him that he wanted to hide from God. He was beginning to suspect, however, that there could be no hiding ever. This he had done, this he had been driven to do, and this he would have to live with always.

Standing on the landing of the wooden stairway that slanted up like a ladder alongside the house to Allbright's living quarters, John tried to think what to do next. Thought faltered. His presence was here on the landing with the sun pressing down, the year's first huge deluge of light, but his being was disembodied a few feet away, condemned with Allbright in his room.

With all else in fragments, the scene that had just transpired was sickeningly clear—he had knocked on the door, Allbright had answered his knock, and the distasteful sight of the barber, the immediate Pork Chops/Ham Gravy fawn, was enough to cause him instantly to explode. Fear played a part in it, and along with fear there was repugnance, but never would he be able to say he had acted in rage. Even that excuse was denied him.

"What I have to say I'll say in a hurry. But you make sure you listen! I know everything about my brother—everything, you understand, except where he is—and if you breathe so much as a word, just breathe, I'll turn you over to the sheriff. And this time I mean it! You need expect no mercy from me."

In large part he was lying, since he did not know everything, but the lie was a risk he could not avoid. Allbright's mouth hung open, the droop of his thick underlip disclosing a row of yellow teeth, and there was a ripple in the fat of his throat as he swallowed. "But Mister John——"

"You'll Mister John me no more! That little game is over. What your plan was, I don't know, but if you bargained that I would stand by and do nothing, letting you ruin us all, you bargained wrong! One word and you're done for! I swear it! Do you understand?"

Allbright's face grew sickly gray. "But Mister John! I don't know what you is talking about. You sound like I was planning some harm. If you would just set a spell and calm yourself——"

An intruder onto the scene might easily have been led into believing that Allbright, despite his alarm, was speaking with utmost sincerity. John, however, was not to be taken in. He said, "Save your breath, Allbright! Just remember what I say. One word out of you and I go to the sheriff. My brother's saddle! You realize that's all I need, don't you? A gift? Do you expect the sheriff to believe that? Or me? A saddle worth over two hundred dollars? Am I a fool?"

"No *sir!*" Allbright said. "You is leastways that way of any gentleman I know. But that's what that saddle was, sir, a gift, just like I said. If the young gentleman to who we is referring should step into this room right now, this very minute——"

It was the infuriating episode in Allbright's shop all over again, and John had enough of these evasions, subterfuges, and lies. He said, "I don't believe you, and neither will the sheriff! What I believe, and what the sheriff will believe, is that the saddle was part of the price you exacted of my brother to keep quiet. And you know what that is, don't you? Blackmail."

"Oh Mister John!" Allbright cried out. "How can you think a thing like that?" and the note of pain in his voice (if actually it was pain) caused John to waver momentarily. "All right then!" he said. "I'll ask you again. Exactly what happened? And where is my brother? This thing can't be buried forever. Sooner or later it has to come out, and when it does I want my brother here. He has the right to speak for himself! That much I insist on. Where is he?"

Had Allbright replied, "I don't know," or even "Am I your brother's keeper?" John might have been willing to let it end there—it had never been his intention to put Allbright on the rack, and he loathed this extremity to which he had been driven. But it was Pork Chops/ Ham Gravy who came to the fore. Allbright half smiled, half cocked his head, and arranged his features into an expression of baffled innocence.

He said, "Your brother, Mister John? You mean Mister Cameron? Well sir, like I was saying the other day, I *heard* he was gone away, yes sir, that I did, but as far as me *knowing,*" and John wanted no more of it. He had traveled a long way with Allbright, not willingly, grudging every step, but never actually turning his back on him, not once, and this was the end—he had lived up to his obligations, such as they were, and he could always rest in the knowledge that it was not he who had failed Allbright, but Allbright him. He said:

"You've had your chance. Remember that. And you are also to remember to keep quiet. Don't imagine I'm making any idle threats. I mean every word!"

Allbright said, "Yes sir, Mister John, I know that," and the supremest actor in the world could not have matched his pantomime of sorrow—his face sagged, his mouth turned down at the corners, and a mournful expression filled his eyes. But it was too crude and overdone—Pork Chops/Ham Gravy lost in the depths, Pork Chops/Ham Gravy drowned in despair. "Yes sir, Mister John, I know you'll go to the sheriff all right, and I know that you'll make it hard as you can. You go to the sheriff and say one thing, and I tell the sheriff another, and who's going to believe me over you?" His lower lip trembled and he seemed on the verge of tears. "But *why,* Mister John? Why you want to be hard on me? What I ever done to you? What I ever done to Mister Cameron, or the Governor, or anybody else in your whole fine family? What I ever *done,* Mister John?"

John watched him coldly—truly the man must think him a fool to be taken in by such a spurious display. He said, "What have you done?

293

All these lies about my brother and still you ask? You know better than I what you have done and what you were planning to do. What *was* the plan? Tell me that. Did you have some idea of getting revenge? On my father, perhaps, or me, or all of us? Was that it? But don't you try anything, that's all. Drive me enough and I won't go to the sheriff! I'll take care of you myself. With my own bare hands! As God is my judge, I will!"

The big liver spot on Allbright's right cheek began to twitch, and he looked for a moment at the wall, where a large piece of plaster had fallen, exposing the naked laths. Allbright's high silk hat hung from a nail driven into one of the laths, speaking of church and Sunday's boredom. The barber was wearing one of his brocaded waistcoats, and his gold stickpin was fastened to his shirt. The tin plate from which he had been eating, crusted with hominy, rested on a plank table that stood near a bed without sheets. Hard lumps showed in the mattress. John wanted to get out. The smell and dinginess of the room were like a personal affront.

Allbright, however, was not yet through. He focused his eyes on John, wet, dog-on-a-leash, standing with his head hunched forward. "You hate old Allbright, don't you, Mister John?" he said. "You wish he had never been born."

John stared at him, stunned. What had seemed like an easy victory began to turn into a hideous defeat. "It's the truth, ain't it, Mister John?" Allbright went on. "You *hate* old Allbright. You hate him for being who he is." Some emotion welled up in him, very slowly, as if having to make its way past many hidden reefs and shoals, yet strong enough to cause him to stand erect. "But I *was* born, Mister John," he said, "and I is who I is. There ain't nothing you can do about that, not you or nobody. Oh, yes sir. You'll go to the sheriff, and I'll end up on a work gang in the swamps, and then, yes sir, then there'll be those who will say that that old yellow nigger is where he belongs at last. There ain't no confusement in my mind about that. But me being on a work gang won't change nothing, Mister John. I'll still be who I is. It ain't for me to fly with the eagles, that I know, but that don't mean I have to peck with the crows. I can't be *made* to peck, Mister John."

The sound of his voice appeared to have given him courage. His effort toward dignity took on a semblance of pride. "If what you want is for me to keep my mouth shut, yes sir, Mister John, I'll keep it shut. And it ain't just because you'd go to the sheriff and make things hard for me. That ain't the reason. The real reason, like you must know, like you *ought* to know——"

John's stretched nerves would stretch no farther. "You shut up!" he said. "Who do you think you are, talking to me like this!" and though he might have left it there, he didn't. The words that came must have been waiting to be spoken a long time, bottled up for years. "I'm sick of your airy pretensions," he said. "And since you say you are who you are, remember who you are! Remember, and *stay* there!" and instantly, as Allbright's attempt at pride and dignity fell about him in ruins, John saw the horror of what he had done—the needlessness of it, the shame and the wanton cruelty.

Arrested, the scene was there in all its detail, the bleakness in Allbright's eyes, the tin plate crusted with hominy, the broken plaster and high silk hat, the shine of Allbright's stickpin, the bare mattress with the hard lumps showing, and part of John's anguish was the realization that it would be there always, unvarying, like those magic-lantern slides he used to have when he was a boy. The lantern used to flicker sometimes, and sometimes go out, but memory's lantern never would —this he had done, this he had chosen to do, and this was why, standing some minutes later on the wooden landing with the hot sun pressing down, he wanted to hide from God.

CHAPTER TWENTY-TWO

It would always be difficult for John Bottomley to say how he got through the rest of that afternoon. He went to Thrall & Lockhart to clear up a few things that had to be looked after before he went away, and then to the Light Infantry Club, which was deserted except for the drowsy Negro stewards and the old men sleeping in the library, and though he had to go over columns and columns of figures with Mr. Lockhart and tried to bolster himself with a couple of drinks at the Light Infantry Club, nothing was altogether real. The knowledge of what he had done to Allbright was real, and shame was real, and it was not until sunset, when he was returning to Indigo through the stretch of woods where he had seen Arabella Stanhope and Neville Monckton, that he remembered about Missy's twist of green silk thread.

A few minutes later, anyone who saw him careering back to the more thickly settled part of Pompey's Head, never giving the horse an instant's respite, would have imagined he was on an errand of terrible urgency. And for him it was. Missy wanted a twist of green silk thread, he had given his promise, and after the sins and trespasses of this day he could not fall farther into error—Missy's twist of green silk thread became both a symbol of penance and an instrument of salvation.

In the end, however, it turned out to be simply a twist of green silk thread. Penance was not that easy, nor salvation so handily bought. John slept poorly that night. Early next morning he left for Deerskin, traveling upriver on the *Serena Moore*. Missy thought he looked unwell, and certainly he was cross as a bear, but she said nothing—Johnny was like that sometimes: leave the grumpy thing alone.

John spent the next several days with Wilson. He rode over Deerskin acre by acre with his overseer, leaving final instructions, and there was something about him, a sort of throttled impatience, that reminded Wilson of Corwin Bottomley in the old days, before he started to fail. Wilson was subdued and respectful, agreeing to everything, and though John thought the overseer was looking forward to being in full command, running Deerskin the way it ought to be run, the truth was that Wilson was beginning to admire him for the first time.

Later that week, when the *Serena Moore* voyaged upstream in one of the heaviest rainstorms in years, Captain Bostwick again had a message to bear. Once more John was wanted home immediately. His first thought was that Allbright had sprung a trap—for if the barber had felt vengeful before, how could he not feel more vengeful now? —and it was a measure of his disintegration that he felt almost relieved when Captain Bostwick said Mrs. Bottomley had taken a turn for the worse.

ii

John returned to Pompey's Head aboard the *Serena Moore* on her night trip. The rain poured harder and harder and the river was so rough that Captain Bostwick had to make three tries before he was able to tie up at the Bay Street wharf, and then nearly crashed. It wasn't until the middle of the afternoon that John got back to Indigo, and by then his mother was dead. He was given the details by Missy.

"It wasn't even night this time, Johnny, not really, just after first dark. Papa was home and I was too. Since Mama hadn't taken anything to eat all day except a cup of broth, I thought she might like an early supper. I was fixing the tray, putting some flowers on it, and I sent Elnora upstairs to light Mama's lamp. Knowing Mama was asleep, I told Elnora not to make any noise. I *told* her. Elnora went upstairs with a lighted candle in one of those candlesticks that came down through Grandma Nesbitt, those long thin silver ones, and when she went into Mama's room I heard her bump into something, I don't know what. 'There's that old fat clumsy thing again,' I said to myself, and I *told* her to be careful, and right then Mama started to scream. I was so startled I dropped the tray. There was *that* noise, and Mama screaming and Elnora starting to scream too, the way she always did when Mama had one of her spells, and when I ran upstairs——"

Missy broke down and began to cry.

"You hush now," John said. "I know what happened."

"But you don't, you don't!" Missy shook her head frantically. "That's the worst of it! It wasn't that Mama imagined Elnora was trying to set the house on fire. That wasn't it." She broke down again, shaking her head in the same frantic, despairing way. "What it was, was that Mama thought Elnora had come to kill her. With a knife! I told you she was losing her mind, Johnny, I told you! She thought the candlestick was a *knife!*"

"Don't, Missy, don't. It's bad enough you had to go through it once."

"*Once!* It's all I can think of. I can't get it out of my mind. Mama with her hair all down, screaming, 'The knife! The knife! They've come to kill me with a knife!' and Elnora moaning and praying with the candle beside her, and her big fat shadow all over the room, and Mama not recognizing anybody, not Elnora nor Papa nor me—— Oh Johnny, Mama didn't *die!* We'll never be able to say that or even think it. Mama was frightened to death. It's bad enough to die and be dead, but to be *frightened* to death——"

She looked at John through her streaming tears, baffled, trying to understand and not able to understand, once again shaking her head at the maddening bewilderment in which she was lost. "I hate it, Johnny, I hate it! I hate what it did to Mama all her life, ever since she was a little girl and that bad thing happened right before her eyes, and I hate how Papa sold four of our Rosebank people all the way to Mississippi that time just to *oblige* somebody, and I hate wondering where all the mulatto children come from and having to pretend sometimes that I don't *know*, just because I'm not supposed to know anything about things like that, least of all that we live surrounded by prostitutes and concubines like poor Mama once said, because she *did* say it in just those words, though I wasn't supposed to hear—oh, I hate it, I hate it, I hate it! It's a curse, that's what it is, a curse! Look what it did to Mama!"

"Hush," John said, "hush. You'll tear yourself to pieces." His mother was dead and fear had killed her, fear in the shape of a silver candlestick, *them*, the poison in the soup and the faces at the window and the arsonists on the lawn, and here was what it had already done to Missy, them, still them, and if it were a curse, as Missy said, the mark of the curse was on him too. He knew that now, and never again could he imagine that he was any less blighted than the others. To think of Allbright was to know better. "Hush, hush," he said to Missy, but it did no good. She was crying her heart out and he let her cry.

iii

All during the funeral it rained, a cold slanting rain that dripped from the trees in the cemetery and ran down the tombstones, and it was still raining two days later when John Bottomley left Pompey's Head to take up his duties in the new government. His father and Missy rode in the carriage with him to the station. John kissed Missy good-by before he got out of the carriage, not wanting her to get wet, and though he tried to persuade his father not to walk to the tracks with him, this was one of the times when his father wouldn't listen to reason. John waited until the conductor shouted "All aboard" before he mounted the steps of one of the cars, and it wasn't until the last minute, as the train was pulling out and he stood on the steps waving to Missy, that he saw his father was wearing his "best" best suit, the one he saved for ceremonial occasions only.

John leaned from the steps in the rain, waving a last good-by to Missy and then raising his hat to his father, who lifted an arm in return, and when the train pulled out and he went into the car he was soaked through to the shoulders. Since the train was made up in Pompey's Head, the car was nearly empty. John found a seat by a window and looked at the passing landscape. This was the first time he had been on a train since he came home from Princeton after his graduation. He thought how it was then and how it was now, one thing after the other, this against that, and he sat staring from the window at the drowned fields and dark wet trees until the train began to slow down for the next station. He felt cold in his wet coat, and his bad arm ached when he bent it.

PART FIVE

CHAPTER TWENTY-THREE

Clay Vincent, looking a year older and wearing a major's uniform that was beginning to get threadbare around the cuffs and lapels, brought the flat of his palm down on John Bottomley's desk. He said, "Goddammit, Johnny, General Monckton is right! The present situation proves it! Consider where we were only seven months ago, when we could have captured Washington had we gone ahead and done it, the way General Monckton wanted us to, and look where we are now. The whole war has run downhill ever since Manassas! We could have ended the whole thing then and there, and where are we instead? Roanoke Island gone, Fort Henry and Fort Donelson taken, the Tennessee River wide open all the way to Alabama, Crittenden licked in Kentucky, Price on the run in Missouri, and a whole new Northern army put together in front of Washington while we sat back on our duffs and *looked!* And the war could be over, by God! That's what I can't stomach, the way we threw away our chance! General Monckton is right! The trouble with this government——"

Twelve months in the Army hadn't taught Clay Vincent anything about keeping his voice down. There was even a new kind of bark in it, reflecting the habit of command. "Spare me," John said, indicating a stack of newspapers on his desk and thinking how offensively brandnew his own uniform, a captain's, must seem to Clay. "I read what the trouble with this government is every day. If I can't find it in the Richmond *Examiner* or the Charleston *Mercury*, I can always depend on Gup Monckton and the *News*. Even from the field your general is able to make himself heard. Owning a newspaper has its advantages.

Sometimes I believe he must have a special courier running between him and Gup, on Army time."

Clay's thin, handsome face hardened into an expression of anger. He said, "That ain't true!" and John, remembering it was Clay who had helped bring about the trouble with Ules Monckton the night of the Light Infantry Ball, and not liking to be barked at, held onto his patience. "Now who said anything about its being true?" he asked. "Where's your sense of humor? But please don't remind me what the trouble with this government is. The trouble with this government is that it is run by a crowd of timid old women who have handed the initiative over to the other side. Am I right?"

"Can you deny it?"

John wished they had found a less difficult topic of conversation. After the months they had not seen each other, Clay at the front and he at this desk, they should have been able to find other things to talk about besides what was wrong with the government and the series of disasters that had lately befallen the South. That sort of talk, however, was everywhere. Here in the capital one heard little else. The new government had been torn by dissension from the day it started. Frustrated ambitions had gone sour, outs were jealous of ins, and the sullen and disappointed made common cause. Nonetheless, up to the battle of Manassas, when the enemy broke and ran, when Washington lay defenseless and for a few hours it seemed as though the war would be ended with a single stroke, there had been an era of at least relative good feeling. Manassas put an end to that. There was as much bitterness and hatred as in the days of the old Union, and a whole new set of feuds.

"Look what's happened!" Clay said. "Would we be where we are now if we had taken out after the bastards the way we should have? Didn't we throw away our chance? Can you deny it?"

John reached into the bottom drawer of his desk for a box of cigars. "I neither deny nor affirm," he said. "The conduct of this war is not my responsibility. My job is cotton. To see that it is not exported illegally and that it does not find its way into enemy hands. That's as far as I go. Have a cigar."

Clay took one and stabbed at the air. He said, "Don't try to tell me you don't know the way things have been bungled! Most likely you know a hell of a lot more about it than I do. Tell me this. Why was it, two weeks after Manassas, when General Monckton practically got down on his knees and begged the government to order an attack on Washington——"

"Begged? You call that begging? The ink is hardly dry on the commission making him a brigadier general——"

"Do you grudge him that?" Clay broke in. "Didn't he deserve it? I was at Manassas and I saw what happened! If it hadn't been for him, moving up his battery just when he did, and then, when the Yankees tried to move across the turnpike——"

John had no choice but to let Clay fight the battle of Manassas all over again—Clay had been in the battle, and he hadn't, and he owed Clay the courtesy of his attention. Besides, he was interested: Clay had always been a good storyteller and this was a good story he had to tell—"So that's what happened. He gave them hell on the turnpike and it was he, more than anyone, who got the men on our flank into new position when the Yankees tried to move across the turnpike to the top of Henry Hill. That was their big mistake. That's where we licked them. After that they didn't have a chance. And there was a time there, maybe a half hour, maybe longer, when it was General Monckton who was in command. Ask anybody! Read the official report! So the least they could do was to raise his rank. What he did back home was no flash in the pan. He's a genius, that's what! And if they had taken his advice when he practically got down on his knees and begged——"

John found it hard to think of Ules Monckton on his knees begging, even in a figure of speech. "That's where we disagree," he said. "I have to deny that it was begging. Consider what happened. He sends in a report all on his own, going over the heads of his superior officers—a purely unofficial report, I'll admit, a statement of what it pleased him to call his views, wrapped up in what was theoretically an acknowledgment of his promotion—and then, even before it is received, it appears on the front page of the *News* along with one of Gup's noisier editorials demanding that his plans be carried out. And so it has been ever since—he is right, the government is wrong, and anybody who doesn't see things his way is absolutely blind. My God, Clay! That's no way to fight a war! There has to be some sort of chain of command! Here. Light your cigar."

Clay sat in a tempest of smoke, looking resentful. Drawn temperamentally to General Monckton to begin with, he was now his aide-de-camp. He said doggedly, "But he was right, goddammit! We should have marched on Washington! This war could be over by now!"

"Could it?"

"Yes, you're damned right it could! The jugging politicians threw away our chance!"

Belligerently, with deep hollows in his cheeks, Clay puffed on his cigar. A scratch of pens came from the adjoining room where the clerks in John's department had their desks. Somewhere in the vicinity troops were drilling, the commands of the drillmaster and a roll of drums. A bugle sang out. Clay shifted his position, causing his sword to hit against his chair. He said:

"What happened, Johnny? Who thought up the idea that we ought to fight a defensive war? Was it the War Department? Or was it Mr. Lord High Muck-a-Muck himself, thinking he has the best military mind in the country and trying to take all the credit for Manassas when he didn't even get there until the whole thing was over? He's spiteful as a woman! All the credit has to be his. What he really wants is to be dictator. Maybe that way he'd be satisfied!"

John again wished he and Clay had found something less controversial to talk about. The lost opportunity at Manassas had become a running sore. There was an administration party, and an anti-administration party, and the suppurating quarrels had a noisome smell. Evading the issue, John said, "You forget what I told you, Clay. The conduct of the war is not my responsibility. My job is cotton," but Clay was not listening.

"A defensive war!" Clay said. "All you have to do is to look at a map to see how impossible it is. Christ! How can we be everywhere at once? The way things have shaped up, the way we've *let* them shape up, they have only Washington to defend. Our side, though——" He bit savagely on his cigar. "They've landed at Roanoke and Port Royal, they're on the Tennessee River, and what happens if the Mississippi goes? Suppose we lose Vicksburg and New Orleans? We'll be split in two." He hawked, cleared his throat, and spat into a brass spittoon that stood near John's desk. "All winter long we've sat looking on, and all winter long they've been building up strength. We can hear them drilling from our forward lines! But it's not too late. We licked them once and we can lick them again. That's not the problem! The problem is to get the government to change its way of thinking and give our men a chance. It's time to switch back to the attack again. That's what General Monckton is here for. He asked for an audience. They tried to get out of it, but he wouldn't let them. Some of his friends in Congress stepped in. He's come to make a personal appeal."

John said, surprised, "General Monckton is here? In the capital?" and Clay nodded. "We got in last night," he said. "What did you think? That I took off to make the rounds of the cathouses?" He grinned, looking sly. "Not that it would be such a bad idea. It's been a long, cold winter. But tell me about you. What's all this stuff about cotton?"

"You mean what I'm doing?" John said. "I doubt your interest. But cotton, as probably you've heard, is still our principal weapon. Read your general's brother in the *News*. Listen to our most eminent statesman. Cotton can win the war for us. All we have to do is to hang on and wait for cotton starvation to set in. The North is bound to collapse in another few months. But even if by some miracle it doesn't, England will. She will be forced to recognize us. If necessary she will come in on our side. And where will the North be then? Cotton can win the war without our firing another shot."

"Jug!"

"Gradually I'm becoming inclined to say jug too, close to treason though it is. But whatever we say, the strategy is unchanged. Let us maintain ourselves until cotton starvation sets in. Meanwhile, to help starvation along, no cotton is to be exported except what is permitted

309

by the government to run the blockade. The rest stays where it is."

"So?"

"So unfortunately it doesn't. Cotton is being smuggled out of the country all the time, mostly to Nassau in the Bahamas. There is almost nothing we can do about it. This department has neither the men nor the money. We have to depend for the most part on our own loosely organized Committees of Safety. Most of them are about as efficient as you would expect."

Clay, if not enthralled, began to look interested.

"Yet this department is theoretically responsible for every bale that runs the blockade," John continued. "A large part of my day is spent signing what we call certificates of release. The way it works is this— Planter Brown has a thousand bales credited to his account in one of our warehouses, we send him a certificate releasing two hundred bales, and he is then free to ship his cotton on the first blockade-runner he can find, paying an export tax of one eighth of a cent a pound."

"What's wrong with that?"

"Nothing, except that it doesn't always work that way. There are too many loopholes. Though some sort of government paper is generally needed to move cotton, the paper isn't too hard to come by. It can be issued by most of the departments, especially War, whose quartermasters may impress any quantity of cotton to meet Army needs. My guess is that as much as a fifth of the cotton sold in Nassau is contraband. We're not losing a bale or two. They run into the thousands. Huge fortunes are being made."

"The traitors ought to be hanged!"

"Yes, possibly. But what stands in the way is that it isn't a hanging matter. There isn't a real law on the books, much less a penalty. Smuggling cotton is hardly more than a breach of honor."

"The more reason they ought to be hanged!"

"It might involve a lot of hanging, Clay. And we might find ourselves stretching some of our best necks. Nor am I sure that hanging would be a deterrent. There's too much money to be made. Do you remember the time when fifteen-cent cotton seemed fantastic? Well, today it's bringing around fifty cents on the wharves in Nassau, and it may well fetch a dollar if things keep up as they are."

"One-dollar cotton? That's crazy!"

"Yes, but so would fifty-cent cotton have seemed crazy a short time back. And at fifty cents it takes only a modest amount of smuggling for a man to get rich. Figure it out for yourself. Four hundred pounds to the bale at fifty cents a pound makes it two hundred dollars a bale. A hundred bales would bring twenty thousand dollars. Five hundred, a hundred thousand dollars. A thousand, two hundred thousand dollars. Grant that by the time you paid off your confederates your profit might be cut in half, still, half of two hundred thousand dollars——"

But Clay had had enough of infamy. He said, "And you mean they get away with it! By God, they *ought* to be hanged! Hundreds of our men are drilling with broomsticks, we're already running short of shoes, and if we'd had to fight another twelve hours at Manassas some of our batteries would have been up hell's own creek for gunpowder. And here's all that money being pocketed when it could buy the things we need! Why doesn't the government do something? If these jugging piss-ant politicians——"

Clay stopped short, his anger turning into embarrassment, and it was only good manners to try to put him at his ease. John said, "It's all right, Clay. I'm getting used to it. According to the newspapers, one of our worst failures is this department. And I'm obliged to agree. All I would say is that were it not for this department things would be worse than they are. We have managed to plug a few loopholes here and there. That, however, isn't much of a defense. I admit it."

"Hell, Johnny, I didn't mean——"

"I know you didn't, Clay. At least I hope you didn't. But the newspapers do. Take your choice. For the most interesting choice I'd suggest the New Orleans *Picayune*. The *Picayune* and our own *News*. Gup Monckton has never forgiven Senator Stanhope—Colonel Stanhope now—for getting into the cabinet. That cut went deep. He began his attack the day the Senator received his appointment and he hasn't let up since. Firing at me, he fires at the Senator. I'm one of those slackers who ought to be shouldering a gun."

Clay tapped away the ash of his cigar, avoiding John's eyes, and it was not hard to imagine what was running through his mind—had he been so offended he would call Gup Monckton out, except how could he call out his revered general's own brother? Though the problem was not his, the dilemma was. He said:

"Well, Johnny, I reckon that once you took this job——"

Clay's prickly discomfort made John smile. He said, "You're right, Clay. Once I took this job I asked for it. Did I seem overly sensitive? I didn't mean to. Actually, I don't mind Gup and the *News* as much as the *Picayune*. Gup has reason to dislike me. My father helped spike his plans and, if you remember, his brother did try to kill me. But with the *Picayune* it's different. I find myself wincing when it is implied that I'm probably not above doing a little smuggling myself on the side. That's the latest. I was reading about myself just before you came in."

"Oh hell, Johnny——"

"It's interesting what you can get used to. Back when my father was governor I used to wonder how he stood some of the things that were said. Now I know. The first time it happens you want to call down the lightning, the dirty sons-of-bitches, and then you want to go off somewhere and hide. You discover that the cruelest offenses—almost the only offenses—are the offenses to the ego. But gradually you toughen. You become a brother to the alligator. You find yourself almost looking forward to what is going to be said next. Take Gup, for instance. He can't train his guns on this department every day—there's bigger game, by far—and when he doesn't, I feel neglected. My wounds want salt. I seem to need to be reminded that they're there. That I'm there. And lately Gup has been a disappointment. He appears to be running out of invective. His present theme is the one he started with—the Senator is a sawdust statesman, I'm incapable of bearing even a quill, and the public welfare would best be served if all the members of this department were forced to resign. And I imagine your general is of the same opinion. Especially so far as I am concerned. I doubt that he holds me in any higher regard than he did the night of the Light Infantry Ball."

Clay shifted uneasily, again hitting his sword against his chair. He said simultaneously with the clank, "That was a long time ago, Johnny. Things change," and the suggestion was that General Monckton, from his new eminence, could hardly be expected to remember so paltry a grudge. The silence prolonged itself and Clay wasn't any happier with silence than he used to be. He said restlessly, "I hope I didn't take up too much of your morning, Johnny. I'd best be getting along. The general may need me for something. He's at the hotel, working on what he's going to say."

"I appreciate your dropping in, Clay. When do you go back?"

"It's hard to say. It all depends on the general. I understand about a week."

"Good. I'll hope to see you again. And the general's appearance?"

"Appearance?"

"You watch your tone, Clay! I meant no offense. His report. His speech. His whatever you want to call it."

"I'd call it his putting them straight!"

"All right. But you may hear other definitions. When is it?"

"Three o'clock this afternoon. Why? What's on your mind?"

What was on John's mind was too complicated to explain. There wasn't time enough, and it would bring Clay to the boiling point. General Monckton wanted an offensive war, and in his loyalty so did Clay, and how would he take hearing that General Monckton was asking to be hanged?

"Go on! What is it?"

Officially John knew nothing. He was an obscure junior official in the most obscure of all departments. But even so he heard things, and one of the things he heard was that the publication of General Monckton's "Views of the War" had put his head in a noose. Bad enough to say there should have been a march on Washington and a fruitful opportunity lost: to lay the blame on those highest in power was to call down the lightning. The way John heard it, General Monckton was a doomed man—arrogant, disrespectful, presumptuous, ungrateful, insubordinate. Severe measures would have already been taken had it not been for his popularity. The conqueror of Forts Signal and Lookout and the hero of the turnpike at Manassas could not be summarily sacked. Public opinion must be considered. The administration had to bide its time.

And then, throughout the time of biding, those intemperate editorials in the *News*—attack after attack on the government by a newspaper whose ownership everyone knew. If by publication of his "Views of the War" General Monckton had put his head in a noose, each outburst by Gup drew the noose a little tighter. And for the general to have insisted on today's audience, bringing his admirers in Congress into it, anti-administration to the man, was to invite the trap to be sprung.

"Why don't you come out with it?" Clay said. "What are you thinking?"

John hesitated an instant longer. "What I'm thinking, Clay, is that General Monckton is braver than anyone knows. I don't like him and never have, but his courage I must admire. What time did you say? Three o'clock?"

"Yes. Why? Will you be there?"

John nodded. "Yes, Clay, I'll be there. Colonel Stanhope is off inspecting the railroads and I'm sitting in his place. That gives me a few privileges that ordinarily I don't have. You'd have to shoot me to keep me away."

ii

With Clay gone, John resumed his interrupted routine. One of the clerks brought in the latest accumulation of paper and John piled it on his desk. The desk was already a quagmire. Paper bred paper like a warren of rabbits. Days behind, John was months dejected. The whole department consisted of Colonel Stanhope, three clerks, and himself. Cotton was his charge. The colonel preferred larger affairs.

Concerning his superior, John no longer had any illusions. Colonel Stanhope was an amiable incompetent. He liked to display himself in his handsome uniform; to grace receptions; to be expansive; to preside as host at Lydia's expensive parties; to go on tour; to hint knowingly of important secrets; to move in the aura of authority. There were times when John felt that all the disagreeable work fell on him, and frequently he wanted to quit. With all his friends and acquaintances in the service, it was becoming cowardice to sit at this desk. His resignation was already made out. It needed only the date to be filled in.

Lighting a fresh cigar, he settled to his task. The detritus of paper had to be gone through. The first thing that came to hand was a report from the Committee of Safety in Mobile. Not much there. The report from the Charleston committee was no more fruitful. The next document, however, meant work. It was a report from the Navy Department listing the vessels from Southern ports that had arrived in Nassau since the first of the year. The length of the list told him there had been a mistake somewhere. He soon saw what it was. The list covered the six-month period from July 30, 1861, to February 1, 1862. He and his clerks had already closed out 1861, but at least the accounting was up to date.

Alongside the name of each vessel, the list gave the name of her captain, the port from which she had sailed, and the nature of her cargo. One could tell that the blockade was closing in. In October, fifteen vessels had made the run to Nassau; in November, twelve; in December, nine. For the month of January just past, however, only five ships were listed—the steamship *Decatur*, Captain Lockwood, New Orleans, cotton; the sloop *Belle*, Captain Carlin, Savannah, rice; the schooner *Alert*, Captain Scott, Jacksonville, naval stores; the steamship *Nashville*, Captain Haggett, Charleston, cotton; and the schooner *Celeste*, Captain Sabistan, New Orleans, cotton.

Despite having fallen into the habit of being suspicious, John could find nothing out of order. That the ships were known to the Navy meant each had been properly cleared. But still there wasn't a vessel on the list that couldn't have had a few hundred bales of contraband stowed away. Checking the list more carefully, John saw the *Alert* and the *Decatur* had each made two round trips to Nassau since August and the *Belle* one. The *Celeste*, however, had slipped through the blockade three times.

Going to the door that led to the adjoining room, John called in his chief clerk, a thin, sallow, middle-aged Mississippian named Rawlins. He had a milky cast in one eye and was trying to support a sick wife and three children back home on sixteen hundred dollars a year, paper money. John said:

"Mr. Rawlins, here are five more. Two we don't have to worry about, the *Belle* and the *Alert*. The one carried rice and the other naval stores. The other three we'll have to put through the mill—the *Nashville* out of Charleston and the *Decatur* and the *Celeste* out of New Orleans. Check their manifests against the reports from the superintendents of the Charleston and New Orleans warehouses, and also against the certificates of release that should have been sent back to this office. You know the procedure. Can you put a man on it right away? I'd like to have all our January figures in hand by the time Colonel Stanhope gets back. That gives us over a week."

Rawlins studied the list. "Only five ships in January, sir?"

"Yes, and I know what you're thinking. It could be, though, that it's not only the blockade. We had bad weather all along the Eastern seaboard last month. Anyway, let's see where we stand. I doubt that we'll turn up anything, but we may be able to learn if the tax was paid."

Rawlins thought a moment, sitting in profile so that John saw only the eye with the cast. "If we had a few agents of our own——"

"Yes, Mr. Rawlins. Around five hundred. Plus a naval patrol and all the money we needed. Is there anything else you want to talk over?"

"You're not too busy?"

"Not that I can't take fifteen minutes or so. What's wrong?"

Rawlins looked grave. "I wouldn't say that anything is *wrong*, sir," he said, taking a folded sheet of paper from the pocket of his coat. "It's this report from the New Orleans warehouse, Superintendent Morris. Mr. Morris is fairly new there, and we have to make allowances, especially since the former superintendent, Mr. Adair——"

"Yes, Mr. Rawlins, I know. Mr. Adair went into the Army without giving us much notice and Colonel Stanhope appointed Mr. Morris in his place. But that was four or five months ago. Mr. Morris should have the hang of things by now. What about the report?"

Rawlins looked even graver. "You remember your asking me yesterday had it arrived and my saying it hadn't? I was mistaken, sir. It had arrived. It was on Colonel Stanhope's desk."

"Yes, Mr. Rawlins?"

"The report only came to me this morning. It was with those other papers that Colonel Stanhope passed along before he left. He had it for nearly a week, it seems. Young Abernathy tells me that the colonel asked that it be brought to him the moment it arrived. He seemed quite concerned about it, Abernathy says. Perhaps, sir, if the colonel hadn't left in such a hurry——"

It was unlike Colonel Stanhope to bother himself with a superintendent's report, which was the sort of tedium he went out of his way to avoid, but John couldn't see that it mattered. He said, "I wouldn't worry about it, Mr. Rawlins. The important thing is that we have the report. What's the difficulty? You seemed concerned."

"I am, sir, a little. Mr. Morris's report is off."

"Off? How?"

"Short. It doesn't account for eight hundred bales."

John couldn't share Rawlins's alarm. The department had always been able to depend on the honesty of its superintendents. Each had several thousand bales to account for every month, and a few slips had to be expected. Two months back the Wilmington report had shown an error of thirty-five hundred bales, which the Treasury had impressed for immediate export to England, working directly with the Navy. The impressment papers, instead of being returned to John's department as properly they should have, were sent instead to the Treasury office, where they were promptly mislaid for weeks. John said:

"Are you sure it's Mr. Morris's mistake and not ours?"

Rawlins's cloudy eye seemed to grow cloudier. "It's not our mistake, sir. According to Mr. Morris's report, we sent him certificates of release for forty-three hundred bales. But the certificates he returned account for only thirty-five hundred bales. These tally with the copies in our files. Here they are, sir. We sent New Orleans twelve certificates in January, fewer than usual—five hundred bales were released to Busby & Brown, seven hundred and fifty to Whitmire & Church, three hundred to L. M. Toussant, Inc.——"

"There's no need to run through them all, Mr. Rawlins. As I understand it, Mr. Morris claims we sent him certificates that would have released forty-three hundred bales. Our records show thirty-five hundred. Which leaves eight hundred bales unaccounted for. Is that it?"

"Yes sir."

"I wouldn't be too concerned, Mr. Rawlins. It's possible that some other department may have needed them, though I wish they would keep us informed, and it could be some more of the Army's doings. We'll have to do some checking, that's all. It may turn out to be simply an error in arithmetic."

Rawlins's milky eye grew stern. "I'm sure it's not that," he said. "Mr. Morris's figures show a disbursement of forty-three hundred bales. I went over them three times and then had young Abernathy check me, just to make sure. There's probably some explanation, as you say, but it's no error in arithmetic."

John still couldn't see that it needed much worrying. He said, "Send Mr. Morris a telegram. Ask for an explanation."

"I'm afraid we can't, sir."

"Can't?"

"That's right, sir. Colonel Stanhope's orders."

"Orders? What are you talking about, Mr. Rawlins?"

"This note from the colonel. It was pinned to Mr. Morris's report. It says we are not to question Mr. Morris about the discrepancy and are to hold the report until the colonel returns."

"Let me see the note. Does it say why?"

"No sir."

The note, in Colonel Stanhope's hand, was as Rawlins reported. John shrugged his shoulders. He said, "I don't understand what this is all about, but orders are orders. Is there anything else, Mr. Rawlins?"

"Not right now, sir. But with the exception of Mr. Morris's report, we can work up our January figures. I could have them for you this afternoon. Would three o'clock be convenient?"

John started to say yes and then, remembering, shook his head. "No, Mr. Rawlins. Let it go till morning. There's not that much hurry. I have to be elsewhere at three o'clock this afternoon."

CHAPTER TWENTY-FOUR

Word must have got around. The small chamber was like a crowded courtroom, with men backed up into the hall, and there was the same air of tension that attends the opening of an important trial. John Bottomley stood hemmed in against the wall near the door. He hadn't arrived until nearly three o'clock, and it was the best place he could find.

It never occurred to John that it would be an open hearing. No longer a stranger to politics, he realized there was more here than appeared on the surface and that some large event was in the making. Under ordinary circumstances General Monckton would have been asked to appear in secret session. As it was, however, with his supporters in Congress having stepped in, a secret session would have been interpreted as a gag. Besides, there was always the *News*. Within a few days whatever General Monckton had said would have appeared on its front page, as well as in the other opposition papers, and it was less hazardous for the administration to risk an open hearing than to have it said that it had tried to prevent General Monckton's views from becoming known. There might be a war on, but politics was politics. Whatever the administration might lose in one way, it stood to gain in another—it had its supporters too.

Looking over the heads in front of him, John saw that the meeting was going to be presided over by a tall, burly planter, almost as huge as Mr. Lockhart, who sat behind a wooden table facing the room. A former United States senator and now a Southern one, he was the most talented, feared, and outspoken member of the anti-administra-

tion forces. Puzzled to find him there, John gradually began to understand what was happening. This was not so much a meeting as an anti-
administration conclave: all the government's enemies seemed to
have gathered round. It could be, however, that the administration
was being shrewder than might appear. Had General Monckton been
called into secret session, it might have had its hand forced. This way,
by throwing the meeting wide open and permitting it to be presided
over by an outside person, the administration could divorce itself from
it completely, waiting until it saw which way the wind blew before it
decided on a course of action. Should General Monckton overstep
himself, measures could be taken: should he call a change of tune,
he could even be rewarded. For all the standing it had, the meeting
might just as well have been held in one of the public squares.

The gathering was divided almost equally between civilians and
men in military dress. John noticed a bearded general from Florida
who was known to favor a more aggressive war, a congressman who
was one of General Monckton's more enthusiastic champions, a number of junior officers, a colonel from the quartermaster corps who
seemed always to be needing cotton, and more clerks than should have
been there. John couldn't see a person in the room, however, who
had any standing in the administration; from that quarter, General
Monckton was being pointedly snubbed.

He sat in one of the chairs that had been placed up front. Clay
Vincent stood a few feet from him, resting his hand on his sword and
looking perhaps more self-conscious than warlike. Though John could
not see Ules Monckton's face, he recognized the droop of his shoulders
and his thin, corded, sunburned neck. He looked more unkempt today
than usual. The creases in the back of his coat had a shine to their
edges, the cloth was bunched up around his shoulders, and the three-
starred insignia of his rank was higher on one side of his collar than
the other. His own needle must have sewed it on.

It was incomprehensible to John that Ules should lend himself
to the purposes of this meeting. To say that he was being used as
a cat's-paw might be going too far, in that he and the opponents of
the administration shared a certain community of interest, but cer-

tainly he must realize it was he, more than anyone, who ran the risk of being burned. His relations with the administration were strained enough and his whole future in the Army depended on its good will. Or didn't he care? That, however, John couldn't believe. So intense a man must care intensely.

The senator at the table rapped for quiet, using his knuckles as a gavel. His strong point was invective. The apparent broad-mindedness of the administration placed him at a disadvantage. He said so. He also said that though it might be hoped the dark clouds of despotism were beginning to lift, he, frankly, was not going to make the mistake of believing that one ray of sunshine made a summer's day. He said that the conduct of the war had been gravely mismanaged and that the administration must be held accountable. It had been given a formula for victory which it chose to reject. Had the advice of certain military commanders been heeded—the advice of one commander in particular—there was every reason to believe that the war might now be over. The South and North would each be going its own way. The formula for victory, however, might still be applied. It was not too late. But it had not been his intention to make an address. He had come to listen. It gave him pleasure to present General Ules Monckton.

The moment was too solemn for applause. General Monckton rose to his feet with only the scrape of his boots to break the silence, and when he faced the audience John was astonished to see how much he had changed. He was beginning to look like an old man. His scraggly mustache was completely white, and so was his rapidly receding hair. The wrinkles on his forehead cut deep as scars. Though he had paid tribute to ceremony by buttoning up his coat, the brass buttons looked dull and dingy and his scuffed campaign boots were run over at the heels. John watched him fall into that lank, ungainly stance of his, with the dull flat look in his eyes, and when he began to speak it was in an almost inaudible monotone—he appreciated the good offices of the senator and his other friends; he had not expected so large a meeting; he was glad of this opportunity to put forth his views.

John imagined it was going to be like the time the Light Infantry was welcomed back from the forts, when Ules seemed too bored and listless to make a speech—a defensive policy was bound to fail; it should have been apprehended from the start that the South must invade or be invaded; the first mistake was to permit the enemy to cross the Potomac; the South was now paying the price of that error, not only in Virginia but elsewhere.

Gradually Ules's voice began to ring out and his eyes to come alive. He became braced with the same confidence that had dominated the gentlemen of the Agricultural Society so many years before. He said that the North must be invaded, that it was not enough to defeat the enemy armies in the field. He could not agree with his good friend the senator that there was room within the boundaries of the former union for a Northern and a Southern country. He felt that his good friend the senator was in error. The purpose of the war must be the destruction of the North as a political unit, and the war must be made as terrible as possible. War was not a pastime or child's play. Wherever the Army passed in the North the sign of its passing must remain for fifty or a hundred years. The civilian population must also be warred upon, without mercy, and the North brought utterly to heel. For only then could the South feel secure enough to go about the creation of its own society, claim its rightful empire, and show the way to the rest of the world.

Listening and remembering, John thought it might be the meeting of the Agricultural Society all over again—possessed by his vision, made blind, Ules could not see that his audience was deserting him. Lay waste the North? Make war on the civilian population? Burn, plunder, and pillage? War was war, yes, but even in war there were civilized standards to maintain. Was the chivalry of the South to sink to the level of a tribe of murdering Indians?

Amazement hushed the room. The rebuked senator sat with his massive head sunk forward, staring at the floor; the general from Florida braced himself straight, hostility showing in every line; a young lieutenant barely old enough to shave watched with an astonished look that John thought must be like his own look the night he heard

Ules Monckton say that Thomas Jefferson, misreading nature's most fundamental law, had attempted to erect a government on a foundation of sand.

Seemingly unaware of the less cordial atmosphere, General Monckton returned to a discussion of military affairs. He gave his ideas on how to defeat the several Northern armies, smaller than the force that had crossed over into Virginia, that had elsewhere invaded the South. He said that in these areas large-scale battles should be avoided. Everywhere outnumbered, the South could not put that many men into the field. The lesson should be drawn from the French and Indian wars, from Francis Marion in the swamps of South Carolina during the War of Independence, and from the guerrillas who had harried the French when only a small corner of Spain was left as England's last foothold on the continent during her long struggle with Napoleon.

Although the main army must be kept intact, ready to invade the North, the other Southern forces should be broken up into small, independent units composed principally of mounted men. Ceaseless punishment must be their purpose: the tactics of hit and run. Give these irregulars free rein. Let them take the enemy in ambush, snapping at his flanks and attacking his rear guard. Let them blow up his depots, raid his horses, cut his lines of communication, and destroy his supplies. Everlastingly harried, forced to be on guard everywhere at once, never knowing where he would be hit next, the enemy would soon lose heart. What little fight he had would be demoralized out of him.

Against his will and despite his prejudice, John began to be persuaded—Ules's program would make him no friends among the West Point generals, pledged as they were to the conventions of chessboard warfare, but when had Ules Monckton ever wanted to make friends? Here truly was a large design—the carrying of the war deep into enemy country, the wearing down of his isolated forces, the elimination of the North, and then the marching on of the victorious Southern armies to new conquests in Mexico and the other tropic countries that were waiting, like Jericho, to fall at the bugle's first blast.

It was to this theme that Ules now returned: but here again, as at the meeting of the Agricultural Society, his vision was too intense. These other eyes were unaccustomed to looking into that blaze—could it be that the man was slightly mad?

It was not until Ules enlarged on his program of irregular warfare, however, that he came fully to disaster—he said that the tactics of hit and run must be accompanied by the torch. Wherever the invader had penetrated the South, that part of the South must be laid waste —barns, crops, dwellings, stock, bridges, railroads, villages, towns. The day must be as night with smoke and the night as day with flame. The enemy must find himself lost in a desolation such as had never been seen before.

Somewhere in the room a man snarled, animal-like, driven past the limits of endurance, and there was a tangled protesting outcry—"Our own homes and firesides!" "Helpless women and children whose men are at the front!" "Ask us to be heartless barbarians to our own!"— and John was one with them. It was Indigo that went up in flames. But still the notion nagged him that Ules Monckton might be right. Great ends are not accomplished without great sacrifices. Given his vision——

No! It was not so much a vision as a tragic myth, the hallucination of a slave empire that by its profit and example might lead to the creation of a whole slave world. These men in this room were right to shout him down. Only madmen follow madmen. Except for these, Ules Monckton must learn to stand alone.

Learn? One glance at him and you knew the lesson had long gone home. As he had been willing to bide his time before, so would he again. He would not pander nor try to please. The flat, empty look came down like a blind across his eyes, the intensity in his voice fell off, and his whole loose stance was one of disdain. He persisted to the end, however, just as he had the night of the Agricultural Society meeting, and it was as though he were determined to damage himself as much as possible—"All that might have been achieved by bold, aggressive action has been neglected, and nothing has retrieved our reputation but the boldness of our soldiers in the field. Every plea for action has been ignored. Merely to urge a determined movement against the enemy has been to encounter censure, to provoke hostility, and to inaugurate a quarrel with the powers above."

Rash though it sounded, John knew it was not rashness alone. The concept of duty was involved. Just as Ules Monckton was the same man who had addressed the Agricultural Society, so was he the same man who had captured the forts—rashness was duty, duty permitted no escape, and if it was demanded that he risk his future by opposing the administration, he had no choice. It was the future of his country that mattered, not his, and if by chance both futures should prove to be bound together, it must be seen as history's will, beyond his power or any man's.

Looking to see how Clay Vincent was taking it, John could tell that his friend's loyalty was being stretched extremely fine. Clay was getting more than he had bargained for—first that business about warring on the North's civilian population, then that worse business about burning up the South, and now this recital of ineptitude that was sure to send the powers that be into a vengeful fury.

For all his noise and temper, Clay Vincent was a practical man. Unlike Ules Monckton, he was not indifferent to his future, nor was he sustained by the belief that the turn of history's wheel would someday prove him right and perhaps, alone of all men, call him to the fore. He was probably thinking that there are rosier futures than that of aide-de-camp to a general who was practically demanding to be sent to some distant graveyard theatre, never to be heard of again. Clay's dismay was understandable. This was one set of demands the administration would be glad to meet. The conqueror of Forts Signal and Lookout and the hero of the turnpike at Manassas had been a thorn too long. Though he could not be sacked he could be buried, and John gave the administration no longer than a fortnight to act. He felt rather sorry for Clay.

CHAPTER TWENTY-FIVE

A body of troops was marching down the street, a new batch of Texans by the look of them, and John Bottomley, on the way back to his office, joined the crowd on the sidewalk that had gathered to watch them pass. For the second week in February the day wasn't so cold that one couldn't linger, and the late afternoon light was still good. Standing near the curb, John saw that some of the young ladies of the capital, wrapped up tight, were handing out loaves of bread, slices of ham, tobacco, taffy, and other presents to the passing men— "showering gifts," the newspapers would say in the morning.

Though the war was no longer a holiday, moments like this were. New troops meant new excitement, and Texans were a rarer novelty than men from the Gulf States and the Carolinas. More than patriotism and the joy of good works flushed the cheeks of the young ladies. All that rangy devil-may-care had something to do with it. "Say, Captain," one of the men called out to John. "Either take off your shoulder straps or fall in with us. Maybe you didn't know there's going to be fighting up ahead."

It was nothing but raillery, the unbloodied impudence of a raw recruit who wanted to show off, but John was caught in a sore place. Made to feel conspicuous, he thought that what the Texan saw was what everyone else saw, an able-bodied man in uniform (well, nearly able-bodied) who was amusing himself in the capital when he should be at the front. He pretended not to have heard, looking past the Texan and holding his crooked arm as straight as he could. His discomfort, however, must have been more glaring than he realized.

"Shame on you!" one of the wrapped-up young ladies said to the Texan, snatching back the parcel of tobacco she was about to hand him. "Can't you see the captain has been wounded! A fine thing! Wait till you've proved yourself as brave before you talk so big!" She was more nice-looking than pretty, with a high-bridged nose and a wide, generous mouth, and there was something in her spirited voice that reminded John of Missy—his sister would have said "A fine thing!" in just that way. He was unable, however, to be grateful. The Texan was right. Now that they were in this war why wasn't he in it all the way?

Turned upon so unexpectedly, the Texan glanced at John worriedly. He tried to say with his sun-bleached eyes why was it people couldn't take a joke, and then, moving on, gave the rolled-up blanket slung across his shoulders a needless, belligerent hoist. The implication of the hoist was that life on the plains was never like this. A man didn't expect to be scratched at by a woman. Why couldn't the fellow look out for himself? Was he her husband, brother, sweetheart, what?

Her softer emotions played upon, John's defender ran after the Texan and thrust the parcel into his hand. A few words passed between them, his face brightened, and life here and life on the plains weren't so different after all—the last thing he wanted was to offend a brave, honorable man who bore the scars of battle, and the last thing she wanted was to make one of our boys, no less brave and honorable and so very far from home, feel unwelcome and unappreciated.

Glad to have been forgotten, John continued on his way. He could hardly have felt more cast down. This was always a bad time of day anyway, the onset of twilight and nothing to look forward to except another evening in his hotel, and as he walked down the street he fell into a restless melancholy like that which used to settle upon him at Deerskin. The thought that Ules Monckton might soon be getting his comeuppance added to his depression. He could not possibly like the man, and it never failed to make his blood run cold to remember how much Ules had wanted to see him dead, and yet, because of that and the mark Ules had left upon him, this slightly crooked arm that he must carry to the grave, there was an unwelcome bond. There were times when he hated it, Ules being too much with him and too indelibly impressed, but over a year's consideration had given him a better perspective of his enemy. To say that Ules was slightly mad was merely another way of saying that he had taken the Southern position and brought it to its logical extreme—if the peculiar institution was correct in one state, why not in all states: if in one country, why not in all countries? The only way to fault him was to fault the basic Southern premise. And who would go that far?

John's spirits fell lower and lower. It grieved him that so large a part of the war involved a defense of what he believed was indefensible. And yet, all that to the side, why wasn't he moving on to the fighting up ahead? Charlie Rhett had been killed at Manassas and little Jack Wendover had lost a leg, the same burst getting them both, and what happened when that shell went off was that an impersonal war was made personal, exploding in the midst of the picnic at Happy Chance and destroying a way of life forever.

Into the confusion of his thoughts there entered the presences of Professor Adam Sedgewick and Miss Clarissa Drew, Miss Clarissa's face warmed by the firelight of a chill Philadelphia evening and Professor Sedgewick's dark bright eyes in piercing contrast to the benign grandfatherliness of his beard, but before he could tell what they were doing there or what they had come to say, his attention was distracted by the Stanhopes' carriage, driven by Mallory, the colonel's coachman.

Impulsively, believing that Lydia must be in the carriage and hoping to put an end to loneliness, John stepped into the street. There were other carriages going past, as well as buggies and buckboards, men on horseback and other men on foot, mostly soldiers, and though it was beginning to get darker and colder by the minute, there was still enough light to see by. One glimpse into the carriage was all he needed. Instead of Lydia it was Arabella. There was a man in uniform with her, Neville Monckton.

Averting his face, John stepped back onto the sidewalk and hurried off. Though he was thankful he hadn't been seen, more than thankfulness he felt anger. The war had relaxed convention. It was now permissible, and even patriotic, for an unchaperoned young woman to go out riding with an admirer, especially if he was just back from the front. But even so there were limitations. *An unchaperoned young woman didn't go riding in a closed carriage with a man in the dark.* And dark it would be in another few minutes. Assigning intimacy to the carriage's shadowy little cave, and remembering the day he had discovered Neville Monckton and Arabella in the woods, John clenched his teeth. The fool she was! The silly unthinking fool! Walk long enough on the razor's edge and someday the razor is bound to slip. Was that what she wanted, to do herself some irreparable harm?

What had happened was all too clear—Neville had contrived a way to get to the capital with Ules, he had sent some message to Arabella beforehand, she had willingly fallen in with his plans, and what Missy had been writing could not be discounted.

I hear that Arbell has more followers than a Highland chief. Is it true that even a general is in love with her, mooning like a calf? You'll get mad when you hear this I know, because you always get mad at Arbell, no matter what, but in the last letter I had from her she said she still thinks she may be in love with Neville Monckton. Generally I'm able to understand almost everything about Arbell, but this I can't. What I believe is that she isn't in love with him my little finger's worth. Think! May! You don't think you're in love with somebody. You know!

Of course as far as Arbell is concerned the whole thing goes back to his getting wounded the time the Light Infantry captured the forts, but in all fairness he seems to have been very brave at Manassas and I guess that that has something to do with it too. But even so I can't for the life of me imagine what she sees in Neville Monckton, especially when that pompous stuck-up Gup brother of his keeps writing those things in the News about the colonel and you. If I were Arbell I would want to scratch his eyes out. I just hope she doesn't go ahead and do something foolish, that's all. It would break my heart.

Something foolish? What in God's name could be more foolish than the spoiled impossible girl's riding with Neville Monckton in a closed carriage in the dark? Again the dark implied intimacy, the yielding mouth, the surrendering bosom, and what Missy could not understand, John could—this would not be the first time a young woman of gentle breeding had been attracted to a handsome upstart beneath her station.

The dark fell faster, with lights coming on in the windows and the branches of the trees black-purple against the sky, and John's imagination began to run riot—it was rather the way it had been the first months after Lydia's marriage, the images that flared in his mind. He charged himself with being jealous of Neville Monckton, his good looks, his bravery under fire, even his sexual successes, and swept the charge aside—it was purely and simply that the man was still the shady skipjack of Liberty Street, not of Arabella's class. This was the way he would feel if Missy were involved, although if it *were* Missy he would damn well call the fellow out. The fantasy took hold of him that he should find Neville Monckton and provoke a quarrel (not firing into the air this time!) and then, aware that his behavior was no better than a schoolboy's, he shook himself free—if Arabella came to grief it would serve her right. It would hurt Missy, and for that he would be sorry, but it might be just as well if she got over some of her notions.

CHAPTER TWENTY-SIX

Mr. Rawlins was still working. A fire was going in the potbellied stove, causing the iron to glow, and after the cold of the evening the air in the room where the clerks worked was stale and bad-smelling and stifling hot. John said, "What? Still here, Mr. Rawlins? Why haven't you gone home with the others?" and he instantly regretted the slip. Rawlins had no home. A few weeks ago he had asked and received permission to sleep in the basement. The cheapest boarding-house was asking ninety dollars a month, and with a sick wife and three children back in Mississippi, Rawlins couldn't afford it. He looked tired and seedy and in need of a wash, one more man without a woman.

"It's the January figures, Captain," Rawlins explained. "The reports from South Carolina were mislaid. Young Abernathy tied them up with some Army requisitions by mistake, the New Orleans ones for December. Colonel Stanhope asked to see them. I'm almost through, though. It's getting colder, ain't it?"

"Yes, some," John said, wanting to add that a drop in temperature didn't mean they had to turn the office into a roasting oven. "But why don't you call it a day, Mr. Rawlins? There's not that much hurry about those figures. Just so long as they're in hand by the time Colonel Stanhope returns."

"Yes sir, I know. But I thought that since I'd started, and with all the work that's been piling up——"

He looked up with his milky eye, evasive and uncomfortable, and what he was saying was what else did he have to do—walk the streets?

write another letter home? use up the evening's only diversion by finding a cheap eating place for supper? go down to the basement where it wasn't even warm?

His sharp face and long jaw brought someone to mind, not very distinctly, and it took a few seconds for John to decide it was Wilson, his overseer at Deerskin. There was the same conformation and cast of bone. He said, as much to Wilson as to the man before him, "I'm going to have a drink before I sign my letters and call it a day, Mr. Rawlins. Will you join me?"

Rawlins's face lit up in a way that Wilson's never had. "Glad to, Captain," he said. "You'll find everything that needs your signature on your desk. And I was thinking, if you had a few moments to spare——"

"Yes, Mr. Rawlins. What is it this time?"

Rawlins fumbled through the papers on his desk. The knotty movement of his fingers seemed to summon an invisible cloud, smelling of dust and glue and souring ink. Finding what he wanted, Rawlins said, "It's the New Orleans warehouse again, sir. These Army requisitions——"

Though John could tell that Rawlins believed he had discovered something important, he was in no mood for another problem. He said, "Come into my office, Mr. Rawlins. We'll talk about it there. Let's have that drink first."

The fire in John's stove had died down, but still it was disagreeably warm and close. He opened a window, admitting a draft of night air and a disharmony of male voices joined in a drunken chorus of "Old Friends Are Gone," and then, going to his desk, brought out two tumblers and a bottle of whisky from the drawer where he kept his cigars. He poured a drink for Rawlins and another for himself. "Your health, Captain," Rawlins said, tossing off the drink and giving a shudder. "Anything tastes as good as this does shouldn't cause a man to make a face, but somehow it does. A reminder, my daddy used to say, to heed the words of St. Paul. Take a *little* wine for thy stomach's sake."

"You care for another, Mr. Rawlins?"

"Thank you, Captain. It does a man good. I reckon it would keep within the definition of little."

He smiled, showing long, tobacco-stained teeth. "Much as I hate to admit it," he said, "these Virginians make better whisky than we do. Sometimes they run it through charcoal, I hear. Is that the practice in your country, Captain?"

"No, Mr. Rawlins, I think not. We're not that patient."

"Just so long as it drinks good, eh, Captain?"

"I believe you could say that's the general idea. Now what's on your mind? Did Superintendent Morris make another slip?"

Rawlins's face took on the expression of an earnest, worried ferret. "I don't know that you would call it a slip, Captain. It's the worst puzzlement I've ever seen."

"Why don't you tell me about it?"

"It's these three requisitions, Captain. If you will examine the signatures, first this one and then——"

"Just a moment, Mr. Rawlins. Let me try to get a few things straight. What I gather is that you've turned up another error in Mr. Morris's January report. Is he short more than those eight hundred bales we were talking about this morning?"

Rawlins's worried look persisted. He said, "It's not the January report, Captain. It's the December one. As I started to say when you came in——"

John was getting confused. "The December report? We closed it out several weeks ago. You yourself initialed it as being correct. So did Colonel Stanhope."

Rawlins nodded. "Yes sir, that's right. So we did. But at the time——" He broke off, wrinkling his brows. "Maybe, if I went back to the beginning——"

"Must you?"

"Yes sir, I think I ought to. You remember my saying that the January reports from the South Carolina warehouses were mislaid and that young Abernathy tied them up with some Army requisitions by mistake, the New Orleans ones for December?"

"Yes, I remember."

"That's how it started. How it came to my attention, I mean. If it hadn't been for young Abernathy's putting things in the wrong place——"

"But what *is* it, Mr. Rawlins? What are you getting at?"

"These three requisitions, sir. They were drawn against the New Orleans warehouse, two in December and one in November."

"My God, Mr. Rawlins! Do we have to go back all the way to November?"

Rawlins's cloudy eye began to fill with a hurt expression. "I know it sounds complicated, Captain. I'm only trying to do my job."

"My apologies, Mr. Rawlins. It's been a trying day. Let me see if I understand you. The South Carolina reports were mislaid, and you found them tied up with the New Orleans requisitions for December. Then, in some way or another, your attention was drawn to the requisitions we have here, two for December and one for November."

"Yes sir, that's right."

"Which brings us to the requisitions. What is it that upset you?"

Rawlins started to speak, changed his mind, and began anew. "It's going to sound impossible, sir, and I don't know what you'll make of it, but the two December requisitions, these two here——"

"Yes, go on."

It was as though Rawlins, standing on some high, fearful precipice, was being commanded to hurl himself into space. He said, taking the plunge, "I believe they're forged."

Outside in the dark a noisier chorus of "Old Friends Are Gone" rose nearer the window. "Forged?" John said, and it was as if he had been dragged along by Rawlins on his dive, landing in the same spot with the same shock, miraculously alive and wholly dazed. "Forgery is still a crime, Mr. Rawlins. Are you sure of what you're saying?"

Rawlins nodded assent. "I don't see how there can be any other explanation, sir. If you will look first at the signature on the November requisition, signed by Major Howell Angry——"

"Major who?"

"Howell Angry. It's an unusual name, that I'll admit, and it was that—well, sir, if it had been a more ordinary name, Cobb or Johnson or Williams or Smith, then, perhaps, with the hundreds and hundreds of requisitions that pass through the office——"

"Yes?"

"What I mean, sir, is that I might not have noticed. It was that, Major Angry's name, that caused me to look up the November requisitions drawn against the New Orleans warehouse, just to check. Then, when I did, I realized the two December requisitions had to be forged."

"*Had* to be? That's strong language, Mr. Rawlins. Let me see the requisitions."

Examining the three slips of paper that Rawlins handed him, John found that each bore the signature of a Major Angry, an Army quartermaster in New Orleans, and that although there might be some slight difference in the way the *g*'s and *y*'s were formed on the December requisitions, the variation was much too insignificant to warrant, much less substantiate, a charge of forgery. John said:

"I'm no handwriting expert, Mr. Rawlins, but I don't think it will wash. Unless you can back up your charge with something more substantial——"

Rawlins began to look desperate. He said, "I know, sir, I know. That's what makes the whole thing so hard to believe. Do you recall that little engagement at Pohick Church here in Virginia the middle of November?"

"Now wait a minute, Mr. Rawlins! Can't we get some kind of order into this? What has a skirmish at Pohick Church——"

"Major Angry was killed there. He's dead."

"*Dead?*"

"Yes sir. That's what I've been trying to say. And if he was killed in Virginia in November, how could he sign these requisitions in New Orleans in December?"

The back of John's neck began to prickle. It was a sensation he associated with getting close to a deer or a flock of wild turkeys. Trying to sound calmer than he was, he said:

"Not so fast, Mr. Rawlins. Are you sure Major Angry was killed at Pohick Church?"

"It's the name, Captain. If it had been less unusual, as I've said, I don't think I would have remembered. Major Angry was a local man. His death was written up in the *Examiner*."

John finished his whisky. The chorus outside the window had moved on. He said, "There are still a lot of unanswered questions. For one thing, if Major Angry was quartermaster in New Orleans, then how——"

"How did he happen to be killed in Virginia?"

"Yes?"

"It was Manassas, Captain. It said in the *Examiner* that Major Angry, after Manassas, decided to seek active duty in his home state. He was in business in New Orleans when the war broke out, married to a New Orleans lady, but he felt he ought to come home."

"And then he was killed at Pohick Church?"

"That's what it said in the *Examiner*."

"Are you sure of all this? Positive?"

"If you mean what I read in the *Examiner*, yes sir, I'm positive. Had it been a less unusual name——"

John said, "There's one other thing we have to consider. You don't imagine there could be two Major Howell Angrys, do you?"

Rawlins thought a moment. "Well, sir, I suppose there could be, anything's possible, but under the circumstances——"

"I daresay you're right," John said. "It's hardly likely. Still, just to be on the safe side, send one of your men over to the War Department in the morning and have him examine the rolls."

"First thing, Captain."

"Let's consider these requisitions. If you are right—*if*, I say—the one with the November date was properly signed by Major Angry, and the signatures on the two later ones, the ones with the December dates, are forged. Is that the way you see it?"

"Yes sir."

"How much cotton is involved? As represented by the December requisitions? What's this date? A two or a seven?"

"I make it a seven."

"Two hundred bales on December seventh, another two hundred

on December fourteenth, or four hundred bales in all. That's a sizable amount of cotton, Mr. Rawlins."

"Yes sir, it is. And if you add the eight hundred bales that are short on Superintendent Morris's January report——"

The back of John's neck began to prickle again—eight hundred and four hundred added up to twelve hundred bales, or around two hundred and fifty thousand dollars' worth of cotton at the going rate on the Nassau wharves. John said:

"Let's keep quiet about this, Mr. Rawlins. I believe I know what's in your mind, that Superintendent Morris may be involved, but we don't want to stampede. We have upward of twenty people employed in the New Orleans warehouse, a number of whom have considerable authority. Any one of them——"

"Yes sir, I've thought of that."

"There's something else, too. Assuming there is a forger, then why was it, if Major Angry left New Orleans early in November and was killed a few weeks later——"

"Why didn't the forger know about it?"

"Yes."

"I think he did."

"You do?"

"Major Angry was a long-established New Orleans resident. He was connected with some of the best people. He left a wife and children. There was bound to be something in the New Orleans papers about his death. And if you put yourself in the forger's place——"

"I'm not sure I want to."

Rawlins's thin lips drew back in a smile. He said indulgently, "I'm less particular, sir. I've been pretending that I stood in his shoes, trying to think as he might. And what I thought of last is what I should have thought of first. Dead men tell no tales. Don't you see, sir?"

John reflected a moment. "I'm not sure. I suppose it could have happened as you say. Any way you look at it, though, the fellow ran a dangerous risk."

Rawlins this time gave the impression of trying not to smile. He said, "Yes sir, that he did. But much less of a risk than if he had forged the name of someone alive and present. Besides, I reckon he was willing to run a risk or two."

"You speak with a curious authority, Mr. Rawlins."

Rawlins gave a soundless laugh. "You're right, Captain, I do. Every day I handle slips of paper that represent thousands of dollars' worth of cotton. A man gets notions. Knowing what I do about the procedure of this department, and given a small amount of capital, I could make a fortune."

Quickly he raised a hand. "I'm speaking a poor man's daydreams, Captain, not his plans. But the possibilities of forgery have often occurred to me. Risks? What are they? Hundreds of requisitions come to this office every month. What is one slip of paper? How can we prove the genuineness of every signature? We'd have time for nothing else."

"I'm not sure I like what you are saying, Mr. Rawlins. Am I to understand that we are letting forged requisitions get past us all the time?"

Rawlins's milky eye narrowed shrewdly. "I'm sure they do. Not many, perhaps, not when you consider the temptations, but certainly more than a few. It goes back to what I said. How can we be sure of every signature? There's not enough time. Haven't you had the same suspicion?"

"Often," John admitted. "I try not to think of it, however. There are many things about this department I try not to think of."

"I understand the way you feel, Captain. But if this could help tighten things up a bit——"

"Thanks to you."

"A bit of luck, sir."

"And we're still a long way from home. Even if it turns out to be forgery, all we know is that someone has stolen four hundred bales of cotton from the New Orleans warehouse. But who? Superintendent Morris? I doubt it. He could be completely innocent. These are Army forms. The likelier probability is that the wrongdoer is a man in uniform. It wouldn't be the first time it happened—there was that scandal in Savannah, you will remember. So let's not be so quick to assign criminal behavior to Superintendent Morris."

Rawlins's silence implied that he had other ideas, and the suspicious look on his face, which could be the whisky beginning to work, again reminded John of Wilson—deal with a back-countryman and you automatically dealt with distrust. John said, "I sense a few reservations about Superintendent Morris on your part. This is hardly a time to be secretive."

"If I could be sure I was at liberty to speak," Rawlins said.

"Why do you doubt it? Nothing you say will go any farther. Now what is it about Mr. Morris that's troubling you?"

Rawlins appeared to be having second thoughts about what he had got himself into. He said, "It's the way Mr. Morris received his appointment. After Mr. Adair resigned we had over a hundred applications for the job, as you will recall."

"No, I don't recall," John said. "Patronage is not one of my privileges, and Colonel Stanhope doesn't always take me into his confidence. I believe, however, that I'm beginning to understand. It was your impression that there were worthier candidates than Mr. Morris and that Colonel Stanhope may have showed some favoritism. Is that it?"

Coming a little more into the open, Rawlins said, "Mr. Morris didn't even apply for the appointment. Colonel Stanhope approached him. I wrote out the letter for the colonel after he made a rough draft in pencil, the way he does with most of his correspondence, and I remember thinking at the time that Mr. Morris must be a friend of his."

There was plainly more than that, however, in Rawlins's mind. John searched his memory, trying to think if he had ever heard Colonel Stanhope mention the name Morris or if the name by itself meant anything, and came up with nothing. He said:

"I can't find anything irregular in Mr. Morris's appointment, and I'm sure the colonel satisfied himself as to his suitability. What else is bothering you?"

For an instant, shifting his gaze, Rawlins appeared anxious to escape. He said nervously, "I don't want to lose my job, Captain."

"Nor would I like to think of your losing it. You must know your value to this department. I doubt you have anything to worry about on that score."

Rawlins seemed unable to make up his mind. "It's not only the way Superintendent Morris received his appointment, Captain. It's not even the irregularities in his reports. What it is——"

"Yes, Mr. Rawlins?"

"It's Colonel Stanhope," Rawlins blurted out, and then, as if a release of tension had loosed his tongue, though it could have been the whisky taking further effect, "Why is he so interested in the New Orleans reports?" he said. "He never asks to see any of the others. Why is it then, even before this last report of Mr. Morris's came in——?"

John listened with a sinking sensation. From being a seedy backwoodsman who lived in the basement and needed a wash, Rawlins came close to being a dangerous enemy. Let him air these suspicions, and let the anti-administration newspapers get hold of them, Gup Monckton and the *News*, for instance——

"I wonder if you know what you're implying, Mr. Rawlins," John said. "I must warn you to be careful."

"You asked me what I thought——"

"Yes, and now I have to ask why you thought it. I advise you to weigh words carefully. You may be called upon to repeat them in the presence of others."

Rawlins probably saw his job going out the window. He said, "I can't shut my eyes, Captain! I can't pretend that I don't find a few things peculiar when I do! You asked me what I thought——"

"So I did. But you've far from explained yourself. All you have done is to speak the wildest set of notions imaginable. Follow them out to the end, and what we come up with is that Colonel Stanhope, acting in collusion with Mr. Morris—— Good God, Mr. Rawlins, how can you think such a thing!"

Rawlins said nothing, his milky eye warily watchful, and John knew he walked on dangerous ground. Arouse a back-countryman's suspicions, let him believe a piece of mischief was afoot, and no more than a bulldog would he let go. John said:

"Apparently you find it curious that Colonel Stanhope should be interested in the New Orleans reports. But why? Although it's true that I have been put in charge of cotton, the whole department is under the colonel's direction. Is there anything peculiar in his wanting to keep his eye on things?"

But even as he spoke he was convinced there was—since Colonel Stanhope had never before given so much as a glance at the warehouse reports, why should he suddenly become so interested in what was happening in New Orleans? John said, extemporizing:

"Actually, now that I think of it, it could be that the Colonel is planning to drop in on some of the warehouses on this trip, besides inspecting the railroads. He didn't say anything to me about it, that's true enough, but he was in such a hurry to get off——"

A cold gleam in Rawlins's eye brought him up short and he watched the clerk with added concern. Lydia's extravagances were the talk of the capital, and it was an open secret that Colonel Stanhope had severely overstretched his means. He had enough cotton in Louisiana to bring in nearly three quarters of a million dollars in Nassau, and some fourteen hundred bales of it were stored in the New Orleans warehouse.

John drew back from the threat of his own thoughts. Trying to be stern and realizing how false he sounded, he said:

"I doubt, Mr. Rawlins, that we need continue this conversation. Shall we say you fell into an excess of zeal?"

Rawlins wouldn't say it. If his job had gone out the window, he might as well be hung for a cow as a calf. His voice was sharp with challenge.

"And that note he left?"

"What note?"

"The one that said we were not to communicate with Superintendent Morris."

The day had been so crowded that John had forgotten the note completely. He said, off balance, "Oh, that. The way I see it, it lends

345

proof to what I've said. Apparently Colonel Stanhope caught the error in Mr. Morris's report and decided to make a personal investigation. It looks like he beat us to the gun."

Rawlins would not be put down. "And the forged requisitions? Why should they be on his desk? Why should he have asked young Abernathy to get them from the files?"

"Well, since he didn't take me into his confidence——"

"That's just it! Wouldn't he have? Would he start an investigation without saying a word? Aren't you in charge of cotton? Would he have left you out completely?"

John didn't like to be so closely hemmed in. "One thing you seem to forget," he said. "This is Colonel Stanhope's department. It is not for me to question his conduct, and, if I may say so, neither is it for you. Let's understand each other. I'm going to forget this conversation and I want you to forget it too. Do I make myself clear?"

Rawlins sat without moving for a few moments. He said, "Yes, Captain, you make yourself clear," and John knew, as had happened with Wilson, that their relation would never be the same.

"Why don't you go and get some supper?" he said. "You've worked too late as it is. I'll sign my letters and then lock up. There's nothing else we have to discuss, is there?"

"No sir, not that I know."

"I'll see you in the morning then. Good night."

"Good night, Captain."

Watching Rawlins's thin, narrow back as he walked through the doorway, John was reminded of the day Wilson strode off, and he felt some of that same kind of loneliness, in the same kind of way. He hoped Rawlins would remember St. Paul. Let him stretch the definition of "little" to the point of getting drunk, and start talking, and he could bring the whole department down on their heads.

CHAPTER TWENTY-SEVEN

Meals in John's hotel were communal affairs. Some thirty long, narrow tables were set out in the dining room, placed close together. Each accommodated from fifteen to twenty men, most of whom were in uniform. Ladies ate in their rooms. Before the war the hotel had had a few modest aspirations toward elegance, drawing a large part of its trade from the tidewater gentry, but now, after a year of military patronage, it was beginning to look shabby and run down.

In the early days of the war, prior to Manassas, the atmosphere of the dining room had been one of easy, if occasionally quarrelsome, comradeship. Now it was different. There were those who had been under fire and those who hadn't. Belonging as they did to a society that made a ceremony of smearing a boy's forehead with the blood of his first buck, the men who had seen action were not inclined to overlook this newer initiation—they had risked, they had endured, and they had come through. And the ones who had panicked had found excuses. The white feather was not truly their plumage. Since few remembered, they were willing to forget.

Sitting between two of the veterans, a red-faced Alabama captain and a slight, soft-spoken major from South Carolina, John felt the lesser man. They had won through to some right he was denied. "Well, Captain," the South Carolinian said, "I see you stopped one too," and John fell into a piece of dishonesty that up to now he had managed to avoid. Instead of replying, "No, this happened before the war," as ordinarily he would have, he said, "Yes, I did," and although he could tell himself that it was not strictly a lie, the lie cut deep. He wasn't hungry. He pushed back his chair and left the table.

Going into the lobby, he looked around for a place to have a cigar, but all the seats were taken. He went into the bar, hoping to find someone he knew, Clay Vincent perhaps, and then, unsuccessful, left the hotel. The night was much colder and there was a smell of frost in the air. He started to walk, turning off on a side street, and Rawlins walked with him. A man from the backwoods made a dangerous enemy. He shot from ambush and set fire to barns. Generations of poverty and isolation bred a meanness in him and even when he partially escaped, as Rawlins had, some of the meanness remained.

Those suspicions of Rawlins's, however, were absurd. What he saw as cunning could be coincidence. Not could be—*was*. What had happened, most surely, was that Colonel Stanhope, cleverer than they knew, had smelled a rat and gone to New Orleans to investigate. But still John was plagued—why hadn't the colonel said anything?

Rawlins's presence was like a ghost. "He wouldn't advertise it, would he? Wouldn't he want to cover up? And why did he leave in such a hurry? Don't it look like something happened to make him nervous? Use your head, Captain."

John stopped walking, the better to think. Leave out the question of guilt or innocence—ask only if Colonel Stanhope had any inkling of the mischief. Should he be ignorant, the matter of guilt or innocence naturally did not arise. The whole answer would seem to hinge on whether or not he was going to New Orleans and there was one way to find out. Lydia would know. The colonel would not have left on a trip of more than a fortnight without telling her his plans.

John wished he knew what to do. He had made a point of never calling on the Stanhopes when there was a chance Lydia might be alone. To see her in company was bad enough. To be alone with her would be intolerable. Aware of the penalty he might have to pay—the frustration of promise made all the worse by the remembered nearness of promise—he decided to take a chance. Because of Rawlins's memory and Major Howell Angry's improbable name, he had stumbled on what looked like a conspiracy. He needed help, and Lydia could help him. He was simply a man with a job.

Turning off on another side street, he began walking toward the residence Colonel Stanhope had rented in the capital. At first it seemed easy. He need see Lydia only for a few minutes, and he felt confident of his ability to get through the interview without being disturbed. All went well until he came to the corner of the block where the Stanhopes lived. Self-righteousness vanished. It wasn't doing a job that had brought him here, it was Lydia. He had been thinking of her constantly ever since Colonel Stanhope left on his trip. His heart beat slower and then faster, and he began to pray he would find her alone.

ii

The moment was poorly chosen. John was aware of it the instant Amos, the butler, opened the door. The Negro's face was too impassive. John knew the look. It implied eavesdropping and loyalty. It meant that something had gone wrong, that the white folks had been quarreling, and that they must not be given away.

The silence in the hall was like a heavy curtain, drawn so hastily as still to show the ripples in its folds. John knew the curtain also. There was one kept handy in every household, ready to be run out at a moment's notice. Behind it tempers were being calmed, manners composed, and features arranged—whoever the intruder was, there must be presented a united front: let it never be said this isn't a happy home!

It was Arabella who came to greet him after his arrival was announced. "So it's true!" she said. "I couldn't believe Amos when he said it was you. What brought you out of that grimy office of yours? Somebody set fire to it?" and then, since he stood in that middle ground reserved for those who were less than family and more than friend, she brushed the curtain aside and gave him a cross, sullen look. "You're thin as a rail," she said. "I can't say it becomes you. And where's your sword? I think a man in uniform looks half dressed without one."

She was dressed to go out, wearing dark red velvet and a narrow black ribbon round her neck, hung with the same jewel she had worn the night of the Light Infantry Ball. Her hair was piled high on her head, lending an engaging and entirely misleading impression of frankness to her face, and the glow of color on her cheeks, breaking close to the surface, told of a rush of recent anger that also showed in her troubled, too bright eyes. She said, "I wish you were Missy. Why won't she come to visit? Your father can't need her all that bad," and then, "Why did you decline the Taylors tonight? They're going to have an orchestra. You're getting more and more of a stick." John knew this mood of hers and her habit of hitting out at the first person who came along, but the mood was higher-pitched and more finely drawn, strummed from a set of tighter nerves.

He wondered how much of it was traceable to Neville Monckton, how much to Charlie Rhett, and how much to that McKenzie boy from Georgia. A legend of fatality had begun to attach itself to Arabella. The word was that she was a dangerous talisman, worn at enormous risk. Charlie Rhett had fallen completely in love with her, and the McKenzie boy was blindly adoring, and when they were killed at Manassas they were each wearing one of her scarves—up to Manassas the war was like that, the jousts and tournaments of plantation parties brought to a larger, hardly more dangerous field.

Arabella said, "There's no need just to stand there. Come join us in the parlor," and part of the change in her, John decided, was that she wasn't merely Missy's best friend any more, or the gangly child who had run through the dust of the track at Happy Chance. She addressed him in her own person and right, a young woman who knew she was attractive and with whom many men were in love, and what she meant when she said he was a stick was why couldn't he see how desirable she was, and why didn't he ever respond?

John found himself being put off again—no woman should need that much attention. It hinted at some painful insecurity. Catching his look, Arabella apparently divined the substance of his thought. "You're bad as a blue-nose Yankee," she said. "You should have been a preacher or something," and then, holding her chin up, she led the way into the parlor.

Lydia was also dressed to go out, wearing blue. It had become her favorite color. Rarely now was she seen in anything else. She and Arabella avoided looking at each other, as if afraid of striking sparks, and John understood that it was no ordinary quarrel he had interrupted but a bitter, impassioned scene.

If Arabella was high-strung and edgy, Lydia was fiercely controlled. Strain corseted her figure. Her face had a drawn, pinched expression that made her seem almost ill. She said, "Why, Captain Bottomley, what a happy surprise," and though she tried to sound friendly, forcing a smile, there was a repressed tremble in her voice, and the smile was no more than a nervous grimace—her eyes had a peculiar, staring look, icy cold.

Responding to Lydia's greeting, John saw Arabella's lip curl with scorn. He didn't like what it did to her face or what he had stepped into. He said, "I see I have come at a bad time. I should have known you were going to the Taylors'. I came to ask the colonel's present whereabouts, but it's actually not that important. If you will both excuse me——" And it was Arabella, before he finished, who first replied.

"Don't go, Captain," she said in a tone of hollow cheerfulness. "At least take something to drink. You couldn't have come at a better time. My papa's pretty little wife was giving me another lecture and I'm afraid I put her all out of patience. We were being hateful to each other, weren't we, dear?"

What little color there was in Lydia's face drained away completely, and John thought she would start from her chair. Somewhere in his mind there was the recollection of an earlier scene he had blundered upon, hinging on Lydia's having put Amos into plum-colored livery, but whereas then it had been a contest between an experienced woman and an immature girl, now the combatants were evenly matched—if anything, it was Arabella who had mastered the deadlier thrust.

When Lydia spoke, her voice was dry and thin. "I wonder, Captain Bottomley, if you would excuse me a moment. I seem to have forgotten my gloves. Arabella will be glad to entertain you, I know, and we can talk about the colonel when I return."

The silence was so heavy that John imagined he could see it divide where she passed. He watched her walk down the hall and turn to mount the stairs, and she looked so slight and fragile, so open to disaster, that a feeling of pity went through him, sharp as pain.

Arabella waited until the sound of Lydia's footsteps were lost behind a closing door. She said, "That wasn't very nice, was it? I suppose you think I was hateful."

"I don't understand you, Arabella. What makes you lash out the way you do?"

"Me? Lash out?"

John preferred not to argue. "Oh come, Arabella. You do it all the time. You let go with both barrels the moment I walked in. And then, what you said to Mrs. Stanhope——"

"You mean Lydia, don't you?"

"I mean your father's wife. It doesn't become you always to be quarreling. You know how people talk. What you don't seem to realize is that your father, holding the position he does——"

Arabella's eyes began to light up. "You don't have to bring my father into it. That's not necessary! You can take up for her if you want to. You always have. I know that."

"Then you know more about it than I do. I don't propose to quarrel over nothing. But if what you were being lectured about was the unwisdom of riding out in a closed carriage after dark, I urge you to listen."

Arabella spoke in a rush. "That wasn't it, what it was was something I said to that ditchwater old general, thinking he's so grand," and then, breaking off, she began to color vividly. She said, "You know then?" and John, nodding, wished he did not. It was hard to look at Arabella and think she might have been pawed over—it shouldn't have made that much difference, but it did.

He said, "Yes, Arabella, I know. I just happened to see you," and that much, anyway, was out in the open. Arabella stood still a moment, looking into his face.

"Ah, Johnny. Be my friend."

"My being your friend isn't the easiest thing I know. What's the matter with you? Certainly you don't need me to explain things. You're no child. Even if your father wasn't so involved, even if there was no Gup Monckton and the *News*——"

Arabella silenced him with a wave of her hand. "I know, Johnny. There's nothing you can tell me. I've thought and thought. The thing of it is——"

She broke off, pressing her lips together. John waited for her to continue, and, when she did not, "The thing of it is what?" he asked.

"I know it's none of my business——"

"Don't say that, Johnny, please. That's not true. Can't you be my friend?"

"When have I not been? But I can't see that it signifies. Missy writes that you think you may be in love with him. Are you?"

"I don't know, Johnny. Sometimes I think yes and sometimes no. I know that perhaps I shouldn't be, that I shouldn't *let* myself be——"

"Then why——"

Arabella's eyes lighted up again, brighter than before. "I told you I didn't know, didn't I! Maybe I'm in love with him and maybe I'm not. And it's something I have to know! Is that so hard to understand? Or can't you understand anything any more? If all you came here for was to make me feel ashamed——"

"You can't think that."

"I'd like to know why I can't! I ask you to be my friend and you look at me with your eyes like broken glass! What's made you so hateful? I could slap you!"

"Listen, Arabella——"

"Why should I? Do you listen to me? Maybe I'm in love with him and maybe I'm not! Make out of it what you like! I don't care! And what if I did ride out with him today? What's wrong with that? He has to go back to the front in a few days, and sooner or later there is bound to be more fighting, and when I think of what happened to poor Charlie Rhett——"

Her eyes grew moist, and John hoped she wasn't going to cry.

353

"What is it you want, Arabella? What are you looking for?"

Her too full eyes began to overflow. Stepping closer to him, she made as if to rest her head against his chest. "Don't ask me any more questions, Johnny. Just hold me. Please hold me! Say you love me," and then, as he held himself aloof, worried that they should be discovered in such an intimate pose, she must have read caution as rejection.

"But why should I beg you for anything!" she said. "You or anybody! And what do I care what you think? I don't care my foot's worth! You want to know if I love him—yes, yes, I do! He's brave and he's handsome, he knows how to treat a girl, and he doesn't go around like a blue-nose Yankee preacher always trying to make people feel bad! So now you know! I love him! I'll run away with him if he asks me to! I'll do anything! And if you want to tell your little friend Lydia about it, mooning around in that sickening way of yours——"

Were she a man, John would have had her by the throat. He said hoarsely, "I'd stop now! You've said enough!" and Arabella's mouth hung open—she wasn't used to being talked to like that, nor to that much rage. A door opened on the second floor, and Lydia's footsteps could be heard descending the stairs. The dart of Arabella's eyes was like a physical start. Giving a bright, nervous laugh, she said:

"Ah, Johnny, what a dear you are. But I don't believe a word of it! I never heard such a thing in my life. And don't forget what I told you. See if you can't make Missy come for a visit. All I get out of her is that she isn't able to leave your father," and there was nothing for John to do, as comprehension sank in, but to follow her lead and join in hanging up this new curtain as fast as possible. Trying to match her lightness of tone, he said:

"I'll do what I can, Arabella, though I don't think there's much hope. It's true what Missy said about not being able to leave my father. He's not well. He caught cold more than a year ago and has never been able to shake it off," and when Lydia returned the curtain was all in place and he and Arabella couldn't have been chatting more cozily.

Or was it too cozy? Lydia paused in the doorway, holding a pair of long white gloves. She said, "You two seem to be having a nice visit.

You must come to see us more often, Captain Bottomley. You put Arabella in a good humor. I think she has been missing you," and though she inclined her head prettily and pretended to smile, her eyes were still icy cold.

John tried to ease the heavy expression he knew was frozen on his face and could not—it was Arabella who came to the rescue. She said, "He does put me in a good humor, and why shouldn't I miss him? He's my oldest, dearest friend," and John, caught in the cross fire, not so unknowing as to imagine that the words being used had any conceivable relation to what was being said, felt an enormous sag of relief when the knocker on the front door rapped out—he couldn't have stood much more of this; he was thankful he didn't have to live under the same roof.

Arabella ran to the door without waiting for Amos. Lydia lifted her eyes at this latest breach of deportment, as if to inquire, really, what was to be done? and while she again went through the pretense of a smile, no trick of artifice could conceal the effort that composure demanded, or that, wherever her attention lay, it wasn't here—the stare of her eyes might have been directed a thousand miles away.

Amos came into the room at a half trot and John wondered how much of his conversation with Arabella had been listened to. The butler, given a sign by Lydia, went back to the kitchen, looking peevish at having made his trip for nothing, and what he was, John thought, along with every other Negro in the South, was a keg of powder that might explode at any minute—we love and trust our people, even in the midst of this war we love and trust them, but five of the Deerskin Negroes had joined the runaways who had deserted to the Northern camp after the fall of Port Royal in South Carolina, including the girl Glory, making their way through forty miles of swamp, and how could it be imagined that there was a single one of them who hadn't given the larger part of his hope and loyalty to the other side?

"You look troubled, Captain Bottomley," Lydia said. "Is anything wrong?"

"Wrong?" John quickly brought up his guard. "No, what I was thinking——"

355

What he was thinking was that the free man in the North was free in a way that the free man in the South could never hope to be, living where the air was lighter and clearer and much less charged, but now, confronted with Lydia's fixed inquiring stare, he spoke the first thing that came into his mind. "What I was thinking is that if it gets any colder we may have ice by morning. Back home it's nearly spring by now."

Lydia's face became slightly more relaxed. "You miss it, don't you, Captain?"

"What?"

"Old Pompey. Home."

"Yes, I do."

Out in the hall Arabella laughed, honestly this time, and soon she returned with a tall, dark-haired young officer, splendidly good-looking, who wore the uniform of one of the fashionable Virginia cavalry regiments. How much he was attracted to Arabella was only too obvious. He could have been in church, saying his prayers. The introductions completed, he diffidently explained to Lydia that his aunt was waiting in the carriage outside—"My *great*-aunt, ma'am. She'll be sixty-eight come September, and, if I may say so, begging her pardon and yours, it ain't as easy for her to get in and out of a carriage as it used to be. She requests that I convey her apologies and respects, and says she hopes she will see you at the party. And now, ma'am, if you'll excuse us, and you too, Captain——"

John liked him. He was too young, as all men in their early twenties are too young to a man approaching thirty-two, and although it might be said that he was too rigidly encased in the pieties of the tidewater aristocracy, at least he looked like somebody and was of Arabella's class. His error lay in being too worshipful. Arabella seemed restless already. She said, "Isn't it a bit early for us to be leaving? We don't want to be the first ones there," and as the lieutenant furrowed his brow and started to look baffled, Lydia stepped into the breach. She said, "Late as it is, you'll hardly be the first ones there. Besides, the lieutenant's aunt mustn't be kept waiting. Even the tightest carriage can get uncomfortable on a night like this," and while John no less than before could understand what was going on, or the compulsion of these two women always to scratch, he was able to tell that it was now Lydia's turn to chalk up a score.

Arabella's face clouded. She said, "Yes, I suppose so. Shall we go, Lieutenant? Good night, Johnny. Give my love to Missy when you write. And don't forget to tell her that the answer to what she wanted to know is yes," and all these double meanings and cunning insinuations were getting much too exhausting to follow, like a barely defined trail through a jungle of fern—he was glad to see Arabella and her escort go. The front door closed and the house was quiet. Lydia said resignedly:

"I'm afraid I made Arbell angry again. It's probably no secret to you that I always do. She has resented me from the start. But you didn't mind my getting rid of them, did you? Senator Fenchurch is taking me to the Taylors' and will be here most any minute."

Composing herself on a sofa, she said, "Sit down, Captain, please. What can I do to help? I believe you said something about wanting to know the colonel's whereabouts. Why? Has something gone wrong?" and there was a strained overeagerness in her tone that warned him to tread lightly. He said:

"Yes, it could be that something has. Rawlins, my chief clerk, has stumbled on what seems to be a whole nest of irregularities in the New Orleans warehouse. Do you know if the colonel planned on going there? I may have to get in touch with him."

Lydia turned into a pillar of fright—there was no other way for John to describe it. The image that came into his mind was that of Lot's wife. She appeared to tremble with a deep, racking shiver, and her face was so pale that the three little freckles on the bridge of her nose stood out like a disfigurement.

John watched her with a hollow feeling—he remembered that it was she who had urged Colonel Stanhope to invest in Louisiana cotton land and that there were fourteen hundred bales credited to his account in New Orleans. Begin with her greediness, go on from there to the colonel's precarious financial position, add to that the enor-

357

mous influence she exercised over him, and an ominous pattern began to form. John said:

"I'm merely speaking my suspicions, you understand? All these irregularities may well be cleared up. If there is any wrongdoing in the New Orleans warehouse, however, the department should act immediately. My problem is that I don't want to proceed without the colonel's consent. That's why I asked if he planned on going to New Orleans. I thought that if an investigation is needed, he could make it."

He watched Lydia intently, hoping to detect a sign that might lead him to believe his suspicions were wrong—any sign would do. Even as he watched her, however, he watched himself. And the incredible thing was that he wanted her no less than ever. Standing in this room, he also stood in the greenhouse at Happy Chance.

"What about the colonel?" he asked. "Is he going to New Orleans?"

Lydia, with an effort, roused herself. "Not—not that I know. I don't think so. He said he intended to travel no farther than Mobile."

John was beyond thinking straight any longer. If she was telling the truth and if his earlier reasoning had been correct—that Colonel Stanhope's not going to New Orleans would mean he was unaware of any wrongdoing there, much less being involved in it—then the colonel stood absolved. But if she was lying or, if not lying, telling less than she knew, then, in that case—— His mind refused to function. He said:

"I don't mean to be alarming, but what we are dealing with is more than the usual thievery of a few stray bales. There seems to be a real conspiracy. Even forgery may be involved. What worries me as much as anything is Rawlins. I go no farther than to say there appears to be a conspiracy. He, however, is convinced there is. He belongs to the same order as those sand-hill whites back home. You know how suspicious they are and how quick to develop a grudge."

He looked to see what impression he was making, but Lydia's face was a blank. He said, "That much, the grudge part, I'm afraid I've accomplished already. What I believe Rawlins wanted was for me to fire off a telegram telling the New Orleans police to arrest everyone in the warehouse immediately. Let him smolder enough, or happen to drink too much, and he is quite capable of airing his views outside the department. He may be having such notions already."

Lydia sat straight up on the edge of the sofa, holding her long white gloves. The demure blue color of her gown heightened her look of virginal innocence. John said:

"My worst fear is that Rawlins will talk and that the newspapers will get hold of it. Those correspondent fellows are always hanging around, especially the one for the *News*. If there actually is a conspiracy and we leave it to be uncovered by the newspapers, the department might as well close its doors. I'm thinking that perhaps I ought to communicate with the colonel in Mobile. He may want to go on to New Orleans."

Lydia looked as though she had been brought to the edge of hysteria. John said, "Do you know where the colonel will be staying in Mobile? The Battle House?" and Lydia reminded him of his brother Cameron, floundering in panic and wanting to run. "*Must* you?" she cried out. "Isn't my poor husband overworked enough as it is? Can't you at least wait until he returns?" and two thoughts ran through John's mind simultaneously—that only in a humorous sense could Colonel Stanhope be described as overworked, and that she was fighting for time.

His first shock over, and now convinced that Colonel Stanhope was smuggling cotton and that Lydia had a hand in it, John began to think of himself—obviously he could remain in the department no longer: his ties and loyalties were at an end; once the scandal broke, every enemy of the administration would be thirsting for blood, and he was under no obligation to be present when the pack closed in. Only then, with that much decided, did he try to think what to do next. Again his mind refused to work. It veered off on a tangent, worrying about what this was going to do to Arabella, and then he discovered that what he most wanted was to save Lydia. In the final analysis, it was Colonel Stanhope who was responsible, not she—whatever her blandishments, he could have resisted: he shouldn't have been that weak.

"Perhaps you're right," he said. "It may be best to wait until the colonel returns. Another week or so won't make that much difference. We'll decide what to do when he gets back."

His mind was now working the way he wanted it to, and he began to see what might be a way out. The government needed foreign exchange—how easy for Colonel Stanhope to drop in on the Treasury Department, to say that he had been selling cotton on his own initiative for the government, and then to turn over such moneys as he had accumulated, making a great big patriotic thing of it. If there was a medal for disinterested public service he would be decorated; even without a medal he would be wrapped in the mantle of noble behavior: he might even be considered for Vice-President the next time around—as, if the rumors making the rounds were true, Lydia was determined he should.

Lydia said, "Thank you, Captain. The colonel will appreciate your thoughtfulness," and now that the moment of immediate peril had passed, she seemed less distraught. John wished he knew what wheels were turning in her mind and what plans were being made. But whatever they were, it made no difference—she and Colonel Stanhope were trapped, and they would have to do whatever he said, down to the last humiliating detail. It gave him no pleasure to think so. Lydia could only hate and despise him, which was as good a way for it to end as any, and Colonel Stanhope, hollow though he was, had always been a friend.

"You are very silent, Captain."

"Am I? I hope not to the point of being rude. If you will excuse me——"

"Not back to your office, I hope."

"No, not this evening."

The knocker on the front door rapped out again, and after bidding Lydia good night John followed Amos down the hall. The new caller was Senator Fenchurch. John bowed to him, a short, stocky man with a bushy beard who had been recently widowed and was known to be greatly taken with Lydia, and walked back to his hotel. He went into the bar and drank more than he should have, but he knew what he was doing. He wanted to be able to sleep. He hoped he wouldn't have too much of a head in the morning.

CHAPTER TWENTY-EIGHT

Some days in the department were busier than others. Although it was not yet ten o'clock, John had already interviewed five visitors—three office seekers, a member of the Wilmington Committee of Safety, and a Brownsville, Texas, businessman who wanted a permit to trade with Mexico. John turned down the office seekers, tried to make the member of the Wilmington committee feel more important than he was, and told the Brownsville businessman that his request would be considered. Actually there wasn't a hope. To grant the permit would be to open another possible door to the contraband trade, and enough cotton was being smuggled out of Texas as it was.

In between visitors there had been a brief session with Rawlins. Three days had passed since he had brought up the matter of Major Howell Angry and the questionable situation in New Orleans, and he had been stiff and standoffish ever since. John regretted having tried to be stern with him. Up to then he and Rawlins had been on good enough terms. Even the awkwardness caused by Rawlins's sleeping in the basement had been surmounted. It had not been easy for Rawlins to ask permission, nor was John especially taken by the idea. Back-countrymen like Rawlins were extremely conscious of social distinctions. More often than not their sole claim to status was the color of their skin, and the surest way to make an enemy was to cause one of them to imagine he was being treated with less than proper respect. As a class, they had little enthusiasm for the war. They saw it as a rich man's affair.

So because of John's effort to be stern Rawlins had his back up. He spoke only when spoken to, and his "yes sirs" and "yes Captains" had an empty ring. That which should be done was to draw his sting, but at the same time he must not get the idea he was being catered to—he would instantly conclude that somebody was trying to hoodwink him, that he was being played for a fool, and he was too smart for that, by God! There was something crooked going on and he wasn't going to let it get past him. He might have to sleep in the basement and maybe hadn't had all the advantages, but he was an honest, sincere, patriotic man.

John decided the least dangerous course would be to play to Rawlins's sense of importance—he placed no small value on being chief clerk. Perhaps he might be asked to write a report on the New Orleans situation, or it might be suggested that he take over a few slightly more important duties. However, regardless of the procedure, John knew he would not like it: it came too close to blackmail.

Rawlins walked in with a new batch of papers. He said, carrying his head like something sacred, "Here are this week's requisitions from the War Department, Captain. They need your signature," and John decided that this was as good a time as any to try to bring him round. He said, "Thank you, Mr. Rawlins. Do you have a few minutes? I've been thinking about the New Orleans situation and I'd like to discuss it with you," and Rawlins, less rigid, came close to being pleasant for the first time in days.

He said, "Glad to, Captain. Any time you say. But you have another visitor. Major Vincent. He just this minute arrived," and John was not adroit enough to avoid another mistake. "Show Major Vincent in," he said. "We'll talk about the New Orleans situation later on," and Rawlins, in his readiness to be affronted, took it as another rebuff. He said, "Yes, Captain. You give the orders, sir," and John was ready to give up—these sand-hills spooked quicker than wild turkeys. "Right away if you please, Mr. Rawlins," he said. "Major Vincent may be going back to the front," and that was no help either. What if this biggity-big plantation major was going back to the front? Was that a reason why a man should be sent packing like a field hand?

Rawlins withdrew to the clerks' room, and John brought out the bottle of whisky from his desk. Clay Vincent would be wanting a drink. The curious thing about Rawlins, John thought, was that he was really an Abolitionist at heart. It was only the status symbol of his skin that kept him on the Southern side.

ii

John had already heard the news. General Monckton had been ordered to the West. Deciding to act, the administration lost no time. Word of the general's banishment had leaked out that morning. There had been a great scurrying about of correspondents and by afternoon the newspapers would be full of it.

Draining his glass, Clay Vincent said, "You knew it was going to happen, didn't you? Why didn't you tell me? That's a hell of a way!"

John was in no mood to be attacked. He said, "Knew it was going to happen! How could I? Am I the Chief Executive? Do they take me into their confidence at the War Department?"

"You must have had some idea."

"Yes, so I did. Your general hasn't exactly gone out of his way to make friends. Did he the other day? He practically asked for it. He's been asking for it for quite some time."

"You should have told me."

"Told you what? And why? To rub you the wrong way?"

Clay changed his position in his habitual restless fashion. He said, "Maybe it's true what you say, that he doesn't know how to make friends, but still this is no way to treat him. Not after all he's done." John freshened Clay's glass, and Clay nodded his thanks. "I hate politicians," he said. "I hate them up and down. What they've got against the general is that he's too popular. And not only with the public. Wait till the men hear about this. They ain't going to stomach it one bit."

Clay looked out the window. It was a cold, gray day. "But there's this much I can tell you," he said. "The politicians ain't heard the last of him yet. That you can count on. I admit some of his ideas may be a little out of the ordinary—like what he said about burning up the South—but in the field he's a genius. You don't believe it, do you?"

"I'm not qualified to say."

"You don't *want* to say. You've got this grudge against him on account of what happened back home——"

"What am I supposed to do? Lead the cheers?"

"Nobody's asking that. Just give him credit, that's all. And don't forget this—what happened at Manassas can happen over in Tennessee. Maybe his being sent there will be a good thing. Maybe he'll put some starch into those fellows. Retreat! A defensive war! Christ Almighty! How are we ever going to get anywhere that way? All you have to do is look at a map——"

John didn't want to get into that again. He said, "What else do you know, Clay? Have you been having a good time since you've been here?" and Clay half emptied his glass. He said clinically, "I got me a frig, if that's what you mean. After all that time it was like dipping it in cream. It came high, though. The price of everything is going up. I bought me a pair of twelve-dollar boots and had to pay twenty-five for them. In gold. U.S. gold, at that. If things keep up the way they're going, our own money will be worthless. And what's to prevent? This damn government does everything wrong!"

He rolled the remaining whisky around in the glass, swallowed it, and made a face. "Why the hell don't we fight this war and get it over?" he said. "And now I have to haul ass all the way to Tennessee. I'll never be able to get home now, not till the war is over." He slumped in his chair, stretching his legs. "You hear any news lately? How's Missy and the Governor?"

"Missy's well, but I'm worried about my father. He's been sick off and on for over a year and he's still trying to look after everything himself. And your father, Clay? How is he?"

Clay looked more cheerful. "That old gentleman is going to outlive us all. He was eighty-three month before last, and you know what he did? Went on a deer drive and shot himself one of the biggest bucks ever." Clay's face sobered. "You think it'll ever be like that again, Johnny, the way it was before the war? Jug! Trouble with me this morning is that I'm homesick. That's what's wrong with the troops too. You let them hang around camp with nothing to do, like it's been all winter, and homesickness plays holy hell. Most of them have never been away from home before. Now you take me, a funny thing—up till the war came I hadn't been out of Marlborough County in sixteen years. You been home since you came here?"

"I haven't had time."

"In your place I'd of made time. Don't you do anything but work? I looked for you at a party last night, some local people named Harrison, but you weren't there. Don't you ever go to parties? You missed the Taylors' too. You hear about Arbell Stanhope last night?"

"No, what's there to hear?"

Clay found another drop of whisky in his glass and drank it. He said, "She tried to play both ends against the middle and got caught in the squeeze—but by God she's good-looking! She had on a green dress, maybe a little tighter than it should be, and the way she's filled out——"

John found himself resenting Clay's analytical tone. "But what happened?" he said. "What did she do?"

Clay shifted his gaze. "Oh hell, Johnny, it ain't that important. I shouldn't have opened my mouth," and John began to feel uneasy. He said:

"I'm beginning to think you may be right. But you can't stop now. Just what did she do?"

Clay shrugged. "I reckon you'll hear about it sooner or later. She damn near caused two men to call each other out, that's all. The reason I'm sorry I said anything is because of Arbell and Missy—the way they are practically like sisters, I mean. And then, not only that——"

John could sit on his impatience no longer. "Damn it, Clay, why don't you come out with it! The more you hem and haw, the worse you make it sound!"

"Now don't you get so hot under the collar," Clay said, narrowing his eyes. "I ain't one of your clerks! All right—you want to know what happened, so I'll tell you what happened. Arbell Stanhope's no charge of mine. It ain't my fault that she seems hell-bent to get herself talked about. She went to the Harrisons' party with this Virginia fellow, a man in the cavalry, the same one who took her to the Taylors'——"

"I know him."

Clay raised his brows. "There ain't much you *don't* know about Arbell, is there? Anyway, if you know this Virginia fellow, you know how bad he's got it. Me, I felt sorry for him. I said to myself, 'You poor moon-struck bastard, I'd like to have a silver dollar for every man she's had tailing around.' It's just like my sister Lucy says—Arbell can't do with just one man, or even two or three. She has to have a regiment."

For John to entertain such thoughts was one thing, to hear them uttered by Clay Vincent another. "I can't see this is getting us anywhere," he said. "And I would have thought you'd be more careful. Your talking about Arabella like this isn't going to help any."

Clay's low boiling point was reached. He said, "I don't propose to be given any lectures by you. Me talk about Arbell Stanhope! That's a good one! She goes to a party with one man, while he ain't looking she runs off to the garden to meet another, and you tell me not to talk!"

"Who was he? The man in the garden."

"Do you have to ask?"

"I'm asking, am I not?"

"And suppose I tell you to jug it?"

"I doubt that you'd dare."

"You ain't daring me, are you?"

"Am I supposed to be afraid to?"

They had gone as far as they could—one more word and somebody would be obliged to call somebody out. John said, "Look, Clay. If you didn't like my tone, I didn't like yours. That's as much of an apology as you'll get. Just because you're graveled about General Monckton's being ordered to Tennessee——"

"Damn if I am as much graveled as you are about Arbell Stanhope! But I accept your apology. I didn't know you felt this way."

"What way? Just because I don't like the idea of Arabella's being talked about?"

Clay shrugged his shoulders. "Let's forget it. It ain't worth another argument. But as far as her being talked about is concerned, well, if that's her idea of how to behave——"

"Who was the man in the garden?"

Clay looked straight at him. "You know who it was. You know damn well you do. That's the big reason I'm sorry I said anything. The way things stand between you and the Moncktons, I didn't want to cause any more bad blood."

John looked at the litter of paper on his desk, remembering the work he was neglecting—he'd be here half the night again.

"You're not thinking of doing anything about it, are you?" Clay said.

"Like what?"

"Like using a whip on him. Hell, Johnny! What good would it do? Maybe he is a tomcat, which is what you're thinking, but do you think he'll stand there and take it, just because he's prowling where you don't think he belongs? Besides, you're not involved in what happened last night. If you go out of your way to pick a fight——"

"Was there much of a scene?"

"I'm afraid so. Trouble was that he wasn't even invited to the party. The way I see it, he and Arbell arranged to meet in the garden beforehand. I can't figure that girl out. Could it be she's in love with him, do you think? Granted he's not her kind, and if it was my sister Lucy I wouldn't take to it a single goddamn bit, but still, if she was willing to run a risk like that——"

Seeing John's expression, he cut himself short. "You asked me to tell you, Johnny. I should have had more sense than to get started. Maybe you wouldn't have heard about it, though I don't see how. It's bound to be all over by now. I reckon I'd best be getting along. What I dropped in for was to tell you good-by. We'll be leaving in a couple of days and the general has me all tied up."

"Tell me this, Clay. Was Mrs. Stanhope there?"

Clay nodded. "That she was, waited on hand and foot by some

369

senator—Fenchurch's the name, I believe, a widow fellow with five children. She sure has changed since the last time I saw her. Most of the time she looked like she wanted to jump out of her skin. That senator fellow didn't get far, I'm afraid, and that business about Arbell didn't help any. If looks could kill, Arbell wouldn't be here this morning. Those two sure go at each other, don't they? According to Lucy——"

"According to everybody," John said. "Well, you take care of yourself, Clay. Where do you go from here?"

"Right on to Tennessee. The general's not inclined to waste any time. And, Johnny——"

"Yes?"

"Why don't you talk to Arbell Stanhope?"

"Me? Why? What about?"

"You know what about."

"Take care of yourself, Clay. Let me hear from you if you find time."

"No offense intended, Johnny. I just figured——"

"You figured wrong."

"Yes, so I see. Well, good luck, Johnny. I'll be seeing you. Come summer we may all be home."

"That's a nice idea. Let's hold it."

CHAPTER TWENTY-NINE

John's big task of the day was to clear the requisitions sent over by the War Department. All that was required was that he validate the requisitions by signing them, thus making it possible for the War Department to draw upon the various government warehouses for the cotton it needed, but it really wasn't quite that simple—there were times when the War Department seemed determined to get its hands on every bale in the country: sign every piece of paper it passed along, and there wasn't a warehouse that wouldn't be stripped clean.

Picking up one of the requisitions, John found himself immediately drawn into the sort of tedious detail that made this the dullest part of his job. The War Department wanted another two hundred and fifty bales from the Mobile warehouse, and he was practically certain it had already used up its Mobile quota for the month. It was part of Rawlins's responsibility to check the requisitions beforehand, on the lookout for just such conflicts, and also to provide an itemized statement of the number of bales currently on hand in each warehouse. Unable to find the statement, and irritated with Rawlins for not doing his work properly, John went to the door to call him in.

The other clerks were busy at their desks, but Rawlins's chair was empty. John saw him standing in the corridor, engrossed in conversation with the correspondent of the *News*, a tall, lanky, horse-faced Virginian who seemed to be always hanging around. Rawlins stood with his head bent forward and slightly to one side, as if the better to hear, and his companion, to judge from the rapidly changing expressions that crossed his face, was making some kind of plea.

By now the morning was nearly gone. Enough time had passed for the news about General Monckton to have been put on the wires and for the correspondent to have received a set of instructions in reply. It was not hard to imagine what they were. General Monckton would probably have accepted his fate philosophically. But not so his brother. Gup would be wanting revenge.

Entering the clerks' room, John walked to a filing cabinet that stood in one corner. He deliberately passed the door that led into the corridor, and both Rawlins and the correspondent of the *News* saw him at the same time. He swept his eyes past them, went to the filing cabinet, shuffled through a few papers, and returned to his office. Within half a minute Rawlins entered. He said:

"I went to get a drink of water, Captain. Did you want something?"

John felt relieved. If Rawlins was ready to talk, he hadn't talked yet. Any defection, and he would have gone deeper into ambush. He would not be using this conciliatory tone. Rawlins said:

"Mr. Clinton just happened to be in the corridor."

"Just happened?" John lifted his brows. "That I doubt, Mr. Rawlins. My notion is that Mr. Clinton made a deliberate point of it, acting on instructions from his editor. You've heard about General Monckton, I suppose?"

"Yes sir. It's all over town."

"And you know that General Monckton is the proprietor of the *News*?"

"Yes sir."

"And that one of his brothers is the editor?"

"Yes sir."

"Need I continue?" John paused a moment. "Is it too much to believe that General Monckton and his brother would like nothing better than to damage the administration? Might they not welcome a chance to discredit this department, not caring how?"

Rawlins looked uncomfortable. "Yes sir, I see what you mean."

"I hope you do, Mr. Rawlins," John said pointedly. "I don't want to issue any orders, but I would like to suggest that we might be wise not to do anything that might play into their hands. Do I make myself clear?"

"Yes sir, you make yourself clear."

Sensing an increase of antagonism, John decided to let Rawlins stew in it. The worst thing he could do would be to try to appease. He said, "This requisition, Mr. Rawlins, drawing on another two hundred and fifty bales from Mobile. Hasn't the War Department already used its Mobile cotton for the month? I count on you to verify such things."

"I can't do all the work, Captain." Rawlins's voice was strained. "I had to divide up the requisitions among other clerks. It's not my fault if they're not up to the job."

"Whose fault it is doesn't matter," John said. "You're supposed to be in charge out there. All I want to know is if the requisition is in order. I can't sign it if there is any question, and if I don't sign it I will be asked to explain. Not that that will save an argument. You know those people in the War Department as well as I do. And what about the warehouse statement? Did you forget?"

"No sir, I didn't forget. It's with the certificates of release you have to sign. Is there anything else?"

"No, not right now. But will you check the Mobile situation immediately? These requisitions should go back not later than three o'clock. We'll never make it, but we ought to try."

Rawlins left the room, again holding his head like something sacred, the Holy Grail or a piece of the original cross, and John was once more reminded of Wilson, full of bile and bitterness because the Deerskin people had been given an afternoon off. He lit a cigar, went back to work, and soon fell into an uninterrupted, quieting routine. It was some time before he became aware that Rawlins, from the sound of him, was standing on his dignity.

A VISITOR: *Is Captain Bottomley in?*

MR. RAWLINS: *I don't know.*

THE VISITOR: *Could you find out? I would like to see him.*

MR. RAWLINS: *There is his door. You can ascertain for yourself.*

THE VISITOR (in a voice that John was beginning to find disturbingly familiar): *Now see here. I asked you a civil question in a civil manner.*

MR. RAWLINS (testily): *It is not civil to presume that I am acting in the capacity of a messenger or a doorkeeper. I am the chief clerk of this department.*

THE VISITOR (whose voice John was now sure he recognized): *Oh, so that's it. Well, Mr. Chief Clerk, what do I do? Walk in?*

MR. RAWLINS: *You may please yourself.*

John hurried to the door. He looked at his visitor, an emaciated young man who wore a wide black hat and a shabby suit ripped at one elbow, and his visitor looked steadily back. There was a cut on his forehead and a front tooth was missing. His nails were dirty and he needed a shave. John said, stepping aside, "You want to see me? Won't you come in?" and his visitor, moving past Rawlins, whose desk was nearest the door, followed him into his office. John shut the door carefully. He said:

"Of all people! Sit down, Cam. It does me good to see you."

Cameron eased himself into the chair. He looked not so much thin as withered. A desperate illness could not have wasted him more. He took off his hat and held it on his knees. His long hair fell in a hook over one eye, the last trace of his boyishness. He said:

"Damn if I think much of the railroad as a means of transportation. I got in on the midnight train, nine hours late, and I've been hunting for you ever since. You wouldn't have a drink for a thirsty man, would you?"

No "Good morning," no "How are you?" no "How have you been?" John said, "Sure, Cam, of course. But where have you been all this time? Don't you realize the worry you've caused?"

Cameron laughed softly, showing his missing tooth. "Same old Johnny," he said. "Always wanting to know do I realize." His laugh subsided and he looked around the room. "So this is where you've been mismanaging our cotton, letting it be smuggled out of the country right and left. Don't look so surprised. I've been reading all about you, you and the Senator. Except now he's a colonel. He's a colonel and you're a captain. Times do change, don't they?" He looked around the room again and then across the desk. "How did you get yourself into this, Johnny? Was it the old man's idea?"

"Partly."

"That's what I figured. I made myself a bet."

John expected him to ask about their father, to begin to pick up the threads, but Cameron's thoughts had moved on elsewhere. He touched the cut on his forehead, fingering it gently. John started to ask about it and the missing tooth and decided he would rather not hear. He said, "Where have you been, Cam?" and Cameron, gazing at his hat, made no move to reply.

"Why didn't you come home? Why didn't you send us word?"

Cameron drew in a deep breath and expelled it slowly. Then, lifting his eyes:

"How about that drink, Johnny?"

"You had breakfast?"

"We ain't talking about breakfast. It's a drink I could use."

John brought out the bottle and a single glass. Cameron, pretending not to watch, watched greedily. There was no sound for a few seconds but the splash of the whisky. Reaching for the glass, Cameron said, "Here's to you, Johnny. Health and prosperity," and his adam's apple was sharp and bony as he drank.

"Tell me about things. How's Missy?"

"She's well. She and Gordon Carpenter are going to be married. The wedding will be as soon as Gordon can get home. He's here in Virginia, but not with the Light Infantry. It's been broken up. The mounted fellows have gone into the cavalry, the others into the infantry."

Cameron, listening abstractedly, took another swallow. He said, "I always thought Missy and Gordon would marry. And Mama? How's she?"

John told him what had happened, and Cameron gazed at his hat a long time. John said, "Father keeps going along more or less as usual, but I'm worried about him. He's developed this chronic cold and hasn't been well for nearly a year," and Cameron, with an abrupt, throttled movement, drained his glass. He said:

"What I came for, Johnny, one of the things, is this. In case you don't know it, you're getting frigged. Royally. I've been reading the *Picayune*."

"In New Orleans? Is that where you've been?"

"Most of the time." Cameron began to look shifty. "I had the idea of going to Texas at first, and then on to California or maybe Mexico— it was gold mining I had in mind—but I didn't get any further than New Orleans." His voice dropped off and he lowered his glance. "I got robbed."

"Did you?" John tried to sound sympathetic. "That's too bad. I've always heard you had to be careful in New Orleans. How have you been managing?"

Cameron looked into his empty glass. He said, "I've been managing. You don't have to worry about me," and finally raised his eyes. "You wouldn't mind if I had another, would you, Johnny?"

"Must you?"

"We ain't going to start that all over again, are we? If so——"

"No, of course not. Why don't you pour your own?"

Cameron filled the glass nearly to the top. "The best way to raise a thirst, I've decided, is to travel by the cars. All I did was to breathe in cinders." He put the bottle on the desk and took a long, hungry swallow.

"About my getting frigged," John said. "I don't think I understand. And how does the *Picayune* come into it?"

"Those editorials. They made it sound like you were up to something crooked. You saw them, didn't you?"

"A few."

"A few would have been enough for me. I'd of reached for a shotgun."

"One can't always. But you still haven't told me——"

"I will." Cameron paused long enough to drink again, almost emptying the glass. "You won't like it, but I will."

"Why don't you then?"

"It's your friend Lydia Stanhope."

Needing time to recover, John reached into the drawer where he kept his cigars. He said, lighting one, "Yes, go on. What about her?"

"She's smuggling cotton."

John glanced toward the door. Rawlins's desk was just outside and the door wasn't nearly as thick as it might be.

"I knew you wouldn't like it," Cameron said. "I told you."

Seeing that the outside wrapper of his cigar had pulled away, John pressed it back into place. He said, "Like it? Of course I don't like it. It would be strange if I did. I wonder, though, if you understand what you're saying. Can you prove it?"

Cameron said, "How do you mean, prove?" and the old familiar look of belligerence began to harden his face. "If you mean by going to court with a lot of documents and that sort of stuff, no, I can't." He looked at John steadily. "You've been soft on her for a long time, haven't you?" he said, his eyes narrowing to slits.

All John could think was that rarely are we as clever as we imagine we are, and how poorly he must have dissembled—under a different set of circumstances it might be laughable. He said:

"Yes, Cam, I suppose I have been. I just didn't realize it was that obvious. So what you say does come as a shock. It would be foolish of me not to admit it. However, unless you have proof——"

"What's the matter? Are you afraid to listen?"

Cameron's hand reached for the bottle, and John almost asked him not to. It required an effort to hold his tongue. He said, "Yes, Cam, I'll listen. You must have some reason to make such a charge. Why don't you tell me about it?"

"Ain't much to tell." Cameron held the bottle poised over the glass. "You remember a telegraph operator we used to have back home, man named Morris? You never knew him, but I did. He used to sit in those games on Liberty Street. Big heavy man with a big red nose. George Morris. Don't you remember?"

At first John did not remember, and then, almost immediately, he did—the picnic at Happy Chance: Jeremiah Lake trying to be pleasant to Lydia and how flustered she was; Blue Fly's stirring finish and

Arabella tearing through the dust, wearing her crown of leaves. He said:

"Mrs. Stanhope's cousin?"

"The very same. And do you know where he is now?"

John had already bridged the gap. Cameron said, "Superintendent of the cotton warehouse in New Orleans," and John wished he would keep his voice down. "It ain't pleasant to be frigged, is it?" Cameron said. "Now you know how it feels."

John looked at his brother, the cut on his forehead and his missing tooth, the week's growth of stubble and how dirty he was, and all of a sudden he didn't care. Not about anything. At that moment he didn't believe he would care about anything ever again.

"And they're in it together? Mrs. Stanhope and her cousin?"

Cameron nodded. "I said you were getting frigged, didn't I?" There was the suggestion of a smirk on his face, and in his voice a trace of malice. "Good old Johnny. Letting himself get frigged right under his very nose."

John still didn't care—dully, the mind's reflexes working nonetheless, he cautioned himself not to imagine that Cameron now was any different from Cameron then. Being an older brother is not always the most fortunate of identities, and it was too late in the day to pretend that Cameron had ever really liked him. He said:

"What about the colonel? Where does he stand in this? Does he know?"

Cameron frowned and scratched his head. Now he was enjoying himself truly. "The colonel? You mean the Senator? Our dear friend and neighbor? The one with the pretty little wife with the pretty little——"

"Yes!"

Digging into his bag of tricks, Cameron began to grin—his little-boy-being-naughty-and-well-knowing-it grin, the one he had been using ever since he was ten years old. He said, "Well, they are pretty, ain't they? Or can't you say yet?" and his grin became wider, marred by the missing tooth.

"About our dear friend and neighbor, it's hard to say. Seeing that she's his wife, though, and that Morris got his appointment through her——"

"How do you know that! You're not mixed up in this, are you?"

Up to a point Cameron could always manage. Maintaining his poise, he brought out one of the trump cards of what used to be his charm—the casual, honeyed, teasing tone. "Why, Johnny! What a thing to say! You should know better than even to think that. I just heard a few things, that's all."

John fought down his anger as best he could, and for an instant, as he watched the greedy ripple of Cameron's adam's apple, he was not himself but his father, glaring across the dinner table in a prelude to one of those terrible scenes. He said:

"You didn't come here to play games, did you? What *did* you come for?"

One of Cameron's largest talents was the ability to look innocent.

"What did I come for? I figured that maybe I could help you out. That's one thing."

"Yes, and I believe I know the other. I'm still a branch office of the Merchants & Mechanics Bank. What kind of mess are you in this time? Oh for God's sake, Cam. Don't you realize——"

"Realize, realize!" Easy as it was for Cameron to look innocent, it was even easier for him to look ugly. He said, "Hell! If that's the thanks I'm going to get, putting myself to all this trouble just to help you out, breathing in smoke from here to New Orleans——"

"Goddammit, you shut up!" Perhaps it was Cameron's appearance, perhaps his whining tone, or perhaps everything in general—though John had never been able to understand why his father had disavowed Cameron, now he did. He said, "Probably it makes no difference to you, but I'm responsible for the cotton affairs of this department. You can't walk in here and make these wild charges and expect that to be the end of it! How did you find out? Have you been part of this thing? Is that how you've been managing in New Orleans?"

"I told you I've been managing, didn't I?" Cameron's smoldering resentment broke through. "That's all you have to know! I don't pry into your affairs, do I? All right then! You keep your nose out of mine! You're just like Father! You're even beginning to look like him, the old bald-headed bastard."

"He's your father, Cam."

"You don't say!" Prodding himself with anger, Cameron reached for the bottle. "Ain't that a piece of news! Then why didn't he ever act like a father instead of always complaining and finding fault, making me feel I was no better than a piece of dirt since as far back as I can remember. Sure, sure, I know! I'm a trifling good-for-nothing that ain't worth the powder to blow him to hell. That's what he thinks and that's what you think. But what do I care? What difference does it make to me?"

Pouring another drink, he sloshed some of the whisky onto his trousers. He cursed under his breath, drawing his lips back over his teeth.

"I think you're being unfair, Cam," John said, "but, if it pleases you, have it your own way. The important thing is what you've said about Mrs. Stanhope. I'm still waiting to hear how you found out."

Cameron, shaking his trouser leg with thumb and forefinger, looked up slowly. It was the look of one wrestler measuring another, seeking the likeliest grip. He said, "I've got this friend in New Orleans. He used to work in the warehouse. This Morris ain't half as smart as he thinks he is. He made a mistake, a big one, and my friend caught him in it."

"So?"

"So my friend ain't no fool! He got Morris to take him in. A hell of a lot you know, sitting up here being important! More cotton is being smuggled out of New Orleans than is shipped regular. Why should my friend be left out? Why shouldn't he get his share?" Glowering, but more at some distant recollection than at John, he dropped his voice to a less combative tone. "I ain't going to tell you my friend's name, though. I don't want to cause him any trouble."

"With your generous nature, of course you don't," John said. "And actually it doesn't matter. There is one thing, though, that I'd like to know. This friend of yours—did he ever tell you whose idea it was, Morris's or Mrs. Stanhope's?"

Cameron watched him cautiously. "The way I heard it from my friend, it began with Morris. The way he tells it, Morris came up here after he got his appointment. You didn't know that, did you?"

"This is a big place. I can't keep up with everybody."

Somewhat more at ease, Cameron was more inclined to talk. He said, "I believe my friend said Morris's visit was last October. And it was after that, he says, that the smuggling started. The way I got it from him, Morris and Mrs. Stanhope worked it out when Morris was here. He says it was Morris who thought it up. That, though, is just what my friend heard. He hasn't been in on everything."

"He has been in on a lot, though, hasn't he? Did Morris pay him well?"

"That I don't know. I reckon he did all right, though."

"But it all slipped through his fingers?"

"That I don't know, either. It costs money to live in New Orleans. Those boardinghouse keepers are a bunch of bloodsuckers."

"It costs money to live anywhere these days," John said. "And your complaint about boardinghouse keepers is a common one. You ought to talk to my chief clerk. He's the gentleman who didn't like being mistaken for a doorkeeper."

"Mean-looking devil, ain't he? What's the matter with his eye?"

"I've never inquired."

"It would give me the fidgits. I wouldn't want to have him around."

"He does his work and that's what he's paid for. But let me go back to what you said, what your friend said, about Colonel Stanhope. As I understand it——"

"I've already answered that. The way I got it from my friend, it's all between Morris and Mrs. Stanhope. The Senator—or the colonel, as you keep calling him—doesn't seem to be involved. So far as my friend can tell, he doesn't know anything about it. However, seeing as she's his wife, it stands to reason——"

"Yes, that's one way of looking at it," John said, and yet the more he thought it over, the more it did not stand to reason. The many points of Colonel Stanhope's odd behavior must still be explained, and also his hasty departure, but without his being able to say why, yielding to some prompting of intuition, John stood ready to believe, as he had not been before, that Colonel Stanhope had no part in this.

"What are you going to do?" Cameron asked. "It's no crime to smuggle cotton, you know, not according to law. That's why my friend was willing to take a hand."

John's cigar had gone out. Relighting it, he said between puffs, "A wise man, your friend," and continued puffing until the cigar began to draw. Waving away the smoke, he said, "The truth of the matter is that there isn't much I can do. Not about the cotton. It belongs to the Stanhopes. None of it has been released for export—I'd know about it if it had: I would have had to sign the certificates of release— but I imagine Morris was shrewd enough to get around that. It would have been simple enough for him to withdraw, let us say, one hundred bales from government supply and then replace them with one hundred Stanhope bales. Except for their gin marks, all cotton bales look alike, and gin marks are easily altered or defaced. The exchange would never be detected. No one would ever know."

Watching Cameron closely, John puffed on his cigar. "So I don't think your friend has too much to worry about. Except possibly for one thing. That chief clerk of mine, the one you wouldn't like to have around, has turned up a couple of forged requisitions. They may make a difference. There is no penalty for smuggling cotton, as your friend says, but forgery remains a crime. I don't know if any punishment is attached to aiding and abetting a forgery, or to profiting from one, but if there is, then all those people may find themselves in trouble." He ground out his cigar on the heel of his boot and dropped the frayed end into the brass spittoon. "In this case, however, since smuggling cotton is not illegal, I doubt that aiding and abetting would apply. My suspicion is that your friend is pretty much in the clear. Unless he's the forger. You wouldn't happen to know anything about that, would you?"

Cameron said, "My friend ain't no forger. That much I can swear to," and John felt relieved. If Cameron had been lying, his face would have given him away.

"And now you, Cam. I appreciate your coming all the way from

New Orleans to help me out, but what did you really come for? Money?"

Cameron said, put upon:

"Don't think I couldn't use some! It cost me my last cent to get here."

John nodded understandingly. "Yes, traveling does come high. But much as I appreciate what you've done, I may have to disappoint you. Money isn't as plentiful as it used to be."

"Don't start that, for Christ's sake! One thing I can't stand is your talking poor-mouth! And if you're going to start throwing things up to me——"

"How much did you have in mind this time?"

Cameron said, "This time! There you go again!" and what this new expression meant, this outraged glare and distorted mouth, was that, with no more tricks in his bag, he was trying to dose himself with anger, trusting it to do the work of courage. "Here I came all the way from New Orleans, spending my last cent——"

"How much, Cam?"

Cameron hesitated briefly. "I know I owe you fifteen hundred, and there was nine hundred before that, but I've still got that eleven thousand coming to me when I get married——"

"I wouldn't count on that eleven thousand if I were you. There's a war going on. If we lose it, which is not impossible, we'll all be impoverished. Can't you understand?"

Cameron had never been a graceful petitioner, and there were no more tricks in his bag. He said, "All I understand is that it gravels you to help, just like it always did! A war going on! As if that made any difference to you! Didn't I read in the paper that the government bought up nearly all last year's crop of rice? You didn't get your share, I suppose?"

As a matter of fact, John had—thirty-five hundred dollars for the whole turnout, the smallest crop in years, sold through Thrall & Lockhart and paid for in government bonds. That, however, was gross. John's net came to a little under seven hundred dollars, and the government's paper had already declined to sixty per cent of its face value, provided you could find someone foolish enough to redeem it in coin. John said:

"Have it your own way, Cam. Keep on believing I'm a rich man. I'll help you get on your feet and keep you going until we straighten a few things out, assuming they can be, but the old days are over. How would fifty dollars do?"

"Fifty dollars!" Cameron sounded strangled. "How am I going to get to California on fifty dollars?"

The slip made, he was obliged to bluster it out. He said, "Why shouldn't I go to California? There's a lot of opportunity out there. A man could start all over, make a fresh start." More openly belligerent, he pressed the attack. "What are you looking at me like that for? They don't need me in the Army. They've got more men than they know what to do with. What do you expect me to do? Join up, so they can stick me off somewhere and let me rot?" Genuinely aroused now, he said, "What about you? I don't see you in the Army! You didn't waste any time looking after yourself! Why don't you practice what you preach?"

Unaware that he had been preaching anything, John was willing to concede that his expression was probably one of reproach. He said:

"What about what happened back home? Have you forgotten you killed a man? Are you going to keep on running the rest of your life?"

That Cameron had never liked him, John didn't need to be told: that Cameron could hate him required a few moments to sink in. Anger he had anticipated. What he was not prepared for was to hear himself called a son-of-a-bitch. He was a son-of-a-bitch, a dirty *rotten* son-of-a-bitch, he had always looked down his nose, pretending to be better than everybody else, while all the time he was sniffing around after another man's wife, he cared about nothing except to pile up money in the bank, and he was as bad as his father and maybe worse —the grotesque notion leaped into John's mind that abuse, for some fevers, was probably more helpful than Pittman's Ague Cure.

Cameron exhausted himself. "Now it's my turn," John said. "You make sure you listen," and though it was rather like standing over Cameron with a whip, the way it had been with Allbright, he could tell himself that this time the unfairness was not all on his side. He said, "Sometimes I wonder who you think you are. Let any other man talk to me like that, and I wouldn't wait to call him out. You, though, you have privileges. You can say what you like. But at least I know what's been bottled up in you all these years. That, however, doesn't matter. The important thing is what you intend to do about what happened back home? Is California your answer to killing a man?"

Huddled within himself, sunk for a moment in apathy, Cameron did not answer. John said, "If you're wondering if the whole town knows or if the sheriff is looking for you, the answer is no. The sheriff couldn't be bothered, and then the war came. What you did got lost in the shuffle. Father doesn't know and neither does Missy. I stumbled on it purely by accident."

"How?"

"I don't have time to explain. Not everything. Mr. Roundtree was sick again and I happened to see that girl. And no, I didn't get it from her. Not at first. I put it together myself, out of what I was able to pick up."

Recovering, Cameron came close to sneering. "And that's all?"

"For me it's enough. The fact remains you killed a man. His name was Shamus O'Connell and you were fooling around with his sister. Any other man in your place, finding someone as rare as she, that beautiful and with so much to give——"

He broke off suddenly, realizing too late his mistake, and Cameron leaped to press the advantage. He said, "I'll be damned, so that's how it is! You get soft on them right and left, don't you? Somebody that rare and beautiful. I'll be damned! Ain't that something to put in the book!"

John's vision began to blur. He said, "You watch what you say! I've never hit you yet, but by God if you keep this up——" And then, defeated, he clasped his hands together and dug the joints of his thumbs into his forehead. "Ah Christ!" he said. "Brothers, and this is how we do! Go to California! I'll give you my last cent. It would be worth it just to get you out of our lives forever!" and when he raised his head, already regretting his outburst, he found that nothing had changed and that it was still imperative to try. He said, "Does it make no difference that you killed a man? I know you acted in self-defense——"

"You're damn right! He jumped me with a knife!"

"Just like that, I suppose. No warning of any kind. He simply jumped you. Would it be believed in court? It may not have been murder, but certainly it was manslaughter. You could go to prison."

John was unable to see that mentioning prison had made any difference. Nor was he too surprised. A society prone to violence takes a lenient view. Whatever the circumstances, a man has the right to protect himself. Going to prison was the last thing Cameron had to fear. But why then had he run away? Trying a different approach, John said:

"Why don't we try to stop fighting? All I'm asking is that you tell me what happened. Her brother found you together, didn't he?"

Cameron was a little less on guard. He said tentatively, "It all depends on what you mean by together. If you mean did I have her drawers down, giving her a frig——"

It was sympathy Cameron wanted, the understanding ear of a considerate ally, but John found it hard to sit in the same room. Looking past Cameron, he saw that the girl was watching them, come out of nowhere. Her eyes were wounded beyond all bearing, and John willed her away. He said, turning back to Cameron, "Where did you pick up that expression, on Liberty Street or in New Orleans?" and when Cameron replied, "Don't you try to get high-toned with me. You don't fool me none," they stood where they were before, inflamed and at swords' points and ready to brawl. John broke the silence first. He said:

"I detest bargains, but I'll make one. Either you tell me what happened, everything, or you don't get a cent. How was it that his body was found on River Street? Was that where you asked her to meet you, somewhere on the wharves?"

It was one of Cameron's characteristics that he could hold out for just so long. He said, "Goddammit, just because you've got me down," and John knew from past experience that a corner had been turned.

"None of that!" he said. "We'll begin at the beginning and go straight through to the end. Where were you?"

"On River Street, like you said."

"Was that the best you could do? A doorway? A pile of cotton on the wharves? You weren't too particular, were you?"

Cameron was not so defeated that he couldn't fight back. "You always know so much, don't you? Where else was there? The parlor at Indigo? I can just see it! You'd have been the first one to turn up your nose."

"Not if you were in love with her."

"Oh for Christ's sake! Who said anything about love?"

John was glad the girl was no longer there. He said, "So the best you could do, the best you wanted to do, was some alley on River Street. A warm, decent, courageous girl, and as beautiful as anyone I've ever seen——"

Cameron was close to hate again. "Why don't you shove it! Who are you to get so jugging moral with me! The thing that's graveling you, the thing you won't admit, is that you would have liked to do it to her yourself." Glaring, his whole face like a snarl, he paused for breath. "Warm, decent, courageous! Who are you trying to fool?" He clenched his teeth, breathing hard. "And it was she who started it in the first place, wagging it around when I went to collect the rent, just like I reckon she wags it at every man who comes along. What was I supposed to do? Run the other way? Is that what you did? Well, Mister Man, I didn't. I ain't that holy and I don't have me a hot black wench hid back in the swamps. I asked her to meet me on River Street, and I was going to take her to that room of Allbright's above his shop."

A blow over the heart could not have winded John more. He was too stunned to be conscious of any expression that may have been on his face, but Cameron must have read it as a condemnation of Allbright. "And don't start blaming the nigger," Cameron said. "He didn't want to lend me the room. What I told him was that I needed a place to talk to her alone. And even then he didn't want to. The only reason he finally agreed was because he's the only real friend I ever

387

had, the only one who ever understood," and John expected him to go into one of his spells of mawkish self-pity. But instead, on a rising note of defiance, "You want to know something, you mealymouthed son-of-a-bitch? That old nigger made me feel like he was proud of me, proud just to know me! Who else was proud of me? You? Was ever the old man? Sure, being like him, you and him could get along, but me?—what did I ever get but one lecture after the other and in between lectures, when I was little, sometimes the strap!"

Borne headlong, the floodgates open, he paused only to catch his breath. "You never liked that yellow nigger, always looking down your nose, but I did! That's all he is, a yellow nigger pumped full of airs, but I could talk to him. He'd listen. The day I stopped off at Deerskin—did you listen? Were you interested? Could I talk to you? Well, I could to him. That's the important thing. I could *talk* to him. And if ever I happened to get drunk or something and was afraid to go home, not wanting to hear another lecture——"

There was no way in the world for John to keep Allbright from entering the room. He stood quietly against the wall, withdrawn, keeping his distance, wearing his Sunday clothes and one of his brocaded waistcoats, his big gold tiepin catching the light. His head was hunched forward in the way reminiscent of Corwin Bottomley, the same general build, the same general stance, and though he might have been wearing a look of victory, or even disdain, his expression was one of profoundest sorrow.

John said, "And it was he, after the fight, who took care of everything. The girl ran home, Allbright cleaned you up and got you quieted down, as much as anyone could get you quieted down, and early next morning you went to Cornwall." He rested his elbows on the desk, noticing a spot of ink on the cuff of his coat, just above the braid. "But couldn't the fight have been avoided? You've always been good at talking your way out of things. Couldn't you have explained?"

"Explain what! That I was hoping to do it to his sister? Besides, he gave me no chance. We were standing by those steps on the side of Allbright's shop, and she was beginning to scare off, not that she had agreed to it in the first place—that I can't lie about—and then *he* comes out of the dark. He must have been listening, me trying to get her up the steps and she not wanting to, and right away he starts trying to bully me around. What he said was that I would have to marry her. Why, for God's sake! I hadn't even touched her. The way he had it figured, I had been giving it to her right along. All he could say was that I would have to marry her. What the hell! I wasn't going to be bullied. What I told him was that I would just as soon marry one of the nigs."

There was a long, forsaken silence, the desolate silence of an endless stretch of burned-out woods, and when John recovered, the girl was back in the room, come to join Allbright. She stood defiant and unflinching, able to endure because she had to endure, looking at Cameron with icy contempt and saying to John, merely by the way her feet were planted, that if he had been wondering what it was that Cameron had done, the thing more cruel than the death of a brother, now, finally, he knew.

"You said that? She heard you? You said it where she could hear?"

Whatever else John might have added, the things he wanted to say would never be spoken—as Allbright's presence now prevented, so would memory stand always in the way. For what Cameron had done to the girl was no less than what he had done to Allbright, the same cruelty, the identical shame, and if it was a curse that lay upon them, as Missy in the wisdom of sorrow was able to perceive, the stain of the curse was on him too. Eventually he managed to speak.

"That's why you gave Allbright your saddle, wasn't it? He admired it and you were grateful. But I still don't understand why you ran away. There would have been a trial—that we couldn't have avoided—but you could have pleaded self-defense. The girl herself would have testified for you. Why didn't you stand up to it? Why did you run away?"

Cameron, starting to speak, swallowed his words. "Why did you?" John said. "You must have known the sorrow you'd cause, especially to Mama and Missy," and it was with a feeling of despair that he saw Cameron was going to try to bluster it out. He held up a restraining hand, but Cameron, launched, would not be stopped.

"Trial! Self-defense! Why should I stand trial? I didn't kill him. It was an accident. He pulled a knife when I said what I did, and we started to wrestle. I got him by the wrist, the wrist of the hand with the knife, and though he was bigger than I was, and stronger, I ain't been wrestling all my life for nothing. I spun him around, tripping him, and when he went down he fell on the blade. He had the knife the whole time," and John knew that Cameron, despite the bluster, had managed to tell the truth.

"All the more reason why you didn't have to run away," John said. "It makes less sense than ever. I suppose there would have had to be an investigation, with the grand jury being called in——"

Cameron was too agitated to listen. "Investigation! Grand jury! You don't know that bunch! He wasn't her only brother. She has another, mean as they come! And what about her old man? What about her uncles and cousins? You think they would have waited for the grand jury? They would have cut my heart out. It can still happen, any day!"

Once more stunned, knowing that his jaw had sagged and that his mouth hung open, John waited for his mind to start functioning again. He studied the spot of ink on his coat, wondering how it had got there, and what must be understood about Cameron, in the same way as it was understood about the color of his eyes or that he had always been something less than stable, was that Cameron was a coward.

But quietly, quietly. One false move and you'll jump the wary bird. John looked at his brother as through a dense concealment of leaves. To say that Cameron was a coward was not enough, nor, again, was it enough to say that he fell too quickly into panic. He lived with panic. All his life he had been possessed by it, running, panic snapping at his heels, and he would keep on running until the day he died. But still quietly. Say that Cameron Bottomley is a coward, and panic's thing, but also say, in mercy and pity and a prayer for the dead, that he is his mother's own true son.

"Don't you want to go home, Cam, even if only for a few days? I'll arrange to go with you if you like. We can clear up everything in no time at all. It will give you a chance to see Missy and Father, and then——"

"Then what?" If Cameron was aware of the different, more considerate note in John's voice, he was not inclined to respond in kind.
"Then you and the old man can decide where you want to ship me
off? Is that it? I told you I wanted to go to California. What's the
matter? Ain't that far enough away for you?"

"Very well, Cam. If you can live with your conscience——"

"I don't have anything *on* my conscience," Cameron said. "What's
eating you, anyway? You want me to go all the way to Pompey's Head
just so the grand jury can say that I can go free? What's the point in
it? I didn't do anything. It was an accident. If you were half willing
to help——"

"How?"

"Lend me the money to get to California."

"I don't know what to say, Cam. If that's what you want——"

"That's what I want." Cameron spoke up eagerly. "You help me
this one last time and I'll never bother you again. I swear it! There's
a lot of opportunity out in California. A man could strike it rich."

"Yes, I suppose a man could. I'm a little tempted to join you. Are
you sure about this?"

"I'm sure."

"You have no intention of going home?"

"Why should I? Maybe I will someday, after I've showed you all
what I can do, but not now. What's the point of it?"

A man could try and keep on trying, but there was always a point
beyond which it was foolish to persist. John said, "If going to California is what you really want, why not? Let's see where we stand.
So far as money is concerned, our paper currency won't do you much
good, and all I have left in gold is a little over four hundred dollars.
Some of it I'm obliged to keep for myself. I can let you have two
hundred, however. That ought to be enough."

Cameron thought a moment. "Yes, I reckon so, if it's in gold."

"You ought by rights to have a safe-conduct to get through our
lines. The War Department has been handing them out as freely as
theatre tickets and I'm sure it can be arranged. Getting you one won't
take more than a couple of days."

"That's too long. I can manage."

"Not if you have to go through our lines. You might be shot as a spy. You have to have some kind of paper. What I can do, the best I can do, is to write you a letter making you one of our agents. How does that sound?"

Cameron looked uncertain. "No strings attached?"

"No, no strings attached. But I wish you would rest for a few days. You can share my room at the hotel."

"No, thanks. I want to be moving along."

It took John only a few minutes to open his strongbox and then write a letter saying that Cameron was one of the department's agents. Only once he paused. He said, glancing up, "How shall I make it out? Have you been using your own name?" and Cameron looked the other way. He said, "Put down William Smith," and as John did so, thinking of Indigo and his father and all those generations, it was as if, with these few scratches of a pen, he was expelling his brother from existence.

Cameron put on his hat. He said perfunctorily, "I'm much obliged for the kindness. I won't forget," and John walked with him into the clerks' office. John said, "I'll see you to the street. I could use a breath of fresh air," and Rawlins, who had been making a point of being busy, hunched over his desk, was unable to continue the masquerade —he shot them a quick, distrustful glance, his cloudy eye seeming to peer like a lookout around a corner of his nose.

John and Cameron went down the corridor. When they came to the door that led to the street, Cameron forgot to shake hands. He said, "You take care of yourself, Johnny. I'll be seeing you," and it wasn't until John extended a palm that he stopped in the doorway. John said, "Let's keep in touch, Cam. Try to write," and then, standing on the steps, he watched Cameron walk down the street, his black hat conspicuous amid a crowd of aimlessly drifting soldiers. There was something almost jaunty in the way he walked, two hundred dollars in his money belt and California up ahead, and the only trouble was that he would never get there. He was too far gone. Though he might imagine he was on his way to California, he was actually walking into oblivion.

When John returned to his office he told Rawlins he was not going to be in to anyone for the rest of the day. He closed the door and sat thinking for a long time, and once, very briefly, he held his face in his hands. When he brought them away he noticed that the space under the nail of one of his thumbs was black with ink. Though he couldn't remember how it had got there, it explained the spot on his cuff.

CHAPTER THIRTY

Several hours later, his work pushed aside, John Bottomley read over what it had taken him all this time to compose.

TO WHOM IT MAY CONCERN: *This department has received information that an apparently well-organized ring is secretly exporting cotton from the port of New Orleans. It has been reported that the originator of this enterprise is Mr. George Morris, superintendent of the government warehouse in New Orleans, and that one of his chief confederates is Mrs. Robert Stanhope, wife of Colonel Stanhope, the head of this department. The known details are as follows. Major Howell Angry, a former Army quartermaster now deceased . . .*

John read through to the end and stared at his desk. The distress caused by Cameron's visit had more intensified than lifted, and now here in his own handwriting, attested to, certified, was the ruinous greediness of the woman he imagined he loved. He stared at the desk dully, slumped in his chair. Whatever it was he should feel, he felt nothing. The mind's numbness chilled the heart.

Stretching his arms to ease an ache caused by having sat too long in one position, he rose from the desk and went to the window. The sky was low and dark, heavy with rain or snow. Across the street four soldiers at loose ends were sitting on the curb, making a meal of bread and ham and drinking from a common bottle. Remembering that he had not eaten since breakfast, John did not feel hungry. He opened the window to get rid of the smell of cigar smoke and whisky that hung in the unventilated air, and the soldiers, their attention caught, greeted him with whistles and catcalls. One of the men, a huge bearded fellow wearing a blue coat that had surely been stripped from some dead Northerner, held up the bottle, pretended to offer him a drink, and used the bottle to make an obscene gesture.

Ignoring a noisier burst of whistles and catcalls, John turned from the window and began to walk the floor. Rawlins was at his desk with that grudge of his burning like a slow fuse, the correspondent of the *News* might be waiting in the hall this very minute, and something had to be done. What, though, and why him? His responsibility was cotton, not the colonel's wife, and though wife and cotton had somehow been ginned into the same bale—not somehow: because Lydia Stanhope had the soul of a greedy clerk!—it was still the colonel's problem.

Picking up the several sheets of paper on which he had written, John again read them through. He started to tear them up, changed his mind, and acted on a different impulse. After taking an envelope from a drawer of his desk, he opened the door and called in Rawlins.

Curiosity, poorly masked, glazed the chief clerk's face—first there had been the warm welcome extended to that down-at-the-heels young man, followed by the rise and fall of an almost continuous quarrel behind a carefully closed door, and then, after the young man's departure, a period of solitary meditation that had lasted all through the midday dinner hour and up till now.

John said, shutting the door, "Pull up a chair, Mr. Rawlins. I'd like to have a talk," and though he hoped Rawlins would begin to thaw a little, his ramrod intransigence quickly put an end to any such notion. Continuing, John said, "I'm afraid the War Department is in for a disappointment. The requisitions will have to be put off until tomorrow. I've hardly begun on them and it must be nearly three o'clock already."

Rawlins, still standing, moved his chin as though to say nobody need expect any sympathy from him—it wasn't his fault if people didn't keep up with their work. John said, "Sit down, please. This may take a few minutes," and Rawlins, fixed in an attitude of determined indifference, took the chair previously occupied by Cameron. Knowing that his mind was working less well than usual, and trusting that impulsiveness was not leading him into a mistake, John said, "I find myself in a difficult position, Mr. Rawlins. It will probably not surprise you to hear it is related to the situation in New Orleans —or, rather, to speak more correctly, what we suspect the situation to be."

Rawlins sat transient and remote, the lid of his cloudy eye drooping a little, and John tried not to be discouraged. He said, "I haven't decided how to proceed, or even how to begin, but my hope is that, whatever we do, it can be carried off quietly. That's the important thing. We don't want to frighten anyone off, and even less do we want to create a scandal."

Since he had been thinking in terms of scandal, already seeing Lydia Stanhope's name in headlines, it was not surprising that the word had slipped out. But no longer could Rawlins maintain his air of iron aloofness. His lips twitched, a look of furtive shrewdness broke over his face, and it wasn't hard to guess what was going through his mind. Knowing nothing of Lydia's involvement, he was already hitching scandal and Colonel Stanhope to the same yoke—which was exactly what he had figured from the beginning! Hadn't he spotted it right off?

Again John tried not to be discouraged. He said, "What I've done, Mr. Rawlins, has been to write out a report on the affair in New Orleans as I see it. Some of the information it contains I'm obliged to keep secret, even from you, but what I want you to do, if you will, is to seal what I have written in this envelope, and then write your name and the date on the flap in such a way as to make it impossible for the envelope to be opened without defacing what you have written."

Suspicion spread across Rawlins's face—something was going on here, something peculiar, and he didn't like it. He seemed to sniff the air for the scent of wrongdoing, to strain his ears for the sound of its footsteps. He said, in a voice like a croak:

"What for?"

John recognized it as a sign of emotional stress that he wanted to laugh. Rawlins looked like a reluctant anarchist handed a bomb and ordered against every inclination to blow up the royal palace.

"Don't sound so fearful, Mr. Rawlins. What's in my mind is this— I'm worried that what has been going on in New Orleans, what we believe has been going on, may come to light any minute. With so many cooks stirring the broth, it could be that the broth will spill. And all over me. It's my job to prevent cotton from being smuggled out of the country. There will be those who will be wanting my scalp."

Pausing to gauge his progress, John couldn't see that he had gained an inch. He said:

"Try to look at it my way, Mr. Rawlins. I can't bring a lot of charges without having some proof, and until I get the proof I'm obliged to proceed cautiously. But meantime, to put it bluntly, I have to think of my own skin. I can't let it be said that I have been derelict in my duty or, worse, that I have deliberately shut my eyes to what may be going on. This report may not be much, but at least it puts a few things into the record. Here is the envelope, Mr. Rawlins. Will you do as I ask?"

Had he been the worst of all the Borgias and the envelope a packet of deadliest poison, Rawlins could not have handled it more gingerly. He moistened the flap, sealed the envelope, and scratched out his signature and the date, February 18, 1862, writing partly on the flap and partly on the back of the envelope. John said, "Thank you, Mr. Rawlins. I'm much obliged," and when Rawlins put down the pen, with fumes of malice and resentment appearing to be rising within him, John knew that the slow-burning fuse was almost gone—the clock had struck, the cock had crowed, the knell had tolled, and if he hoped to save the situation he had best do something immediately.

What, though, what? Uncertain and on edge, resenting the need to act under pressure, he decided on a modification of the plan he had worked out when he called on Lydia a few evenings before. In the maze of confusing uncertainties, the one thing he could depend on was that the government needed money. Once Lydia had been confronted and a confession wrung, he would insist she drive with him to the Treasury Department and explain to the nice polite gentlemen, with a few of her most becoming blushes, that out of her zeal and devotion she had been quietly exporting some of her dear husband's cotton—her *dear* husband's cotton—with the sole purpose of adding to the government's funds abroad.

The structure was so rickety that John began to believe he could get it to stand. Lydia was after all no obscure housewife, no questionable female from the far end of Liberty Street. She was Mrs. Robert Stanhope, the wife of a cabinet member, one of the first ladies, and that she had been smuggling cotton would be no more thinkable to her listeners than that that baboon in the White House had learned to eat at a table with knife and fork.

Rawlins stirred in his chair. "Anything else, Captain?"

John decided that the immediate need was a few hours' time. Give him until tomorrow afternoon and this sour-tempered sand-hill could talk his head off. He said:

"Yes, Mr. Rawlins, there is something else. How would you like to take charge of the department for the rest of the day?"

Rawlins's face lighted up, darkened, and became a battlefield of conflicting emotions. He said, "Take charge of the department?" and while John had never thought of himself as having any particular talent for duplicity he had to admit he had been wrong.

"That's right, Mr. Rawlins. I have some business outside the office and I would like to leave you in charge. Are you too busy? Do you think it can be arranged?"

Rawlins made an effort to resist, and John suspected that basically he wanted to, but how was it possible? To be in charge of the department even if only for a few hours, to write home about it, to tell his friends and save it up for his old age——

"Yes, Captain, it can be arranged."

John should have sealed Rawlins's acceptance with a handshake, hearty and companionable and man to man, but despite the gift of duplicity he now knew he possessed, he wasn't quite that endowed. He said, "Good, Mr. Rawlins. Undoubtedly there will be a few more office seekers turning up, since we haven't had nearly our quota for the day, but I'm sure you will know how to handle them. Also, because of the way I've had to neglect things, you might sign the rest of these requisitions and, if you have time, the certificates of release. Simply add beneath your signature, 'Acting Secretary.' "

Seeing the expression on Rawlins's face and the way he appeared to have grown a full inch taller, John thought he was being asked to pay an extremely high price for just a few hours' time. He said:

"I expect to come back to work after supper, Mr. Rawlins, but I wish you'd take the evening off. There is going to be a band concert in one of the theatres, a sort of contest, and I got inveigled into buying a ticket. Why don't you use it? My understanding is that the Georgians, the South Carolinians, and our friends from Texas will try to outdo each other. It might be entertaining."

Rawlins melted at last. It was the first time they were on good terms since John had invited him to have a drink. "You're mighty kind, Captain. I'd rather listen to a good military band than anything I know."

"By all means use the ticket then. It's there on the desk."

"I'll be glad to, Captain. You're mighty kind. But I'll see that everything is left in order. You can depend on that."

"Yes, Mr. Rawlins, I'm sure."

John put on his slouch hat and long gray overcoat, a sharp twinge going through his elbow, and left the building. He hadn't walked far before it began to rain. A few flakes of snow were mixed in the rain, and the wind was straight from the north.

CHAPTER THIRTY-ONE

It was one of Corwin Bottomley's favorite observations that a man couldn't think of everything. He was constantly ringing changes on it and John could remember his saying, late one rainy evening by the fire, that if Creation had been left to a mortal creature something would surely have been forgotten and the universe wouldn't be in working order yet—the sun would be cold, the moon hot, the stars always colliding, and pieces of places like China and Africa strewn all over where they had no right to be, like in the middle of France and Switzerland or maybe up somewhere near the North Pole, and all because a man couldn't always think of everything.

Though John had been frequently thinking of his father of late, he could not imagine what had brought him to mind at this particular moment unless it was the fire in the Stanhopes' hearth, the sound of rain upon the panes, and the fact that the one thing he had not taken into consideration was his inability to go through with it —to vow in his office under the rowel of anger that he would wring a confession from Lydia was one thing; to sit in her presence with a fire going and the rain driving against the windows was to wonder how he could have been so brash.

Lydia said, "Won't you take more tea, Captain? You'll be drenched should you leave now," and once again, as had been happening ever since she joined him in the parlor, he felt caught up in an unreality more confusing than a dream—here she was, wearing one of her blue gowns and the glow of the firelight on her cheeks, a smuggler, caught up in the net of her own greediness, the face of innocence and the soul of a clerk, and it was almost impossible, looking at her, to believe it was true.

Lydia seemed much more cheerful than the last time he called. A few minutes earlier, pouring tea, she explained that she had received a letter from the colonel in Mobile, saying he was going to be there longer than he had anticipated but would be returning to the capital in a day or two, and it could be that the letter was partially responsible for her happier mood—had the colonel gone on to New Orleans he might have accidentally stumbled onto something: she could read his letter to mean that the worst of the danger had passed.

"You don't take sugar, do you, Captain?"

"No, thank you. Just as it is, please."

Lydia's face, as she filled his cup, could be seen from the angle he most admired. She said, "I can't tell you how happy you've made me. For our sake, I mean. How good it is to know you don't think there is anything to worry about in New Orleans."

"I don't believe you understood me," John replied. "What I said was that it's properly a matter for the colonel to look into and that I have decided not to take any steps until he returns."

"And I quite agree," Lydia said briskly. "I'm confident he will know how to handle the matter."

She smiled as she handed John a second cup of tea, the fire burning minutely in her eyes, and what she was thinking, of course, was that she, not the colonel, would know how to handle the matter. She said, "I'm sure there is nothing that can't be straightened out. I daresay it will turn out to be nothing but an error in bookkeeping or such," and the incredible thing, as John was beginning to realize, was that with hardly any trouble it could be made to appear as nothing but an error in bookkeeping or such—had he not been thinking so poorly he would have been able to perceive it before.

"I vow!" Lydia said. "Listen to the rain!"

Remembering their conversation of the other evening and the desperate bid she had made for time—it was when he said he thought he should communicate immediately with Colonel Stanhope—John recalled how he had fallen in with her wishes. Already she had doubtless communicated with her cousin, Superintendent Morris, and already he would have started to cover his tracks—actually, for anyone who knew the workings of a government warehouse, it wouldn't be hard. A government warehouse was a busy place. Hundreds of bales of cotton were constantly being moved in and out, and for each bale of cotton there were five or six pieces of paper. Let Superintendent Morris falsify a few figures or lose a few bills of lading, let him forget to make a few entries or enter them in the wrong place, let him credit a given quantity of government cotton to the account of a private shipper or the other way around—a dishonest man could make such a confusion that it would take an army of investigators a year to get to the bottom of things. The worst obfuscation, however, would come from Lydia. She would bend every effort to see that Colonel Stanhope wouldn't want to be bothered. He would have to put himself to all kinds of trouble, spending months over the most boring details imaginable, and if everything appeared to be in order, as by that time it would, then why go out of the way to stir things up?

Lydia, pouring herself a cup of tea, said, "Tell me this, Captain —this clerk in the department you spoke of, I believe you said his name was Rawlins. As I recall, you mentioned you were worried that he might talk to the newspaper people, something about a grudge. Do you still feel apprehensive?"

John thought of Rawlins in charge of the department.

"No, not as much as formerly. I believe we can count on him, at least till the colonel returns."

Lydia bent over the tea-things, helping herself to sugar, and that she was clever John had known ever since the picnic at Happy Chance —what he had not known or wanted to know, the new coloration, was that she was clever all the time, with rarely a word spoken or action taken without some kind of rehearsal. Though it was part of human behavior occasionally to mount guard, Lydia was on guard always. He wondered how it would be to have her in bed (not as he used to wonder, not with that tormented agony) and if, even when swept by passion, a doubtful assumption to begin with, she ever really let go. He saw her as making love with her eyes open, looking far away, and it was that more than anything, how wide open her eyes were, that made him understand he wasn't in love with her any longer and would never be again. It wasn't how calculating and greedy she was, or her duplicity, or that she couldn't be trusted—it was the way she would keep her eyes open, blue and watchful, alertly on guard.

John watched the glints in her soft blond hair reflect the rise and fall of the fire. The awareness that everything was over was not a new set of thoughts, or a set of old thoughts in some new and more perceptive arrangement, but a deep-running physical alteration. And though it should have been attended by some equally deep-running emotion, it was not. There was no more emotion than if a column of figures had been added up, and no trace of sorrow that the figures came out to zero.

"You've heard about General Monckton, I suppose," she said.

"How could I not? It's all over the place."

"I daresay we may expect a new onslaught from the *News*."

"If it isn't in type already."

"How aggravating!"

She sipped from her cup and rested it on the saucer, and though everything was over and no more to it than a candle's going out, he was still able to appreciate how intelligent she was, how naturally bright and alert. For when she said how aggravating, it meant she was thinking of Rawlins and the possible consequences should he talk— Superintendent Morris would by now have covered his tracks to such an extent that it would take an army of investigators a year to get to the bottom of things, but nonetheless it would be awkward if the newspapers set out to make trouble. She said:

"The Moncktons will stop at nothing now, especially that contemptible Gup! He has never forgiven the colonel and never will. That is why I inquired about your clerk. I wouldn't want him to injure the colonel by playing into Gup Monckton's hands."

John was willing to bet that Rawlins had that pile of requisitions signed by now, having checked each one like a hawk.

"I don't believe you have to worry," he said. "I think you can count on Rawlins's being on our side."

Lydia looked at him intently.

"You've changed your mind from the other evening, Captain."

"Yes, but I have my reasons."

He was so pointedly speaking to what he imagined were her secret thoughts that he did not see how she could fail to understand. Her expression, however, could not have been more composed. She smiled at him prettily, but with her eyes never for an instant leaving his face, and again the incredible thing was how easily it could be made to appear as nothing but an error in bookkeeping or such, even with Major Howell Angry and the forged requisitions thrown in.

SUPERINTENDENT MORRIS (being interrogated): *Forged requisitions? These, bearing the signature of Major Howell Angry? Well, now! You don't say! But since the requisitions originated with the Army, it would seem that it's in the Army where the forger must be sought. And it won't be easy, will it, sir?—not with all those hundreds and hundreds of men and the way they're transferred hither and yon. If the requisitions were forged, as you say, the fellow could be anywhere by now. But having no reason to question the requisitions, we naturally surrendered the cotton. The receipts? We send all our receipts straight on to Headquarters. The ones in question must be somewhere in the department files up there, unless some clerk has lost or mislaid them. I don't want to complain about Headquarters, but that sort of thing happens all the time. And as far as that discrepancy of eight hundred bales in the January report is concerned, you've already seen for yourself that it was merely a clerical error. We occasionally make a mistake or two ourselves, I'm afraid. Anything we can do to help——*

It would be foolish to imagine Colonel Stanhope would want to go into the matter—Lydia would be the first to remind him that the department couldn't afford an investigation, not at this time. At the first rumor of an investigation the newspapers would rush into print, and virtue, in this instance, would not be much of a reward. The administration wasn't nearly so firmly entrenched as it might be and to relieve

405

some of the pressure on its center it might decide to sacrifice part of a flank. Already a considerable liability, the colonel might be asked to resign. So why stir things up then? He wasn't *anxious* to resign, was he?

"Is there any other news in the department?"

"Nothing special. It's been a routine day."

Well, perhaps not quite—John could see his brother Cameron going down the street under his broad black hat, two hundred dollars in his money belt and oblivion up ahead, and then, as the fire burned brighter and a sudden gust of wind rattled the panes, he realized that he himself was the only person Lydia had to fear, and even so not really.

Lydia was also watching the fire. She said, "Is there anything more cheery than an open grate? I'm glad you decided to call, Captain. If I may make a small confession, I have a way of getting melancholy when it rains."

John nodded and said nothing. He felt warm and comfortable, wanting to stretch, and now that he wasn't in love with her any longer and would never be again, he could afford to admit that this was one of the fantasies he sometimes had—a rainy afternoon, a fire, a sense of ease, and he and Lydia shut away from the world.

"Is there any late news from the front, Captain?"

"No good news, if that's what you mean."

"I hear a battle is impending in the West."

"So the rumors say. One of the incidental by-products of war is the way it adds to one's knowledge of geography. Had you ever heard of Pittsburg Landing before? Or New Madrid? Or Island Number 10?"

"No, not ever. And now we hear talk of Shiloh. They say that the battle will be fought near there. Where is Shiloh exactly?"

"In Tennessee, the southwest part of the state."

"I pray that our forces will gain a victory. It would make up for our recent reverses. I hear from Senator Fenchurch that those in authority are confident that success will be ours."

Lydia had come a long way, and no one looking at her would ever guess she had once been a schoolteacher at Huntington Hall, but there was still a hint of Gunpowder Street in her voice whenever she spoke of a senator or some other highly placed personage. John started to say he couldn't be as hopeful as those in authority, since the Southern forces would probably be greatly outnumbered, but his mind wasn't truly on the war—armies might be massing, and huge events in the making, and what he was thinking was that although he was the only person Lydia had to fear she need not worry because his mind was made up and he didn't intend to lift a finger. He said, "The rain seems to be slacking off and I ought to be leaving. Thank you for tea."

Lydia was gazing abstractedly into the flames. "There's no need to hurry, Captain. Today is Arabella's day at the hospital, but she ought to be home any minute. She would be sorry to miss you. Did I not have another engagement I would ask you to supper. Will we be seeing you at the Senate Ball?"

"About that I don't know," John said. "It all depends on the colonel."

"The colonel?"

"Soon as he returns I am going to resign."

"Resign?"

She searched his face for an instant, drawing her brows together, and though it had been put in the form of a question it was actually a sigh of relief—tractable though he seemed, he might decide not to leave matters to the colonel after all: his suspicions having been aroused, she could never be completely sure: a resignation would be a safeguard and a guarantee. She said, "Resign? But why, Captain?" and while he had always known she was clever, it was still difficult to make it a part of awareness that there was never a moment when she wasn't clever, always watchful and on guard. He said:

"Why? Because government life is not for me. I am by nature much too restive."

"You intend to seek active service, I suppose."

"Yes, I do."

Lydia picked up a small silver bell and rang it. She said, "I can tell from your manner that nothing will induce you to reconsider," and since she so obviously did not want him to reconsider, the last thing in the world, he said, "No, nothing," and the conversation had to be halted until Amos cleared away the tea-things and returned to the pantry. Lydia said:

"Surely I don't need to tell you how regretful the colonel is going to be? Or how regretful I am already? I know only too well the loss your resignation will mean. But more than that, we shall miss you."

A week ago John would have tried to interpret the affectionate tone of her voice as a sign of more meaningful affection, but now he knew it was simply the voice of an extremely clever woman who could afford to sound affectionate because she had what she wanted and nothing to lose. He said:

"You are much too kind."

Lydia shook her head. "No, Captain, not kind. You must know how much the colonel has come to depend on you and how fully aware I am of the many burdens you have lifted from his shoulders." She shook her head again. "No, not kind, Captain. Grateful. Most exceedingly grateful. Are you sure you won't reconsider? The reason I ask is that the colonel won't be as amenable as I. He is going to argue, I promise. He has plans for you."

"Plans?"

Lydia's gaze returned to the fire. She said, "My husband is looking to the future. Did you know he intends to offer himself as Vice-President in the next election?" and if what she wanted was an exclamation of astonishment or a gasp of surprise, John was unable to oblige. Having brought the Senator this far along, why should she stop now? Or at Vice-President? Had not Arabella been correct when she told Missy that the ultimate goal was the highest position the government had to offer?

"I don't know that I altogether approve of this latest ambition," Lydia said, "the expense of the office and how much it costs to campaign," and John stopped listening. He remembered how the ladies of the Wednesday Afternoon Ladies Society accused Lydia of being too ambitious and overfond of money, and yet they no more understood her than the gentlemen of the Agricultural Society understood Ules Monckton—the presence of a vision and the way it consumed. And if hers was a lesser vision, selfish and tawdry and perhaps even a little obscene, she, like Ules, must follow wherever it beckoned, even if it led to smuggling cotton and possible disgrace. But not for the money, not money alone. Because of a vision, the expense of the office and how much it cost to campaign, and because of the way a vision consumed. Though John had never seen the Northern Lights, it was as if their brilliance were cascading across his mind.

Outside the day was beginning to fade and the rain was almost over. Lydia went on to say that in making his plans the colonel had naturally been planning for his friends. She said, "Is there nothing we can do to get you to reconsider?" having what she wanted and nothing to lose, and John shook his head. "No, I'm afraid not. My mind is made up. And now I truly must be going. I don't want to wear out my welcome. Thank you again for tea."

Lydia walked with him into the hall. She stood beside him as he got into his overcoat, the three tiny freckles showing very plainly on the bridge of her nose and, except for the ticking of the clock, slow and meditative, the quiet of the hall was like the quiet of the greenhouse at Happy Chance—John bent and kissed her, and her lips parted ever so slightly, and for a moment she didn't move.

"One thing I must tell you," John said. "I've been wanting to for years. You will never know how much I used to love you. When you married the colonel I didn't believe I would ever get over it, I felt that deserted and betrayed. There were times at Deerskin when I was so desperate for you I thought I might lose my mind. I used to look in the direction of Pompey's Head and call your name, trying to bring you closer. I wanted to marry you and I believe I could have made you happier than you are."

Now that the rain was over, the ticking of the clock seemed louder than before. Lydia stood rapt and still. She said, "You leave me speechless, Captain," and now that he did not want her he knew he could have her, and if he did, she would not necessarily make love with her eyes open after all. He said, "Now you know and I'm glad you know. It's something I had to say. I loved you so very much," and then, in a way he had always imagined, she raised a hand and placed it gently on his chest. She said, "Thank you for speaking, Captain. I shall always remember. Always," and now that everything was over they were close and together for the very first time.

She said, "Take care of yourself. You will be much in my thoughts. Come see us whenever you can," and it was at that moment that Arabella ran up on the porch and opened the front door. There was more than enough time for Lydia to withdraw her hand and John to rearrange the expression on his face, but Arabella apparently sensed the moment of intimacy she had walked into—she looked mystified and then astonished, and the astonishment gave way to a contemptuous glare, and though John wanted to cry, "Wait, Arabella, it's not what you think," by then she had swept past them, leaving a wake of perfume and cold—John heard her footsteps running up the stairs.

In his discomfort he expected Lydia also to be discomfited, but the interlude of closeness was over. She was her usual self again, competent and controlled. She said, "Good evening, Captain. I enjoyed your little visit. The colonel will be glad to know I have not been neglected," and while he could easily have been mistaken, he thought he detected a note of satisfaction in her voice, as if, in the long struggle between her and Arabella, she had scored another victory.

Outside it was dusk. The trees were wet and there were puddles in the street. Walking to his hotel, John argued that Arabella couldn't have seen anything, since in all truth there had been nothing to see, but nonetheless he felt uneasy. He didn't believe Arabella would let it go at that. What put him off was her timing. He hadn't expected her to take matters into her own hands quite so soon.

CHAPTER THIRTY-TWO

"You!" Arabella said. "And you my father's friend!"

A single gas jet was turned low in the clerks' room, burning with a faint hiss like the sound of a small plume of steam escaping, and in his office, which was also equipped with gas, John Bottomley, before this interruption, had been working by the light of a kerosene lamp. At Deerskin he had had none of the modern conveniences, and without wanting to quarrel with those who held that gas represented a marvelous stride in illumination, clean and trustworthy, he preferred the more restful glow of a lamp.

"You're in love with her, that's what you are!" Arabella said, thrusting her hands deeper into her muff. "As if I haven't always known!"

Rawlins had kept his word about leaving things in good order. The various papers and documents John had left scattered about were neatly arranged, a new point had been put in his pen, a fresh bottle of ink had been brought from the supply room, and the glasses from which Clay Vincent and Cameron had drunk stood on the far side of the desk, rinsed out and dried. Returning to his office after another communal supper at the hotel, John thought that perhaps it was Rawlins who should have this job—he had the proper temperament and took pride in his work.

"Aren't you going to say anything!" Arabella said. "Are you just going to sit there!"

John had no sooner settled down to work than she arrived. The envelope containing the pages of his TO WHOM IT MAY CONCERN report lay on the desk, and immediately before him, in the light of the lamp, was a sheet of paper on which he had scratched out the opening sentences of a covering letter he was trying to write to Colonel Stanhope.

"Well," Arabella said, "are you!"

John had not yet been able to adjust to her presence. Never before had there been a woman in the office, and his mind was full of the problems with which he had been trying to contend—how best to break the news to Colonel Stanhope and give notice of his resignation, and what to divulge about Cameron's visit and disturbing recital. He said, getting to his feet:

"Good evening, Arabella. You are in a fuss about something, aren't you? What brings you here?"

"As if you didn't know!"

A week ago, even a few days ago, John would have stammered and backed away. He wouldn't have been able to notice that the damp weather had made Arabella's hair curlier than usual, that the cold had brought a flush of color to her cheeks, and that her sullen pout added to her attractiveness. He said:

"Yes, Arabella, I have something to say, if only you'll give me a chance to get a word in edgewise. But first thing of all, please sit down and compose yourself. You didn't come here this time of evening all alone, did you?"

Bright as they were, Arabella's eyes shone brighter. "That's none of your business! And I don't care to sit! I'm going to the band concert and I don't wish to keep my escort waiting!"

John found it agreeable to be in command. He wasn't in love with Lydia any more and never would be, and if Arabella were not standing so close to danger, directly in the line of fire, the episode might be amusing. He said:

"It's something you have an escort. That handsome young Virginian? Is his aunt with you, the one that can't get in and out of a carriage as well as she used to, begging her pardon and yours?"

"That's none of your business either! And if you think you're entertaining, you're not. You *are* in love with her, aren't you? You always have been. But to carry on your flirtation behind my father's back, you of all people——"

Any other young woman would have thought twice before charging in like this, but then any other young woman was not Arabella. Never in her life had she been one to think twice. If there was any china to be broken, the pieces could always be picked up later. John said:

"I don't quite understand what brought you here, and I wish you would watch what you say, but since you've been good enough to honor me with a visit——"

"Oh, stop talking with a mouth full of mush!"

"And you stop trying to look like one of the avenging furies. Compose yourself and sit. I'm sorry I can't offer you a cushion, but these are Spartan times."

Still with her sullen pout, Arabella sat in the chair next to the desk, folding her hands on her muff. The gas jet in the clerks' room began to sputter noisily, as if it might be going out, which happened often enough to cause John to question the trustworthiness of gas, but then, correcting itself, it resumed its normal hiss.

"Now just who is it I'm supposed to be in love with?" John said. "If for any reason you happen to be thinking of your stepmother——"

"Don't call her my stepmother! I despise it when people do. She's nothing to me. And that you, my father's friend——"

John said, "That I, your father's friend, what? If in your foolishness you came here for an explanation, which were I not making allowances I would find offensive, then why not give me a chance? I'm not in love with her. Is that clear? And now, unless you want to be late for the concert, which I imagine your friend and his aunt won't particularly relish——"

"I don't believe you!"

"I must ask you to be careful what you say, Arabella. Merely because I happened to call on Mrs. Stanhope——"

Arabella's chin went up. "Mrs. Stanhope! Mrs. *Secretary* Stanhope! That cold grasping selfish thing! If you knew her as well as I——"

"Such things are not for me to know," John said. "Nor do I care

413

to discuss them. Not even with you. Just what your quarrel with her is——"

Arabella's chin went higher. "*My* quarrel. So even that is my fault. It's *my* quarrel, not hers! Do you think I wanted to be like this, or that I haven't tried? Oh, butter wouldn't melt in her mouth at first, back when she was teaching at Huntington Hall, dear little Arbell this and sweet little Arbell that, and I'm not saying I wasn't fooled. You remember the picnic at Happy Chance, the time I was night-blooming catchfly——"

"Yes, Arabella, I remember. But these confidences——"

"Is it agreeable to be used?" Arabella said on a rising note of anger. "Have you ever been made a pawn?" The lines of her nostrils became more sharply defined, and she began to mimic Lydia's voice. "*You must do your very best today, dear Arbell. Night-blooming catchfly is the nicest, prettiest role of all. I want your dear papa to be pleased with us both. And you mustn't forget to present him to me. I'm sure you have told him what good friends we are.*" Arabella's mouth trembled. "Making a fuss over me so she could win my father's favor! So sweet and simple and demure! The way she sang my praises! And him, poor lonely man, old enough to be her father——"

John rose from his chair. "I don't care to know about these things, I've told you. They are not for me to hear."

"Because you don't *want* to hear, that's why! Because you're in love with her. Don't I know?"

John, who had taken a step toward the window, stopped and turned around. "No, Arabella, you don't know. I've asked you once to watch what you say. Have I proved myself so shoddy that you can't believe me?"

Arabella's face began to lose some of its harshness.

"I'd like to believe you."

"Then do. For if ever I was in love with her——"

"You see! You admit it!"

Wishing that he had had sense enough to know when to stop, John said, "All I admit is what is over and done with, a long time ago.

What is it you want? For me to confess that I was once in love with her? Is that what you want to hear?"

"I knew it! I knew you were! Did she?"

"Did she what?"

"Know you were in love with her? I couldn't stand it if she did!"

First Clay Vincent, then Cameron, then Rawlins, then Lydia, and now Arabella—there came a time when a man was emotionally drained. The gas jet in the clerks' room again started to sputter, and John listened with half an ear until it righted itself. He said:

"Couldn't stand it? Why should it make any difference to you? And though she may have known once, before she married your father, though she should have known——"

In the shaded light of the lamp Arabella's gray-green eyes were almost black. "Oh, how could you, Johnny! You couldn't have been carried away like my father just because she was *young*. You must have known the kind of person she is, unable really to care for anyone except herself, not even a little——"

"Be fair, Arabella. Be fair."

"Fair!" Arabella's eyes again began to blaze. "Why do you take up for her? Why have you always? Is it because of what Missy says, that you started by feeling sorry for her, the poor meek little looked-down-upon-thing, coming from Gunpowder Street and all? Is that the reason? And did you enjoy being in love with her, even after she married my father, knowing how impossible it was? Was that why you buried yourself at Deerskin, because you knew how impossible it was and were *enjoying* it? Oh, Johnny, I don't want to hurt your feelings or make you feel bad, but didn't you know that when the time came she would use you too, just as she uses everybody, even that silly Mr. Wingfield Manning, and that it was she who got my father to go to your father——"

She cut herself short, carried by her agitation farther than she had intended, and her face, as she looked up at John, was stilled by alarm.

"Yes," John said. "Go on. Say it!"

Arabella, in her abjectness, might have been no older than when she was at Huntington Hall—it was night-blooming catchfly, for an instant, who peeped through.

"Say it!"

"Don't make me, Johnny. I was being hateful and I'm sorry. Please don't make me."

John looked at her stonily. "I asked you to say it. She got your father to go to my father—to do what? Do you imagine you can stop now?"

"Please, Johnny."

"Please nothing! You came in here full of malice and spite, not caring what you babble—— Damn it, must I shake it out of you?"

Arabella squared her shoulders. "Just you dare, Captain John Bottomley! Just you dare! And why shouldn't I tell you, you're so anxious to know? You say you're not in love with her any more, but I wonder! Did you think for one moment that it was my father's idea to have you in the department? His idea *first*, I mean? As it so happens, you gallant champion of the meek and looked-down-upon——"

John heard without hearing. Perhaps it was simply a matter of living long enough—live long enough, and wait long enough, and perhaps most of the puzzles came clear. He remembered the day his father summoned him from Deerskin and how, when he called on the Stanhopes and found Lydia alone, he could not understand why, since she seemed so disapproving of his views, almost as disapproving as Ules Monckton, he had been offered a place on her husband's staff— one word of opposition from her, and the Senator would have dropped the idea immediately.

Arabella said, "Don't misunderstand me, Johnny. My father was delighted after she mentioned it to him, but what was back of it, as I heard them discussing one night with Mr. Wingfield Manning, was that it was a sure way of winning your father's support and getting him to use his influence with his friends," and the tumult of rage John felt, the pounding heart and the choked sensation in his throat, was not because of what had been done to him but to his father. A man could lie in bed with a stopped-up nose and see the crumbling of all his hopes—two sons, one gone off like a thief in the night and the other full of doubt and indecision and Yankee notions, and Senator Stanhope's offer must have seemed an opportunity sent down from above.

Arabella's voice sank to a whisper. "I'm sorry, Johnny. I didn't mean to hurt you. Will you ever forgive me? Am I always to do everything wrong, always and always, whenever you're concerned?"

Of all the emotions, surely hate was the ugliest. The pounding of John's heart rang in his ears. "Forgive me, Johnny," Arabella said. "Please forgive me," and though he and Arabella had never been able to get along very well, her not caring what china was broken or ever taking anything into consideration until it was too late, at least she had always been honest and forthright and a friend. She said, "Don't look like that, Johnny. You frighten me. What are you going to do?"

"Do?" He clenched his teeth and faced her squarely. "What I'm going to do is what I was trying to do when you came charging in. I'm going to write my resignation and get out of here. Let Rawlins take care of things until your father returns."

Arabella's mouth hung open. "Resign? You're going to resign? Because of what I said?"

"No, Arabella, not because of what you said! Because I'm tired of worrying about people who are not worth worrying about. Though I may be my brother's keeper, which sometimes I wonder, I am not your father's or your stepmother's. Or yours either, for that matter."

"Mine? What do I have to do with it?"

"What you have to do with it is this. You can't listen to reason, you must have your own way, you caused a scene at some party the other evening that's now all over town, and if what you're hankering after is a shady upstart who belongs on the far end of Liberty Street——"

"Oh, so that's it! If I wanted to, I could believe you're jealous."

"Yes, that you could. Anything to satisfy your vanity! But believe what you like and do what you like. A huge scandal is threatening in this department, and for days I've been trying to think of a way to stave it off. Now, though, I don't care. I'm not Moses, I'm not that fellow who held back the waves, and I'm not even the boy with his finger in the dike."

417

"It's because of what I said. I know it is!"

"That's the amazing thing about you! Always you know how it is! You came in here knowing I was in love with her, and now you know that I am going to resign because of what you said! The earth turns, the sun goes down, the moon rises, and always it's you who stands at the center! But if you truly want to know something, and why I am going to resign, here, read this," and because he had never truly hated anyone before and now hated Lydia Stanhope, he picked up the envelope containing his TO WHOM IT MAY CONCERN report, ripped it open, and handed the sheets to Arabella. "Read it!" he said. "Go ahead and read it!" and then, in the clerks' room, the gas jet sputtered and went out. He said, "That miserable improvement is going to poison me to death someday," and hastened into the clerks' room. He struck a match and relighted the jet, and when he returned to his office Arabella, pale and wide-eyed, had brought a hand to her throat.

"You've made this up," she said. "It can't be true."

"It can't be but it is!" John said. "And that's what I've been fool enough to have been worrying about for the last several days, trying to think of some way out! Why should I? I'm supposed to prevent the smuggling of cotton, not cover up for those who do!"

"I still don't believe it. It can't be true."

"There's no magic to be worked by repeating those same words, Arabella. It can't be true but it is true. Apparently to the tune of nearly two hundred and fifty thousand dollars."

"That much?"

"Yes, that much, though how many ways it had to be split I don't know. But be fair, Arabella, be fair! You mustn't think she did it for the money. You mustn't make the same mistake as the ladies of the Wednesday Afternoon Ladies Society. You must see her as she truly is."

"You did love her once, didn't you?"

Swept along by the rush of his fury, John said, "It's a vision she has, bright and shimmering, and perhaps she hears voices as well. Being Mrs. Senator Stanhope wasn't enough, being Mrs. Secretary Stanhope isn't enough, and if by some miracle she should ever become Mrs. Vice-President Stanhope that won't be enough either! You may not approve of her vision, you may even despise it——"

"A vision like Medusa's head," Arabella said. "It's done that to her, or worse."

It was the quiet resolute tone of Arabella's voice, more than anything, that helped John to regain control of himself—that and the matching expression on her face. She was not Missy's little friend any more, or night-blooming catchfly, but a mettlesome young woman who did not panic and could keep her head. She said: "Tell me this, Johnny. My father—has he had a hand in this? Don't be afraid to tell me. Actually, since all the secrets are out, I wouldn't be too surprised. As you don't need me to tell you, he's changed."

She spoke in the same firm tone, her eyes looking straight into danger and trying not to be frightened, but John could see the effort it cost her. He said:

"About your father, I'm puzzled. He has done a few things I don't understand—a strange note he left, and then this trip to inspect the railroads when less than six months ago he rode the cars all the way from Kentucky to Florida. There are some things I can't make out, but, to answer your question, no, I'm convinced your father isn't involved."

"You're not just saying that? It's not because you think I'll be hurt?"

John gave a short, angry laugh. "I'm afraid I no longer have time for such considerations."

"What makes you so sure about my father?"

John took a few steps toward the window. "Intuition, mostly, and the way a few things combine. Your stepmother's alarm the other day when I asked if the colonel expected to go to New Orleans, and her relief this afternoon when she said he'd written that he was going no farther than Mobile."

"Why is that so important?"

John looked from the window into the dark. He said, as anxious to test his footing as to explain to Arabella, "Shortly after your father left on this trip, my chief clerk here, a man named Rawlins, discovered that he had interested himself in some of the New Orleans reports.

419

That sort of thing had never happened before. If I may say so, your father has hardly immersed himself in the routine of this department."

"You may say so."

"Anyway, when your father left on this trip in such haste——"

"You thought he was going to New Orleans. Perhaps to smuggle more cotton. Is that it?"

John nodded. "At first, yes. Either to smuggle more cotton or, as Rawlins suspected, because something had gone wrong, something that might lead to his being discovered, and he wanted to cover up."

"What changed your mind?"

Arabella was asking the right questions in the right tone of voice, and John hadn't realized how much he needed someone to take into his confidence. He said:

"Mostly your stepmother, but not only your stepmother. Actually, besides what I've told you——"

"Yes?"

"Look, Arabella. Haven't you had enough? Shouldn't you be getting along to the concert? You've probably missed the whole first part as it is."

Arabella avoided his eyes for a moment, looking down at her muff. "That was a story about the concert, Johnny. I hate that brassy noise. I came purposely to see you. I couldn't stand it any longer, thinking you were in love with her, as she didn't waste any time implying after you left this afternoon. More than implied. Practically said. I had to have it out with you, no matter what. Are you going to be angry?"

"And the handsome young Virginian and his aunt? Was that a story too?"

Arabella looked worried. "I didn't say that, Johnny, you did. But I'm glad you're not going to be angry. I was afraid you would be. Now finish what it was you started to say."

Since all the secrets were out, there was no reason why this last struggling secret should not be set free. John said, "I saw Cameron today," and Arabella's eyes went big and astonished, as he expected them to. He said, "Cameron got into some trouble back home, more trouble than he could handle, and his answer was to run away. He need not have, not if he had been willing to face up, but he wasn't willing and perhaps it was partly my fault too."

"Oh, you!" Arabella said. "Always blaming yourself!"

John moved from the window and stepped closer to the desk. He said, "Cameron has been in New Orleans. Apparently he started for Texas but didn't get that far. Would you think me disloyal if I said my brother has turned into a hopeless drunk?"

Arabella looked at him ruefully. "I'm sorry, Johnny. More for Missy than for Cameron, and less for Missy than for you." She reached out and touched his sleeve. "Don't blame yourself. It's not your fault what Cameron does."

John opened the drawer where he kept his cigars and took out the box. "Like it or not," he said, "I'm going to have a smoke, and these are particularly foul cigars. To get back to Cameron, it was he who told me about your stepmother."

"Why don't you call her Lydia? You haven't been thinking of her as my stepmother, have you?"

John struck a match, saying, "No, I haven't. I suppose one of the things I wanted to evade was her being your stepmother. I couldn't permit her to have that identity. Perhaps it was because of Deerskin. You don't know our old Aunt Mim, do you? They say she knows how to make spells, and all the secret words—whose secret words I've never been able to learn. But it seems that there are some words that can't even be used—bad-luck words—and my deliberately avoiding 'stepmother' was equally superstitious. You get to be like them after a time, just that riddled. It's a wonder I'm not wearing a charm around my neck. You don't mind this cigar too much?"

Arabella shook her head. "No, not too much. Just as long as you don't chew. Chewing I can't abide. You know that general who comes to see us, thinking he's so grand? He took me to a review at the fairgrounds and all the while chewed like a cow. And he sort of looks like a cow too, those round wet eyes. I can't stand him. Finish about Cameron."

John went to the window and raised it a few inches. He said, "Gas and cigar smoke make a deadly combination, and I don't want you to perish. What I was saying about Cameron was that it was he who told me about your stepmother—I mean Lydia. He got mixed up in this thing, though not too deeply, I gather—just deep enough to keep himself in alcohol. I asked him about the Senator—specifically I asked him—and he told me he isn't involved. So don't worry about it. Spare yourself. Take your jumps, as they say, with an easy rein."

Arabella gave him a long, quiet look. "Thank you, Johnny. I love you for this. But where is Cameron now? At the hotel?"

"Cameron is still running," John said. "I helped him the first time and now I've helped him again."

Out in the clerks' room the gas jet began to sputter and John paused to make sure it wasn't going to go out. He said, "Cameron wanted to go to California and I gave him the money to get there. Wait till I have to explain that to an investigating committee or a board of inquiry. It's not going to be easy—my only source of information, and I let him get away. Actually it probably makes no difference. That's the interesting thing about this affair. Nothing seems to make much difference. We always get back to the circumstance that smuggling cotton is no crime. The fact of the matter, Arabella, so far as the law is concerned, is that your stepmother can't be charged even with a misdemeanor."

"What about the forgeries you mention?"

John shrugged. "Is she the forger? Will we ever be able to find him? Since they were Army requisitions, we can assume that some man in uniform had a hand in the affair. But how to run him down? Put a detective on the trail of every military man who has ever been in New Orleans? No, Arabella. It would take forever."

"But two hundred and fifty thousand dollars!"

John gave another shrug. "Yes, I'll readily agree it's a lot of money, even when split four or five ways, but even if it were twice two hundred and fifty thousand dollars, smuggling cotton is still no crime. Right now I'd say that Lydia is going to come out of this without a scratch."

"You mean that?"

"Yes, Arabella, I do. It would take forever to prove anything. We don't have men enough or money enough, and even if we did prove it, leaving out proof of forgery, which can't be laid to her, which she may not even be aware of——"

"What you're saying," Arabella said, "is that you don't intend to do anything. What you plan to do is to protect her."

John looked at her crossly. "Weren't you listening, even a little?"

"What did she say this afternoon?"

"Say about what?"

"This. What we're talking about. Didn't you discuss it?"

John expelled a cloud of cigar smoke and waved it away. "Not a word, Arabella. Not so much as a whisper."

"Why not? Do you mean to tell me——"

"Yes, I mean to tell you. This is your father's problem, not mine, his department and his wife. So everything is going to be dropped into his lap—the report you have there, a covering letter, and my resignation. If it didn't please me to believe you don't even know about hard liquor, I'd ask you to join me in a drink. I'm a free man."

Arabella looked straight at him. "Maybe not so free as you think. In other words you *do* intend to protect her."

John snubbed out his cigar. "Look, Arabella. Instead of being stubborn, why don't you listen to reason? And don't start anything, do you hear! If you're worried about its leaking out, the possibility of a scandal, there is a way around that too—all your father has to say is that the cotton was sold to add to the government's assets abroad. He's bound to think of it, just as I did. He will be applauded for his patriotism and everything will be as before. And who knows? It may even help him get elected Vice-President. That's what he wants, isn't it? Lydia certainly hasn't been saving it up as a surprise."

"So nothing will happen to her," Arabella said.

"That's up to your father."

"You know what to expect, don't you? She'll deny everything."

"I wouldn't be surprised."

"And my father will believe her," Arabella said. "He will *have* to believe her. And you won't do anything, either. You're remembering how you used to be in love with her, longing your heart out, and so, because of that——"

John closed the window so hard that the panes rattled. He said, "It's never any use with you, asking you to be reasonable. What would you have me do? Put her in leg irons? Go over your father's head? Is that your idea? Is that what you want?"

"Nothing will happen to her," Arabella said. "She'll do this cheap ugly thing, practically a thief regardless of the law, and absolutely nothing will happen. She'll continue to priss around at parties and balls, being Mrs. Secretary Stanhope, the *charming* Mrs. Secretary Stanhope, and she can think how smart and clever she is. My poor father, though——" She bit her lip and gave a quick high toss to her head. "He's the one I feel for, forcing himself to believe her whether he wants to or not, unable to admit the kind of person she is, because, if he does, just once——"

John rested a hand on her shoulder. "You leave it alone, Arabella. Do you hear me? Probably I made a mistake in telling you this. But you came at a bad time and said too many things. I couldn't help myself."

Arabella reached up and placed a hand on his. "I'm glad you couldn't."

"Are you? Then do what I ask. Leave it alone. Don't go home and have it out with her. It will only make things worse for your father."

Arabella tightened her fingers on his. "Poor Johnny. Always carrying the weight of the world."

"That's nonsense and you know it. Now you get on home or to whatever party it is that you're going. I'll see you to your carriage."

"You don't have to. There's no reason to bother. I've taken up too much of your time as it is."

John stepped back and frowned at her. "What's got into you? Since when have you ever been bothered about taking up too much of my time? Or anybody's?"

It was not until then that John began to worry. At first it was a nameless worry, based on no more than her puzzling resistance to one of the commonest forms of politeness and the stiff, graceless way she carried herself as they walked down the corridor, but then, when they came to the door that led to the street, his worry began to assume a more tangible shape. It was not the Stanhopes' carriage that stood by the curb in the yellow glare of one of the gas lamps, as he had expected, but a rented hansom with a Negro driver. The instant he saw it he knew what to expect.

Arabella held back on the steps, saying "Good night, Johnny. Don't work too late," making a feeble attempt at cordiality, and once again she was night-blooming catchfly, hopelessly out of her depth. John took her by the arm and hurried her along. "My parents took pains with my early instruction," he said. "I was taught always to see a lady to her carriage," and his voice, strained with anger, was so false and theatrical that he might have been one of the players in *The Gladiators*.

Observing them come down the steps, the Negro driver hopped from his seat and opened the door of the hansom. John more pushed than helped Arabella along. She said, "You're hurting me, Johnny. Stop, please," but it had been a long, exhausting day, and a woman was always up to some trick or other, and if he was hurting her perhaps it was time. Arabella said, "Please don't be like this. I wasn't trying to deceive you. I would have told you had you asked," and John brushed past the Negro driver and handed her into the hansom. He said, "Good night, Miss Arabella. Good night, Mr. Monckton," and it was to Neville Monckton's credit that he had enough poise and self-control to incline his head in a bow.

John stood on the sidewalk until the hansom rolled off, a swaying smudge in the dark. His breath condensed in the chill night air and there was a high cold brightness to the stars. He went back to his office and tried to busy himself, but all the while he was like a man treading water. The initiative had passed out of his hands and he could do nothing but wait.

ii

The way things happened, he did not have to wait long. Two days later there was a boxed editorial on the front page of the *News*, black with outrage: TRAITORS IN HIGH PLACES. The editorial demanded an immediate investigation of the government's cotton warehouse in New Orleans, claiming that persons in highest authority were smuggling cotton on a fantastic scale. The editorial added that the names of the wrongdoers were known to the editor, whose information came from an official source within the government itself, and after a few paragraphs of calumny, more virulent than usual, concluded with the promise that no stone would be left unturned until the traitors were exposed: should the government not bring them to justice, the *News* would.

Because of the slowness of the mails, John did not see the editorial until four days later, when that issue of the *News* came to his desk. As he read it, with a hard knot in the pit of his stomach, he thought that this surely was the end. But when that day passed and most of another—no summons to appear before an investigating committee: no roof falling in—he began to perceive that the storm could be ridden out.

Most things are in the eye of the beholder, and what he saw in the editorial others would not. Gup Monckton had been crying wolf too long: a bored populace was disinclined to listen. More important than that, however, and even more important than who might be smuggling cotton, was the military situation. Rumors were rife that the city of Nashville had been evacuated and the whole of middle Tennessee lost. Other rumors said that a Northern flotilla had sailed against New Orleans—who was of a mind to worry about a few hundred bales of cotton when the whole city might fall?

Clamorous though Gup Monckton was, these were louder alarms. Nor could Colonel Stanhope's old enemy, in any further editorials, hope to make himself heard. His only chance would be to spell out names boldly, and that was impossible. Not without proof: not without an army of investigators working a year. Gup Monckton had gone as far as he could. He had used his biggest ammunition and they were still afloat. John began to feel that even Arabella could be forgiven.

His cheerful mood persisted almost to the end of the day. He was at his desk, checking out the latest shipping list forwarded by the

Navy, when Rawlins entered, holding an extra just off the press of the local *Examiner* and looking as though he had tumbled down a flight of stairs—the *Examiner*, on its front page, said that Colonel Stanhope, the night before, had shot and killed himself in the lobby of the St. Charles Hotel in New Orleans.

Gup Monckton, when he heard of Colonel Stanhope's suicide, might have been generous. Publicus, however, he who had coined the maxim that Cotton was King, was by then too far soured. Reminding his readers of his earlier editorial, he said that justice would be served, that the colonel's action was proof of his dishonesty, and that he had been a sawdust statesman all along. The *Examiner* took the same line, as did the Charleston *Mercury* and most of the other opposition newspapers, and the government, its hand forced, was obliged to set up an investigating committee. The ensuing complications were such that John Bottomley was nearly a week extricating himself, and had it not been for a letter Colonel Stanhope had mailed from New Orleans, apparently the day before he shot himself, he might have found it impossible. Gup Monckton had the last insult, but Colonel Stanhope, in his letter, had the last word.

CHAPTER THIRTY-THREE

It was Arabella who sat on the couch instead of Lydia, looking worn and pale, but otherwise the scene was the same—the fire in the hearth, the ticking of the clock, the darkening advance of an already gloomy day, and the dripping sound of rain. Blown by the wind, a few drops fell down the chimney. John said, "It wasn't as bad as I expected, the inquiry today. I came here as fast as I could. The committee has issued a statement to the press. It says that your father was overstrained and overworked, on the verge of a breakdown, and that, as his letter proves, he was a dedicated patriot up to the end."

Arabella, staring into the fire, said, "Thank you, Johnny. It was good of you to come in all this wet. I appreciate it," and John, who had arrived only a few minutes before and was still standing, moved closer to the couch. He said, "So now it's all over. Lydia signed the necessary papers, the chairman of the committee made a nice little speech, and that's the end of it. Why not let it be the end of it for you too?" and Arabella, all in black, her reddish-brown hair burnished a bright coppery tone by the fire, shrugged her shoulders with a faint, weary motion. She said, "End to it? If it wasn't for me my father would still be here. Can anything put an end to that?" and John, faced with the incontrovertible, was for a moment unable to reply. More drops fell down the chimney and there was a hiss and flutter of flame. He said, "You punish yourself too much. Uselessly. The only thing that explains anything is everything, back to the beginning of time. You mustn't forget that others had a hand in it too," and

429

Arabella, again with the same weary motion of her shoulders, shook her head.

"No, John," she said. "Regardless of the beginning of time or the hands of others, it was my hand in the end. What would you have me do? Blame Mr. Gup Monckton for writing what I made it possible for him to write, betraying even you? Am I to lay it all to Lydia, that easy way? I detested her and wanted to see her hurt, more than hurt, dragged down, and if it wasn't for that, the only thing I had in mind, my father would still be here. Do you think I can ever forget?"

Her eyes, seeking his, had an expression of unfathomable candor, too tired to pretend, too exhausted to conceal. She said, in a voice less dejected, "What happened at the Investigation Committee? Did they make it horrible for you? And that letter my father wrote. What did it say? I still don't know," and though she sat straight and un-flinching, willing to take the consequences, John could tell that she had long since come to the end of endurance and was proceeding, not on nerve or determination, but out of a sense of self-respect and the knowledge of how to behave.

Trying to conceal his own disturbed emotions, he said, "No, they didn't make it horrible for me, quite the contrary, and what your fa-ther said in his letter was that it was he who had shipped out the cotton, thinking to add to the government's assets abroad," and it was hard to tell, from the vacant look on Arabella's face, if she had heard. "But that doesn't explain why your father did what he did, does it? Would you like me to put it together as best as I have been able to? And wouldn't you like a toddy? There are times when hard liquor has its uses, even for those who aren't supposed to know it exists."

Arabella made an effort to smile. "I've already had a toddy. My old fat Celina decided I needed it. And it was far from being the first, if I must confess. Add that to all my other sins."

"Or Celina's," John said. "Does she have you packed? Your train leaves at six. And if there is anything I can do——"

"You can tell me what happened," Arabella said. "Most of it is still a mystery. I have been hoping you would call. I was afraid you never would, that I'd made you despise me. And when you stopped by to leave your card, not even asking to see me——"

John brought up his arm in an impatient gesture, forgetting the dull ache that all through this spell of wet weather had been bothering his elbow. He said, "Speak to Celina. I did ask to see you. She said you were resting. She would have no more disturbed you than she would the angel Gabriel."

"Yes, but I thought——"

"Thought what?"

"What I said. That I'd made you despise me, that I'd passed beyond the pale. But tell me about my father's letter. What happened?"

John reached for the poker and briefly tended the fire. He said, "It's hard to tell where to begin. Had I known a few weeks ago what I know now, or had I been bold enough to go through your father's desk——" He leaned the poker against the hearth and stepped back from the fire. "But I didn't. What I am trying to say, Arabella, badly, is that your father had reason to believe something questionable was going on in New Orleans."

"You mean he knew?"

"Knew is probably too strong a word," John said. "Let's call it a wonderment. Make yourself comfortable while I try to follow the sequence of events. Superintendent Morris received his appointment late last August, roughly six months ago. We have a Committee of Safety in New Orleans, headed by one of those Creoles, and the way it seems to have begun, the seed that was planted in your father's mind——"

Up on the second floor a door opened at the far end of the hall, and Lydia's voice called out to Celina. Both John and Arabella turned toward the sound at the same instant, looking at each other. Celina, a Negro woman approaching seventy who bore the same relation to Arabella as Elnora did to Missy, answered from an adjoining room, a low fat rumble, and padded heavily down the hall. Not having seen Lydia since the afternoon she gave him tea, John said, "How is she taking it?" and Arabella was still for a moment, thinking. Then:

"Senator Fenchurch has been a strong staff for her to lean on," she

431

said. "He is seeing us to the depot, and were it not for the sake of appearances he would be glad to accompany us home. She is going to keep this house and come here to live. She naturally couldn't stand the ditchwater society back home any more, or to be locked up with me." Arabella gazed moodily into the fire. "You were saying, about the Committee of Safety in New Orleans——"

"Yes, our Creole friend," John resumed. "We get a report from him each week, even when there is nothing to report. And so all too often it adds up to nothing but rumor, speculation, gossip, and malice. Malice especially. It keeps cropping up in all the committees, as is probably bound to happen when you make it patriotic for people to inform, but here our friend in New Orleans seems to have the edge."

Pausing to look at Arabella, John again doubted that she had heard. Her hands were folded in her lap and her eyes were fixed on the fire. She said, untangling her fingers, "I'm listening, Johnny. What I was thinking was how grateful I am that she intends to return here to live. She'll marry Senator Fenchurch, of course, probably before the year is out, and for that I'm also grateful without being able to say why, unless——" She stopped long enough to frown. "Unless it is because I will never have to think I am associated with her in any way." She brought her solemn eyes to bear on John. "You think I'm being hateful again, don't you?"

"No, this time you're wrong. It's easy to understand how you feel. But what are your plans? Will you be going to one of your sisters? You can't live in that big house of your father's all alone."

"I won't be alone. I'll have Celina."

John studied her face. "Is that what you have decided? Your mind is made up?"

"My mind is made up," Arabella said. "I'll have Celina and the other servants, and Missy will be practically next door. If I went to Julie or Christina's I'd feel a burden, and Julie and her family have moved in with Christina as it is, and not only that but——" She tossed her head impatiently. "Don't make me argue, Johnny. I've thought and thought and it's what I want. Go on with what you were saying. I ask you to tell me what happened and then I keep interrupting. I won't any more. That New Orleans gentleman, the one who is head of the committee——"

"Is a creature of incredible spite," John said. "Spite in a woman is bad enough, but in a man it becomes a deformity. This fellow seems to have it in for half the population of his native city, as well as a patent-leather opinion of himself——"

"Patent-leather?"

"It's the way I think of him," John said. "A bad-tempered hunchback in a pair of patent-leather shoes. My acknowledging his reports was not enough. He felt slighted. He complained to your father. If he was going to be written to, he wanted to hear from the Secretary. No underlings, no clerks. So your father, to keep the peace, took over. All the reports from the New Orleans committee were sent directly to him. After replying to them, he passed them on to me."

The rain, as was its tendency around this time of day, began to slack off. A piece of cordwood fell apart in the fire, crackling noisily. John said, "But there were two reports from New Orleans that your father didn't let me see. One was written last November, the other a little over a month ago. I found them when I went through his desk after——"

Arabella filled in the pause. "After I caused him to kill himself."

There was no other way of saying it, no honest way, and John wished this session could have been avoided. No matter how cautiously he proceeded, there was no way to keep Arabella from being hurt. He said:

"Both those reports were concerned exclusively with Morris. One thing I forgot to say about our New Orleans friend is that his nose is as sharp as his spite. Somehow he managed to find out Morris's salary, three thousand dollars a year in our money, and by last November he was convinced that Morris was living beyond his means. The second report was an elaboration of the same theme. Had they come to me I would have probably dismissed them out of hand as two more exercises in bad temper. Your father, however, having appointed Morris, and knowing him to be Lydia's cousin——"

Arabella's look quickened. "Her cousin? I didn't know that."

433

"He used to work in the telegraph office back home," John said. "I never met him, but he has been described to me as a big heavy man with a big red nose. He seems to have been well known on Liberty Street, one of those fellows who were always hanging around."

"And my father made him a superintendent?"

"More than that. He asked him did he want the job. My chief clerk Rawlins found some of their correspondence in the files. It would appear that Lydia put him up to it. The way I piece it together is that Morris wrote her, asking her help in finding him a government job, and that she used her influence with your father."

"But I find it so odd," Arabella said. "Knowing the way she feels about some things—Gunpowder Street, for instance—I should have imagined that she would have hesitated to claim him, that she might have been even a little embarrassed."

John's thoughts wandered out of the room, back to the picnic at Happy Chance. He said, "Yes, at first it does seem odd. The same thought occurred to me. But perhaps the error we make is in seeing Lydia as Lydia rather than as Mrs. Secretary Stanhope. The first Lydia might well have hesitated to acknowledge Morris. The second Lydia, however, Lydia as Mrs. Secretary Stanhope——" He paused a moment and listened to the rain. "Might she not have been indulging in an enjoyment of power? Did it not give her a chance to prove she was now in a position not only to acknowledge an obscure cousin but, if it so pleased her, to raise him up?"

"Yes," Arabella said, "it could have happened. Except for one thing. Even then, in the back of her mind——"

"No, I can't agree," John said. "Not if you were going to say that even then the thought of smuggling cotton had occurred to her. It was Morris who had that idea. Of that I'm convinced."

"Why?" Arabella's voice had a slight edge. "Are you taking up for her again?"

"Think so if you like," John said. "I have no intention of entering that argument again. My theory is that the smuggling scheme began with Morris. Even to this hour Lydia doesn't know enough about the workings of a cotton warehouse to have evolved it, and it was Morris who felt the full blast of the temptation."

Arabella wrinkled her forehead. "Why did he need Lydia?"

"He didn't," John said. "What he needed was your father's cotton. The government bales were too risky to touch. We don't know too much about our cotton, but we do know how many bales the government has purchased, how many have been shipped abroad, and how much we have on hand. On government cotton we are able to keep a fairly close watch. Cotton in private hands, however, most of it unaccounted for, scattered all over the place——"

"It's too complicated," Arabella said. "I'll take your word. And it was Mr. Morris, you say, who approached Lydia?"

"So I have come to believe. This is like tracking in the woods. You make out the signs as best you can. One of the signs is that Morris made a visit here sometime last October. It would have been when your father was off on that fall trip of his. Morris's excuse, I imagine, was that he wanted to pay his respects to Lydia. At some point during the conversation, however, after a few guarded approaches, perhaps in this very room——"

"I don't want to talk about it," Arabella said. "I'm not trying to make excuses for myself, Heaven is my judge, but if she had been less greedy, less grasping——"

And less possessed, John thought, less goaded and driven. He said, "Yes, Arabella, perhaps. But there was something else that entered—your father's finances. Like all of us, he had been sinking deeper and deeper into debt. The blockade has put an end to commerce in the ordinary sense. Everyone's purse is pinched. And since your father confessed his worries freely, Lydia was bound to know about them. Let us agree that this time it was money that lay at the root of evil. But since your father seemed unable to disentangle himself, and since a bauble like the vice-presidency does indeed come high——"

"I knew you would take up for her!" Arabella said sharply. "As if she did it for my father! As if she ever gave a thought to him! What she is, as you well know——"

"But I don't know," John said. "I'm not as confident as you. I am aware of the words that seem to apply—cold, calculating, greedy, self-ish—these are some I myself have used—but words at best have only a token value. Of course she was prompted by self-interest. When has she not been? But I can't agree that she gave no thought to your father. To rescue a man from financial straits, to help him become Vice-President——"

"But how! *How!*"

"The only way open to her," John said. "By smuggling cotton. Where is the wickedness really? Tedious as it is to keep on saying so, smuggling cotton is no crime. It is Lydia's position that makes what she has done seem reprehensible, Caesar's wife again."

Arabella had been watching him solemnly. She said, "You're always finding excuses. It's just like Missy says. Even when Ules Monckton tried to kill you, you did."

"I gave the man cause."

"I told you! You see!"

"See what?" John shrugged his shoulders. "That living alone at Deerskin caused me to fall into a habit of introspection? That I learned it is easier to construct vast theories about the nature of man than to understand the content of a moment's behavior? That scholars dispute and the case is still before the courts?" He shrugged again. "But we have got far off the track. To return to your father, you can understand why those reports from New Orleans disturbed him. And by the time last November rolled around, our Creole friend was bitter to the point of savageness. He was particularly incensed that Morris had acquired a buggy and a pair of matched bays—Liberty Street's dream of opulence, I might add."

"You know a lot about Liberty Street, don't you?" Arabella said. "Maybe you didn't bury yourself at Deerskin as much as I thought."

She looked at him from beneath lowered lids, frowning dubiously, and then, upstairs on the second floor, the door opened again. Lydia's voice said, speaking to Celina, "You be sure to dress good now. We will have to sit up all night and the cars may get uncomfortable," and Arabella's face seemed taken by a chill. John said, trying to sound brisk and factual:

436

"So that brings us to the end of November. Then the Christmas season began, with all those parties, and it wasn't until about a month ago that your father seems to have become truly alarmed. It was Morris's balance sheet for January that must have done it. His report showed a shortage of eight hundred bales. Any dishonest superintendent can make trouble for the department, but this superintendent, being Lydia's cousin——"

Arabella said, "I see. You're right, of course. But why didn't you tell me these things the other evening? Had I but known, had I an inkling——" She bit hard on her short upper lip, disfiguring her mouth. "It's all my fault," she said. "The whole thing," and John shook his head stolidly. "No, Arabella, you can't take it on yourself. What about me? Had I not fallen into a rage and forced you to read that report I wrote——" He shook his head again. "That's why I say it isn't you, or Lydia, or Morris, or even Gup Monckton. It's everything. Go back far enough——"

"Yes, all that may be true, but if it hadn't been for what I said to Neville——"

"There you force me to agree," John said irritably. "I can't pretend that it was the wisest thing to do. I keep telling myself that it was just a fit of temper, that you couldn't possibly have realized——"

"But I did, I did," Arabella said. "What you would like to do is to put the blame on him, isn't it, making it all his fault? What you'd like to think is that I blurted it out impulsively, not knowing what I was doing, and that he took advantage of—of what? My innocence? No, Johnny. I knew exactly what I was doing. That if I told Neville he would tell his brother, the general, and that the general in turn——"

John turned away abruptly. He was thinking how intimate a carriage could be, and he remembered the afternoon he had come across Arabella and Neville in his father's woods. He said, "Let's not discuss that part of it. Who you fall in love with is no affair of mine. It does seem to me, though, that if the fellow had the smallest speck of consideration, thinking of what such a scandal might do to you——"

Arabella, looking mournful, reached out a hand. "Don't turn your back. Look at me. You confess you were once in love with Lydia, don't you?"

"A long time ago, a long time ago."

"No, not such a long time ago. Until quite recently. Then why, by that same token——"

"I prefer not to discuss it."

Arabella said, "Please look at me, Johnny. The other evening you said you were not in love with Lydia. Now I say that I am not in love with Neville Monckton. That actually I never was. Infatuated, yes. Aware of a physical attraction, yes. Flattered by his attention, yes. But in love with him, no. Not really, not ever."

"I still say that if he had the smallest speck of consideration——"

"And so do I say it," Arabella replied. "*Now* I say it. And if you care to be kind you will not remind me that now is too late. Don't be like a wooden Indian, Johnny. What is it that is raging through your mind? That a man of honor would have tried to shield me, to protect me from my folly? Is that it? Or would you have me understand that he leaped to the chance to damage my father, more loyal to his clan than to me?" Her voice took on a dry, flat tone. "And what else would you have me understand? That I must surely comprehend how little regard he had for me, that all he wanted was a chance to get under my skirts——"

John spun on his heel. He said, "You hush, do you hear!" and Arabella, looking up from the couch, gave a grim, resigned shake of her head. She said, "You always did think I was a silly little fool, didn't you? And now here's the proof. Are you not going to say anything about chickens coming home to roost?" She waited for John to reply, and when he did not, "But what does it matter?" she said. "What difference does it make? I believe you were telling how my father's suspicions were aroused by some statement or other from Mr. Morris showing an error of eight hundred bales."

"Actually it wasn't an error," John said, glad to move on. "We now know that Morris smuggled out somewhere in the neighborhood of sixteen hundred bales, but the apparent shortage in January was a legitimate mistake. And ours, not Morris's. We sent him five more certificates of release in January than young Abernathy accounted for, or, rather, that he accounted for in the wrong place, as part of government exports. As far as your father was concerned, however, the damage was done. Give Morris eight hundred bales to dispose of, and he could well be living beyond his means. I'm not losing you in this maze, am I?"

"Yes, sort of, but I think I know what you're saying. What happened then?"

John said, "Unbeknownst to me, keeping the matter to himself, the Senator had young Abernathy, who was his secretary, bring him the New Orleans papers that covered Morris's term of office—reports, letters, warehouse statements, everything. Among them were the two Army requisitions signed with the name of Major Howell Angry, but the Senator couldn't have known they were forgeries. It was Rawlins who made the discovery. Incidentally, it was Rawlins's belief that the Senator was in this up to his boots, and I might as well confess that I was more than halfway inclined to agree with him."

"How could you have?"

"The shape of things in general," John said. "But most particularly a note your father left, saying we were not to communicate with New Orleans in any way. Now it isn't hard to understand—he didn't want Morris to get any idea the wind was up—but at the time it looked like collusion."

"But still you shouldn't have," Arabella said in a hurt tone. "You should have known better."

John, nodding assent, said, "Eventually I did. Not, however, until Cameron put in his appearance. He named Lydia and Morris and didn't name your father. That was enough. My first thought, my only thought, was what to do. Rawlins occasionally drinks too much and I was afraid he would talk. I could see the headlines in the papers."

Arabella said bitterly, "As you did," and John hurried on. He said, "I'm afraid I lost my head a little. I had a wild plan of wringing a confession from Lydia. That's what brought me here the other afternoon. You, though, letting your imagination run away with you——"

"Did I?"

"Yes, completely," John said. "And one other thing I should have mentioned—this wasn't a trumped-up trip your father made. He did have some railroad business in Mobile, a section of track along the Gulf Coast to inspect, recently repaired with government funds. All the while, however, the question of Morris was nagging him. And notice I say Morris. Not once did your father suspect Lydia. Everything speaks against it. Why would he not have confronted her directly? Why all that brooding and worrying alone? Why a trip to New Orleans?"

The rain was over and the fire was beginning to die down. John said, "For your father did go to New Orleans after all. It's not too far from Mobile, and this thing about Morris apparently wouldn't let him alone. What happened when he reached New Orleans we have to guess. We know he checked in at the St. Charles Hotel on February 22 and that his letter was dated February 23. We also know he paid a call on Morris. Again what happened we can't say for sure. We can only surmise that Morris, faced down by your father, made a clean breast of things. There is a kind of man who can hold out for just so long. In any case, Morris confessed. And that was when your father found out about Lydia. Up to then he hadn't an idea in the world."

Arabella bent her head and started to cry. She said, "How could she, how could she?" and John wanted only to get it over with as fast as possible. He said, "Which brings us at last to his letter. Knowing I would have to turn the original over to the Investigating Committee, I had Rawlins make me a copy. Do you want to read it or shall I?"

Arabella shook her head several times. "You read it."

Bent low as her head was, John could see only the bridge of her nose, the curve of her cheeks, and the coppery sheen of her hair. He reached into his coat, noticing that the spot of ink on his cuff was beginning to fade, and brought out the copy of Colonel Stanhope's letter. "The original was written on the stationery of the St. Charles

Hotel," he said. "Your father must have sat down to it shortly after his interview with Morris."

"Read it, please."

The late afternoon light was almost gone and John could barely make out Rawlins's handwriting. By now, however, he knew the colonel's letter by heart. He said, "The letter is addressed to me, Captain John Bottomley, in care of the department. This is what it says: *Dear John. Immediately you receive this I wish you would go to the Treasury Department and say to the Secretary that, having had an opportunity over the past several months to dispose of a substantial quantity of my cotton abroad, I am now in a position to turn over to the government the sum, in English pounds, of $146,000, now on deposit in the Nassau, Bahamas, branch of the Royal Bank of Canada. For reasons of expedience this sum has been entered in my wife's name, a matter of unimportant detail, and as a consequence the actual transfer must wait until I return to the capital, as I expect to do within the next few days. However, I wish you would convey this information to the Treasury Department immediately, brooking no delay.*"

Arabella raised her head and tried to hold back her sobs. "And to think it was I—— Oh God! What else does it say?"

"Not a great deal. That's nearly the end."

"Read it, please."

"*One other thing, dear John, directly concerning the affairs of your section of the department. I am afraid Superintendent Morris is not the man for his job. I discovered a decided laxness in his operation of his warehouse, a carelessness concerning those little details that make the difference between a good superintendent and a bad one, and I have asked for his resignation. What think you of appointing our chief clerk Rawlins to the post? He has always struck me as being more than ordinarily competent, and, if you will consider the matter, we can discuss it when I return. Incidentally, should you see my wife——*"

Arabella raised her eyes quickly. "Yes, go on."

"*Incidentally, should you see my wife, I would prefer your not men-*"

tioning the contents of this letter. I wish to surprise her with the news. You know her devotion to our cause and it will please her, I believe, to learn that I have been able to aid it in this small way. Please convey my respects to her, however, and give my daughter my dearest love."

John folded the sheet of paper and slipped it into his pocket. He said, "That's the end. Just his best wishes and signature," and Arabella covered her face with her hands. She said, "My poor father," and began to cry. "Don't do this to yourself, Arabella, please," John said, and Arabella determinedly raised her head. She said, "I see what happened now. He wrote that letter, believing he had saved the situation, as he had, and then, before the letter reached you, before you could do what he asked——"

Brave as she wanted to be, that much bravery was beyond her. Her face collapsed into tears. She said dully, "I wish I could die," and John sat on the couch beside her. "Before his letter reached me there came that attack in the *News*," he continued doggedly. "The *News* and the New Orleans *Picayune* have an exchange arrangement. Gup's first editorial appeared on the twentieth, and that issue of the *News* arrived in New Orleans the same day your father wrote his letter. Then, on the following morning, the twenty-fourth, the *Picayune* reprinted Gup's editorial, along with a few comments of its own. Your father had already had one shock, perhaps more than one, since I doubt that Morris went out of his way to protect Lydia, and then, on the front page of the *Picayune*, he finds an editorial saying that the information it contains was received from an official source within the government. What else was he to think but that I had uncovered the mischief and reported it? That Lydia stood exposed and he was ruined? Under such a strain, probably convinced that it was only a matter of hours before all the details would be published, that I had betrayed him——"

"I wish I were dead," Arabella said. "I wish to God I were dead."

John took her by the shoulders. He said, "Listen to me, Arabella. You can't do this to yourself, do you hear? I won't have it," and Arabella, sobbing uncontrollably, wrenched herself free. She said, "Go away, Johnny. Please go away. I can't stand your being sorry for me. I hate it. Please go away," and she began crying so hard that her whole frame was shaken. She turned aside, lowering her head, and John took her by the shoulders again. He said, "Hush, Arabella, hush. Don't, please. For my sake, I beg you."

"Beg me! What do you care? Whenever have you? Go away, I tell you. Leave me alone."

"All right, then. If that's what you want——"

He started to rise from the couch, and then with a small helpless cry she said, "No, Johnny. I didn't mean it. Say that you love me," and with a sudden impulsive motion she put her arms around his neck. "How can I stand your going away?" she said. "You'll get yourself killed, just as poor Charlie Rhett and that McKenzie boy did, and what will I do? I'll die. I know I will. I won't be able to stand it."

John said, "Listen to me, Arabella. Please listen," and she shook her head frantically, saying, "Who wants to listen? Why should I? Don't you know how much I love you? Can't you say you love me too, instead of asking me to listen? Aren't you ever going to?" She brought up her face, the tears tangled in her thick eyelashes, and then, with a stifled moan, her mouth came forward to meet his. He said, "Arabella, my dear," and she said, "Oh, what a fool you've been. Dear God what a fool," and it was not until they heard footsteps in the upstairs hall that they drew apart.

John said, "I'd best go now. It's getting late," and at the door, clinging to him, Arabella again brought up her mouth to be kissed. "Button up good," she said. "Don't take cold. Write to me," and the strike of a clock a few feet away was so unnaturally loud they both gave a start. "And you write too," he said. "I'll come home as soon as I can. Then we'll get married. You will marry me, won't you?" and there was something in his voice or in the look on his face that made her laugh. "I won't say," she said. "I want to keep you guessing." She laughed again, the final note of the clock lingering on the air, and he reached for the knob of the door. She said, "Hold me again, hard.

Harder. I'll say my prayers every night," and when finally he left her and walked through the dusk hung with the cold wet smell of rain, how beautiful she was, the joy and wonder of her, caused him to stand still. Pondering whether he should go to the depot to see her off, he decided not to. He hoped she wouldn't find it too uncomfortable on the train.

PART SIX

CHAPTER THIRTY-FOUR

In after years, whenever he looked back to that time, John Bottomley could see how the afternoon he had spent with Arabella brought him almost to the end of the involvement that had had so many of its roots in the Light Infantry Ball. He became a soldier and he endured. Then, three years later, in the early part of January 1865, when the Northern army that had destroyed Atlanta and marched to the sea was within sixty miles of Pompey's Head, his crippled division, reduced to less than a quarter of its original strength, was separated from the forces defending the capital and sent down by rail, without horses, to bolster the outnumbered and demoralized units that were attempting to oppose the invader.

The move was useless—a whole army was needed, not the remnants of a division. Striking north from Savannah, the federal forces marched almost as they pleased. The principal opposition encountered was the terrain. All this part of the country was a dense tangle of swampland, cut through by numerous small streams now swollen by nearly a month of rain. But even so the Northern march continued. By the second week of February the forward columns were less than forty miles from Pompey's Head.

It was then that John Bottomley saw Clay Vincent again. John was in command of some twenty-odd militiamen holding a rear-guard position on the east bank of the Marlborough River, one of the branches of the Cassava, and Clay rode into camp late one afternoon. Both men were surprised to see each other—when last heard of, the one had been in Virginia, the other in North Carolina. Clay said, "I'll be damned if

I expected to find you here," and John said, "What are you doing in these parts?" and then, after each had explained his presence, the talk turned to the way the war was going.

Clay said, "They're a bunch of criminal thieves and bastards! Atlanta was bad enough, but it only gave them an appetite for more! They've been looting and plundering ever since, and what they can't loot or plunder they burn." Biting off a chew of tobacco—a vicious bite: the clamp of his teeth enforced by a snap of his neck—Clay reached inside his coat and brought out a folded handbill. "Here, read this," he said. "This is the pass we've come to! And none of it need have happened. That's the hell of it! Retreat, retreat, retreat! All the time trying to fight a defensive war! They should have taken General Monckton's advice way back in the beginning. It's the jugging politicians who have done us in!"

John Bottomley, still a captain but wearing a uniform of odds and ends that made his rank unrecognizable, wished he could be glad to see an old friend. Clay's aggressiveness, however, rubbed the wrong way. The weeks of wet weather had pierced John with a clamminess that went down to his bones, his bad elbow ached unbearably, and he was afraid he was coming down with malaria.

He said, "If you think it's been nothing but retreat up in Virginia, you're wrong," and Clay's face, clouding, took on a dark evasive look. Ignoring it, John unfolded the handbill. He turned aside to suffer through a spell of coughing that racked him head to foot, and then, wishing he had a bottle of Pittman's Ague Cure to dose himself with, anything, he ran his eyes over the strident black letters.

CITIZENS

ARISE TO THE DEFENSE OF YOUR NATIVE SOIL! RALLY AROUND YOUR PATRIOTIC SOLDIERS! YOU NOW HAVE THE BEST OPPORTUNITY YET PRESENTED TO DESTROY THE ENEMY. REMOVE ALL PROVISIONS FROM HIS PATH AND PUT ALL OBSTRUCTIONS IN HIS WAY. HIS ARMY WILL SOON STARVE IN YOUR MIDST. BE RESOLUTE! BE CONFIDENT! OBEY ALL ORDERS! I HAVE RETURNED TO JOIN YOU IN THE INEVITABLE VICTORY THAT MUST BE OURS.

Major-General Ules Monckton, Comd'g.

The two men were standing amid a grove of pines within sight of a high trestlework bridge that spanned the river. Ordinarily no more than a good-sized creek, the stream had been turned into a flood. Great mounds of driftwood were caught against the pilings of the bridge, causing eddies and whirlpools to form, and whole trees were being borne along, their dead branches slowly turning this way and that, while the rush of the water, which had overflowed its banks in several places, gave off a ceaseless, rumbling roar.

Wondering what all this rain had done to Deerskin and how much of the silt churning past had been washed from his fields, John returned the handbill to Clay Vincent. He said, "Be resolute! Be confident! Obey all orders! He's lost none of his taste for the grand style, I see," and though he could tell that Clay was growing angrier by the minute, he was more annoyed than intimidated, and even a little bored.

And Clay must have comprehended. Through no fault of his own, he was the less seasoned man. He was still a member of General Monckton's staff, and General Monckton, until recently, had been languishing in exile—so recently that John Bottomley, until Clay's arrival, was unaware that he had been recalled to active duty.

Sending General Monckton to the West had not had the disciplinary effect the government had hoped for. He and the *News* became more critical, not less. The war had been waged incorrectly from the beginning: the same mistakes were being repeated: a more resolute leadership was needed, both in the government and in the field: let the present drift continue and all would be lost—so ran the litany, chanted to the point of monotony and, as General Monckton and the *News* seemed unable to understand, against a growing conviction that this ill-tempered bickering was inimical to the public weal. The luster of the hero of Forts Signal and Lookout began to dim. Less compelled to consider public opinion, the government brought down its fist—General Monckton was placed in command of a small, inconsequential department in North Carolina, miles removed from any of the active theatres of the war.

The universal expectation was that he would resign: there could not have been a more pointed humiliation. General Monckton, however, like a fallen favorite condemned to the darkest corner of Gaul, accommodated himself to obscurity, and Clay Vincent, loyal to the end, stayed by his side.

John Bottomley was between battles in Virginia when he heard the news. It did not surprise him that General Monckton had elected not to give up his sword. The turn of history's wheel would someday prove him right, and his hour was bound to come.

And now, did it please him, he could say that his faith in himself was justified—with the Northern invader marching through the deepest part of the South, and the country in extremest peril, he had been called back to the scene of his early triumph. BE RESOLUTE! BE CONFIDENT! OBEY ALL ORDERS! I HAVE RETURNED TO JOIN YOU IN THE INEVITABLE VICTORY THAT MUST BE OURS!

But still the rhetoric grated: the pose was too heroic and extreme. All moments invest the present moment, and in that moment, standing in a sodden grove of pines with the high trestlework of the bridge like a wooden cobweb on the sky, John Bottomley also stood in Colonial Square, seized by panic and wanting to run. That he should ever have been that afraid gave Ules Monckton a loathsome advantage, and the finger on the trigger belonged to the same hand that had penned the handbill. He said to Clay Vincent:

"And now he has come back to join us, has he—as my father might have said, what does he expect? A medal? We have perhaps twenty-five thousand men, counting militia and reserves, while they have around eighty thousand. We haven't stopped retreating since Atlanta. They've got across swamps and rivers and they keep on coming. And what's the first move of this general of yours? He gets Brother Gup to run off a handbill! It's not that he likes to blow his own trumpet. He *is* a trumpet," and, as had happened so often before, he and Clay came close to that point of punctilio where someone would have to be called out.

Clay said, "You're talking about your new commanding officer. Damn if I can countenance such language," and John, the last of his patience left miles behind, somewhere in the mud and rain along the line of retreat, gave a snort. "Language my ass," he said. "I'm making some coffee, what we call coffee, roast acorns and beans, and I'd be pleased to have you join me. Will you, or are you in a hurry to say what you came for? It's not my intention to quarrel, not unless you're spoiling to, and since you say you've just come from home, I'd like to ask have you seen my wife. But don't expect me to join in welcoming your hero. You've come to the wrong man."

Clay slowly relaxed his belligerent stance. He said, more amicably, "Let me get to my saddlebags. A ship came through the blockade and there was some real coffee aboard. And yes, I have seen your wife. She and Missy are fine. I was sorry to hear about your father. I never knew him well, not as much as I would have liked to, but he was a fine man," and then later, as they sat on a log near John's tent near a fire of pine knots, each smoking a cigar, they again began to discuss the war.

The simplest soldier knew what was happening. The Northern invader must be halted. If he was not, eventually he would get to Virginia, and the worn and ragged troops protecting the capital could not hope to contend against two huge armies combined. But the depressing circumstance was that it was becoming more and more apparent that such an issue was inevitable—nothing had stopped the advance of these Northern columns, and nothing would.

"Or so they say!" Clay Vincent spat out. "That kind of talk is spineless and defeatist! General Monckton has other ideas."

"Like what?"

"Like fighting a different kind of war," Clay said. "Like splitting up into small, mounted units, one or two or three hundred men. We can take to the swamps and the hills. That way, by living off the country and not fighting any pitched battles, we can keep on going forever."

"He still has that notion, has he?"

Clay said, "And why not? What's wrong with it? Guerrilla warfare is our only chance. The North has its belly full of this war, even more than we have. Let us keep it going for another year, just even another six months, and they'll be damn well anxious to make peace. We still can come out on top."

It might have been Ules Monckton speaking, even to the note of passion in Clay's voice—but a lesser Ules Monckton: a Ules Monckton at second hand. Continuing, Clay said, "The only trouble is that they won't listen to him! They never have. Those West Point generals have been jealous from the start! And it ain't as if he was in full command. He still has to take orders from higher up. All the senior officers had a conference a few weeks back. General Monckton tried to get them to agree to his plan, but they voted him down."

"Thank God."

"Why do you say that?" Clay said sharply. "How else can we go on? Look what they did to Atlanta! And will they spare Pompey's Head any more than they intend to spare Charleston? Haven't they called us the twin citadels of secession? Don't they blame us for the war, more than anybody? They won't be satisfied until we're wiped from the earth. They'll ruin us worse than they ruined Georgia. Men! Soldiers! Like hell they are! They're nothing but a bunch of criminal bastards!"

Somewhat comforted by two honest cups of coffee, John studied the end of his cigar. He said, "Of course they're criminals, Clay. We all are. War itself is criminal. Thou shalt not kill. Yet you have and I have. Are we any less criminal than they? How so? By virtue of degree? Because they destroy cities and towns, warring on the whole population? I doubt it will hold. Thou shalt not kill. And once you start killing, for whatever reason——"

"Ah, for Christ's sake!" Clay said. "I don't understand you and I never have! Not since you went North to school! Are you making excuses for them? Are you saying it's right to make war on women and children, to burn for the sake of burning, to destroy whatever lies in their path? Is that it? Are you saying it's *right?*"

A chill went over John, causing his teeth to chatter. Recognizing this newest sign of fever and again wishing he had a bottle of Pittman's to dose himself with, he said, "Right? My experience is that right, whatever we mean by it, is one of the first casualties of a war—right ends up being what helps your side. Suppose instead of Atlanta it had been Washington or Philadelphia that had been destroyed? Where would the right lie then?"

Clay did not answer, his face set doggedly. John said, "Why is it that we have to believe that ours is the sword of the Almighty? How can it be? Or theirs? Or any sword? You keep saying they are criminals. But what are they doing except what General Monckton once proposed? Didn't he say at that meeting in the capital that we should invade the North and make total war, ruining it utterly? Let us assume that we could capture Washington tomorrow? Would we hesitate to turn it into another Atlanta?"

"They would have forced it on us," Clay said. "We couldn't be blamed."

John said, "Of course not. An eye for an eye and a tooth for a tooth. But who are the criminals then? Does one set of atrocities sit on the right hand of God and another on the left? Not wanting to be killed, I'll kill instead. Not wanting to perish, I'll fight to survive. If war has any other right than that, I don't know what it is. Put it on that basis and we can agree—they're a crowd of murdering bastards and I'd see them all in hell."

Clay frowned soberly. "You've had enough of this war, haven't you? You hate it."

"I hate it to my bowels," John said. "We fought to preserve a way of life and because we were invaded—so we believe and say. They fought because of the principles of humanity and to free the slaves —so they believe and say. And what happens? Thousands and thousands slain, as many more thousands maimed and crippled, the nation bleeding as from a butcher's knife, and large parts of the South destroyed. You're goddamn right I hate it! But not abstractly. It's the filth and the stink I hate, the garbage that once was living men, and the things I've seen that I'll never forget. Dear God Almighty, man! I saw Robert Blackford shot down in a burning cornfield, and then—— No, it's an offense to his memory to speak of it. But hate this war? I couldn't hate anything more."

"And so you'd give in," Clay said. "You'd quit. You'd be willing to have the niggers be on top."

453

John dropped his cigar into the mud and got to his feet. He said, "Why do we try to talk? What's the use? I might as well try to talk to this log. You obviously brought me a change in orders, so why don't we get it over with? And if you feel like being insulted, go ahead and be insulted. Call me out and I'll be glad to oblige. Not wanting to be killed, I'll kill instead. That goes for you too. For anybody."

Clay Vincent sat on the log without moving. He wore only one spur, and the mud curled around the soles of his boots. He looked at John and said, "You don't mind flying off the handle, do you? Maybe you better have a drink." Reaching into his saddlebag, which was draped across the log, he brought out a tin flask and handed it to John. "Drink up. You look like you could use one."

John pulled on the flask and handed it back. He said, "I'm obliged for the drink, but I meant what I said. What are my orders? According to the old ones, before your general did us a favor by coming back home, we were to wait here until we learned what happened to Franklin's Station. If the federals captured it and got hold of the railroad, we were to burn the bridge and start falling back to Branchville. What change has there been? Have they got to Franklin's Station?"

Clay nodded glumly. "By now most likely," he said. "The last report was that their cavalry was within a couple of miles and that our fellows were pulling out. They got through the swamps and crossed the Salkahatchie." Clay shook his head. "How they did it, God only knows. We hear they had to corduroy every foot of the way through the swamps, and that sometimes, when the logs gave way, whole wagons disappeared. But even so they got through. Those sons-of-bitches could build a road across the lakes in hell."

"They crossed the Salkahatchie? Flooded as it is?"

Clay threw away the end of his cigar. "That's the worst of it. From what we hear, something went wrong. Our fellows burned the causeways but not the bridge. That made all the difference. They corduroyed the approaches to the bridge and crossed in the night. By morning a whole division had somehow got through the swamps this side of the river and made it to the road. They went in against our fellows five to one. We had to pull out. Franklin's Station is probably leveled to the ground by now."

"So we burn the bridge."

"That's right. The general wants to make sure it's gone. Their whole army is together now, and part of it may come this way."

John paused to think. "But what about our people? If there is to be another retreat, might not some of them also be coming in this direction?"

"Too damn bad. They'll have to ford."

John indicated the river. "Ford *that*?"

"Too damn bad," Clay repeated. "Let them swim. We can't take any chances. Besides, none of our fellows are likely to come this way. They know the country too well—at least I hope they do. Any sense at all and they'll take the road to Moore's Courthouse instead of floundering through that big swamp between here and Franklin's Station."

"But suppose they do?"

Clay gestured impatiently. "Let them swim. The bridge has got to go. The thing we have to remember is that their whole Army is together again. If they corduroy the swamp between here and Franklin's Station and get to the bridge, they can follow the road along the railroad embankment and be on high ground. It's the general's idea that that will be one of their moves. That bummer bastard will probably follow the same tactics as before—send one wing in one direction, a second in another, and hold back his center so as to bring it up wherever it's needed. Come look at the map. This line here is the Atlantic & Central where it crosses the Charleston & Savannah at Franklin's Station. Since it's no good to them, they've been tearing up the Charleston & Savannah as they go along. They say they've built some special machinery to heat and twist the rails."

Clay paused a moment. Then, "Here is Franklin's Station," he continued, "and right about here is where we are, with the bridge. Ten miles to the north, up at Moore's Courthouse, is where the Atlantic & Central branches. The left branch, this one, goes off to the west and then up to Columbia. The right branch takes us into Pom-

pey's Head. Damn if I ever thought this day would ever come—
me sitting on a frigging log in the woods and them so close to home.
You want another drink?"

"It might help. I think I have a touch of the fever."

"A touch?" Clay raised his brows. "Any other time you'd be laid
up in bed. But that's all right. By tomorrow night Arbell will be looking after you."

John hadn't seen her in fourteen months. He remembered their last
night together, their waking to the dawn in his room at Indigo, she
turning on her side toward him, smooth and warm with sleep—it was
several moments before Clay Vincent's hazy image took shape again.

"How is she?" John asked. "When did you see her last?"

"Nine-ten days ago. She's working at the hospital."

"Did she seem well?"

"Never better. She always was beautiful, but now, I don't know.
It's hard to put into words. There's not a man in the hospital who
isn't in love with her. But maybe I'd best not sound too appreciative.
Is it too late for me to offer my congratulations? You're a lucky man."

"That I don't have to be told. And Missy, my sister? And my aunt
Mary Nesbitt? Are they well too? Has Missy heard from Gordon lately?
We were all married at the same time, you know, a double wedding.
It was when I went home after my father died. He never did get over
that cold."

"All three of my sisters wrote me about the wedding," Clay said,
"and every last one of my aunts. The only one I didn't hear from
about it was my father. He keeps writing about deer hunting. I still
say he'll outlive us all."

"But you haven't told me about Missy."

"That little Missy is a wonder," Clay said. "She looks after your
father's properties like she was doing it all her life. You never can
tell about a woman, can you? There she was, apparently not a thought
in her head except how to dance her feet off, and now look at her,
running things as well as any man. But I reckon that that barber has
been a lot of help to her. It doesn't take anything away from Missy,

not in the least, but what they say is that without him she wouldn't have been able to manage nearly so well."

Beneath the discomfort of his fever John felt the stirrings of a deeper, more malignant malady. He said, "Barber? What barber?"

"The one who works for her," Clay said. "That mulatto barber on Bay Street, the one they call Allbright. The way I get it from my father, he's given up his trade and gone to work for Missy. It's all the talk back home, the way she has him eating out of her hand. He keeps her books and acts as agent between her and Thrall & Lockhart, and whenever she has to go upriver, he goes with her. The way my father tells it, he won't let her out of his sight. That's how come he closed up his shop. He's living in that room in your father's stable."

John tried to assimilate this new piece of information—three women alone at Indigo, Arabella, Missy, his aunt Mary Nesbitt, and Allbright living in the stable. "When did this happen?" he asked.

Clay spread his hands. "That I can't say. The way I got it from my father, it's been for some time. What's the matter? I never liked that Allbright myself, no more than I like any free nigger, and he's too full of airs to suit me, but the way my father tells it, so far as the help he has been to Missy is concerned——"

John said, "I didn't know about it, that's all. There's been no mail for months. Let's get back to my orders. You said something about my wife being able to look after me. Does that mean we're going to fall back all the way to Pompey's Head?"

"No, not exactly." Clay took a last quick pull at his flask. "Like I said before, their whole Army is together again, and now that they've got through the swamps to high ground, they can move in any direction they please—to the west in the direction of Aiken, straight up north to Columbia, or to the east against Pompey's Head. Actually, strong as they are, they could move in all three directions at once. Christ! How can we hope to stop them? We're spread too thin as it is! The way General Monckton has it figured, and I believe he's right, is that they're bound to march on Pompey's Head. He says it has a symbolic value to the North, on account of our taking the forts, though exactly what he means I don't know. Sometimes he runs too deep for me."

John said, "But what are my orders? After we burn the bridge, then what? Do we still fall back to Branchville?"

"Not everybody," Clay said. "Just the foot soldiers. General Monckton invites all the mounted men in this part of the line to start riding to Pompey's Head."

A spasm of fever caused John to shiver again. He said, "I don't understand. I doubt we have fifty mounted fellows all along the river. The only one here with a horse is me. If it's cavalry he needs, why doesn't he call on the regular units?"

"He can't," Clay said. "They're not part of his command. The cavalry takes its orders from headquarters. General Monckton has to start from scratch."

"None of this makes sense. What do you mean, start from scratch? And what did you mean when you said he 'invited' all the mounted men to ride to Pompey's Head? Since when has he taken to extending invitations? What brought you here, anyway?"

Clay seemed oddly ill at ease. Putting the flask back into his saddlebag, he said, "I reckon you might as well know the whole story. General Monckton is stepping down. They won't fight the war his way, and he knows better than to try to fight it theirs. What he wants to do is to form a troop of irregulars, more a force than a troop, only men who will volunteer. He already has two hundred or so. It's the only hope we have of keeping the war going. He figures that once we show what we can do we can raise at least a couple of thousand men, probably more. Then, soon as the North realizes what has happened, that we can keep on fighting for years if we have to——"

"So that's it," John said. "That's why you're beating the bushes. At last he's going to have it his own way. Orders are orders but to hell with orders. To him they don't apply. He simply steps down and decides to form an army of his own. And with things as they are, he can't be touched. When does he set sail for Mexico? When does he get himself crowned king of the empire he says we ought to claim?"

458

"You don't have to have any part of it," Clay said coldly. "Nobody's begging you. We only want volunteers."

"So it's 'we,' is it? What rank have you been promised? Count? Marquis? Knight of the Royal Bedchamber?"

Clay said, "You start backing down, do you hear? I've had enough," and John shrugged him off. He said, "Enough of what? My refusing to look on him as Hannibal and Moses rolled into one? Not, mind you, that I don't believe that up to a point he is right. I'll agree that guerrilla warfare is our last chance. But only if we fight that kind of war wherever we have any men left, in Virginia and Tennessee and North Carolina and anywhere else, under some sort of central command. Your proposal is insane. In less than a month your irregulars will become a lawless mob. What could be more 'irregular' than some of our cavalry? Consider the experience we've already had. Cattle shot in the fields, horses stolen, houses robbed, stores looted, food wasted and destroyed. And what happened on the retreat from Georgia? Our own men came to be more feared in some places than the enemy. Is that what you want? Haven't our people had enough?"

Clay, goaded, raised his voice almost to a shout. "None of that don't signify, goddammit! The thing to do is to keep the war going! That's all that counts! It's up to us to show the way! Nobody's begging you to come along. Only volunteers are being asked to report."

"Report where?" John asked, and had Clay thought a moment he might have tried to sound less angry and abrupt.

"Indigo."

"My father's house?"

Without moving an inch, Clay seemed to retreat. He said, "No, not the house itself. That little office of your father's in the garden. We already have a couple of hundred men, like I told you, and those woods of yours are the only place near town for them to camp. We had to have room for the horses."

"So he moved into my father's office. Just like that."

"No, goddammit, not just like that! Your sister gave him permission."

"And if she hadn't?"

459

Clay did not answer, and John, looking at him, could tell that for once in his life Clay was afraid. He was tempted for an instant to further his advantage, to assert his mastery beyond dispute, but Clay was only incidentally present—Allbright in the stable, Ules Monckton in the office in the yard, and a gang of irregulars camped in the woods. He turned away so abruptly that Clay fell back a step.

"Where are you going?"

"To carry out my orders. To get a few of my men and burn the bridge."

"And then what?"

"Guess."

"You don't think you can stop him, do you?"

"Me? Of course not. I just feel like going home."

"You could be shot as a deserter."

"Yes, I suppose I could. I warn you, though, don't miss."

CHAPTER THIRTY-FIVE

Because of the weeks of rain, burning the bridge was no easy task. By nightfall, however, the job was accomplished, a twisting lick and leap of flame that sent great columns of smoke and sparks into the sky, lighting it up for miles. Instructing his men to get to Branchville as best they could, John mounted his horse and started for Moore's Courthouse, ten miles away. When he got there he would be within twenty miles of Pompey's Head as the railroad ran, but more than twenty-five by the route he had to travel.

This was an empty, desolate part of the country, the road no more than a wagon track through a forest of pines. Behind him John could hear the roar and crackle of the bridge, and once a splintering crash as part of the structure collapsed into the river. Slumped in his saddle, he began to doze, waking fitfully. His fever seemed to be abating, and the heat from the bonfires needed to burn the bridge had at least managed to dry his clothes, despite the way he had run with sweat.

Coming to with a start, he found that his horse had wandered from the road and come to a halt in the pines. The glow in the sky was less intense, and he could tell, from where it shone brightest, that he was still traveling in the right direction. But he was too tired to go any farther. He slipped from the saddle, tied his horse to a sapling, and settled down for the night, wrapping up in his blanket and using his hat as a pillow.

When he opened his eyes it was light. A heavy mist shrouded the pines. The horse stood quietly, sleek with wet. John shivered, his teeth chattering, and when he got to his feet, clumsily, pulling himself

461

up on one knee, he stood with his head bent down, waiting for the pain in his elbow to pass.

Hungry, he decided to make some hoecakes and coffee, and when he reached into his saddlebag for his sack of cornmeal he saw that his hands were black as soot—all that smoke and rosin when he was burning the bridge. Bringing out the cornmeal, he also brought out some hardtack that he broke into pieces and fed his horse—that done, he built a small fire, mixed part of the cornmeal with some water from the canteen tied onto his saddle, and cradled the plate in the ashes. ("Ever you get a chance to eat, eat," he was once advised by a wise, bearded Kentuckian back in his greenhorn days. "It ain't ever helped a man yet to get to Kingdom Come on an empty stomach.")

The hoecakes were soon done. John put the coffee to boil as he ate them, found enough sugar left in his saddlebag to sweeten the coffee with, and then, breakfast over, he remounted the horse and found his way back to the road. He felt considerably restored. All that sweating last night must have checked the fever. Something to be thankful for, anyway.

Half a mile farther along the road was crossed by a narrow stream, fed by springs and with a sandy bottom. After watering his horse, John pulled off his coat and what was left of his shirt and did what he could to scrub himself. He dried himself with the least filthy part of the shirt, and then, unable to bring himself to wear it any longer, dipped it into the stream and washed the mud from his boots. He put on his coat, thinking that if he could find a thornbush he could do something about the missing buttons and not go around with most of his chest and belly showing, and carefully adjusted his hat. He bent over the stream, trying to catch his reflection in the water, and what he saw was a scarecrow. It depressed him a little. He was going home and would have liked to look his best.

ii

John had been part of a retreat before and twice had been caught in a rout. The scene he came upon when he reached Moore's Courthouse, however, was something new—it had never been part of his experience to see a nation breaking up.

Moore's Courthouse was one of the way stations of the Atlantic & Central Railroad. When John came within a half mile of it, still in open country, the fields on either side of the road abandoned and thick with last year's weeds, he began to pass groups of straggling soldiers. It was the look on their faces, a sort of belligerent apathy, that first told him something was wrong. And the shouts and yells he heard up ahead, the shatter of glass and the crack of wood, were not the sounds of an army in retreat—the only translation that seemed to fit was a wild, violent Fourth of July.

Like most of the way stations in this part of the country, Moore's Courthouse was built around the depot. During the war the small wooden building had been pressed into service as an Army commissary, and it was here that the shouts and yells were loudest—a crowd of perhaps fifty men had broken into the depot and were looting its contents.

John Bottomley had been hearing of such incidents ever since he had come south from Virginia. He had even read of them in a stray copy of the Charleston *Mercury* that fell into his hands. *There must be radical reform. It is folly to talk of red tape now. We want THE THING! We must have it—reform—shooting—cashiering—order—subordination—soldiers! Not runaways, ragamuffins, ruffians.*

Four years ago, however, the mere notion of runaways, ragamuffins, and ruffians would have been repugnant. The *Mercury* would have spoken of the pride and chivalry of the South. Its anger was the anger of heartbreak. *We are not like this: we have a code: we are a responsible, gentlemanly, well-bred people: What has happened?*

Slowing his horse, John watched the wrecking of the depot. It did not occur to him to try to stop the looters. Seeing the dart of various pairs of eyes toward his horse, and the crafty looks of envy, he rested his hand on his revolver. It was probably his appearance more than the gesture, however, that indicated his readiness to shoot down the first man who made a false move. Compared to the scarecrow he was, most of these fellows looked like fashion plates.

One of the looters edged up warily, holding out a handful of cigars. The invitation was to share the common shame. He was a short round man with the plump smooth cheeks of the fat boy in school, but a fat boy not to be taken lightly—a fat boy reeking of whisky: a fat boy with cold sly eyes: a fat boy who was tired of walking and wanted that horse.

"Have some, Captain," he said, holding the cigars up higher. "You might as well get yours before the Yankees do. They're pouring through at Franklin's Station and will be coming along this way before you know it."

"See that they're made to feel at home," John said. "I'm sure you will."

The soldier looked puzzled (a not too clever fat boy, John thought, one who had trouble with spelling and sums) and then, as finally he comprehended, his face leaped like an animal into a snarl.

"You dirty——"

He made a lunge for the reins, dropping the cigars, and then went sprawling on his back—the toe of John's boot had caught him on the mouth and chin. Several of the other soldiers jumped forward, and John whipped the revolver from his belt. It was a foolish thing to do, since he couldn't possibly cover them all and might have been shot in the back, and again it must have been his appearance that saw him through. At that moment he was quite as dangerous as he looked.

CHAPTER THIRTY-SIX

Three hours later, as he entered Pompey's Head by way of the far end of River Street, with the muddy waters of the Cassava streaked with light, John Bottomley would not have said that this was what he had expected—not a ship nor sail on the river, the stores boarded up, the wharves piled with bales of cotton that some Negroes working under guard were setting on fire, a confusion of wagons heaped with household goods, and a milling mob at the railroad depot trying to climb aboard an already hopelessly crowded train which, in ordinary times, would be the 3:45 P.M. to Columbia, with connections to Charlotte, North Carolina, and points farther west.

And yet, though he would not have said that this was what he had expected, John watched the chaos without surprise—there had been a major breakthrough, the enemy was on the march, and how could Pompey's Head imagine it would be spared? Word must have got around that General Monckton considered the situation hopeless and intended to pull out.

Because of the burning cotton, River Street was full of smoke, hanging low like fog. Except for the Negroes firing the cotton, their sweaty faces showing no more emotion than if they were hoeing corn, the end of the street where John had entered was relatively calm. Most of the consternation was in the opposite direction, where River Street, following the river to the outskirts of town, became a dirt road that led north to Columbia.

John thought Columbia a dubious mecca. Unlike Pompey's Head, it lay directly on the Northern line of march, and sooner or later it would have to meet the massed onslaught of the enemy's whole Army. Far more than Pompey's Head it seemed likely to become another Atlanta, and John hoped Arabella and Missy and his aunt Mary Nesbitt had not joined the hapless pilgrimage.

Into the haze of smoke that filled the street there leaped a ragged sheet of flame. Thick with tar and impregnated with years of spilled turpentine, the wharves were beginning to ignite. The smoke changed from blue to black, dense coiling greasy billows, and the Negroes took to their heels, yelling as they ran. Up toward the depot a woman screamed—a single thin scream that seemed actually to slice like a knife through the other noises, causing them to fall away on either side—and there was a more distant, tinkling sound that John recognized as the shatter and fall of glass. Though it could have been caused by an accident, he didn't think so. It was more likely that a shopwindow had been broken into and the looting begun.

Scattered bursts of flame were beginning to spring up the length of the wharf, and the air was full of sparks and wisps of burning cotton, blowing like autumn leaves. Frightened, John's horse skittered sideways, churning its head and pulling at the reins. There was another shatter of glass, followed by several more, and then the clanging of a bell as the train pulled out of the depot—an enraged howl rose from those who had been left behind.

Digging in his spurs, John guided the plunge of his horse across the uneven cobbles, narrowly missing a man and woman in a buckboard who came tearing through the smoke from the direction of the depot. The horse dodged and reared, and for a moment John thought it was going to fall. He shook free of the stirrups, preparing to slide off, but then the horse came down heavily, stumbling on the cobbles and almost sending him over its head. Jolted, but keeping his seat, John managed to coax the animal into one of the side streets, which ran at right angles from River Street to Colonial Square.

Here, a quieter atmosphere prevailed. The inhabitants stood huddled before their houses, women and children and one fragile old man with the searching expression of the nearly blind, intent upon the pall of smoke rising from the wharves. The menace of an invading army had been for the moment forgotten. A nearer enemy was fire. The old man wore a faded plaid shawl draped around his shoulders, and his broken shoes were laced with bits of twine. A pigpen stood behind one of the cottages in a weedy field that ran off into a clump of trees, and John could hear the hoarse wet snorting of a hog. He was grateful that food in Pompey's Head had never been a problem and that the civilian diet, unlike that in the capital, had not had to accommodate mule meat and rat.

John decided the quickest way to get to Indigo would be to ride to Colonial Square, cut across one of the side streets to the northwest edge of town, and then take the road through the woods. It would be, in reverse, the route he had traveled with Robert Blackford and Jeremiah Lake the morning he fought his duel—Robert killed, Jeremiah lost at sea, and the duel how many aeons ago? When he reached the square, however, it might have been the afternoon of that same day, except for the eerie quiet. It was like a Sunday afternoon late in summer during a hot spell, with everyone taking a nap after dinner, except that even on the sleepiest Sunday there would be some sound somewhere, if only the far-off barking of a dog, or, closer, the keys of a piano touched by some restless, dreamy girl.

John forced his horse into a gallop, the poor skinny beast wanting to get at the grass in the square, and when he passed the corner where the Lockharts lived, he saw a woman's face peep from behind a curtain at one of the windows and pull back with a jerk. John thought it was Jeanette Lockhart, one of Missy's friends, and if she was frightened he couldn't blame her—the fiercest villain couldn't have looked any more rapacious than he, a scarecrow soldier on a scarecrow steed riding hell for leather, one of the heralds of the four horsemen, surely.

ii

Another five minutes and he was in his father's woods. He ached from a day in the saddle, and the fever seemed to be coming back again, but even so his heart beat faster. The woods were green with spring—redbud, wild plum, and the first signs of jasmine. A pounding of hoofs rose ahead, the clink and jingle of harness, and five horsemen came around a bend in the road, yelling as in a charge—they swept by in single file, kicking up spurts of earth, and though John did not want to do them an injustice he was glad he was not one of the local merchants. The *Mercury* might soon have cause to complain further of ruffians and ragamuffins.

As John drew nearer to Indigo, the woods took on the look of a camp. A colony of tents was pitched among the trees, and there were many horses—some tethered, others wandering about, the rest bunched close together in crude corrals made of pine saplings recently cut down. The stumps showed all through the woods, there was a sharp smell of horse urine and manure, and the earth was charred with black patches left by campfires and larger, more uneven patches where the fires had got away.

Only a few soldiers were to be seen. If any sentries were posted they had decided to take the day off. Not once was John challenged. "One hell of a sloppy war this has become," he thought. "I could be that bummer general himself. I could be the whole bummer Army. Keep going, you poor tired bastard horse, we're almost home."

And in another few seconds he was. He emerged from the woods near the Blackfords' barn. The barn was empty and the Blackfords' house deserted, but up ahead, past the line of trees that marked the boundary of the property, a mob of soldiers had gathered before the front porch of Indigo. John judged there were around two hundred or more, spreading across the lawn and trampling down the borders. He noticed that a latrine had been dug in the garden at the rear of the house, not far from the stables, and it could be that his father had picked the right time to die.

By now, his horse slowed down to a walk, John had come to the edge of the crowd. He slid from the saddle, gave the horse a hard slap that sent it toward the stables, and began to push his way toward the porch. Various times his roughness was muttered at, and several of the men started to reach for their belts, but the crowd parted to let him pass. Perhaps it was his appearance again, two weeks' beard and hardly any buttons and black all over, or perhaps it was what might have been taken for his audacity—a man had to be a pretty cool customer to come barging in like he owned the place when General Monckton was making a speech.

As soon as he saw Ules Monckton, John understood. Ules stood on the front porch of Indigo, at the head of the steps, and Monckton's irregulars had been summoned to hear their chief. Still pushing his way through the crowd, John heard Ules say, "And so, gentlemen, there the matter stands. As I believe you have been told, we want only volunteers. Honesty demands that I do not mislead you. We will be living as outlaws in the woods, no longer protected by the rules of conventional warfare. I can offer you nothing but hardship, danger, and a chance to restore the South."

Having reached the forward ranks of the crowd, John stopped before the porch. It was a little like being in a theatre, watching *The Gladiators* with Miss Clarissa Drew, and a little like the pageant at Happy Chance. Three years had passed since he had seen Ules Monckton at the meeting in the capital, but it might have been ten —even then he had looked like an old man, but now, wasted to skin and skeleton, every bone in his face cruelly defined and even the hair on the backs of his hands gone white, he seemed a kind of specter. John thought of the prophets in the desert, consumed by their raging fires, and once again he had to admire—in respect to the war, this man was right and always had been. Of all the commanders of the South, only he showed any true understanding of war's new shape and meaning. Invade or be invaded. Destroy or be destroyed. There are no civilian populations any more.

Ules said, "But this much, gentlemen, I make bold enough to promise. Our cause is far from lost. The South can be restored. All it asks is what it asked in the beginning, your loyalty and devotion," but John no longer listened. Directly behind Ules Monckton, Arabella and Missy stood framed in the doorway. Their solemn faces were close together, and they looked, most puzzlingly, as though they were going to a party. Arabella wore a green dress and Missy a yellow one, and it took several moments for John to realize that because of the blockade they had been reduced to their ballroom best.

"I do not hold out the promise that it will be easy," Ules Monckton said. "It may be required of us that we continue the struggle for years, against hopeless odds," and John, sensing the hypnotic effect Ules was having, the voice of the preacher in the wilderness, turned his attention to the fourth figure on the porch.

It was Allbright. He stood to the right of the front door, near Arabella and Missy, wearing his Sunday clothes and one of his brocaded waistcoats. His big gold tiepin was fastened to his shirt, and his bearing, while withdrawn and respectful, was poised and self-assured. Possibly it was Missy who was responsible, but Pork Chops/ Ham Gravy was nowhere in evidence—wanting to thank Missy, John felt drowned in shame.

Ules Monckton said, "Do I have your support, gentlemen? Do I persuade you thus far?" and a murmur of assent rose from the men. A voice cried out, "Let's ride against them now. What are we waiting for, General?" and the crowd let out a yell. Ules held up a hand, thin as a claw. He said, "Not so fast, gentlemen. I want you to understand exactly what is being asked of you. The swamps are now behind the enemy and he may march at will. How, then, is he to be stopped? Are we to try to oppose his massed might, our few hundreds against his many thousands? Plainly we cannot. Our purpose must be to make it impossible for him to survive. Fire must be fought with fire. Our best weapon is the torch. Let us begin to use it now."

A hush fell over the crowd, as if a wintry wind had arisen. Twice before John had seen it happen, once at the Agricultural Society and once at the meeting in the capital, and now it was happening again. BE RESOLUTE! BE CONFIDENT! I HAVE RETURNED TO JOIN YOU IN THE INEVITABLE VICTORY THAT MUST BE OURS! Victory, however, by what means, and at what cost? John saw Allbright step closer to the front door, glancing worriedly at Missy, and Arabella's face was like a mask. Ules Monckton said:

"It has pleased the enemy to boast he has left a path of destruction thirty miles wide. Let us double that path—nay, triple it! What will he boast of then? He carries no more food than he consumes in a day. He has abandoned his lines of communication. He de-

pends on tomorrow for tomorrow's bread. Our task, our purpose—
yes, and our victory!—requires that he find the larder empty. Soon he
will be hungry and then he will starve. Unable to move forward, he
will find it impossible to retreat. We will be at him on all sides. We
will cut him to ribbons. Witnessing our success, others will rally to
our side. Where we now have one man, a hundred will spring up.
Though we are but a handful, we can show the way."

The crowd was getting increasingly restless, but Ules had not completely lost his hold. He said, dropping his voice to a matter-of-fact
tone, "By my calculations, the enemy is within two days' forced march
of Pompey's Head. We must leave it as he left Atlanta. Some of you
will be asked to lay charges of gunpowder, others to set fires. I have
informed Mayor Warren that the civilian population must be evacuated immediately. By nightfall our work should be well under way,"
and it was only then, and in large part because of Ules's calm, matter-
of-fact tone, that John knew that this man who had once tried to kill
him had finally and unmistakably gone out of his mind.

"A few things need not be postponed until nightfall," Ules continued, almost as if speaking to himself. "The houses in this immediate
vicinity will be burned at once. It is just such edifices as these that
attract the enemy's fancy as headquarters. Once they fulfill his purpose, they are promptly set on fire. Let us deny him the pleasure. Let
him sleep on the ground for a change," and once again, from the peak
of intensity on which he stood, he came close to being right—right,
far-seeing, basing his judgments on proved experience, and wholly,
absolutely mad.

What happened in the next few moments John would never be
able to remember. He found himself on the porch, facing Ules
Monckton. He heard his violent, unnatural voice say, "Harm us
here and I'll kill you. You're insane, you're crazy, you're mad," and
then, rushing from the doorway with a little moan, Arabella in her
green party dress stood by his side. He heard Missy cry out, "Johnny,
it's you!" and Arabella's closer, softer voice say, "Oh, my poor darling,
how thin and sick you look," and though Ules Monckton should have

known him, bearded sooty scarecrow that he was, not a tremor of recognition showed on Ules's face.

"Somebody arrest this man!"

John turned to the crowd of soldiers. The notion passed across his mind that these fellows should be paying good money for this, the way they would if they went to a show. Missy said, "You can't arrest him! He's my brother!" and then, right behind hers, John heard a voice he recognized as Allbright's—"Now you gentle yourself, Miss Missy. There ain't nobody going to arrest Mister John. No ma'am, not *him*. He won't come to no harm. You gentle yourself."

John shouted to the soldiers, "Now listen, you men! This is my house and this is my family. We'll have no more talk of burning. I've just come from the neighborhood of Franklin's Station. It's true that the Yankees may be coming this way, but I doubt that it's likely. I believe we will be bypassed entirely," and he might have gone on indefinitely, making a speech of his own, had he not heard Missy cry out again, "You leave him alone! He's not harming you! Why do you have to be so mean? You shot my brother and now you want to burn our house! Leave him alone, do you hear!"

John spun around—Ules Monckton, his revolver drawn, was threatening Allbright. Ules had apparently tried to get through the doorway, and Allbright was blocking his path. "Where is Aunt Mary Nesbitt?" John asked Arabella, suddenly remembering that tiny old lady and fearful of what this might be doing to her, and as Arabella replied breathlessly, "Gone to the mountains. The Blackfords took her with them," Ules Monckton's voice rang out again, still edged with the habit of command:

"Stand aside!"

"No sir, General, that I can't."

"I command you!"

"I ain't yours to command, General. It's Miss Missy here who I is obliged to."

"Damn you, stand aside!"

It had to be madness at its wildest—too stunned to move, John watched as in a trance, and for a benumbed instant it was like one of those nightmare sessions when his mother was having a spell. A shot rang out, Missy opened her mouth as if to scream and made no sound, Arabella said, "Oh my God! No! No!" and Allbright, a dazed look on his face, disbelieving and frightened, sank to the floor of the porch with a wet red stain spreading across his shirt just beneath his big gold tiepin.

Arabella said, "Johnny, do something!"

She went to her knees beside Allbright, her skirt pulling up and exposing her small white ankles, and John, watching stupidly, saw her twist around, reach under her skirt, and start tearing her petticoat. Missy was less careful. She pulled up her skirt to her chin, squirmed out of her nether garment, and stood for the briefest of moments with her bare legs showing—underwear, it would seem, was a thing of the past.

"I think he's dead," Arabella said. "I think he's gone already."

Less than a minute had passed since the shot rang out, and John could still see the flash of his sister's nakedness before all those men. "You get away from here!" he yelled. "Get the goddamn hell away!" and then he also was kneeling beside Allbright, pushing the women aside. "Uncle," he said. "Uncle."

Missy's eyes were white as chalk and Arabella's deathly still. John said, "Yes, our uncle. Father's half brother," and all he saw for an instant, more vivid than the spreading stain on Allbright's shirt, was the big gold tiepin with the set of initials that were exactly like those on the silver his grandfather had acquired long years before on a trip to London. "I suspected from the start," John said. "Ever since a few weeks after I came home from Princeton and went into his shop for the first time. Look at the initials on his tiepin. Didn't either of you ever notice?"

Missy was crying softly. She said, "I thought there must be something but I didn't know what. And I paid no attention to the initials. They all look the same to me when they're twisted in and out like that. It was the way he reminded me of Papa, the way he sometimes held his head."

"And so was I reminded," John said. "There was that, and the tiepin, and it gave me no peace. One day I went to the courthouse and looked up his articles of emancipation. Grandfather's name was the first one signed. But it was old Aunt Mim at Deerskin who gave me the answer. Once I was sick and she insisted on coming to make a spell. Fine magic! We got to talking and she told me about him. She knew his mother, one of Grandfather's people."

Missy bent her head and began to cry louder. John said, "And we denied him. Not you or Mother or Cameron, since none of you knew, but Father and I. Once, when I came home from Deerskin, I spoke to Father about him, the one and only time. It was just after I had talked to old Aunt Mim. 'All I have is two sisters,' he said. 'I don't have a half brother, or a quarter brother, and least of all any kind of brother who is part nigger to any degree. See that you remember!' And I believe he truly meant it. He couldn't have a half brother he couldn't claim, it was too great a blow to his pride, and so he erased the fact of Allbright's being from his mind. He was there but not there. With me, however, it was different. I knew and couldn't forget. I knew and was ashamed. Ashamed of his being a barber and half black and those fawning ways he had."

"The poor man," Arabella said. "The way he loved Missy."

John said, "That's the worst of the denial. He wanted to love us all. He was proud of us, proud of his relation to us. He loved Cameron, far more than Father ever did, and he wanted to love me. That's my crime—I wouldn't have it. I used to resent his suggestions that there was a tie between us. I tried to pretend I didn't know. And then, after Cameron went away and he tried to protect us, the best he could—— Ah Christ! How can I ever forget?"

Still weeping, Missy raised her head. She said, "Whatever you did, whatever you *say* you did, he forgave you. I know he did. He said only the kindest things." Arabella nodded and reached for John's hand. "It's true," she said. "You have to believe it," and he pulled his hand away roughly.

"Believe what?" he said. "That I didn't deny? And what about the rest of them? Are they to forgive also—the slavery we have kept them in, the denial of the human family, the worse denial of their immortal souls? They scream in the North of the damage we have done the Negro, but how much louder should they bemoan the damage we have done ourselves. There was that morning I had to fight the duel. I gave a silver dollar to Simon, and old Delilah was in her stall close by, and though I could have been going to meet my Maker——"

Missy twisted her head toward the doorway. "There's smoke, Johnny. It's coming from inside. Oh my God in heaven! That crazy man has done it! He's set the house on fire! There's smoke, Johnny, I smell smoke," and once again they might have been down in the pit of one of their mother's nightmare spells—how often she had smelled smoke, them, always them, and now there was no questioning the smoke, beginning to drift from the doorway.

John said, "Let's get him off the porch. He can't stay here. Help me, you two," and as they struggled with Allbright's body, some of the soldiers who were still standing about the lawn, though at a greater distance, came up to help. "Do what you can," John said to Arabella. "Find something to cover him with," and before either she or Missy could stop him, he ran into his father's house.

The heavy curtains in the double parlor were sheets of roaring flame and some of the woodwork had caught fire. Dark splotches on the carpet and a litter of splintered glass explained what had happened —Ules Monckton had thrown one of the coal-oil lamps against the curtains and touched a match to them. Blundering in the smoke, John fell against the case that held the Light Infantry cane. It went over with a crash and the cane rolled out upon the floor. Picking it up, John tunneled through the smoke into the hall—on one of the upper floors he could hear Ules Monckton moving about. He thought, "Maybe in my room. Maybe where we spent our wedding night. I'll kill him. I'll choke him. I'll gouge his eyes out. I'll finish him with my own bare hands."

Fighting his way through the smoke, he tried to climb the stairs. He could get no farther than the second-floor hall. Here the smoke was thicker than downstairs, and there was a crackle and roar from both front bedrooms. "Monckton!" he shouted. "Ules Monckton! Come down, you fool! What was it you wanted to do? Save the South

475

all by yourself, you and your crazy dream? Monckton! Come down, do you hear? You'll never get out," and then, coughing, shielding his eyes with the crook of his bad elbow, he groped his way down the stairs.

Arabella and Missy were waiting on the lawn when he stumbled to the porch. Arabella ran up and took him by the arm, leading him away. "You, you!" she said in a tight frantic voice. "What possessed you, sick as you are and all? Do you know what you put me through? I could shake you to pieces!"

iii

For such a big house, it didn't take long for Indigo to burn. John and Missy and Arabella watched from the edge of the woods. Allbright's body lay under one of the trees beneath a blanket. Missy cried for a while and then stopped. John still clutched the cane. Once he laughed shortly. "You in your party dresses and me with this," he said. "What a silly thing to save."

Arabella held up her chin.

"Oh, I don't know," she said. "Why is it silly? There'll be another Light Infantry Ball."

Al

The Light Infantry ball. [1st ed.] Garden City, N. Y.,
Doubleday, 1959.   *813*
476 p. 22 cm.
I. Title.   *B29*

Full name: Joseph Hamilton Basso.

PZ3.B2965Li   59-9131 ‡
IU InU TNJ OC1 KyU ViU NcU RP MiU
MoSW MH ScU AAP NRU CtY NjP NjR
WU MsSM ViBlbV NIC CLSU RPB NN LU
MnU FTaSU FU OOxM CLU AU CSt OO
OC1W OCU FMU CU GU TxU KU MsU